BEFORE THEY WERE FAMOUS

Babe Ruth

BEFORE THEY

Babe

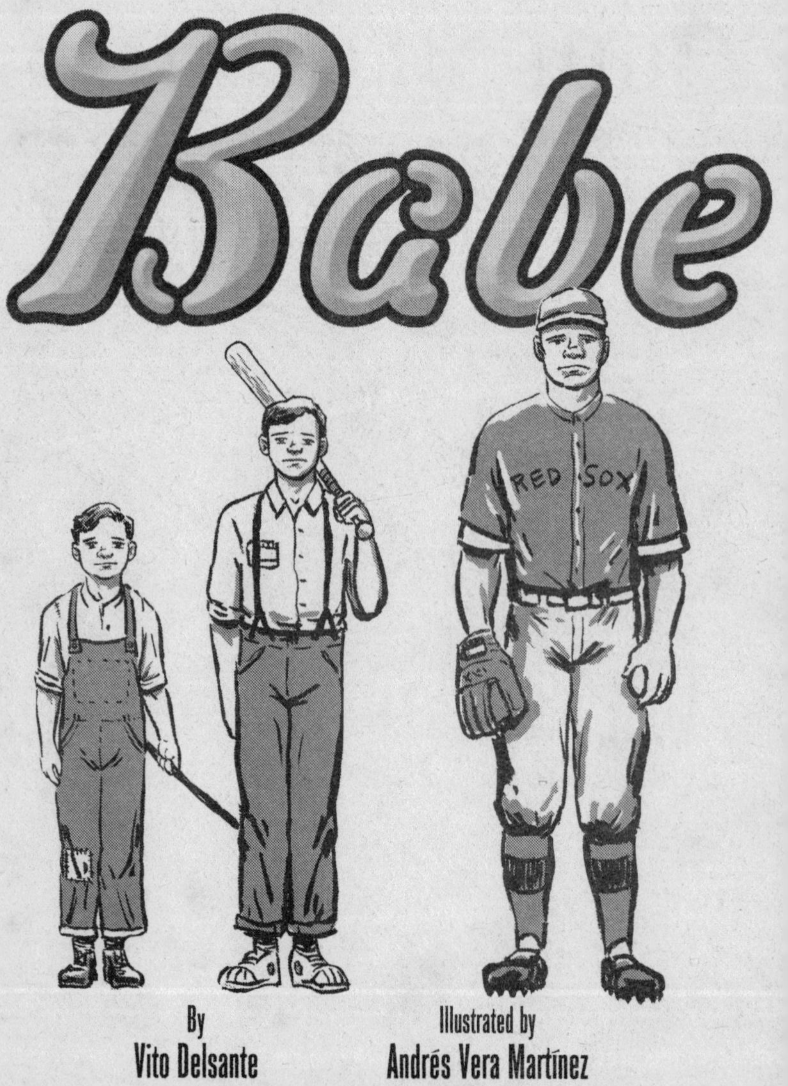
RED SOX

By
Vito Delsante

Illustrated by
Andrés Vera Martínez

WERE FAMOUS

Ruth

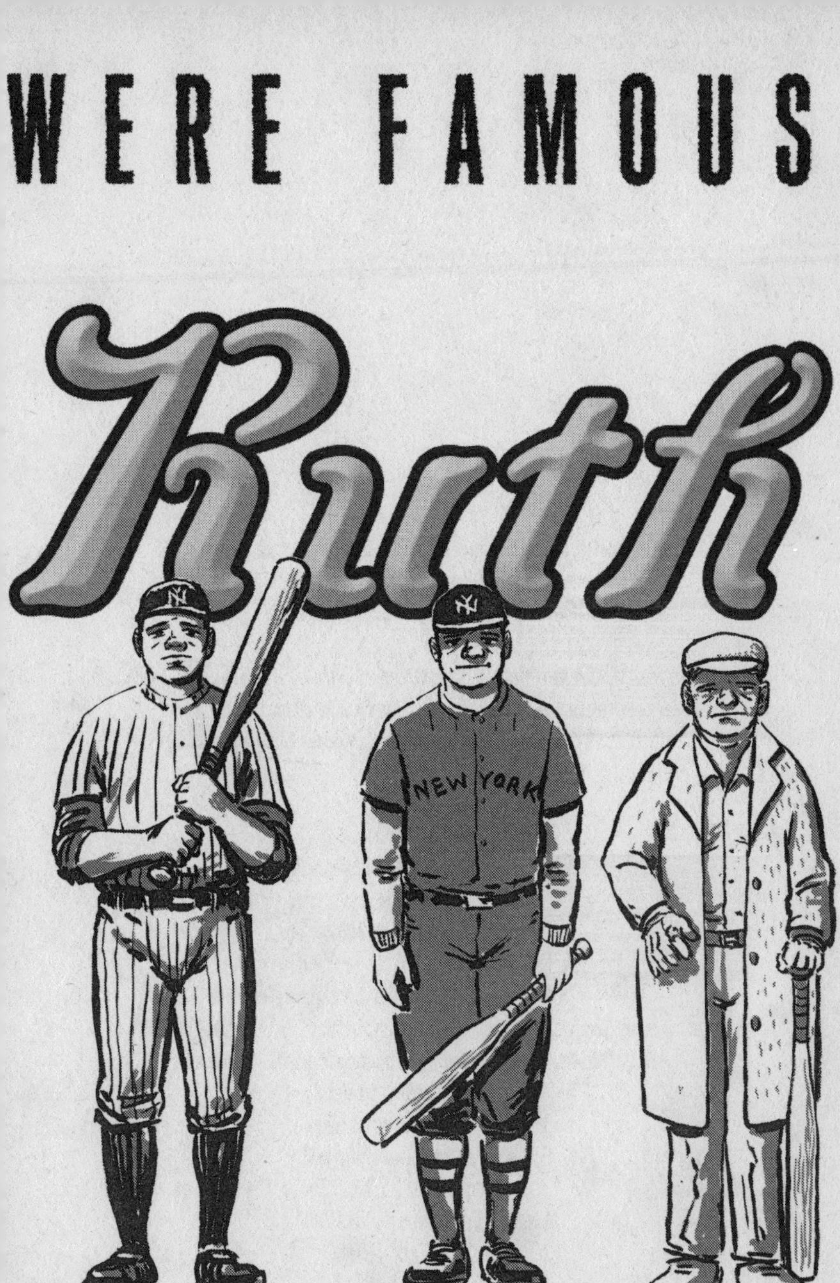
NEW YORK

ALADDIN PAPERBACKS New York London Toronto Sydney

ALADDIN PAPERBACKS
An imprint of Simon & Schuster Children's Publishing Division
1230 Avenue of the Americas, New York, NY 10020
Text copyright © 2009 by Vito Delsante
Illustrations copyright © 2009 by Andrés Vera Martínez
Adapted from Childhood of Famous Americans: *Babe Ruth* by Guernsey Van Riper Jr.
All rights reserved, including the right of reproduction in whole or in part in any form.
ALADDIN PAPERBACKS and related logo are registered trademarks of Simon & Schuster, Inc.
Designed by Christopher Grassi
Manufactured in the United States of America
First Aladdin Paperbacks edition February 2009
2 4 6 8 10 9 7 5 3 1
Library of Congress Control Number 2008929319
ISBN-13: 978-1-4169-5071-4
ISBN-10: 1-4169-5071-0

I dedicate this to my grandfathers, Vito and Emiliano,
who introduced me to baseball in the first place.

I'd like to acknowledge James Owen and Paul Crichton for getting me in touch with Liesa Abrams, a wonderful editor; Mike Lilly, who started this project; Andrés, who finished it and did more than I could ever have imagined with it; and finally Michelle, who is always an inspiration and muse.

—Vito Delsante

I dedicate this book and my work to my wife, Na; my daughter, Mei;
and the rest of my family who inspire me to live the life I love and
love the life I live.

I'd like to acknowledge my teachers from the School of Visual Arts: Marshall Arisman, Kim Ablondi, David Sandlin, Klaus Janson, Sal Almendola, and David Mazzucchelli. I'd also like to thank Brian Rea for seeing my potential and giving me my first break in the business; my agent, Bob Mecoy, for believing in my talent and introducing me to the fine editorial team of Liesa Abrams and Karin Paprocki; Vito, for writing such a charming story; and my interns, Ishmael Forde and Ricardo Blot, two high school kids with bright futures in art. They have all helped make the experience of working on this book easy, creatively fulfilling, and fun.

—Andrés Vera Martínez

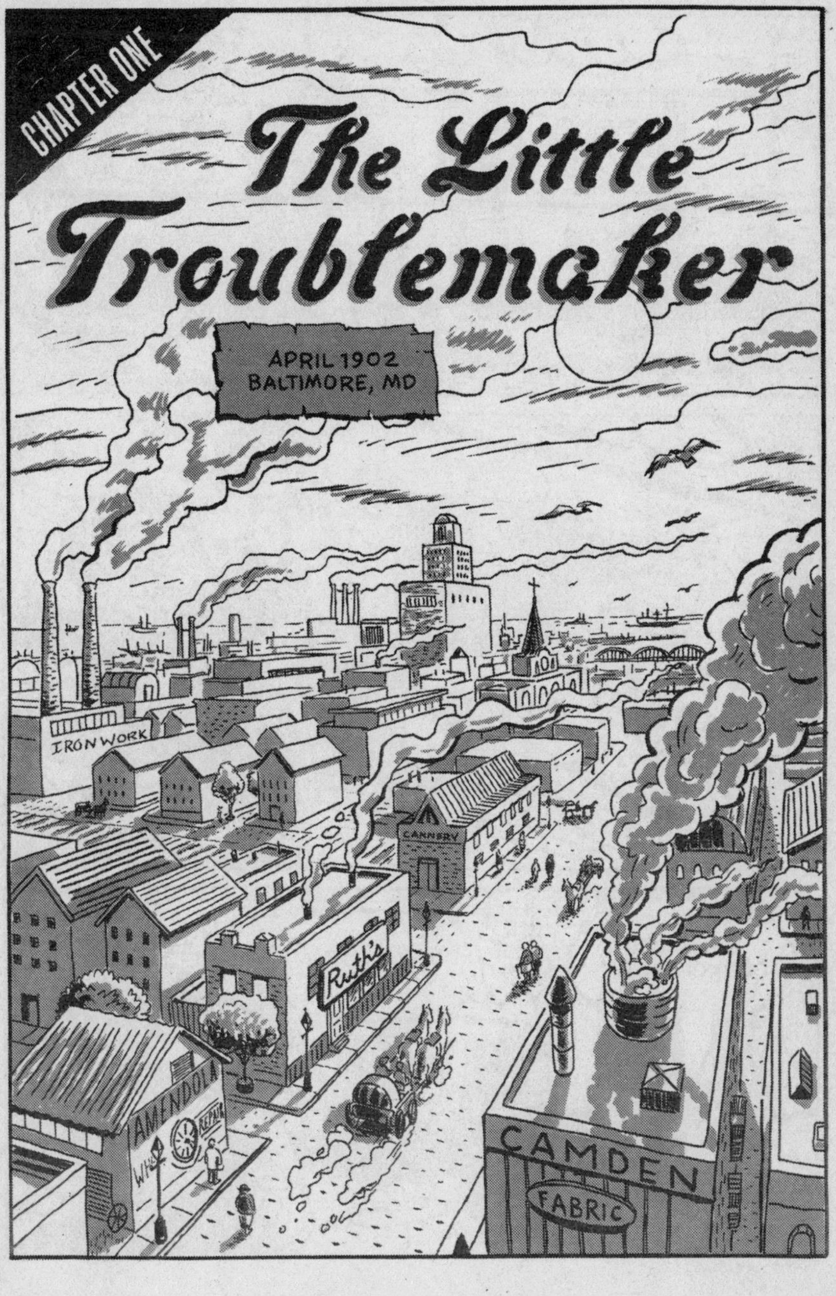
CHAPTER ONE
The Little Troublemaker
APRIL 1902
BALTIMORE, MD
IRONWORK
CANNERY
Ruth's
AMENDOLA
REPAIR
CAMDEN
FABRIC

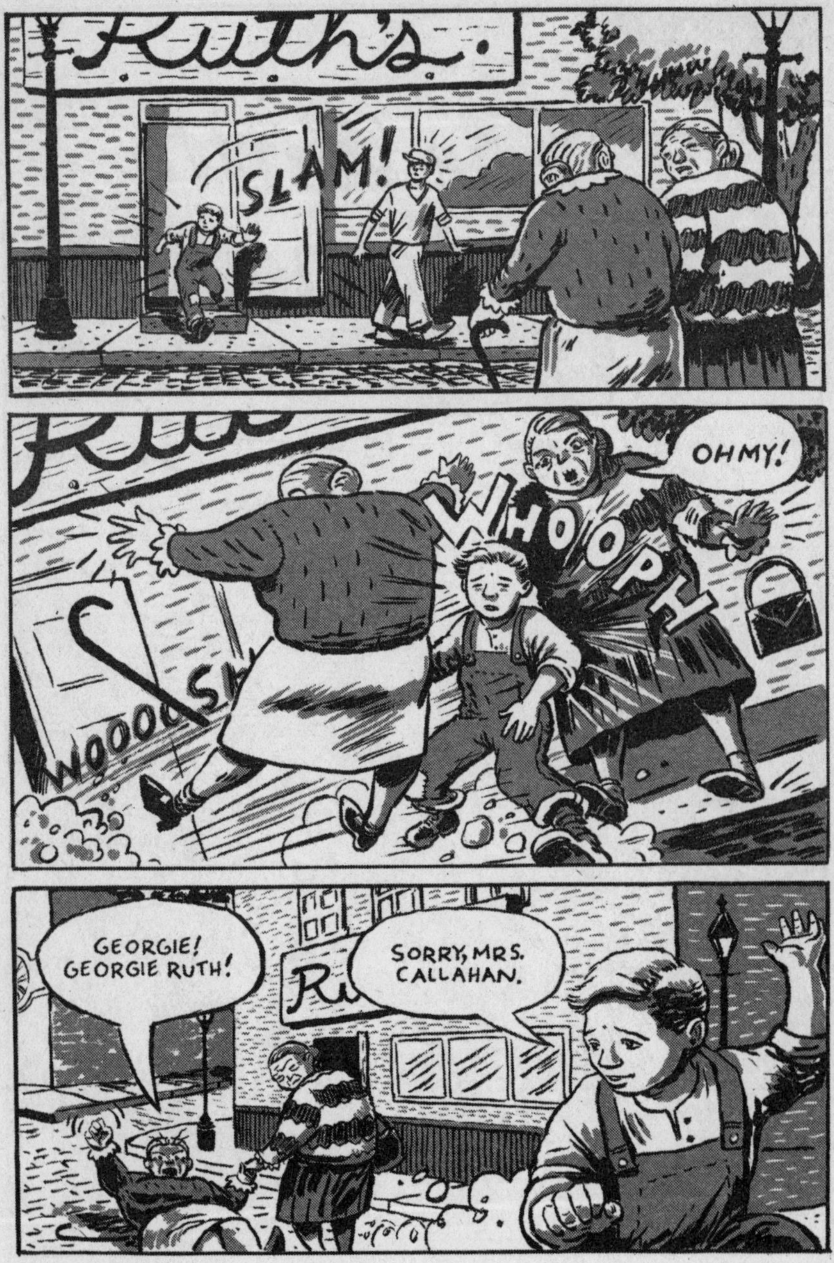
Ruth's
SLAM!
OH MY!
WHOOPH
WOOOOSH
GEORGIE!
GEORGIE RUTH!
SORRY, MRS.
CALLAHAN.

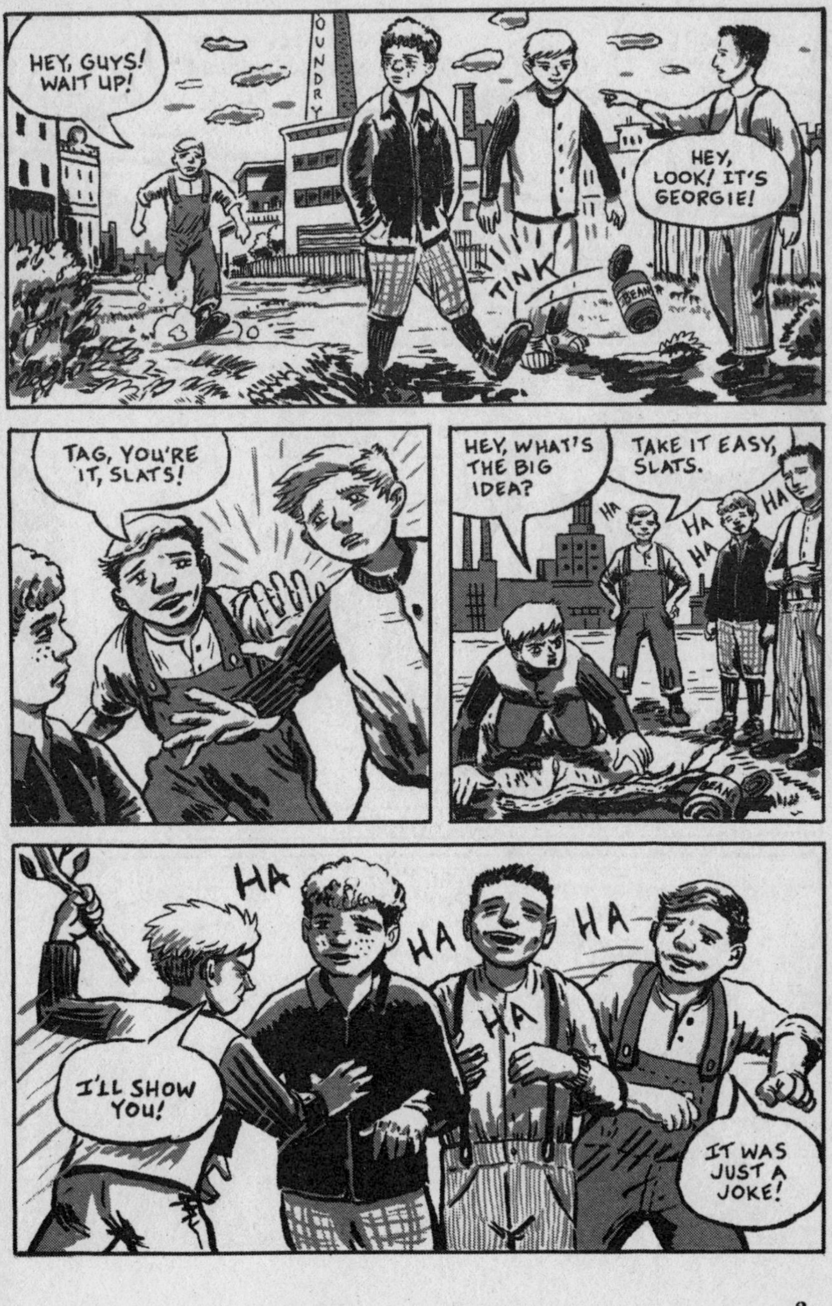

HEY, GUYS! WAIT UP!
OUNDRY
HEY, LOOK! IT'S GEORGIE!
TINK
BEANS
TAG, YOU'RE IT, SLATS!
HEY, WHAT'S THE BIG IDEA?
TAKE IT EASY, SLATS.
HA
HA HA
HA
BEANS
HA
HA
HA
HA
I'LL SHOW YOU!
IT WAS JUST A JOKE!

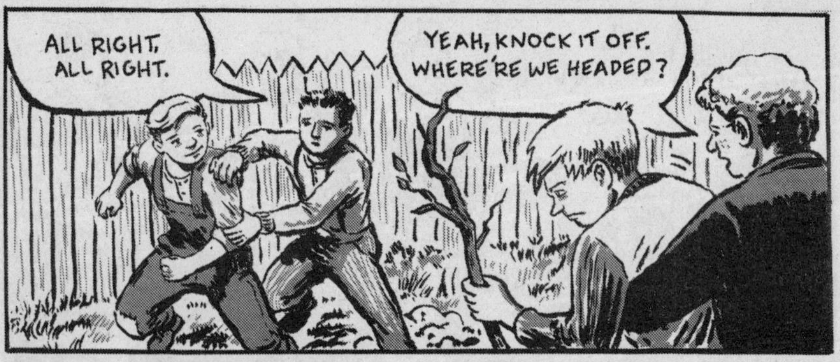
ALL RIGHT, ALL RIGHT.
YEAH, KNOCK IT OFF. WHERE'RE WE HEADED?

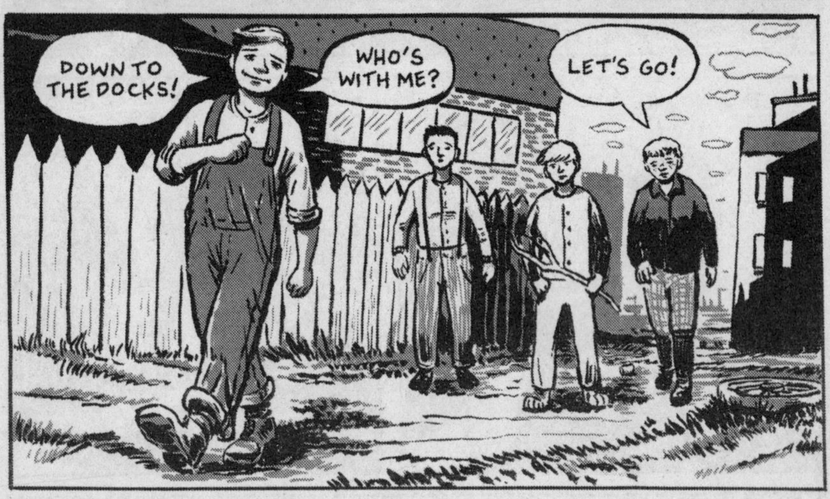
DOWN TO THE DOCKS!
WHO'S WITH ME?
LET'S GO!

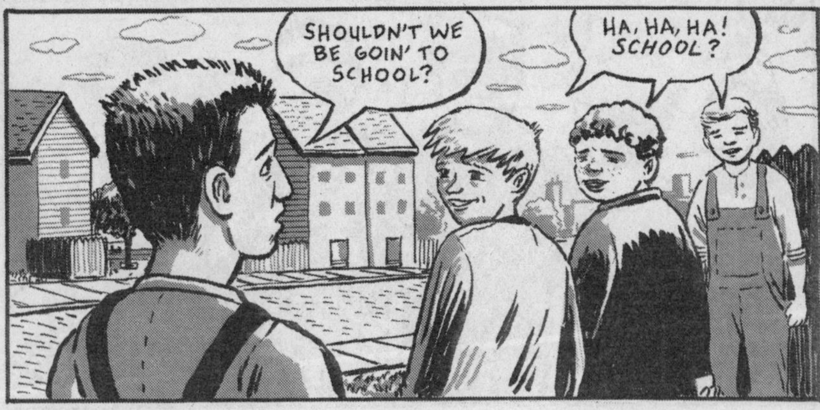
SHOULDN'T WE BE GOIN' TO SCHOOL?
HA, HA, HA! SCHOOL?

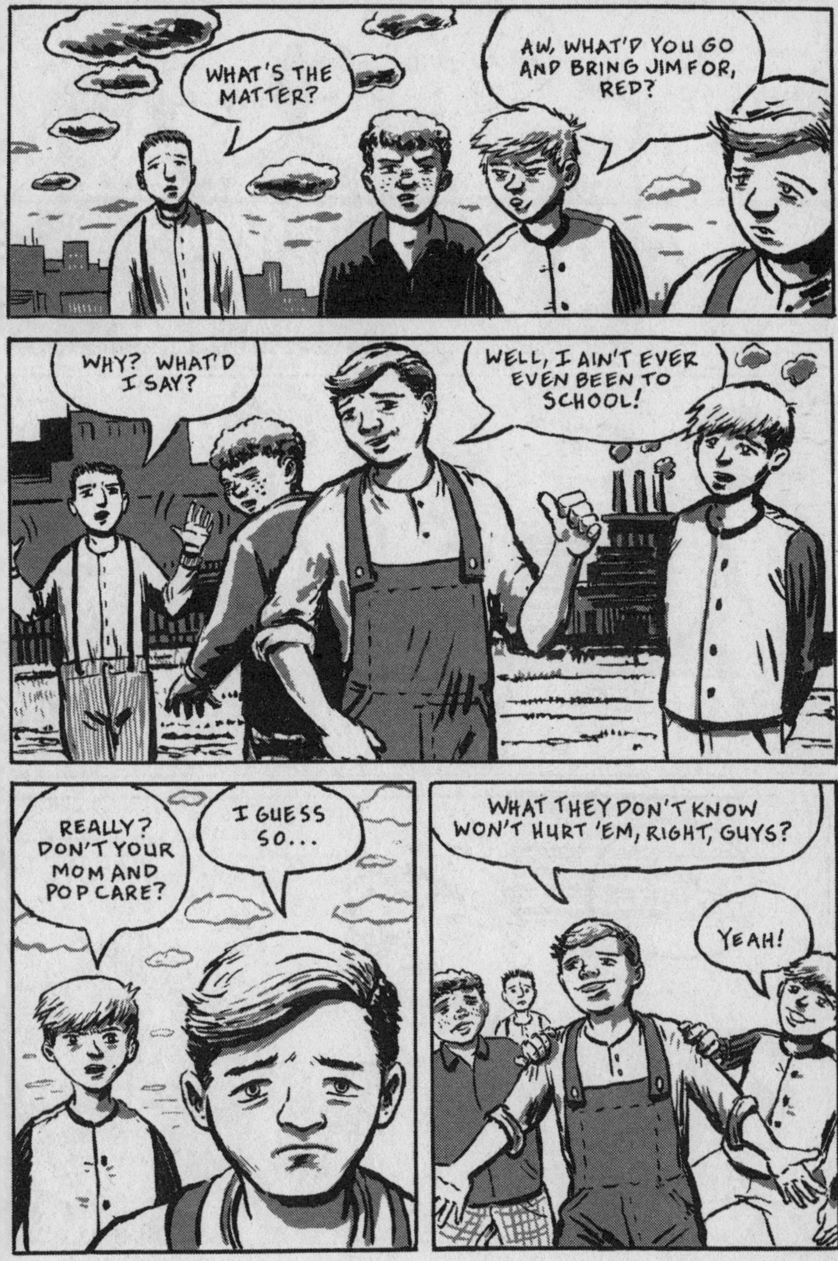
WHAT'S THE MATTER?
AW, WHAT'D YOU GO AND BRING JIM FOR, RED?
WHY? WHAT'D I SAY?
WELL, I AIN'T EVER EVEN BEEN TO SCHOOL!
REALLY? DON'T YOUR MOM AND POP CARE?
I GUESS SO...
WHAT THEY DON'T KNOW WON'T HURT 'EM, RIGHT, GUYS?
YEAH!

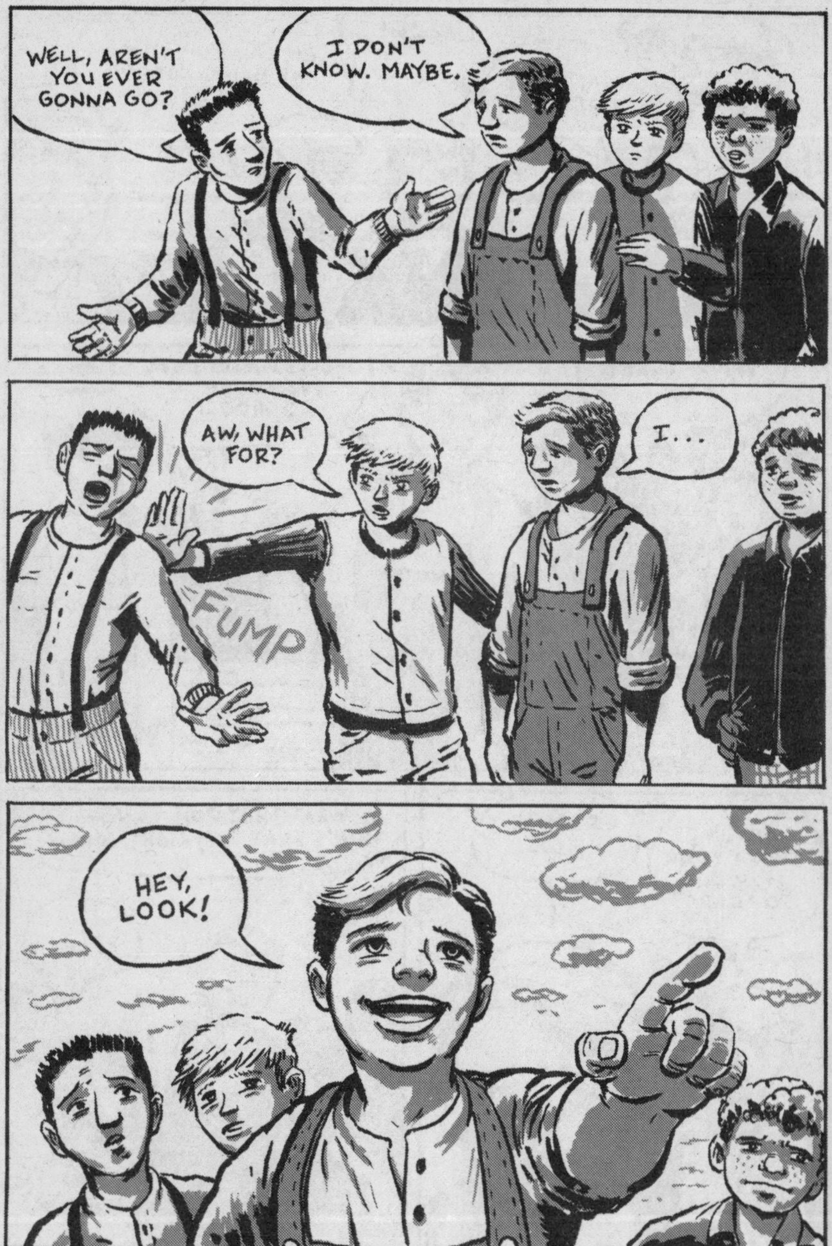
WELL, AREN'T YOU EVER GONNA GO?
I DON'T KNOW. MAYBE.
AW, WHAT FOR?
FUMP
I...
HEY, LOOK!

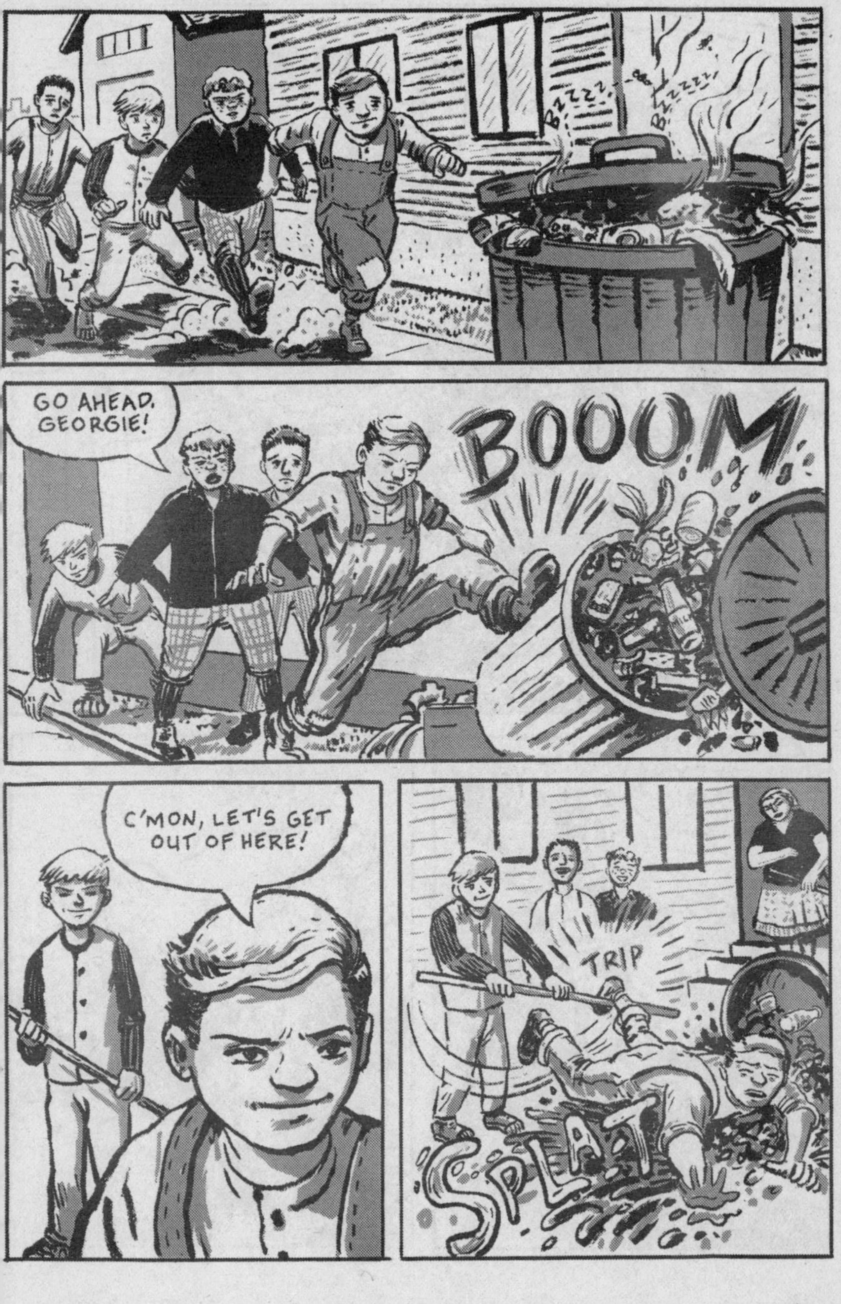

BZZZZ
BZZZZZ
GO AHEAD, GEORGIE!
BOOOM
C'MON, LET'S GET OUT OF HERE!
TRIP
SPLAT

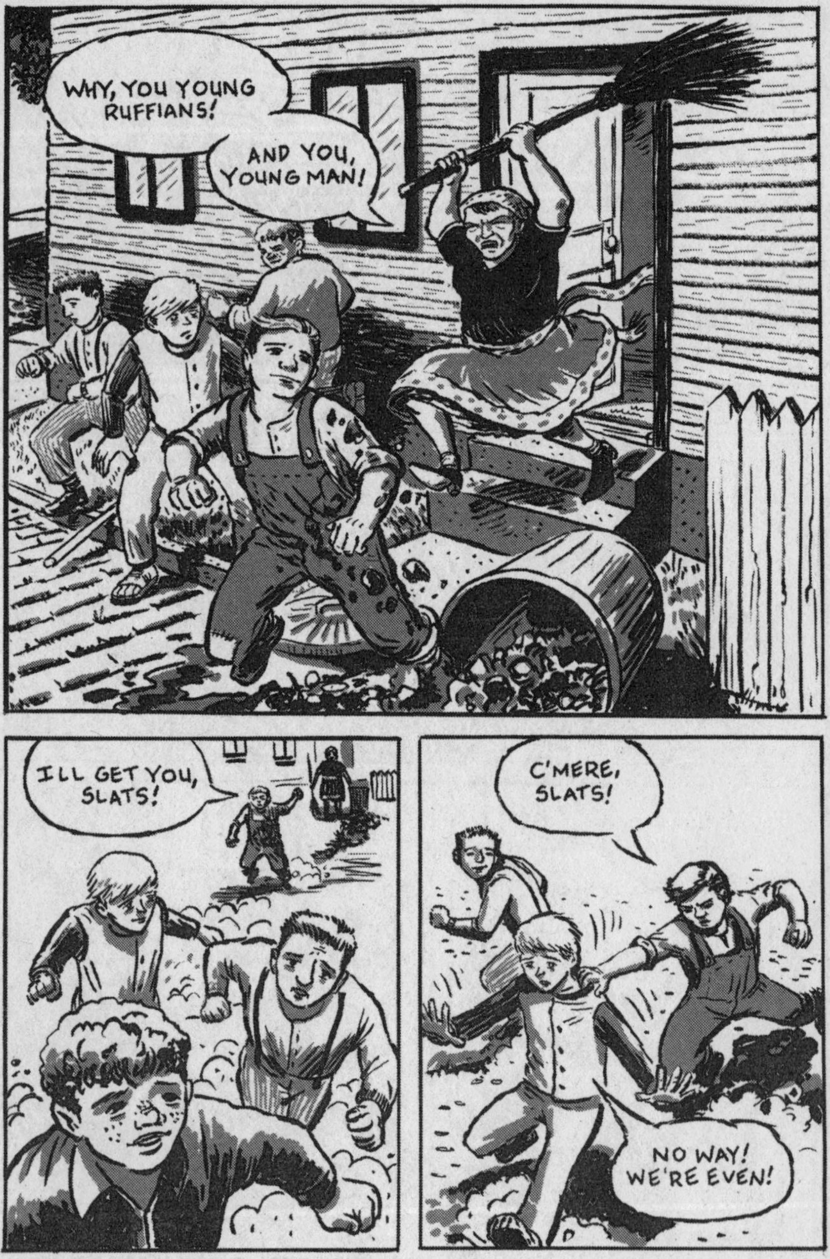
WHY, YOU YOUNG RUFFIANS!
AND YOU, YOUNG MAN!
ILL GET YOU, SLATS!
C'MERE, SLATS!
NO WAY! WE'RE EVEN!

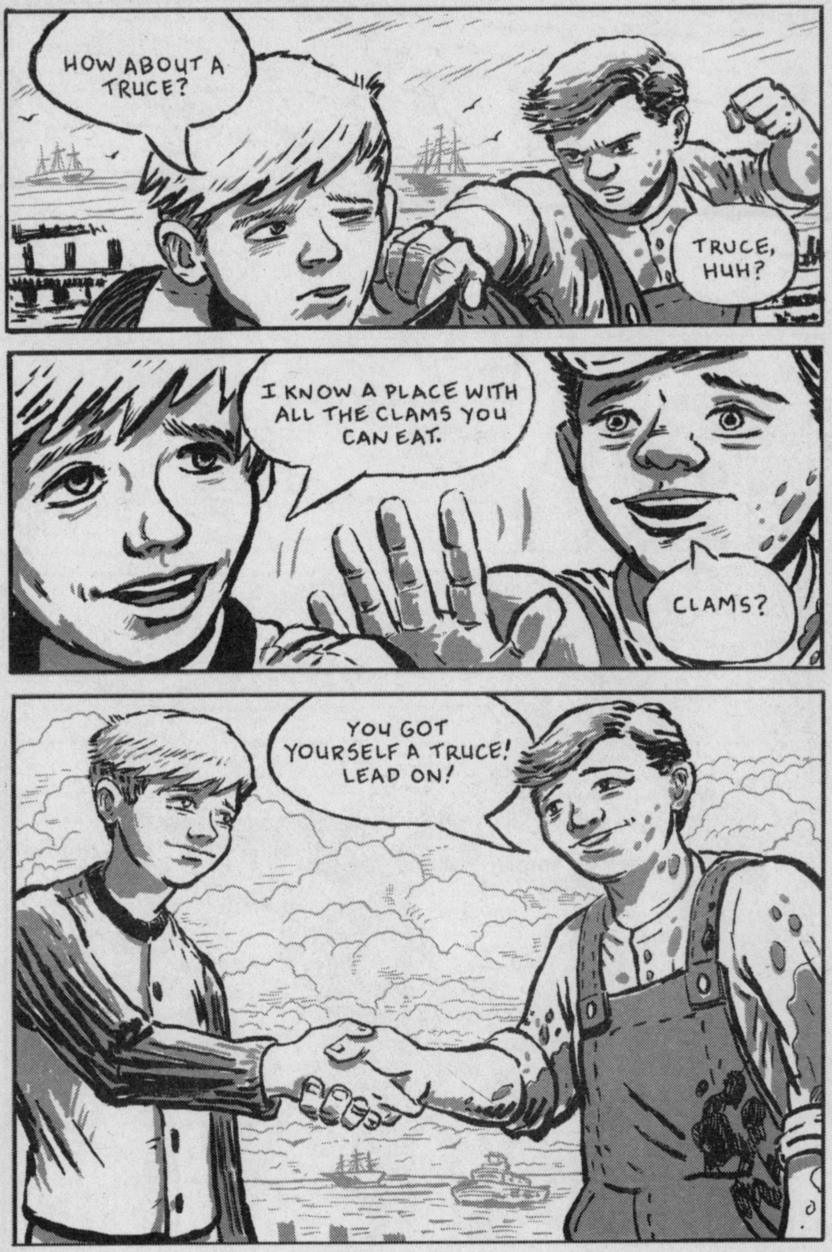
HOW ABOUT A TRUCE?
TRUCE, HUH?
I KNOW A PLACE WITH ALL THE CLAMS YOU CAN EAT.
CLAMS?
YOU GOT YOURSELF A TRUCE! LEAD ON!

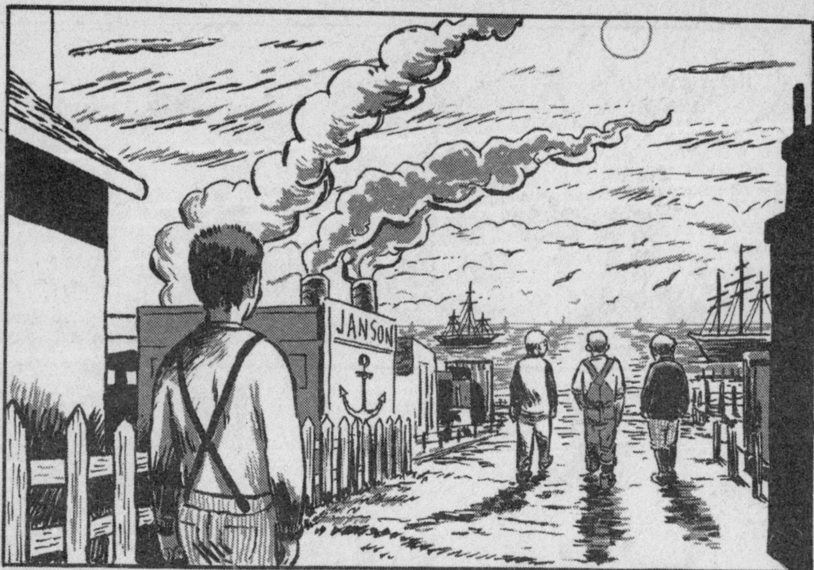
JANSON

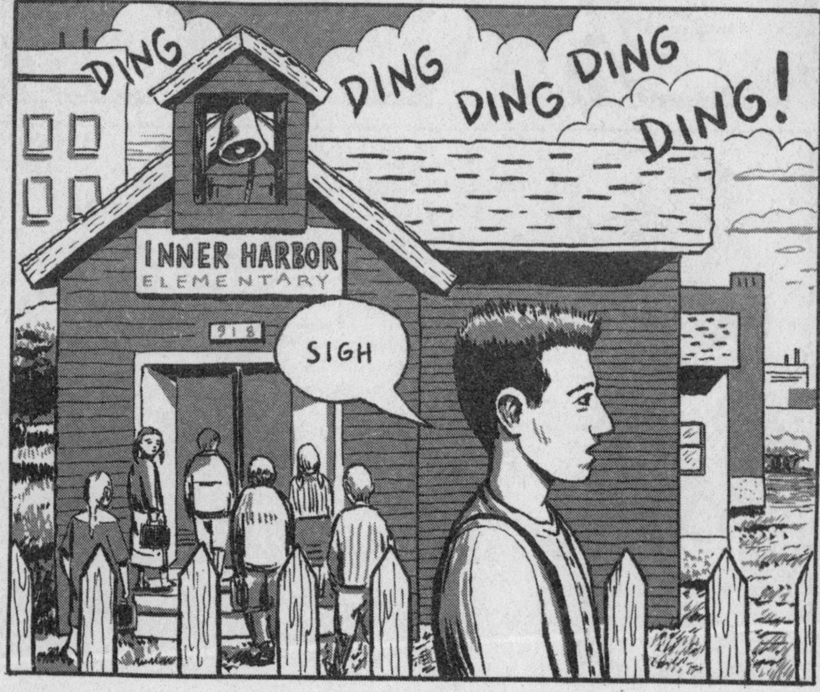
DING
DING
DING DING
DING!
INNER HARBOR
ELEMENTARY
918
SIGH

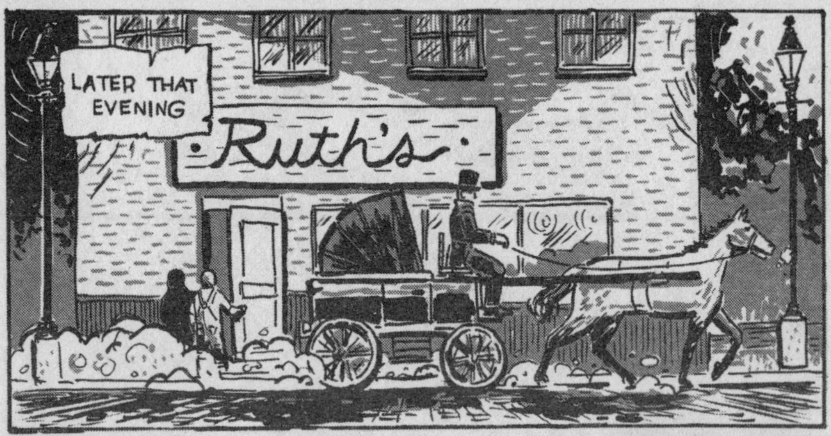
LATER THAT EVENING
Ruth's

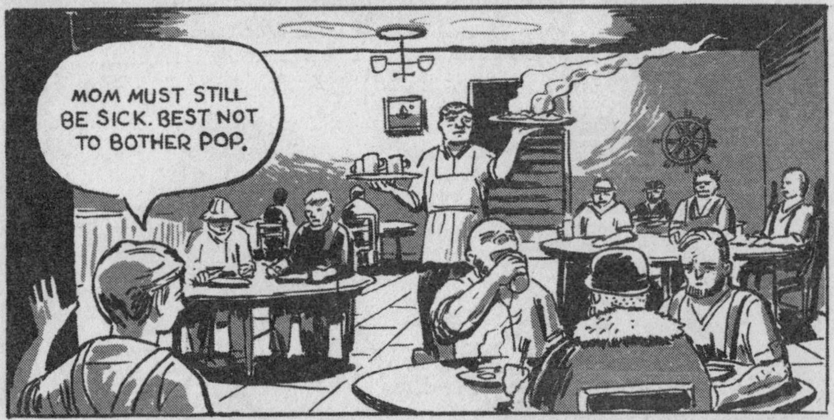
MOM MUST STILL BE SICK. BEST NOT TO BOTHER POP.

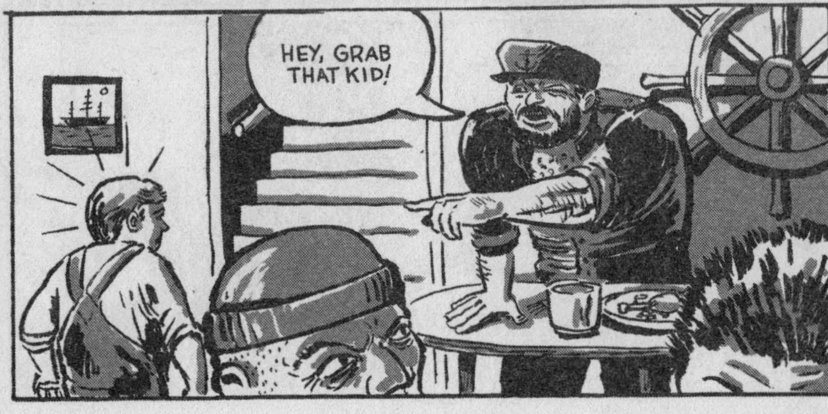
HEY, GRAB THAT KID!

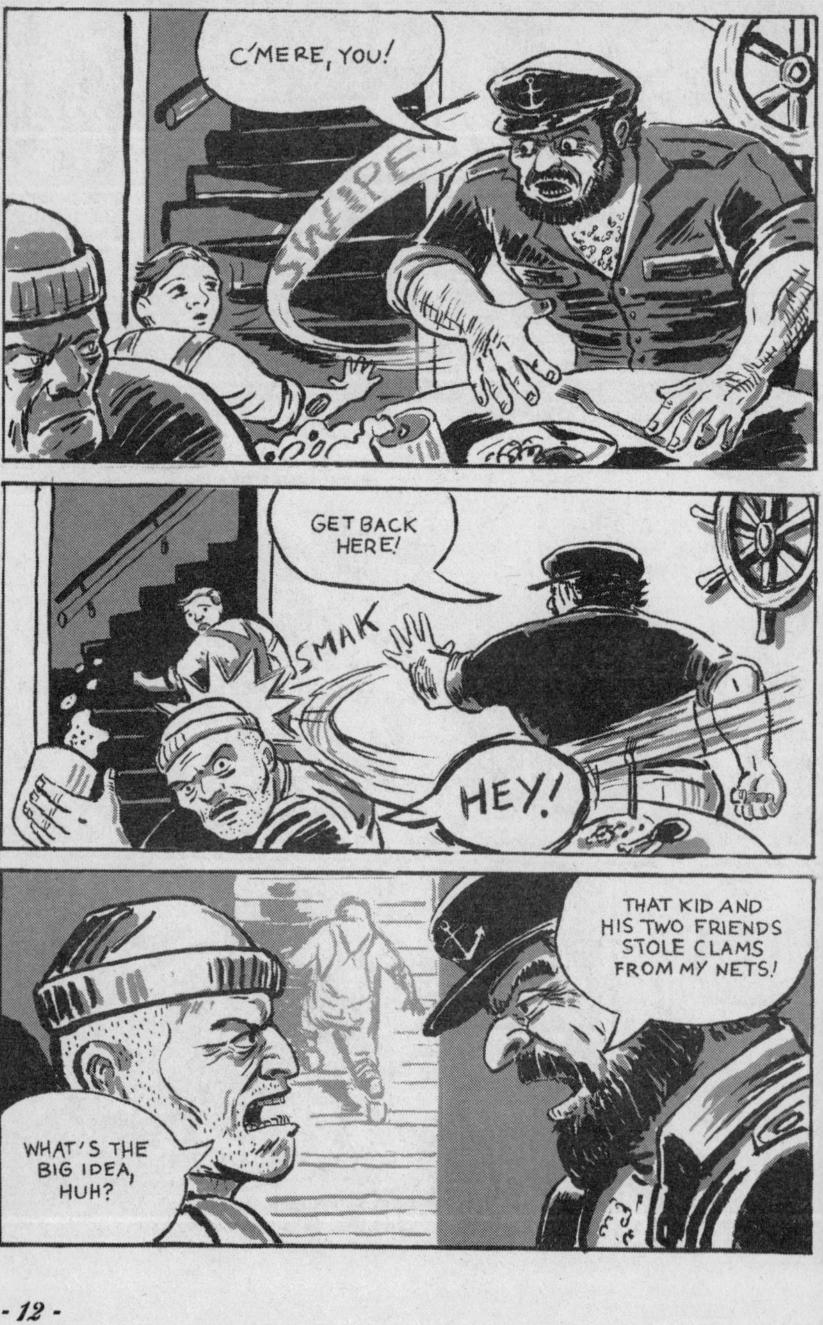
C'MERE, YOU!
SWIPE
GET BACK HERE!
SMAK
HEY!
THAT KID AND HIS TWO FRIENDS STOLE CLAMS FROM MY NETS!
WHAT'S THE BIG IDEA, HUH?

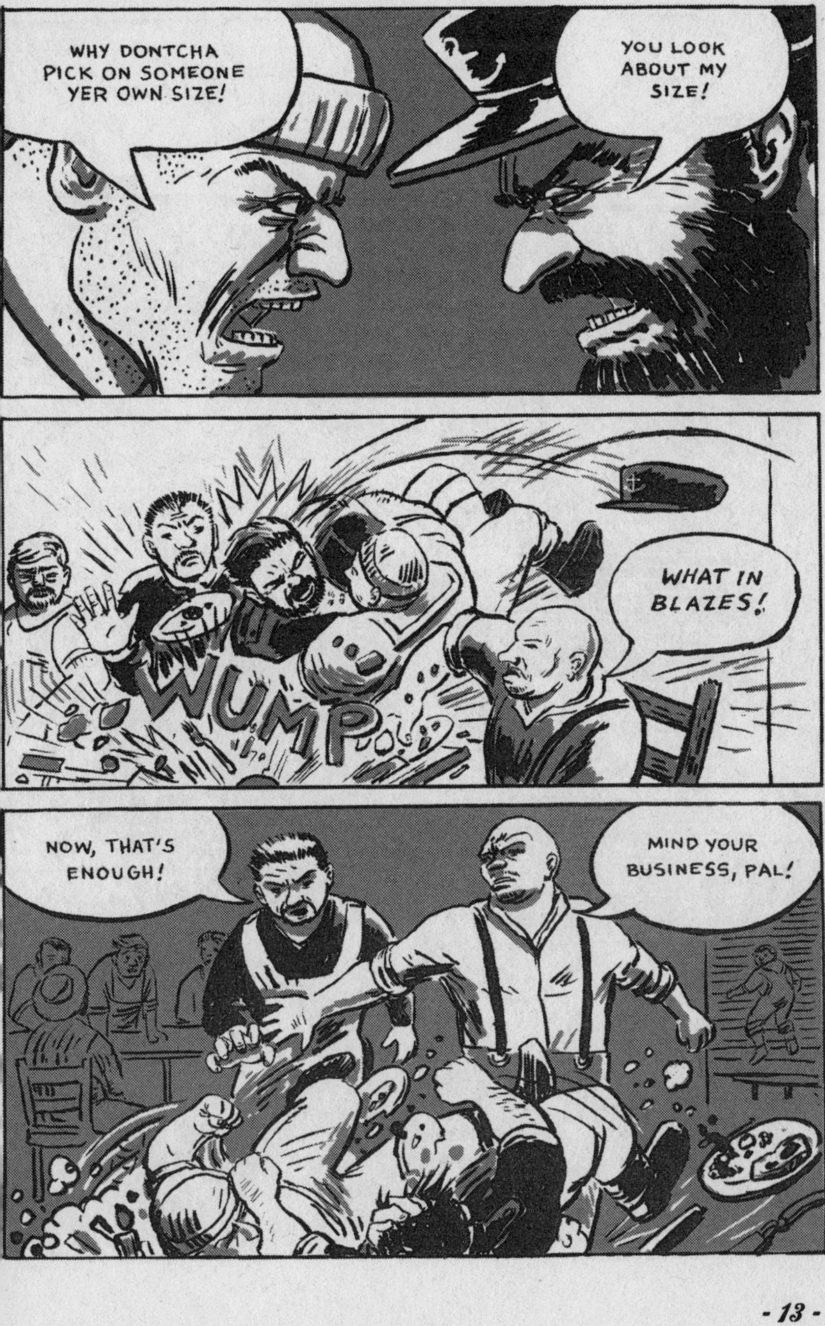
WHY DONTCHA PICK ON SOMEONE YER OWN SIZE!
YOU LOOK ABOUT MY SIZE!
WUMP
WHAT IN BLAZES!
NOW, THAT'S ENOUGH!
MIND YOUR BUSINESS, PAL!

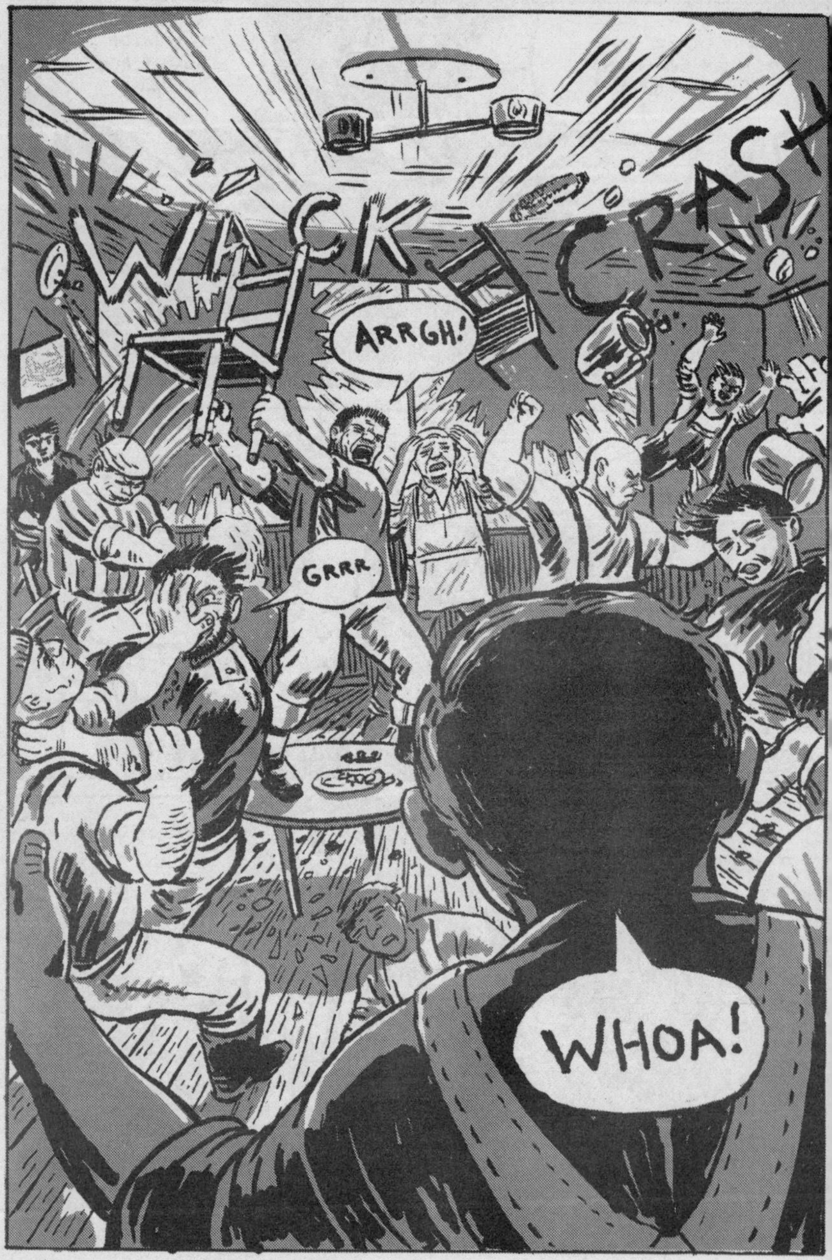
WACK
CRASH
ARRGH!
GRRR
WHOA!

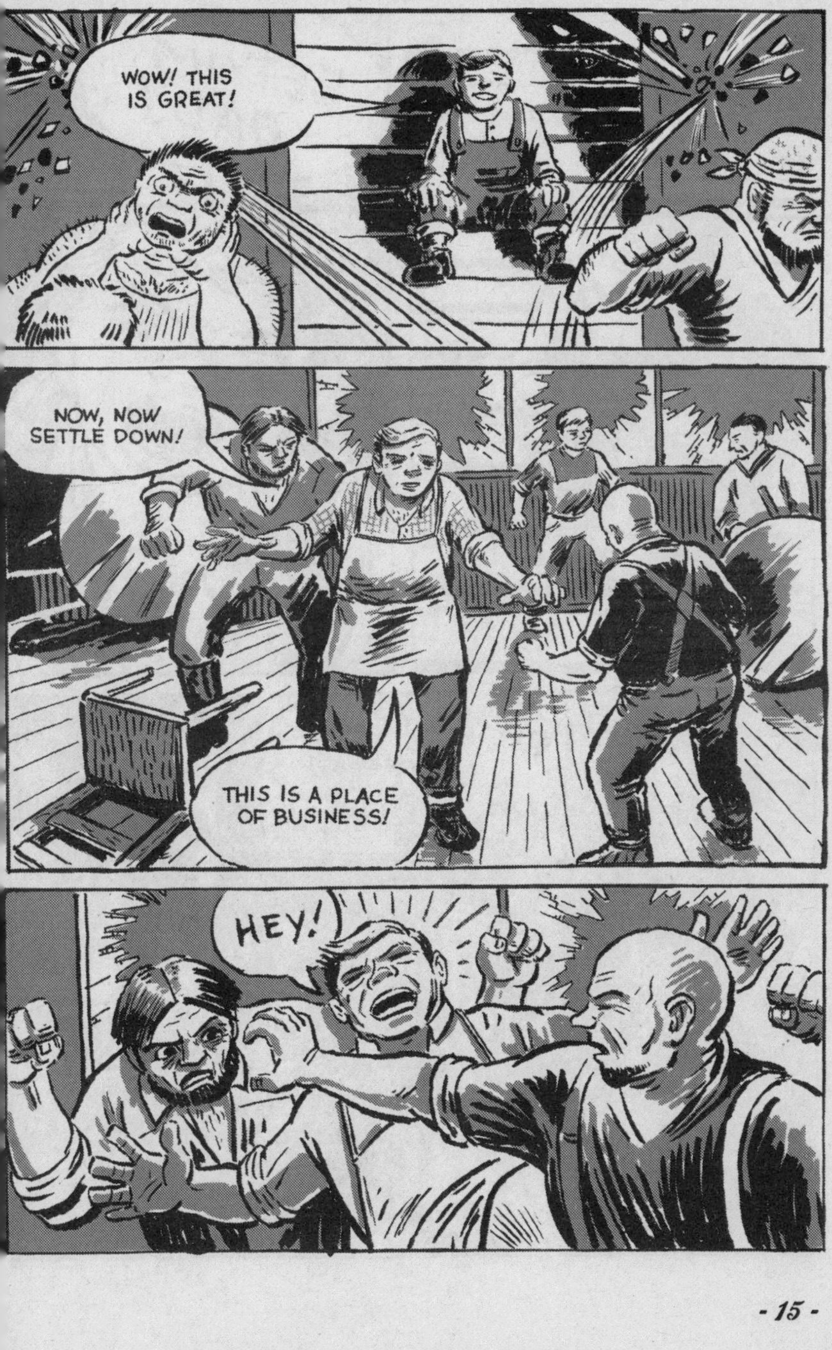
WOW! THIS IS GREAT!
NOW, NOW SETTLE DOWN!
THIS IS A PLACE OF BUSINESS!
HEY!

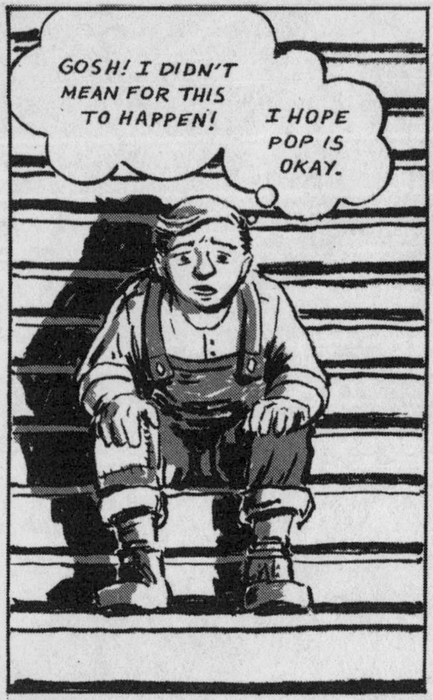
GOSH! I DIDN'T MEAN FOR THIS TO HAPPEN!
I HOPE POP IS OKAY.

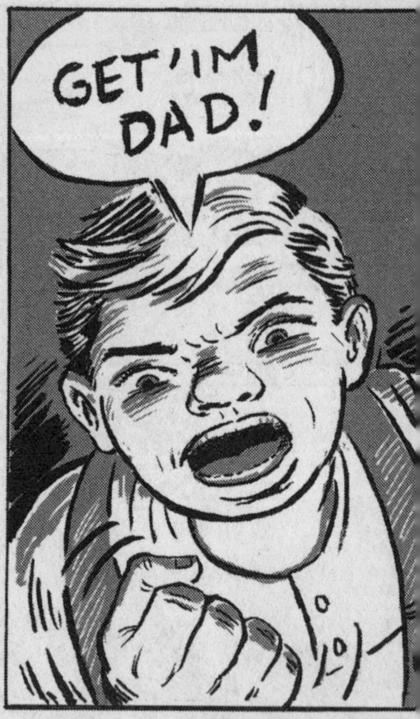
GET 'IM DAD!

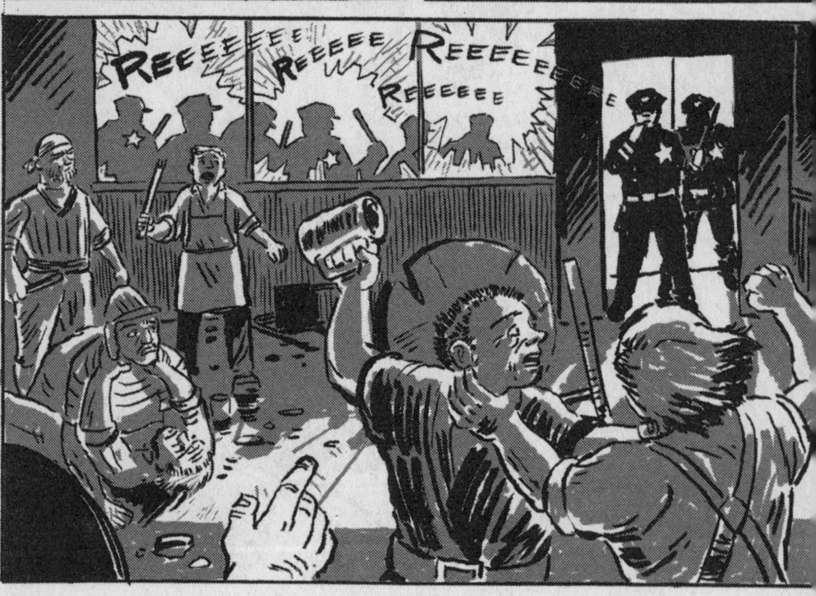
REEEEEEEE
REEEEEE
REEEEEEEEEE
REEEEEE

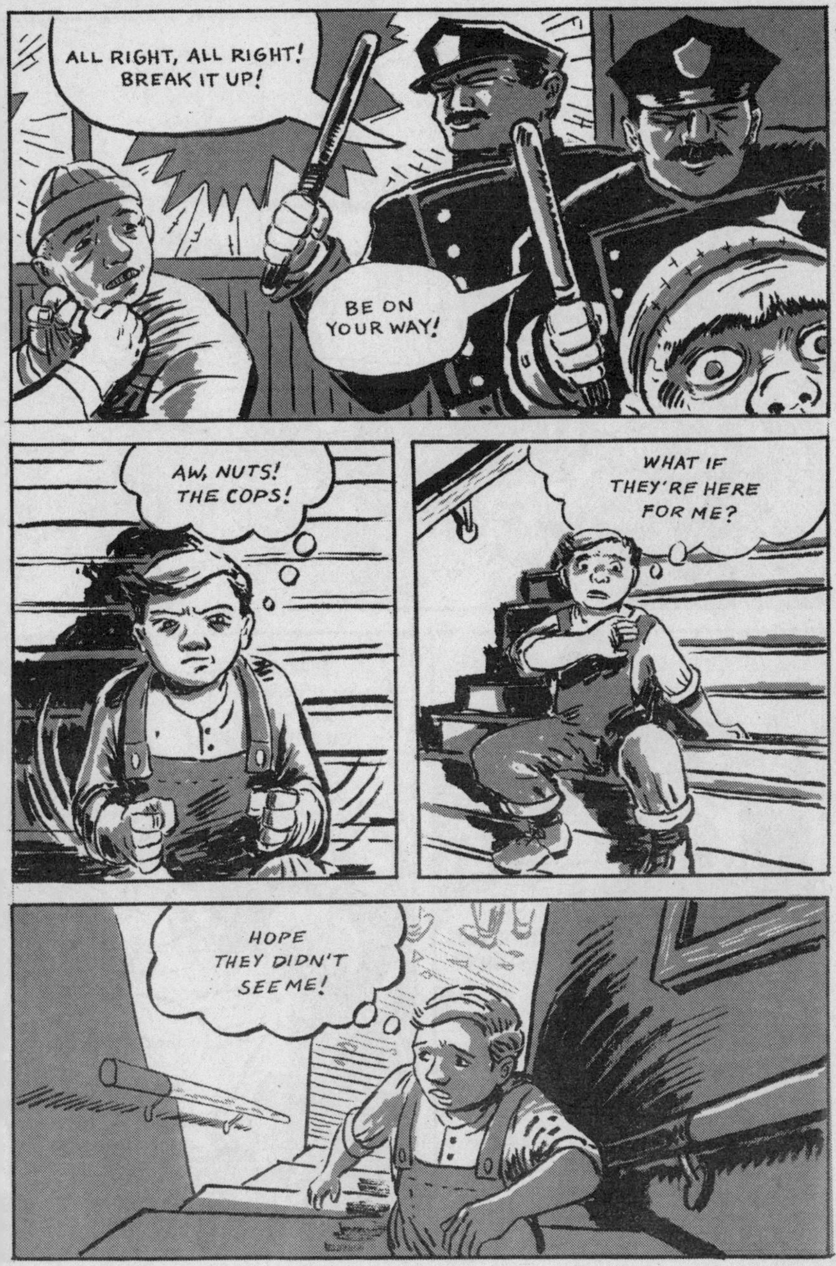
ALL RIGHT, ALL RIGHT! BREAK IT UP!
BE ON YOUR WAY!
AW, NUTS! THE COPS!
WHAT IF THEY'RE HERE FOR ME?
HOPE THEY DIDN'T SEE ME!

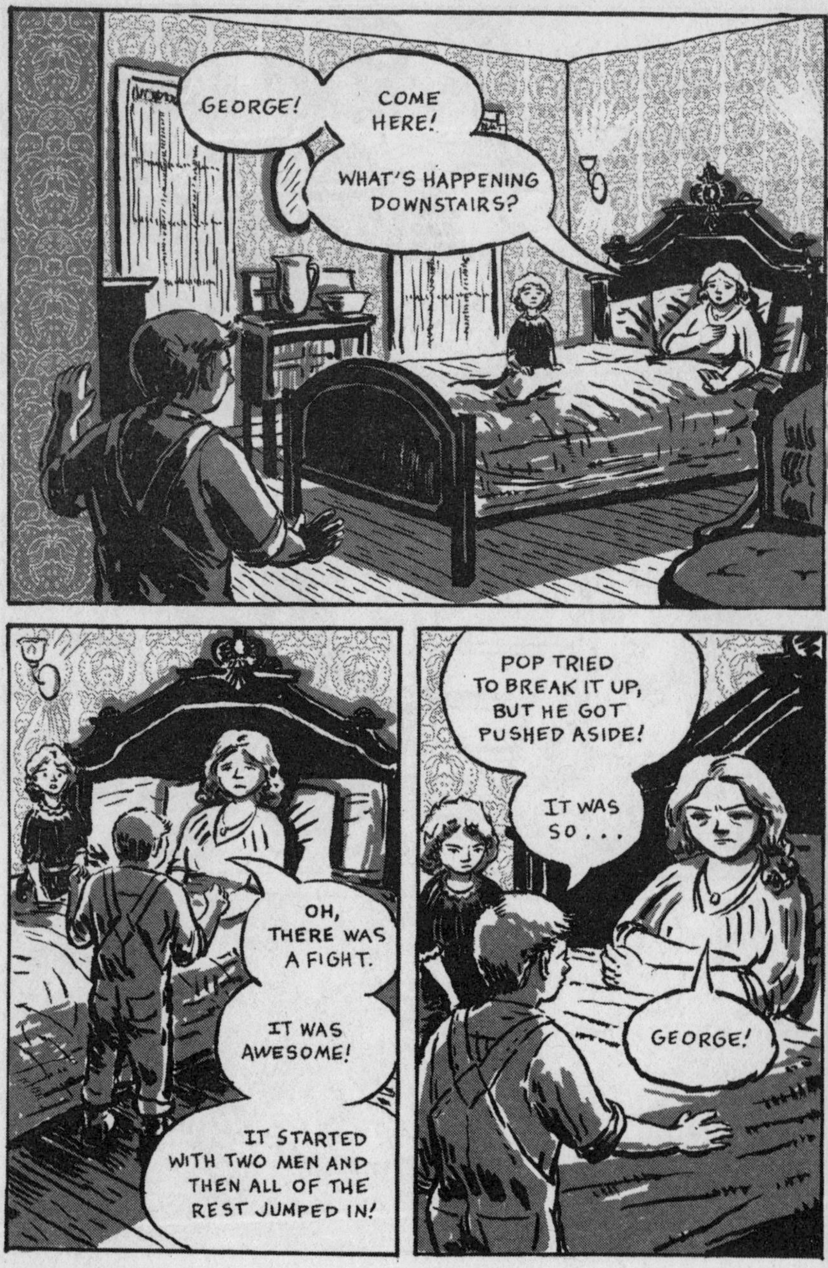
GEORGE!
COME HERE!
WHAT'S HAPPENING DOWNSTAIRS?
OH, THERE WAS A FIGHT.
IT WAS AWESOME!
IT STARTED WITH TWO MEN AND THEN ALL OF THE REST JUMPED IN!
POP TRIED TO BREAK IT UP, BUT HE GOT PUSHED ASIDE!
IT WAS SO . . .
GEORGE!

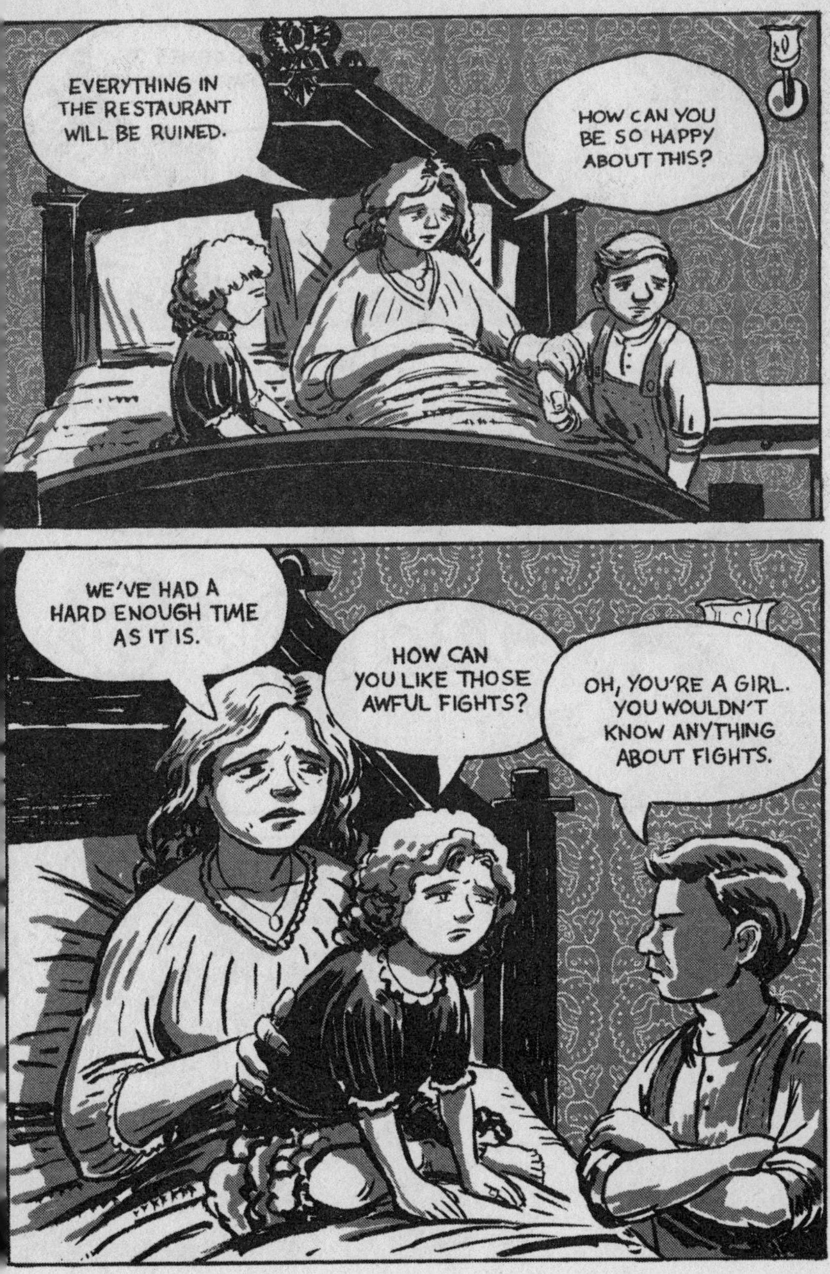
EVERYTHING IN THE RESTAURANT WILL BE RUINED.
HOW CAN YOU BE SO HAPPY ABOUT THIS?
WE'VE HAD A HARD ENOUGH TIME AS IT IS.
HOW CAN YOU LIKE THOSE AWFUL FIGHTS?
OH, YOU'RE A GIRL. YOU WOULDN'T KNOW ANYTHING ABOUT FIGHTS.

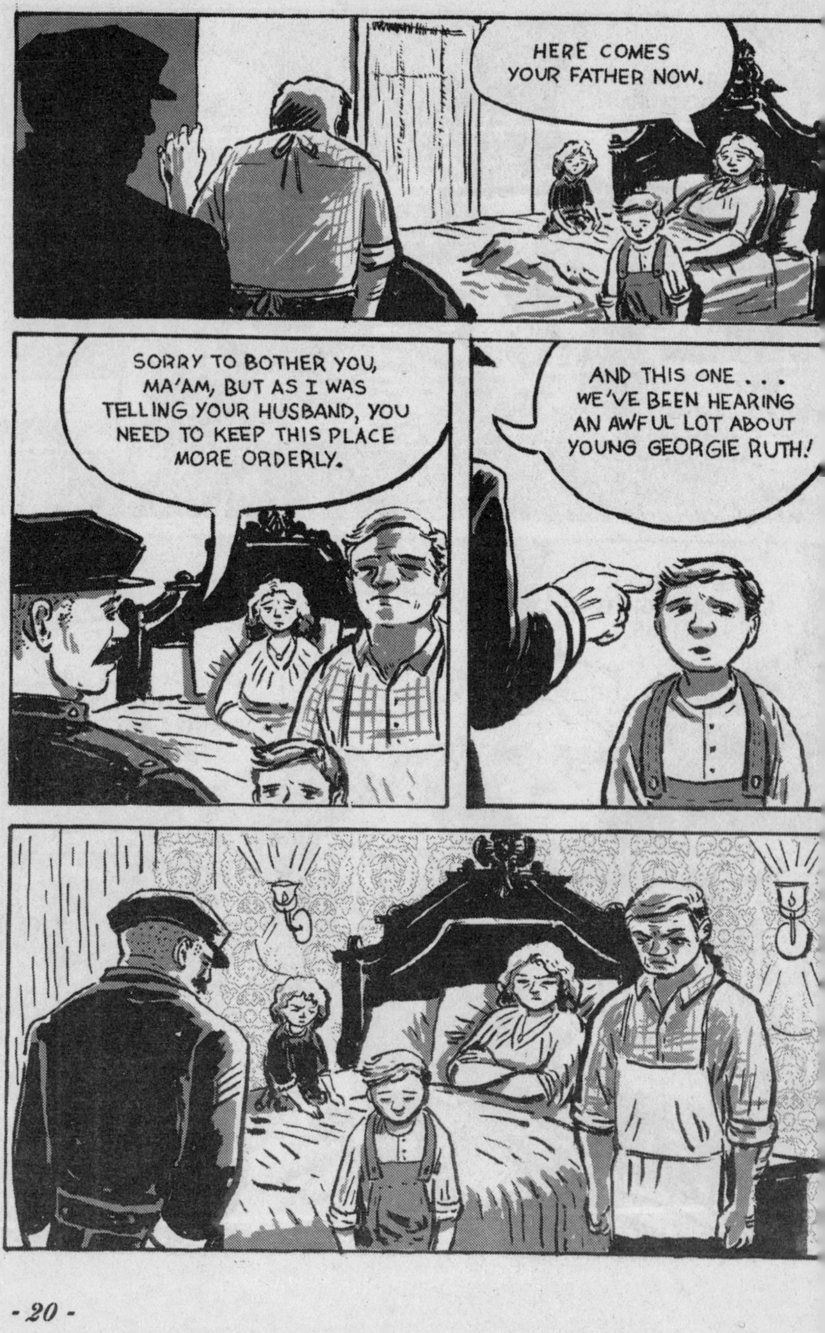
HERE COMES YOUR FATHER NOW.
SORRY TO BOTHER YOU, MA'AM, BUT AS I WAS TELLING YOUR HUSBAND, YOU NEED TO KEEP THIS PLACE MORE ORDERLY.
AND THIS ONE . . . WE'VE BEEN HEARING AN AWFUL LOT ABOUT YOUNG GEORGIE RUTH!

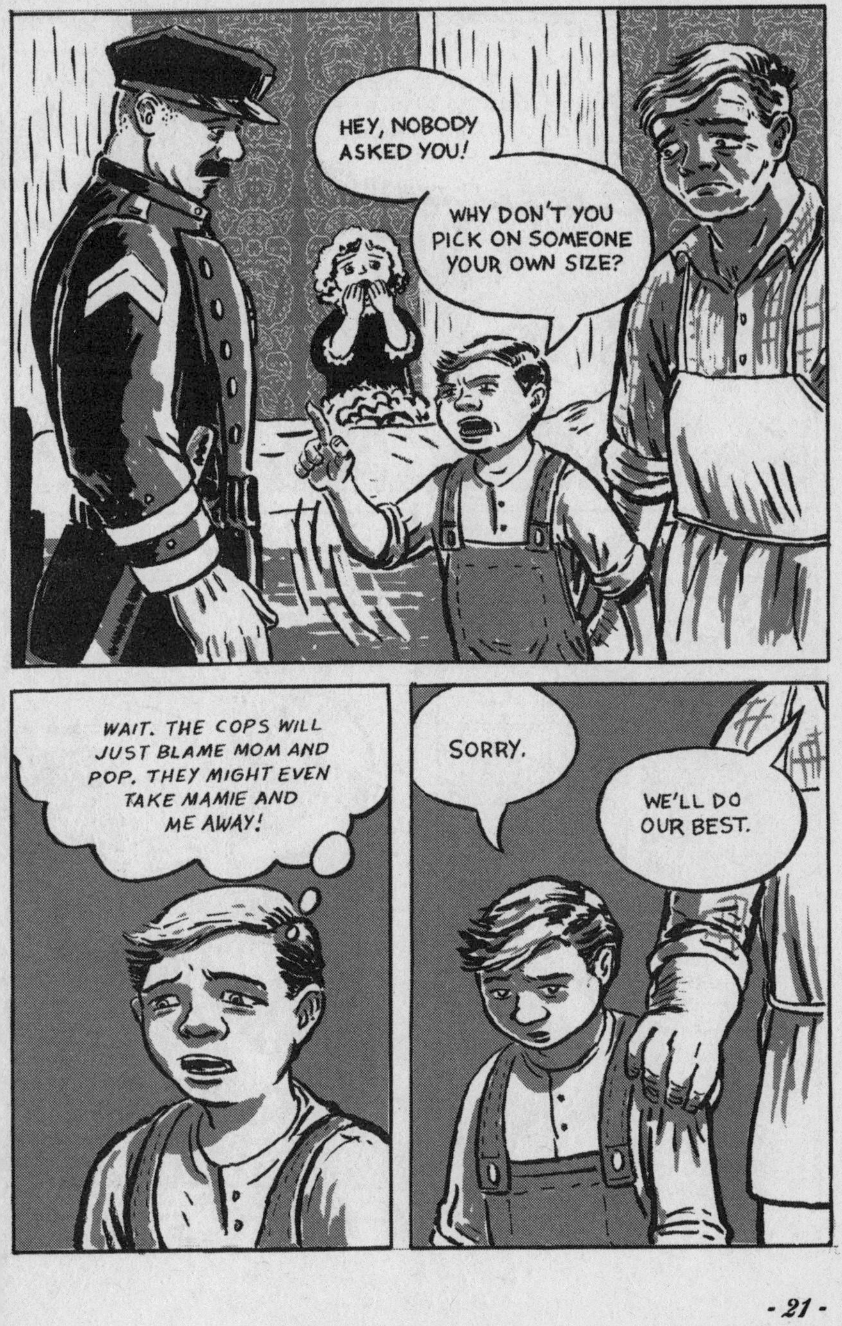
HEY, NOBODY ASKED YOU!
WHY DON'T YOU PICK ON SOMEONE YOUR OWN SIZE?
WAIT. THE COPS WILL JUST BLAME MOM AND POP. THEY MIGHT EVEN TAKE MAMIE AND ME AWAY!
SORRY.
WE'LL DO OUR BEST.

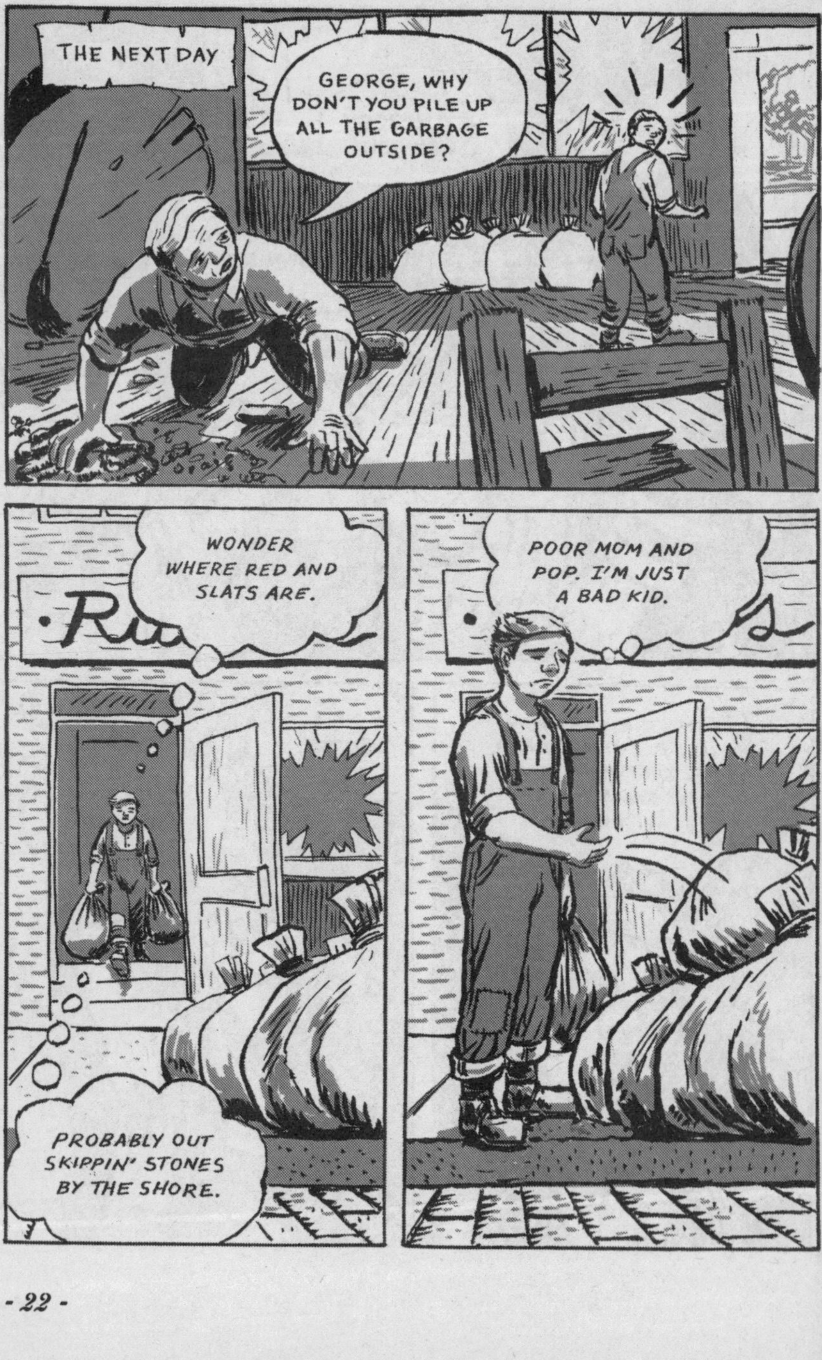
THE NEXT DAY
GEORGE, WHY DON'T YOU PILE UP ALL THE GARBAGE OUTSIDE?
WONDER WHERE RED AND SLATS ARE.
PROBABLY OUT SKIPPIN' STONES BY THE SHORE.
POOR MOM AND POP. I'M JUST A BAD KID.

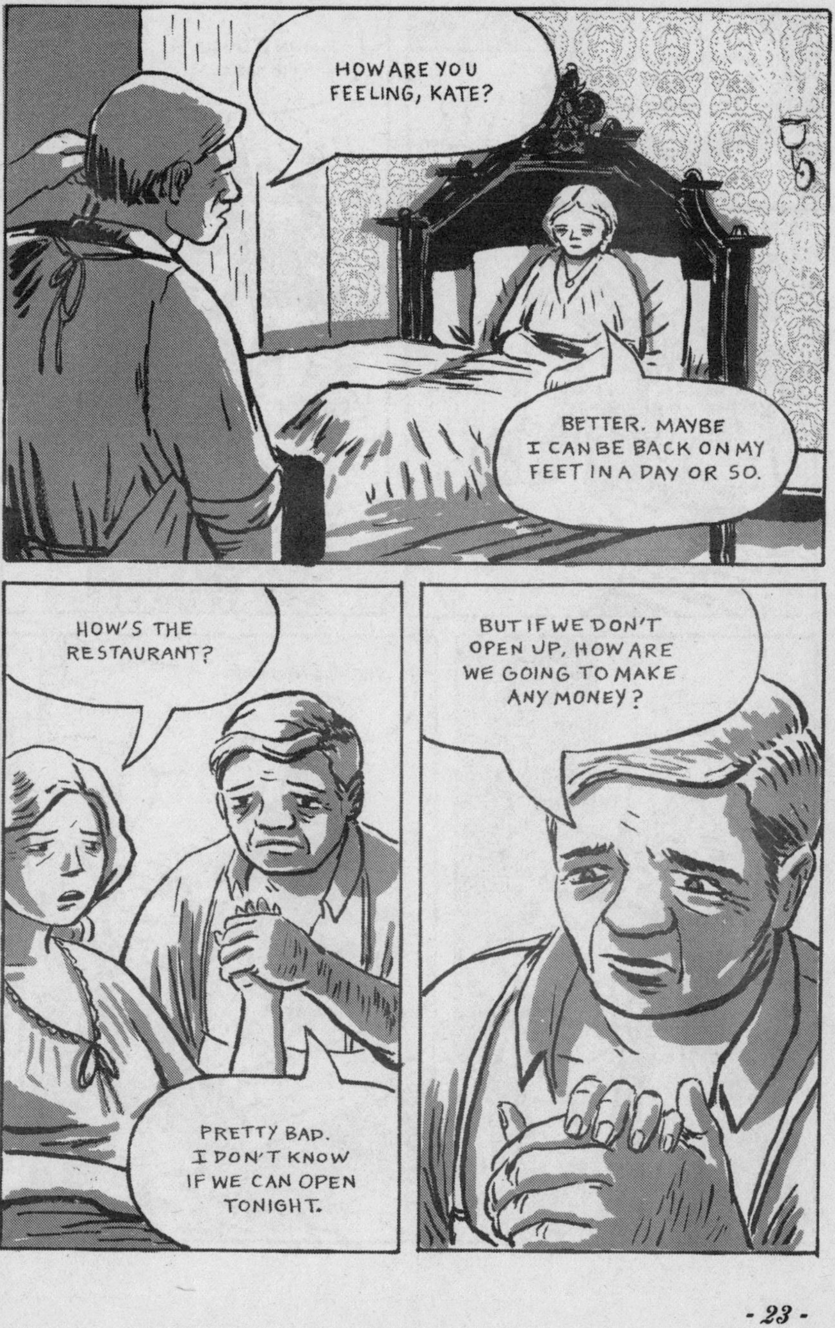
HOW ARE YOU FEELING, KATE?
BETTER. MAYBE I CAN BE BACK ON MY FEET IN A DAY OR SO.
HOW'S THE RESTAURANT?
PRETTY BAD. I DON'T KNOW IF WE CAN OPEN TONIGHT.
BUT IF WE DON'T OPEN UP, HOW ARE WE GOING TO MAKE ANY MONEY?

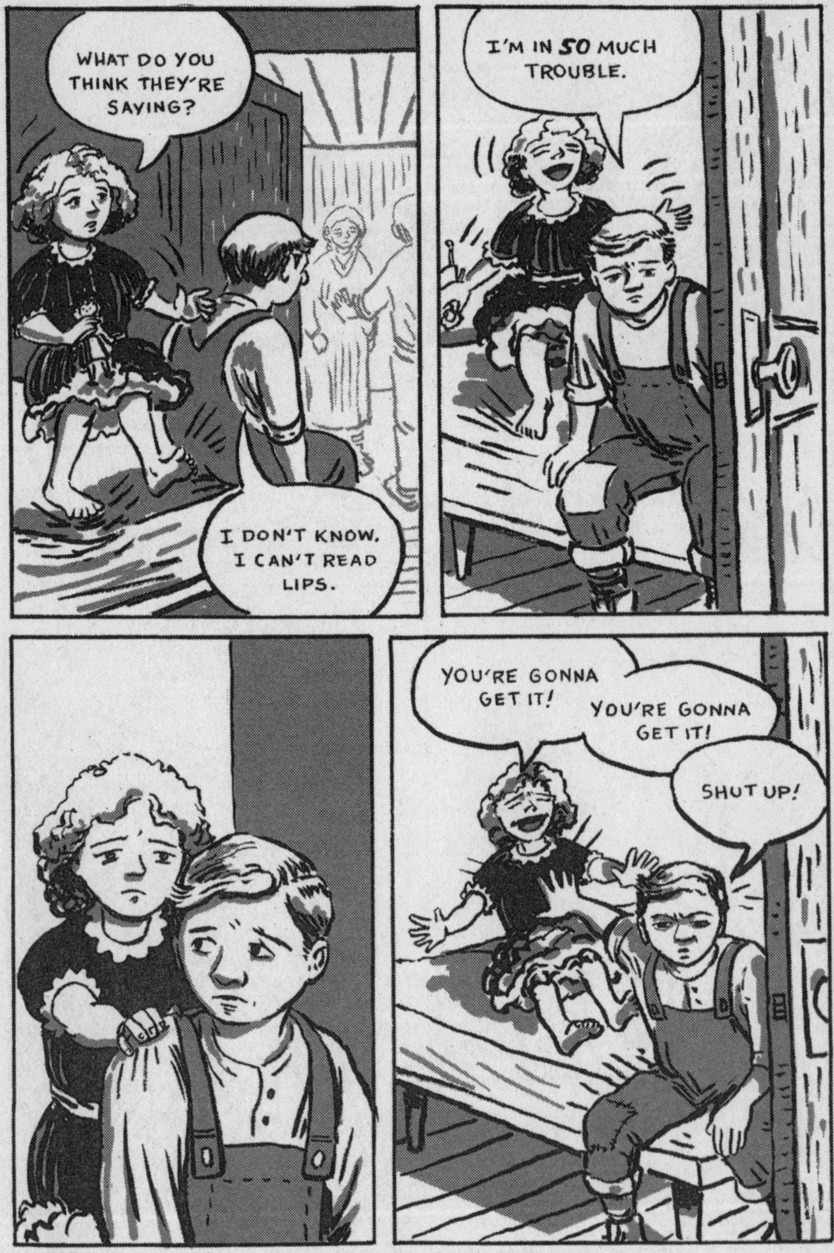
WHAT DO YOU THINK THEY'RE SAYING?
I DON'T KNOW. I CAN'T READ LIPS.
I'M IN SO MUCH TROUBLE.
YOU'RE GONNA GET IT!
YOU'RE GONNA GET IT!
SHUT UP!

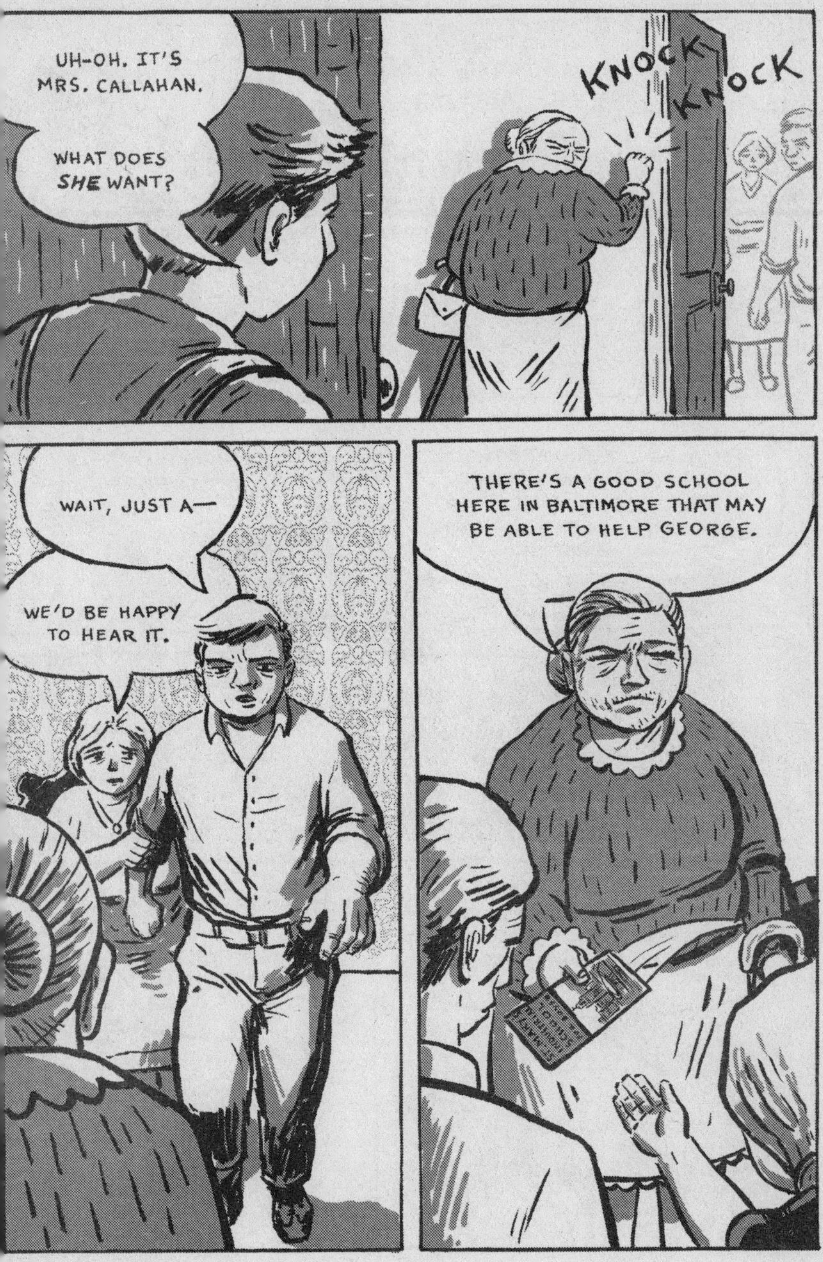
UH-OH. IT'S MRS. CALLAHAN.
WHAT DOES SHE WANT?
KNOCK KNOCK
WAIT, JUST A—
WE'D BE HAPPY TO HEAR IT.
THERE'S A GOOD SCHOOL HERE IN BALTIMORE THAT MAY BE ABLE TO HELP GEORGE.

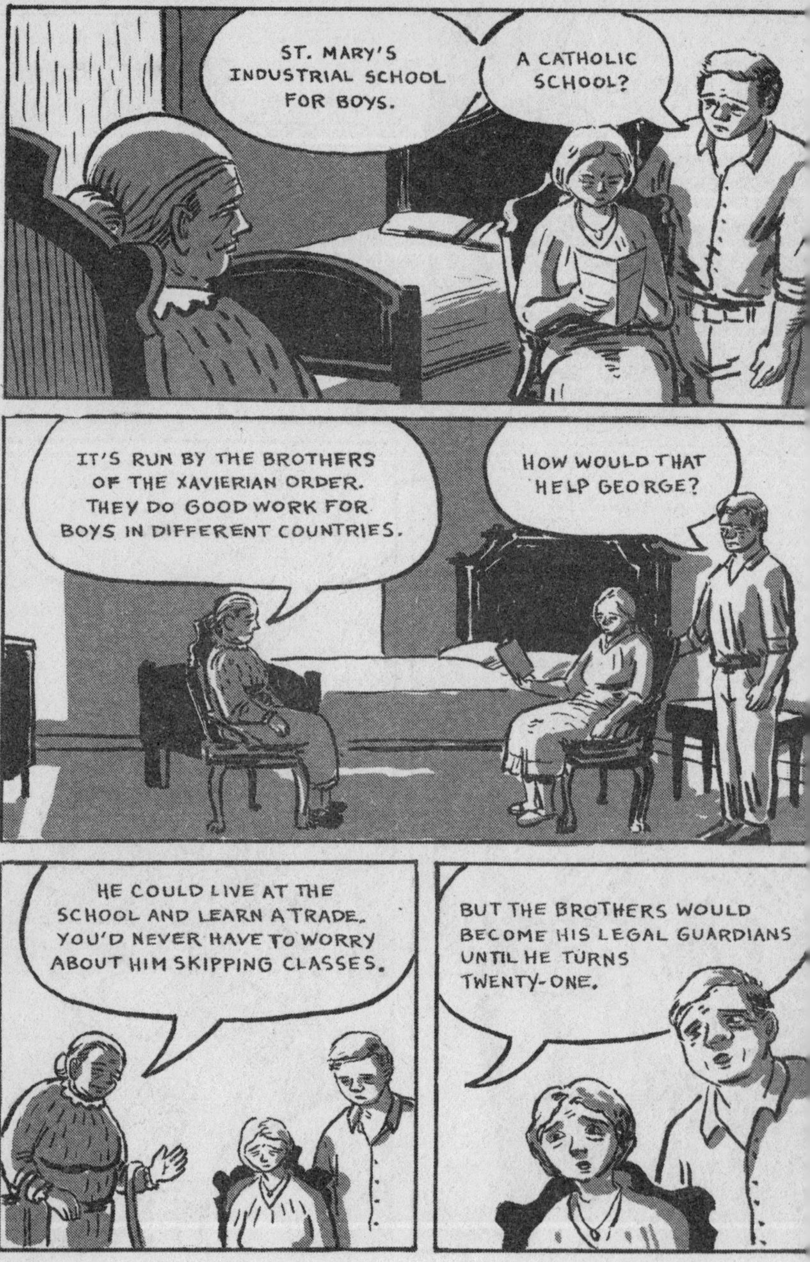
ST. MARY'S INDUSTRIAL SCHOOL FOR BOYS.
A CATHOLIC SCHOOL?
IT'S RUN BY THE BROTHERS OF THE XAVIERIAN ORDER. THEY DO GOOD WORK FOR BOYS IN DIFFERENT COUNTRIES.
HOW WOULD THAT HELP GEORGE?
HE COULD LIVE AT THE SCHOOL AND LEARN A TRADE. YOU'D NEVER HAVE TO WORRY ABOUT HIM SKIPPING CLASSES.
BUT THE BROTHERS WOULD BECOME HIS LEGAL GUARDIANS UNTIL HE TURNS TWENTY-ONE.

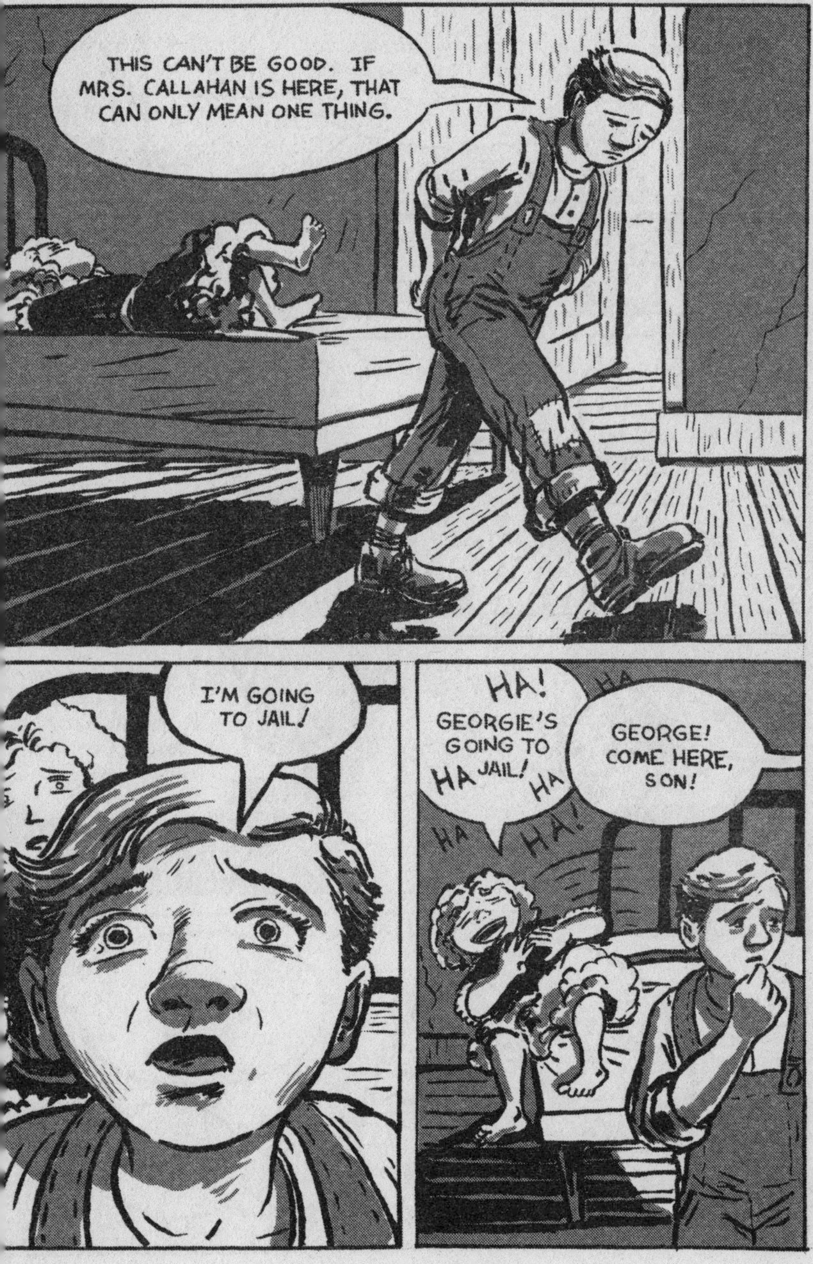
THIS CAN'T BE GOOD. IF MRS. CALLAHAN IS HERE, THAT CAN ONLY MEAN ONE THING.
I'M GOING TO JAIL!
HA! GEORGIE'S GOING TO JAIL! HA HA HA HA! HA HA
GEORGE! COME HERE, SON!

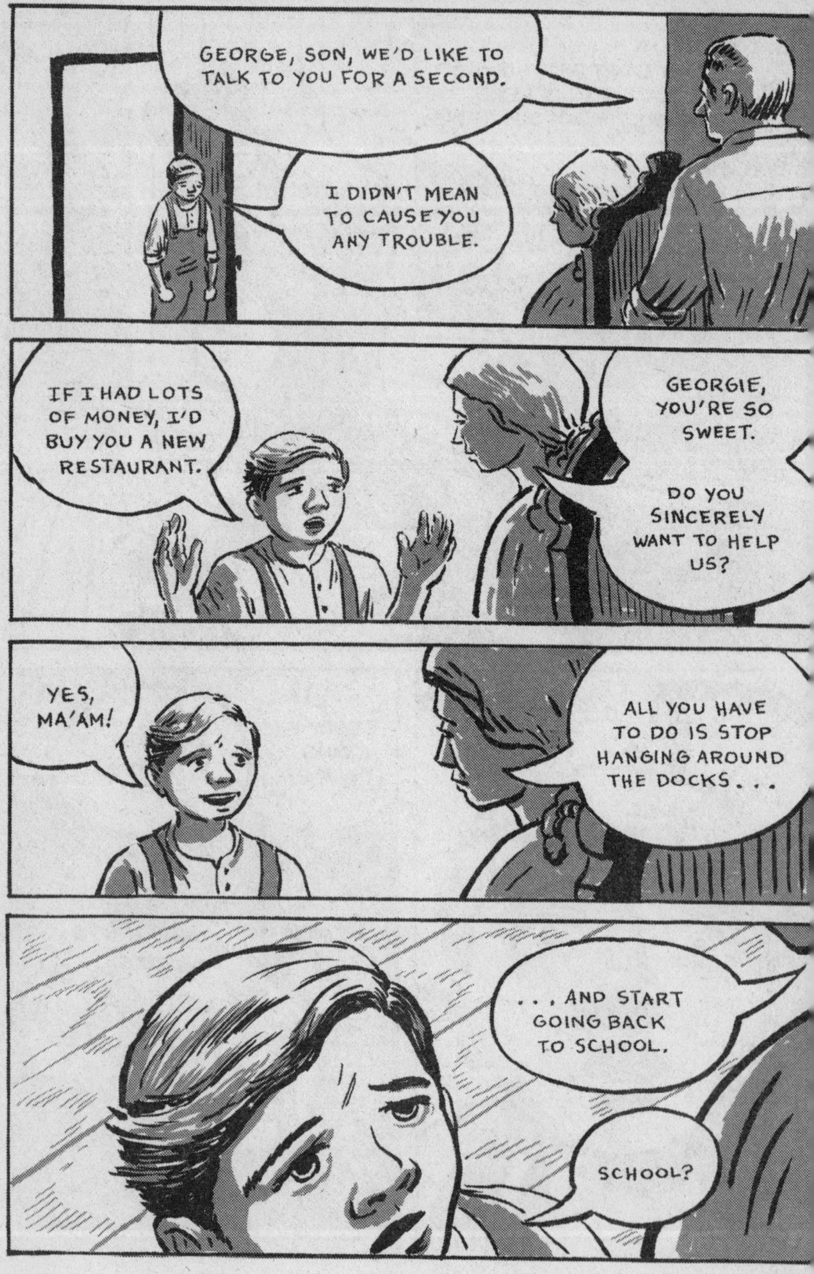
GEORGE, SON, WE'D LIKE TO TALK TO YOU FOR A SECOND.
I DIDN'T MEAN TO CAUSE YOU ANY TROUBLE.
IF I HAD LOTS OF MONEY, I'D BUY YOU A NEW RESTAURANT.
GEORGIE, YOU'RE SO SWEET.
DO YOU SINCERELY WANT TO HELP US?
YES, MA'AM!
ALL YOU HAVE TO DO IS STOP HANGING AROUND THE DOCKS . . .
. . . AND START GOING BACK TO SCHOOL.
SCHOOL?

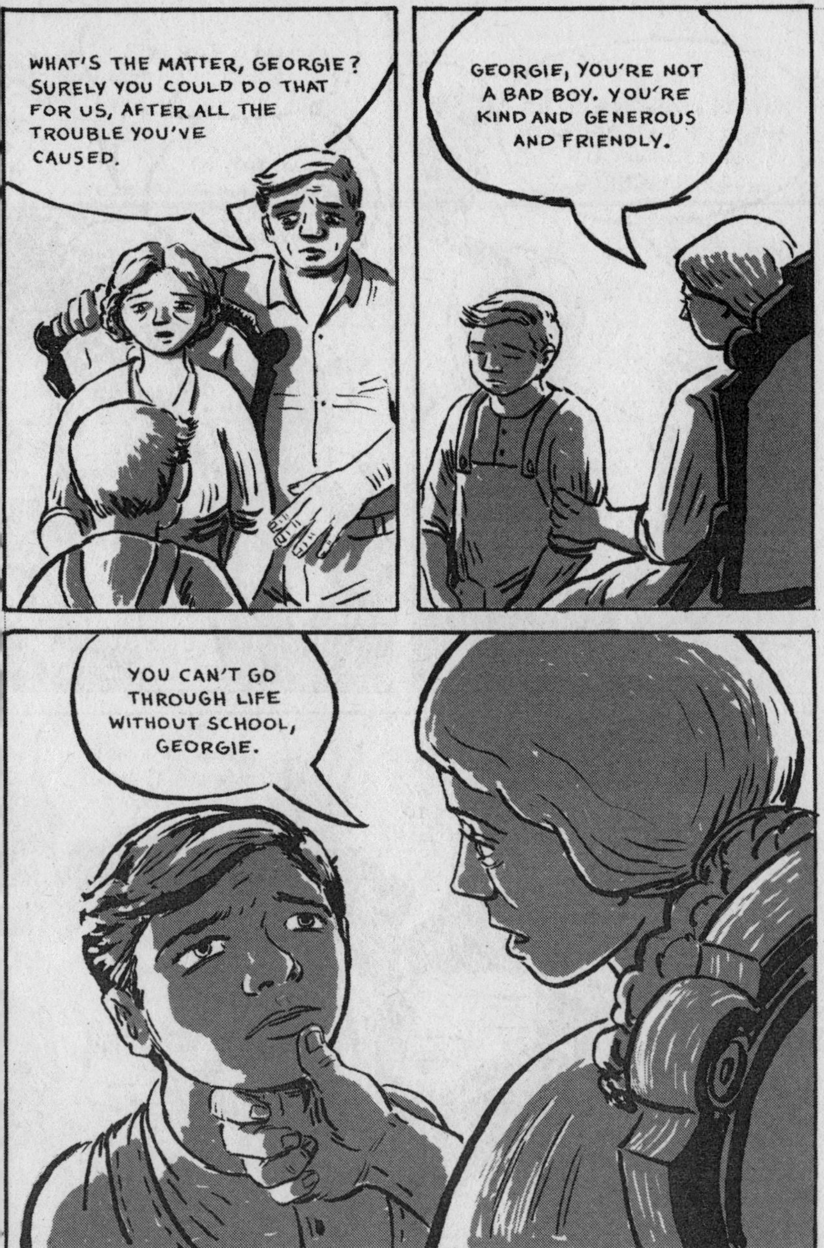
WHAT'S THE MATTER, GEORGIE? SURELY YOU COULD DO THAT FOR US, AFTER ALL THE TROUBLE YOU'VE CAUSED.
GEORGIE, YOU'RE NOT A BAD BOY. YOU'RE KIND AND GENEROUS AND FRIENDLY.
YOU CAN'T GO THROUGH LIFE WITHOUT SCHOOL, GEORGIE.

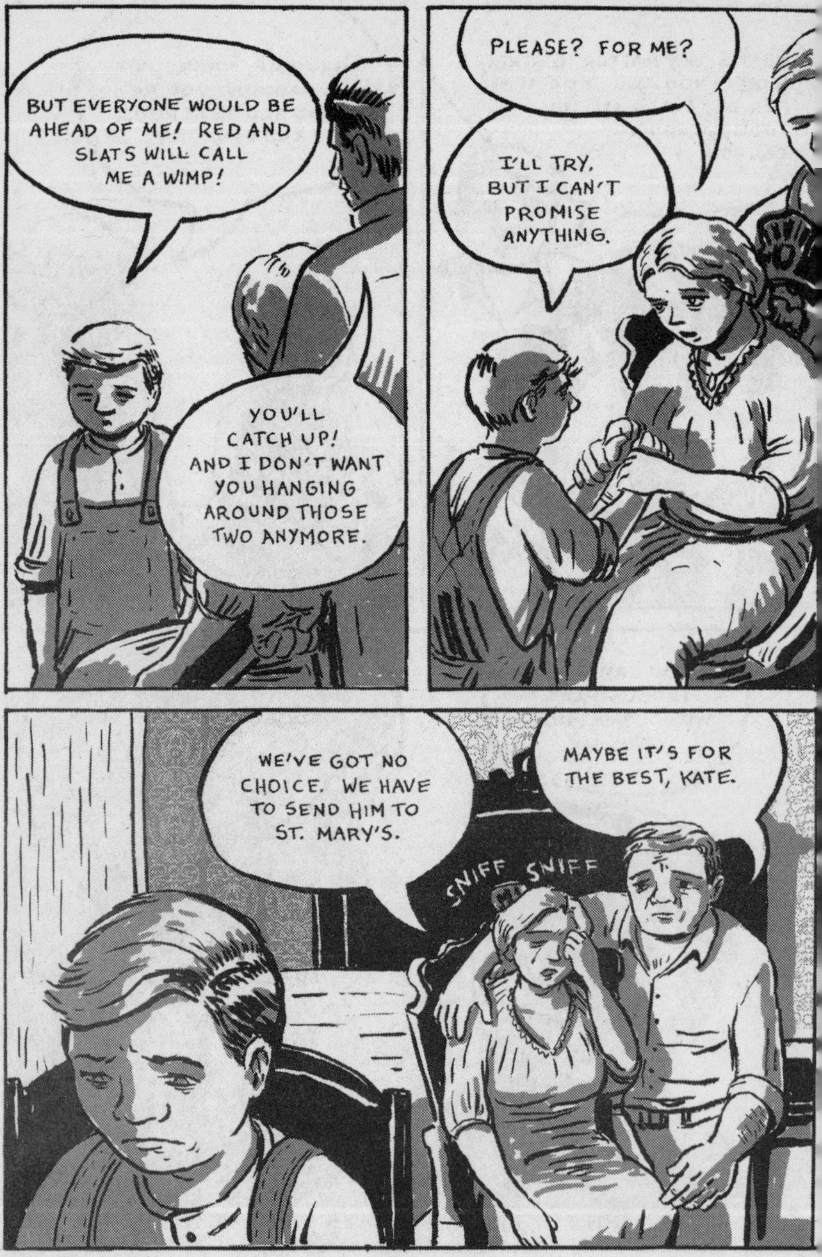
BUT EVERYONE WOULD BE AHEAD OF ME! RED AND SLATS WILL CALL ME A WIMP!
YOU'LL CATCH UP! AND I DON'T WANT YOU HANGING AROUND THOSE TWO ANYMORE.
PLEASE? FOR ME?
I'LL TRY. BUT I CAN'T PROMISE ANYTHING.
WE'VE GOT NO CHOICE. WE HAVE TO SEND HIM TO ST. MARY'S.
MAYBE IT'S FOR THE BEST, KATE.
SNIFF SNIFF

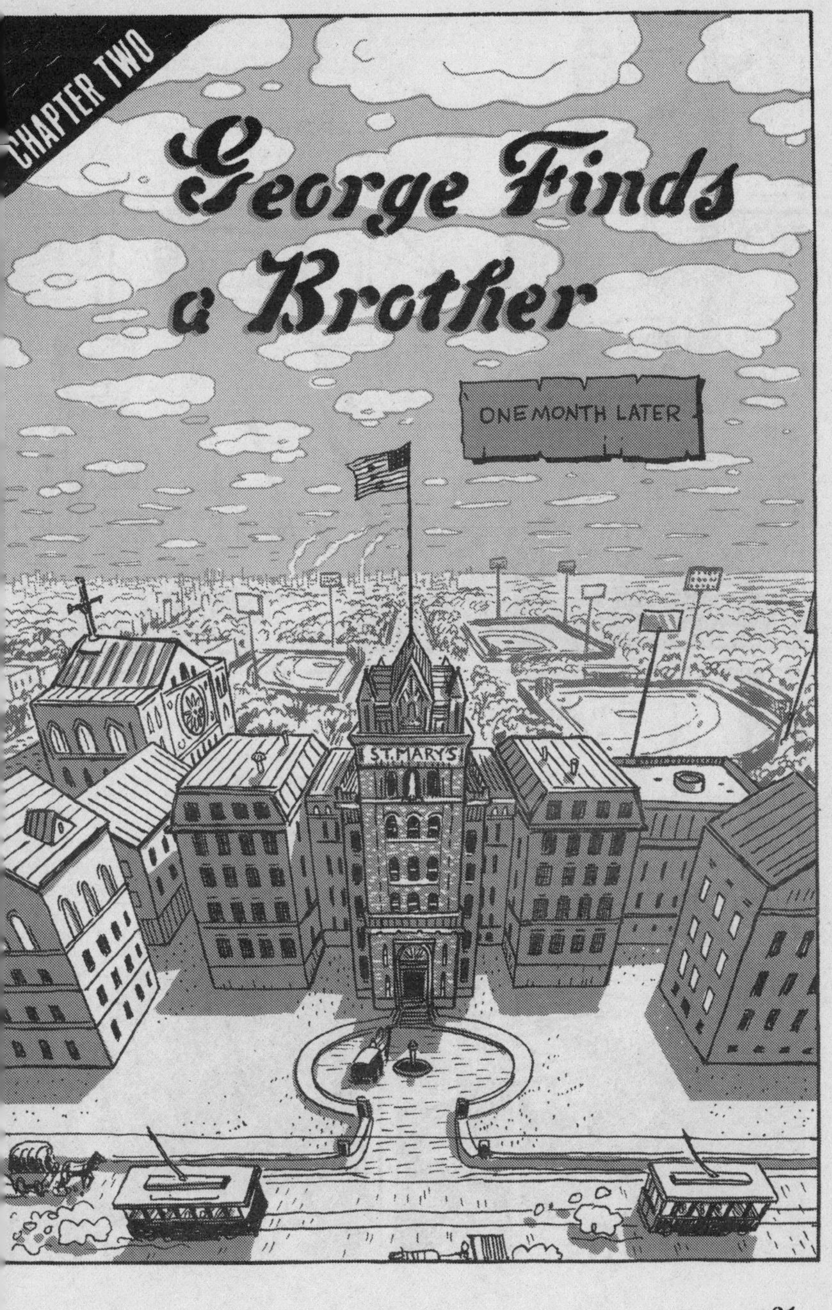
CHAPTER TWO
George Finds a Brother
ONE MONTH LATER
ST. MARY'S

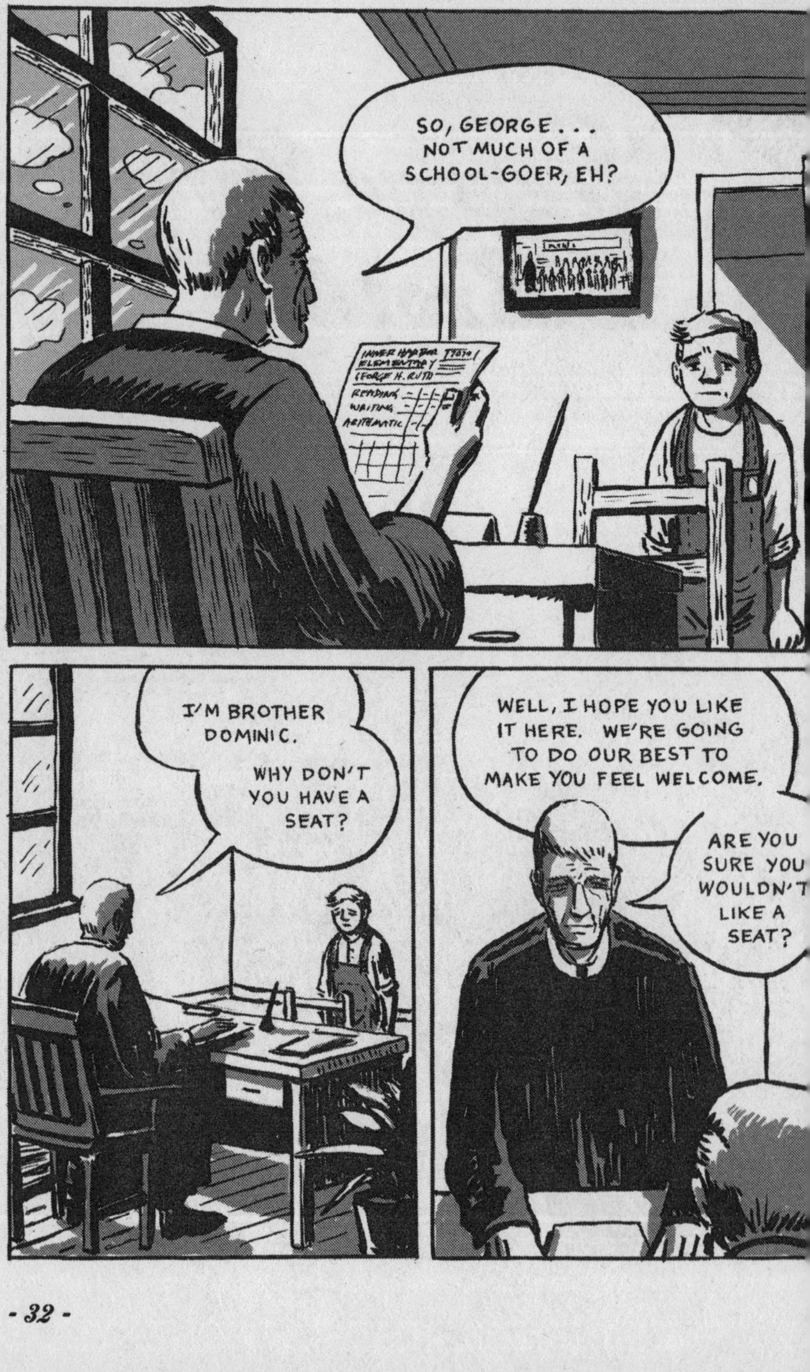
SO, GEORGE . . . NOT MUCH OF A SCHOOL-GOER, EH?
I'M BROTHER DOMINIC.
WHY DON'T YOU HAVE A SEAT?
WELL, I HOPE YOU LIKE IT HERE. WE'RE GOING TO DO OUR BEST TO MAKE YOU FEEL WELCOME.
ARE YOU SURE YOU WOULDN'T LIKE A SEAT?

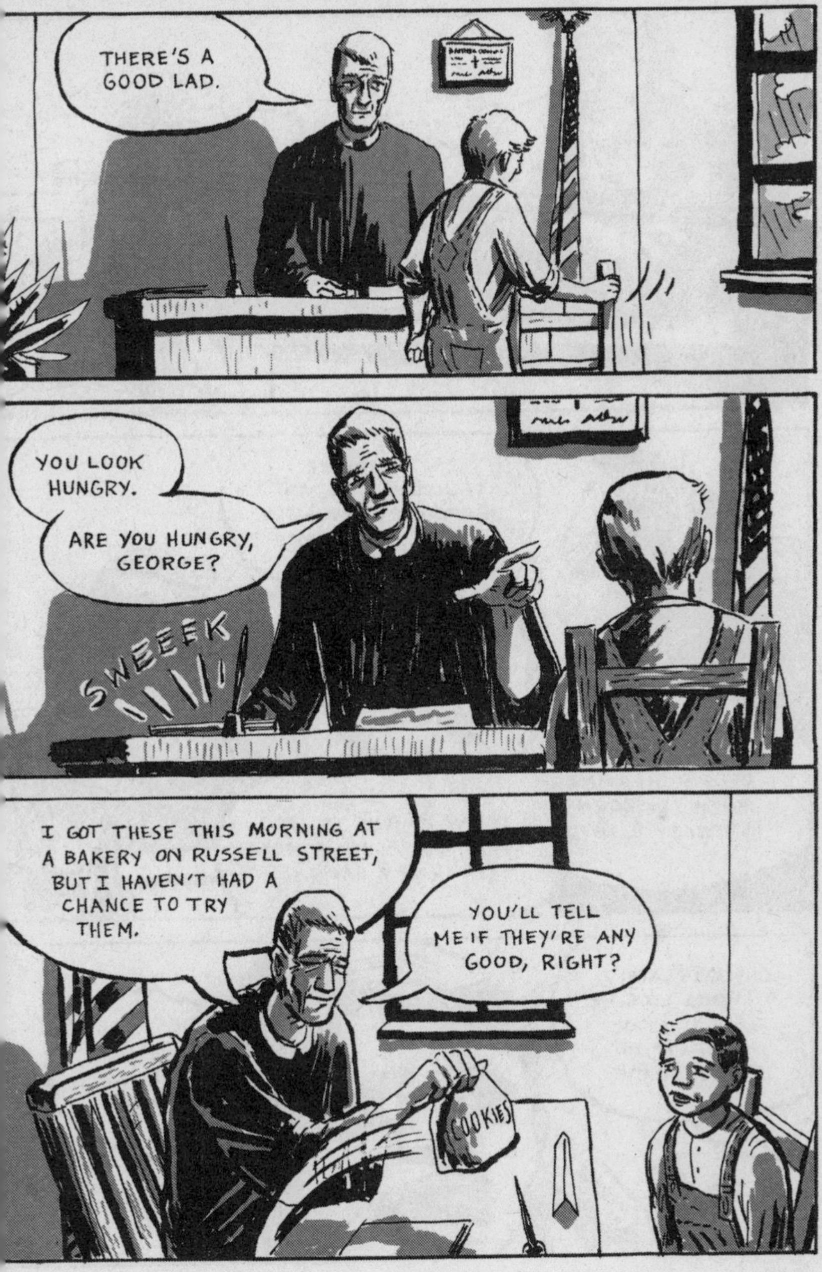
THERE'S A GOOD LAD.
YOU LOOK HUNGRY.
ARE YOU HUNGRY, GEORGE?
SWEEEK
I GOT THESE THIS MORNING AT A BAKERY ON RUSSELL STREET, BUT I HAVEN'T HAD A CHANCE TO TRY THEM.
YOU'LL TELL ME IF THEY'RE ANY GOOD, RIGHT?
COOKIES

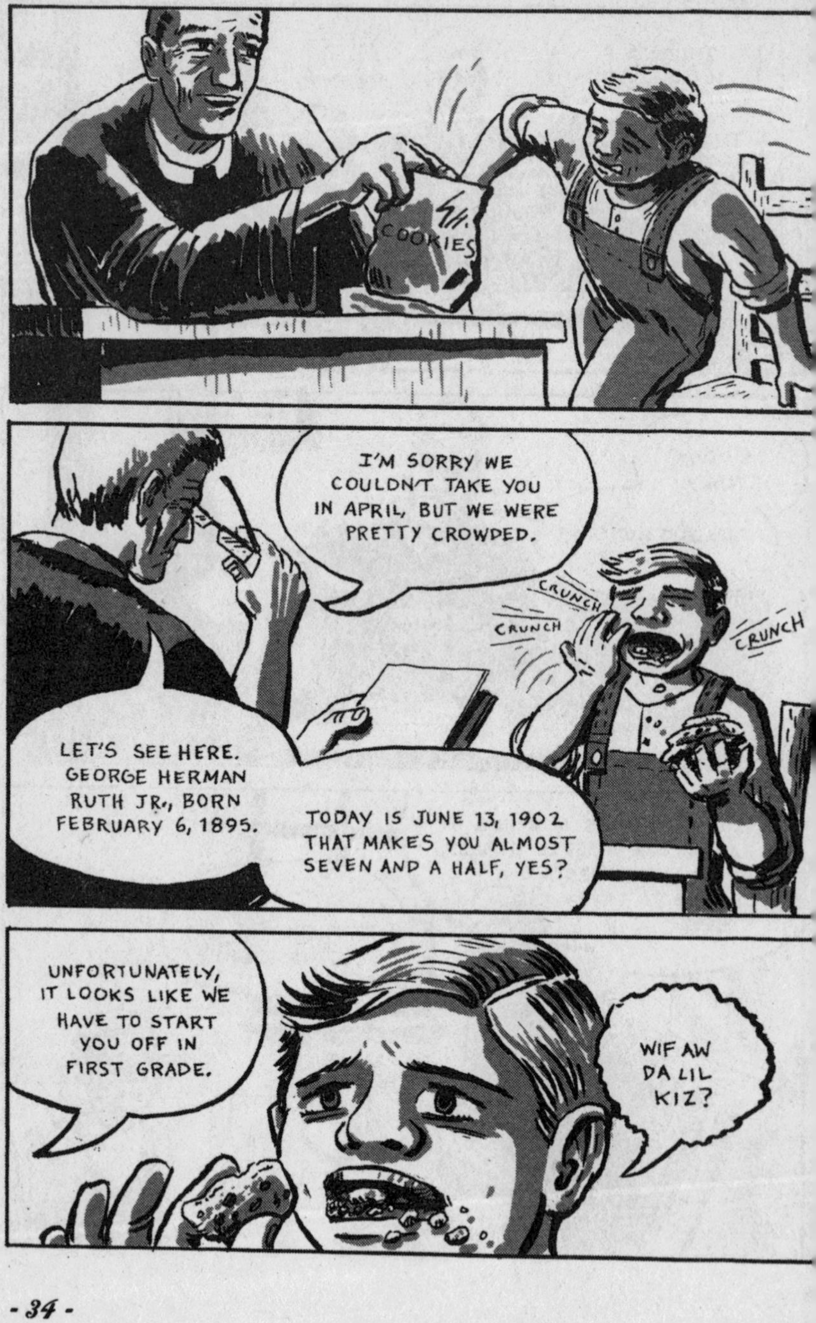
COOKIES
I'M SORRY WE COULDN'T TAKE YOU IN APRIL, BUT WE WERE PRETTY CROWDED.
CRUNCH
CRUNCH
CRUNCH
LET'S SEE HERE. GEORGE HERMAN RUTH JR., BORN FEBRUARY 6, 1895.
TODAY IS JUNE 13, 1902 THAT MAKES YOU ALMOST SEVEN AND A HALF, YES?
UNFORTUNATELY, IT LOOKS LIKE WE HAVE TO START YOU OFF IN FIRST GRADE.
WIF AW DA LIL KIZ?

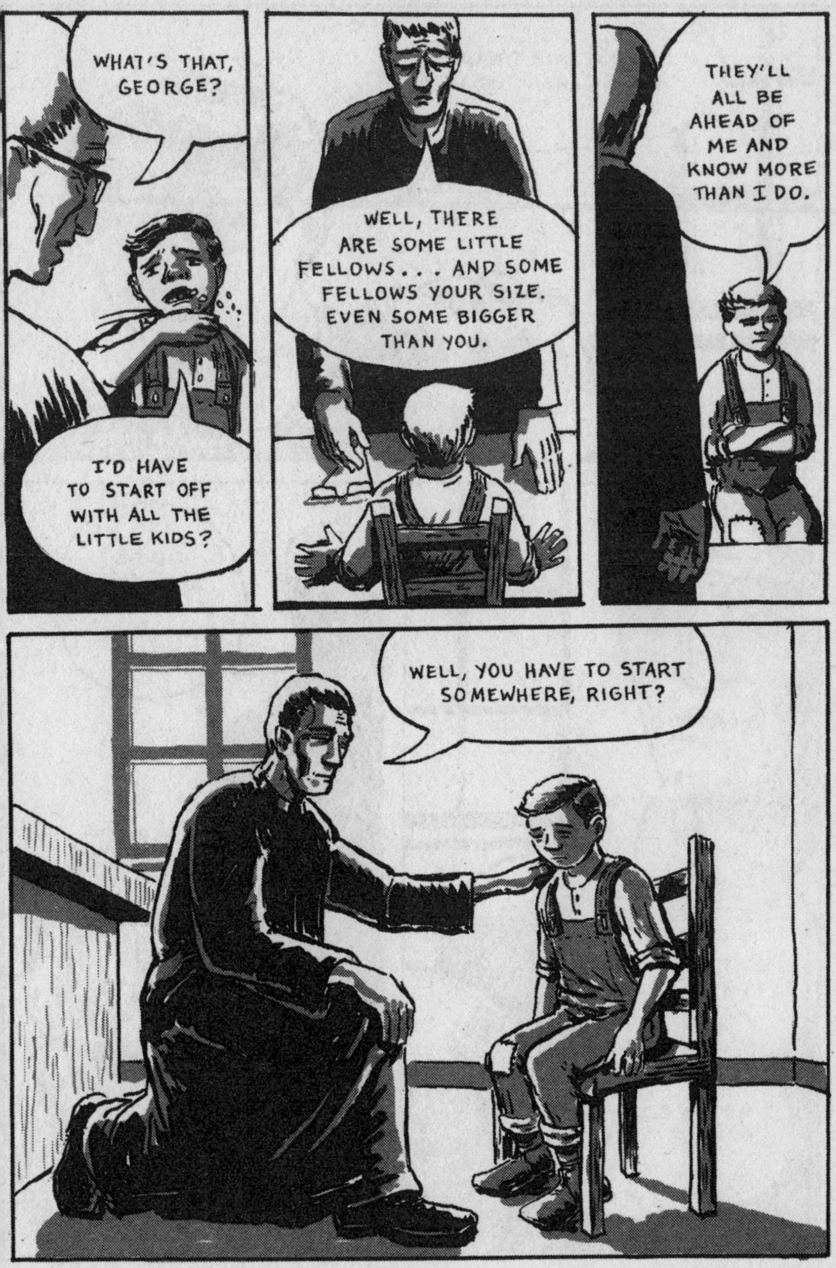
WHAT'S THAT, GEORGE?
I'D HAVE TO START OFF WITH ALL THE LITTLE KIDS?
WELL, THERE ARE SOME LITTLE FELLOWS . . . AND SOME FELLOWS YOUR SIZE. EVEN SOME BIGGER THAN YOU.
THEY'LL ALL BE AHEAD OF ME AND KNOW MORE THAN I DO.
WELL, YOU HAVE TO START SOMEWHERE, RIGHT?

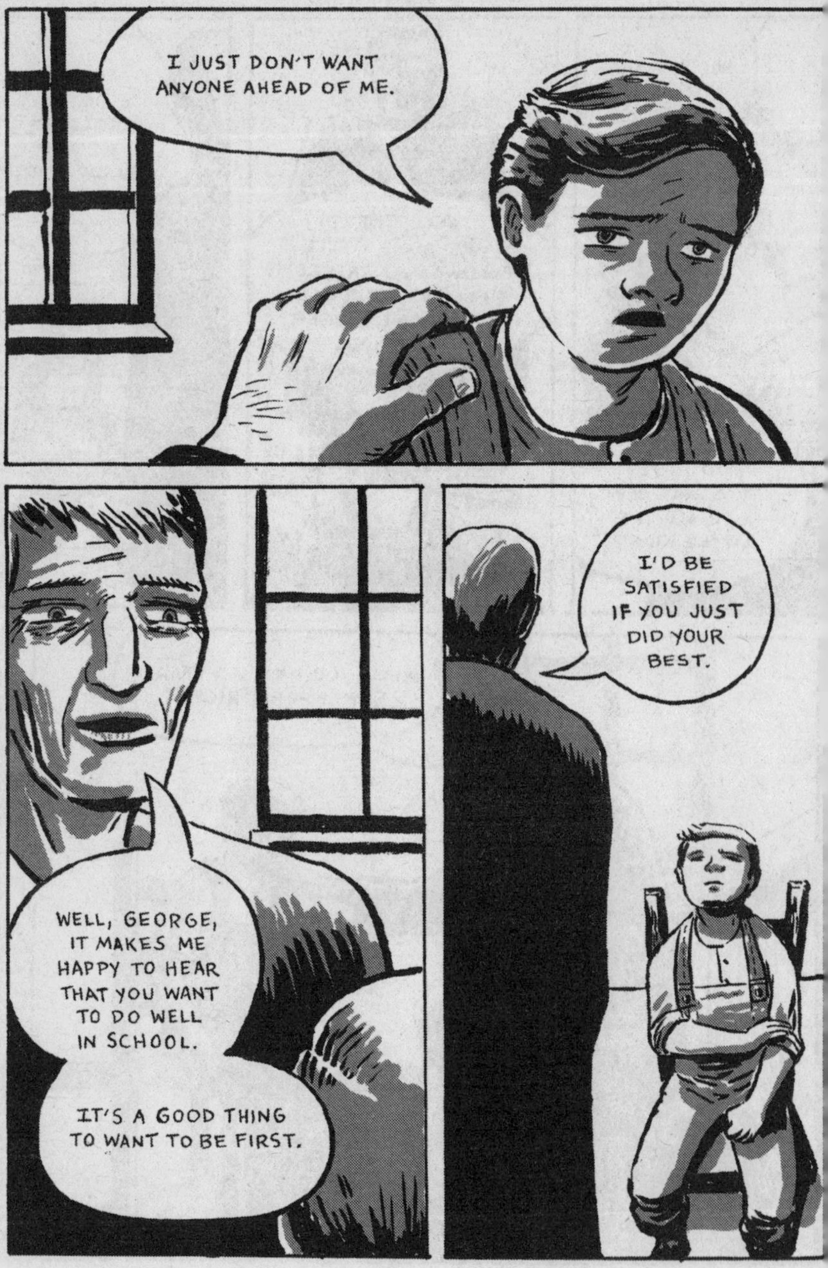
I JUST DON'T WANT ANYONE AHEAD OF ME.
WELL, GEORGE, IT MAKES ME HAPPY TO HEAR THAT YOU WANT TO DO WELL IN SCHOOL.
IT'S A GOOD THING TO WANT TO BE FIRST.
I'D BE SATISFIED IF YOU JUST DID YOUR BEST.

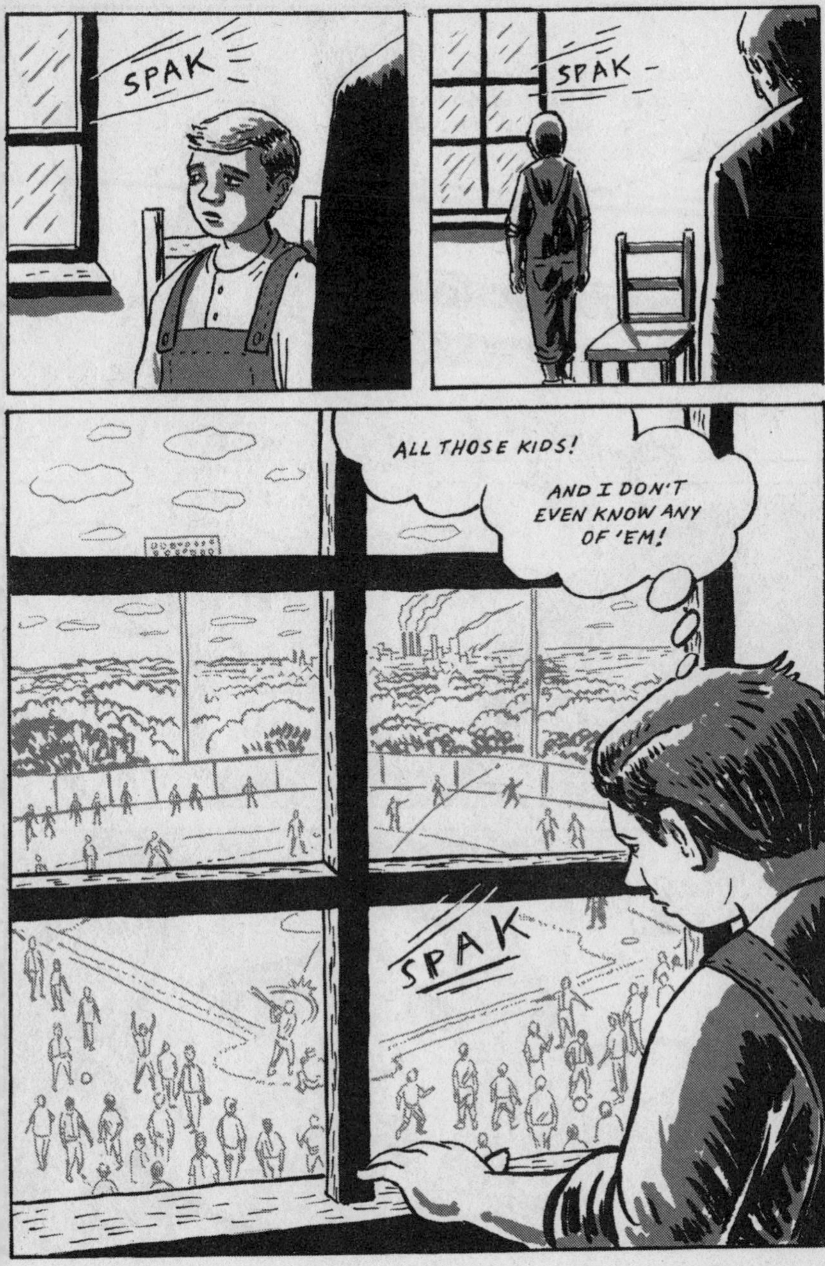
SPAK
SPAK
ALL THOSE KIDS!
AND I DON'T EVEN KNOW ANY OF 'EM!
SPAK

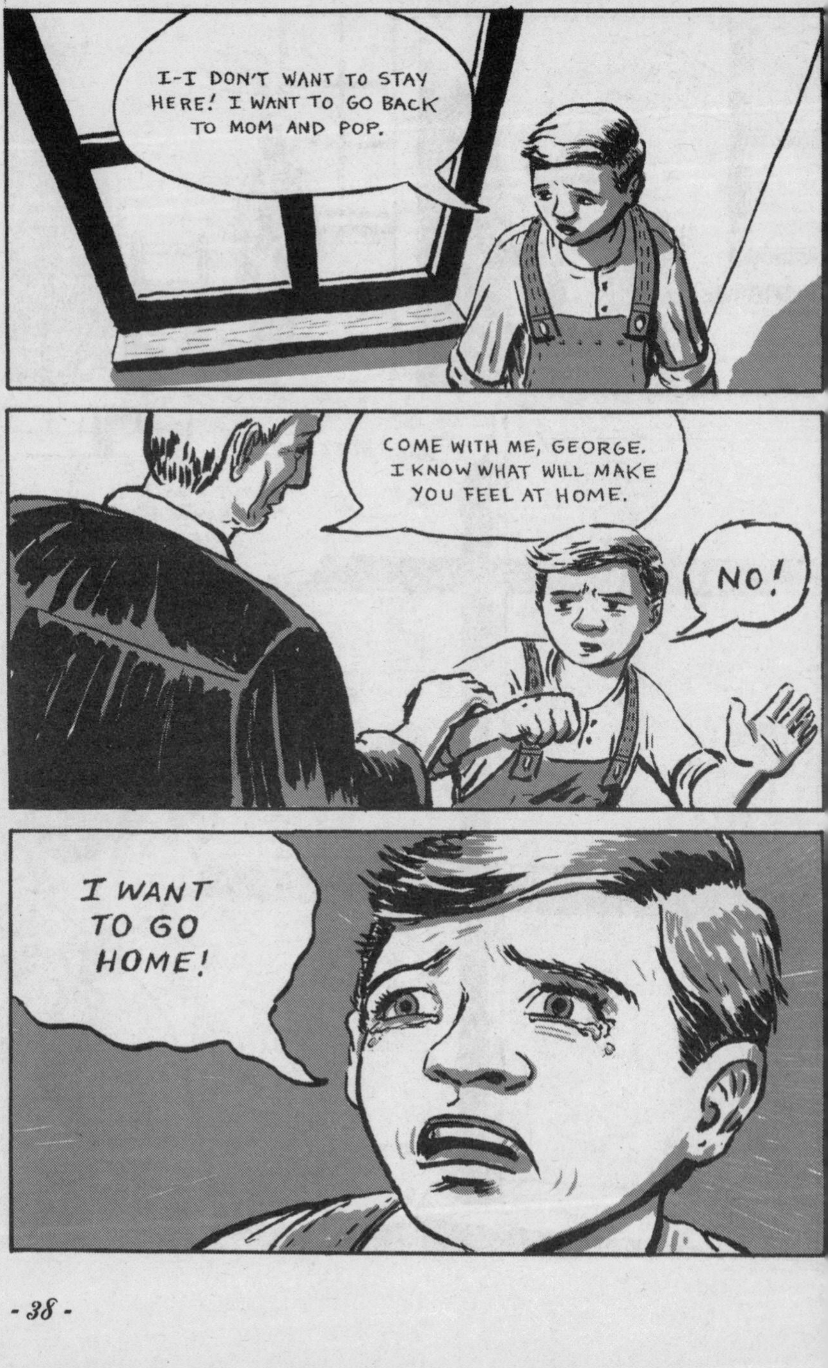
I-I DON'T WANT TO STAY HERE! I WANT TO GO BACK TO MOM AND POP.
COME WITH ME, GEORGE. I KNOW WHAT WILL MAKE YOU FEEL AT HOME.
NO!
I WANT TO GO HOME!

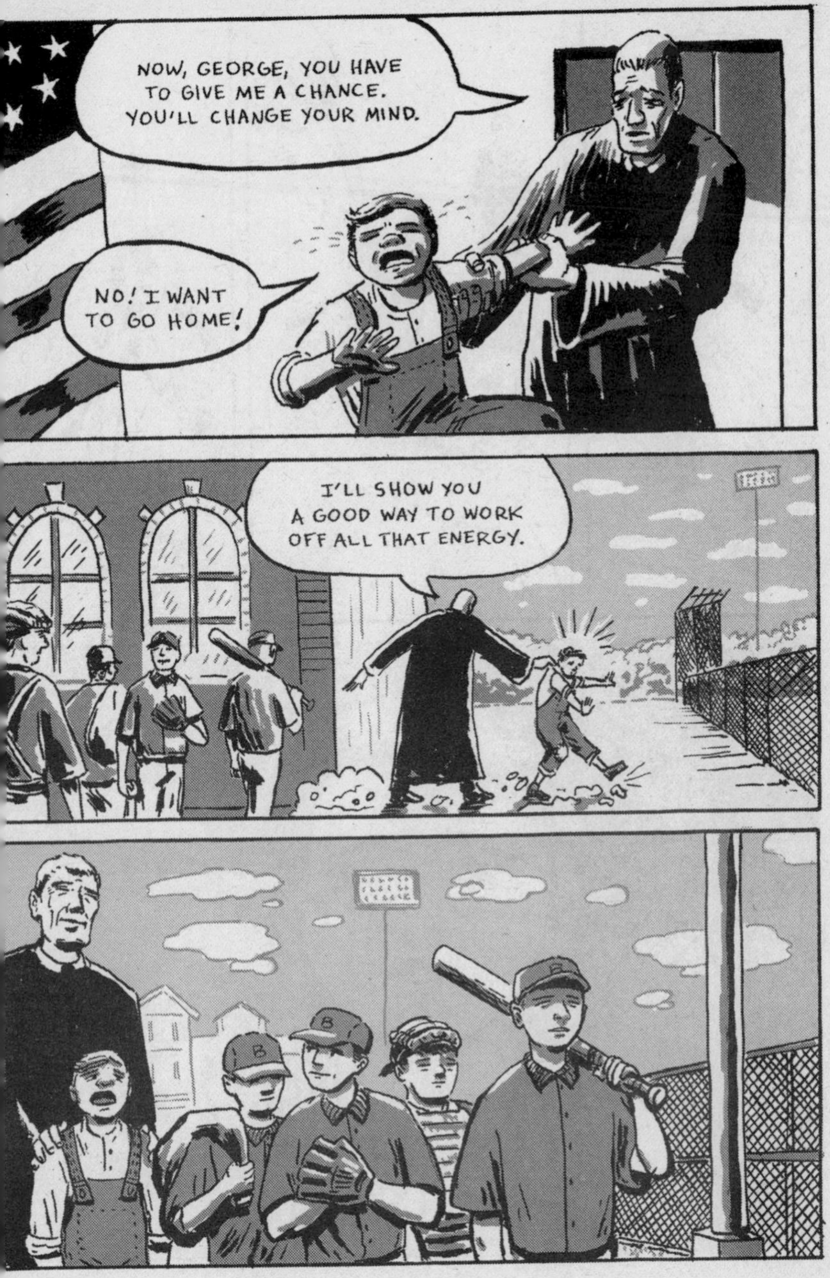
NOW, GEORGE, YOU HAVE TO GIVE ME A CHANCE. YOU'LL CHANGE YOUR MIND.
NO! I WANT TO GO HOME!
I'LL SHOW YOU A GOOD WAY TO WORK OFF ALL THAT ENERGY.

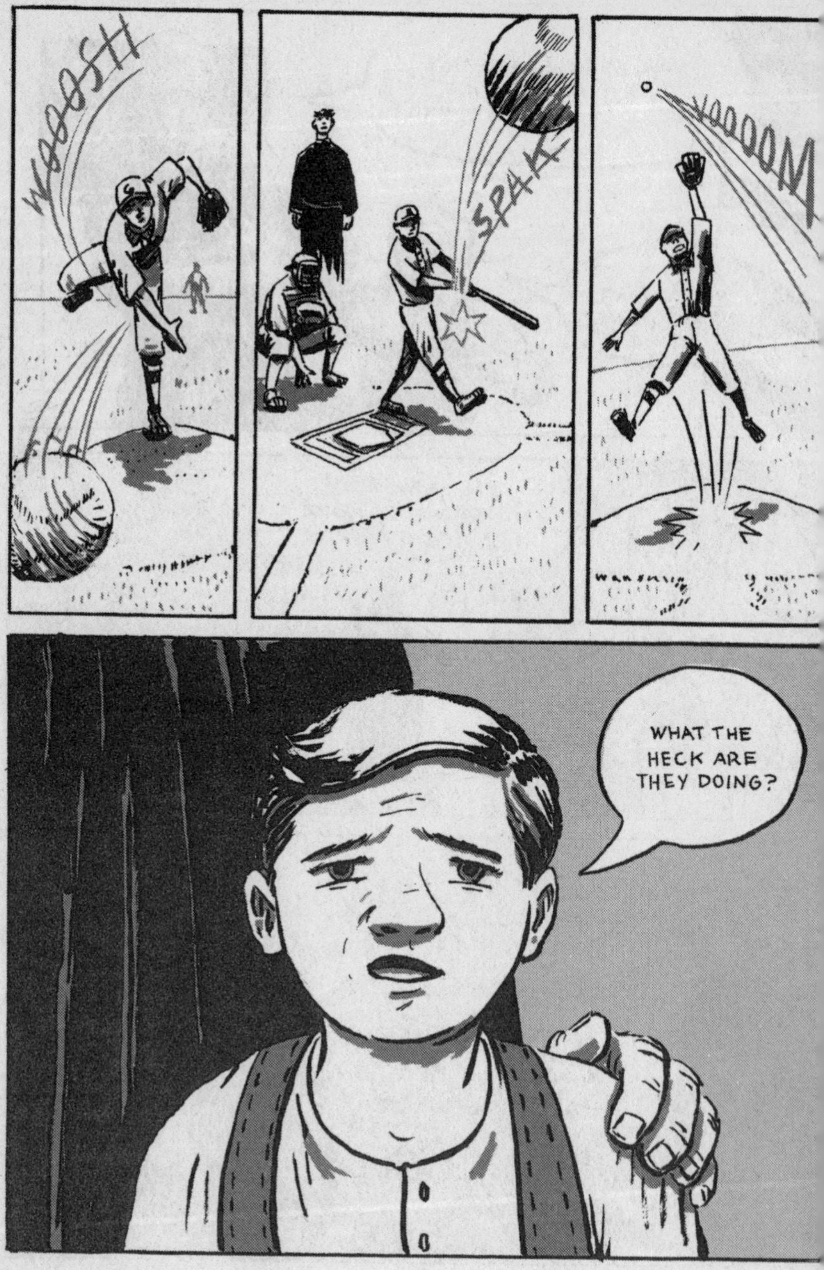
WOOOSH
SPAK
VOOOOM
WHAT THE HECK ARE THEY DOING?

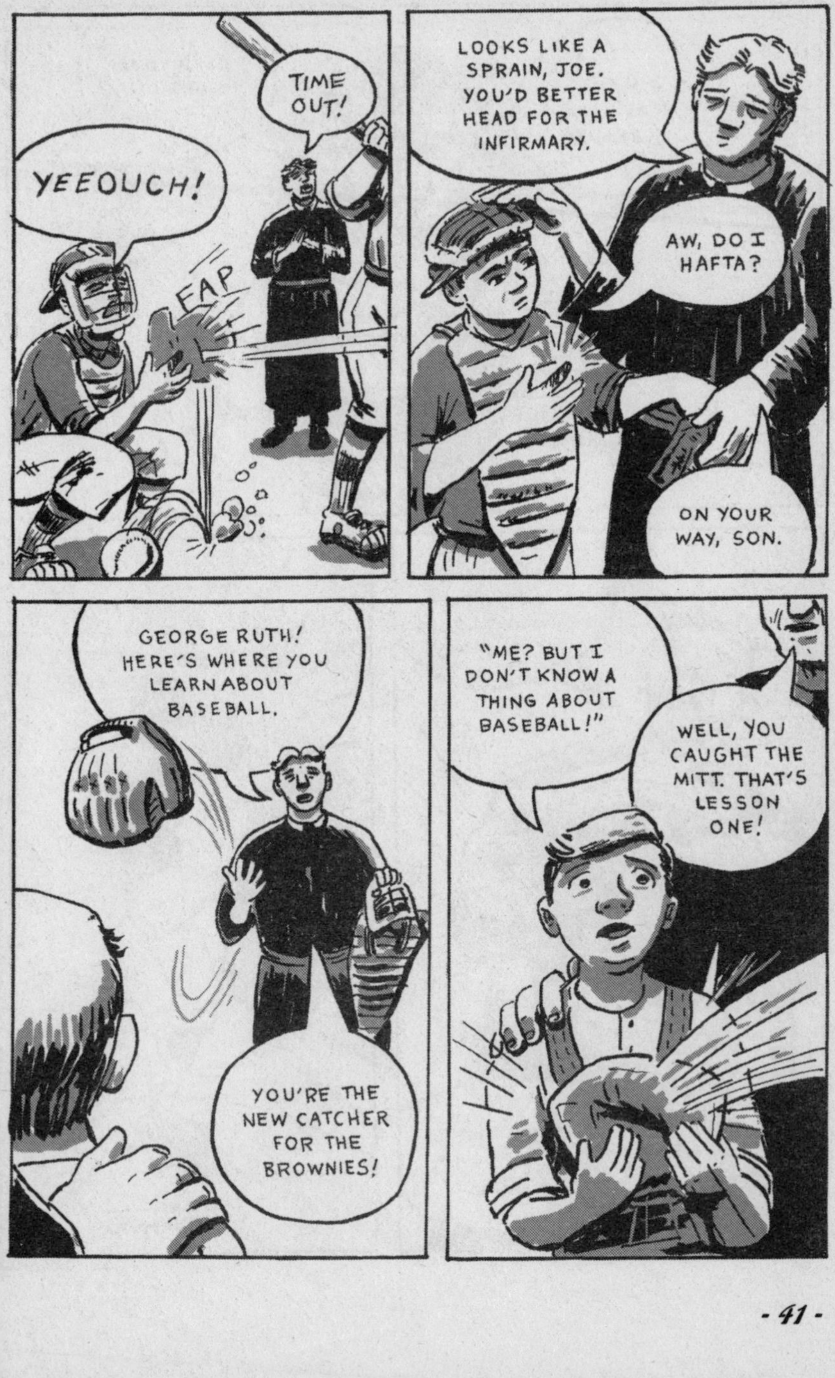
TIME OUT!
YEEOUCH!
FAP
LOOKS LIKE A SPRAIN, JOE. YOU'D BETTER HEAD FOR THE INFIRMARY.
AW, DO I HAFTA?
ON YOUR WAY, SON.
GEORGE RUTH! HERE'S WHERE YOU LEARN ABOUT BASEBALL.
YOU'RE THE NEW CATCHER FOR THE BROWNIES!
"ME? BUT I DON'T KNOW A THING ABOUT BASEBALL!"
WELL, YOU CAUGHT THE MITT. THAT'S LESSON ONE!

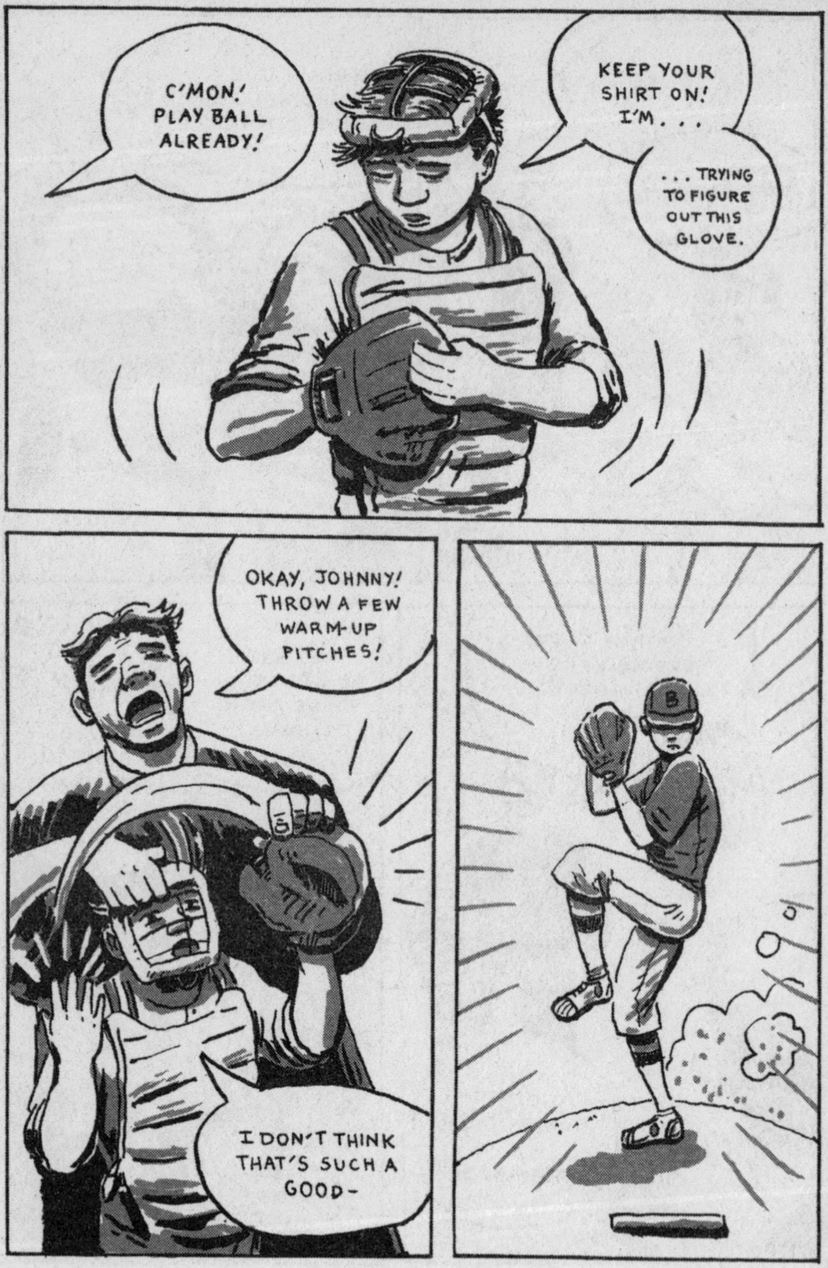
C'MON! PLAY BALL ALREADY!
KEEP YOUR SHIRT ON! I'M . . .
. . . TRYING TO FIGURE OUT THIS GLOVE.
OKAY, JOHNNY! THROW A FEW WARM-UP PITCHES!
I DON'T THINK THAT'S SUCH A GOOD-

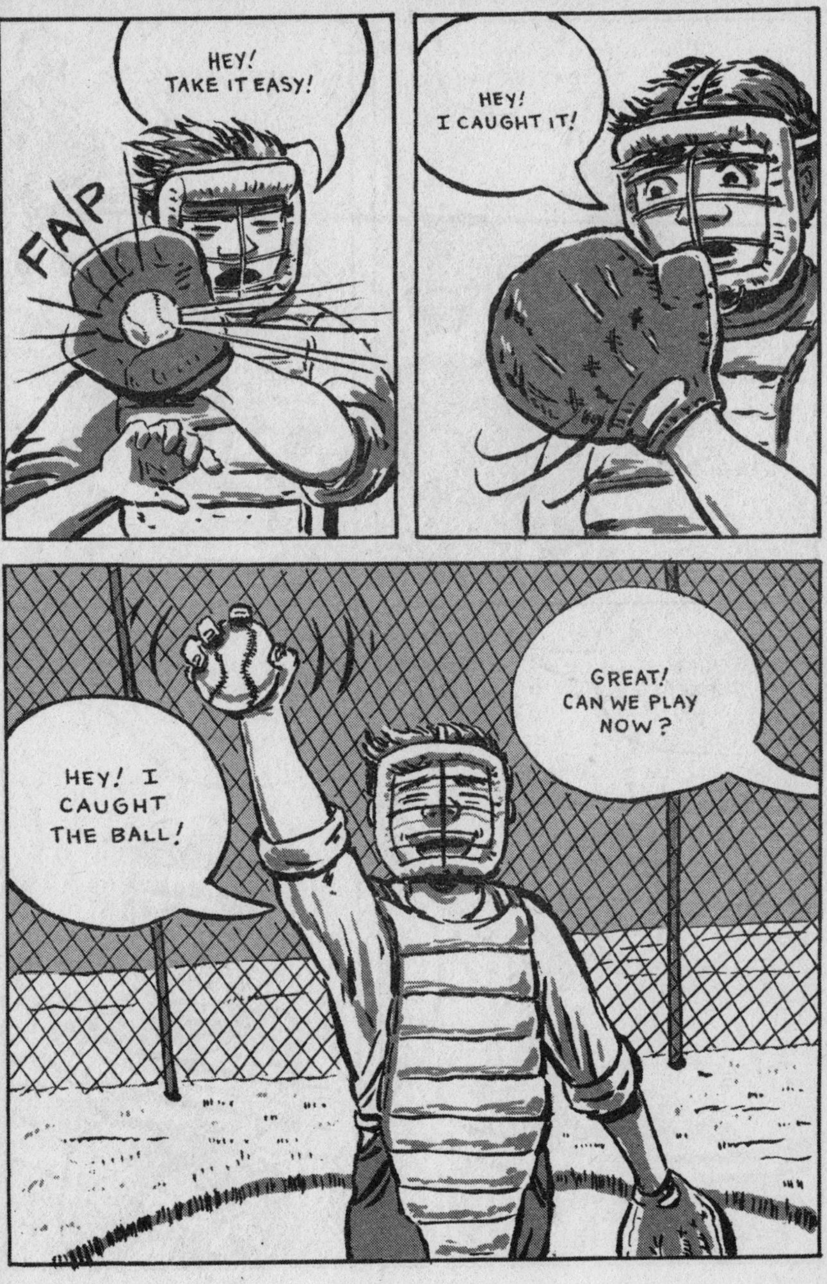
HEY! TAKE IT EASY!
FAP
HEY! I CAUGHT IT!
HEY! I CAUGHT THE BALL!
GREAT! CAN WE PLAY NOW?

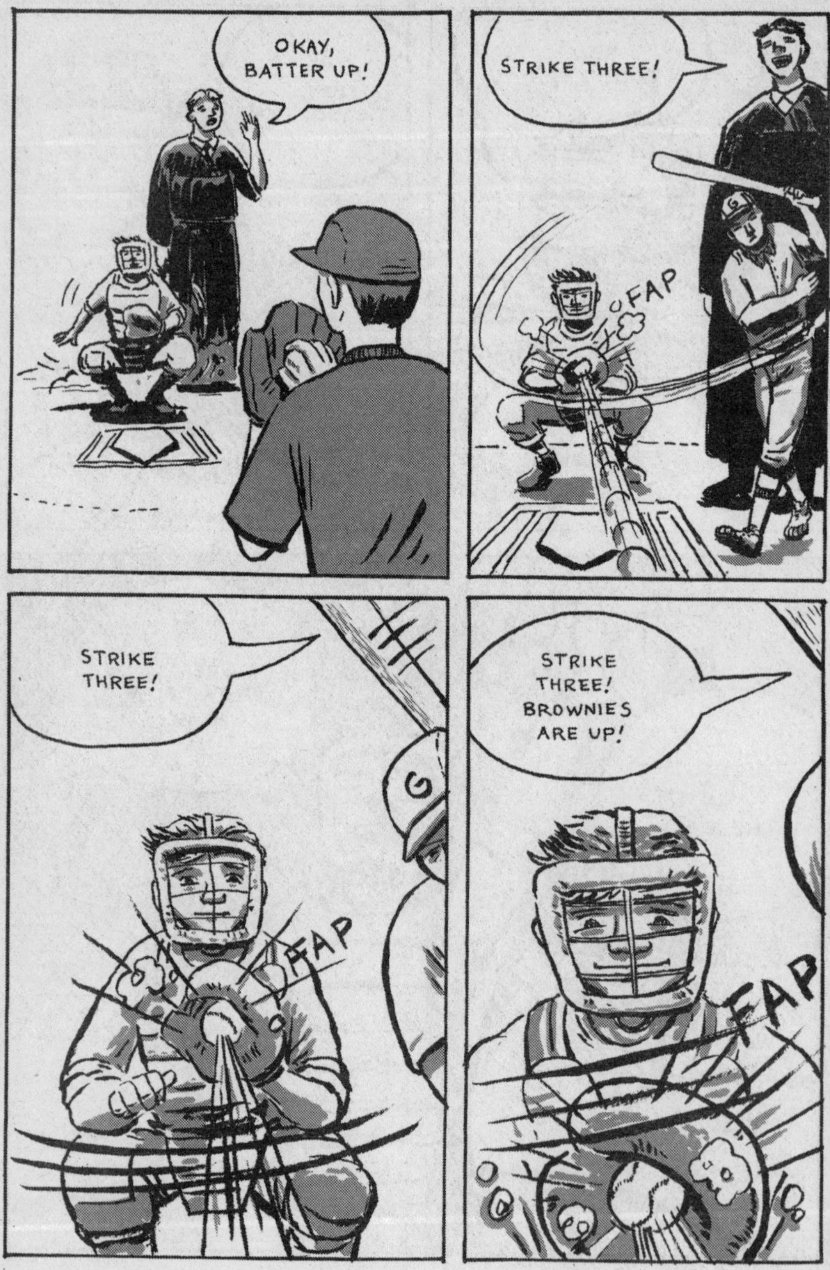
OKAY, BATTER UP!
STRIKE THREE!
FAP
STRIKE THREE!
FAP
STRIKE THREE! BROWNIES ARE UP!
FAP

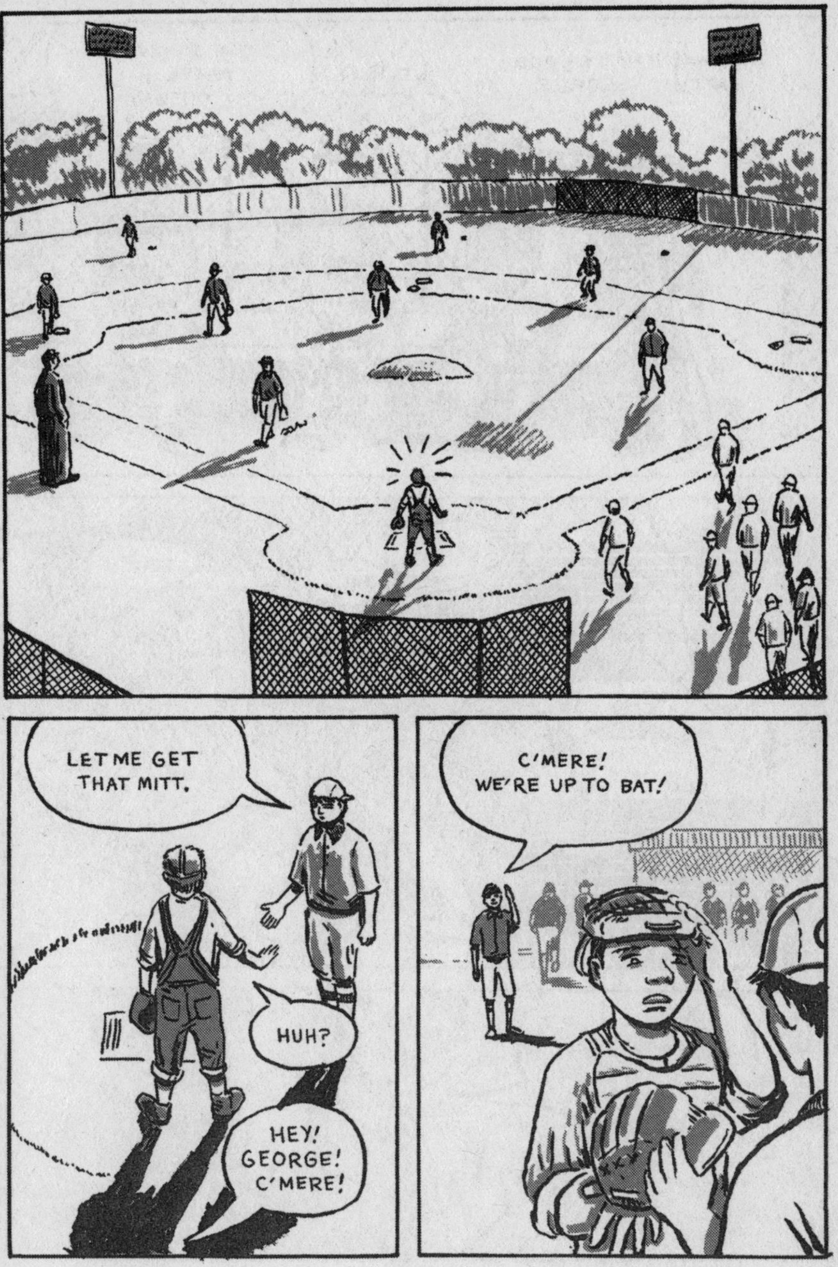
LET ME GET THAT MITT.
HUH?
HEY! GEORGE! C'MERE!
C'MERE! WE'RE UP TO BAT!

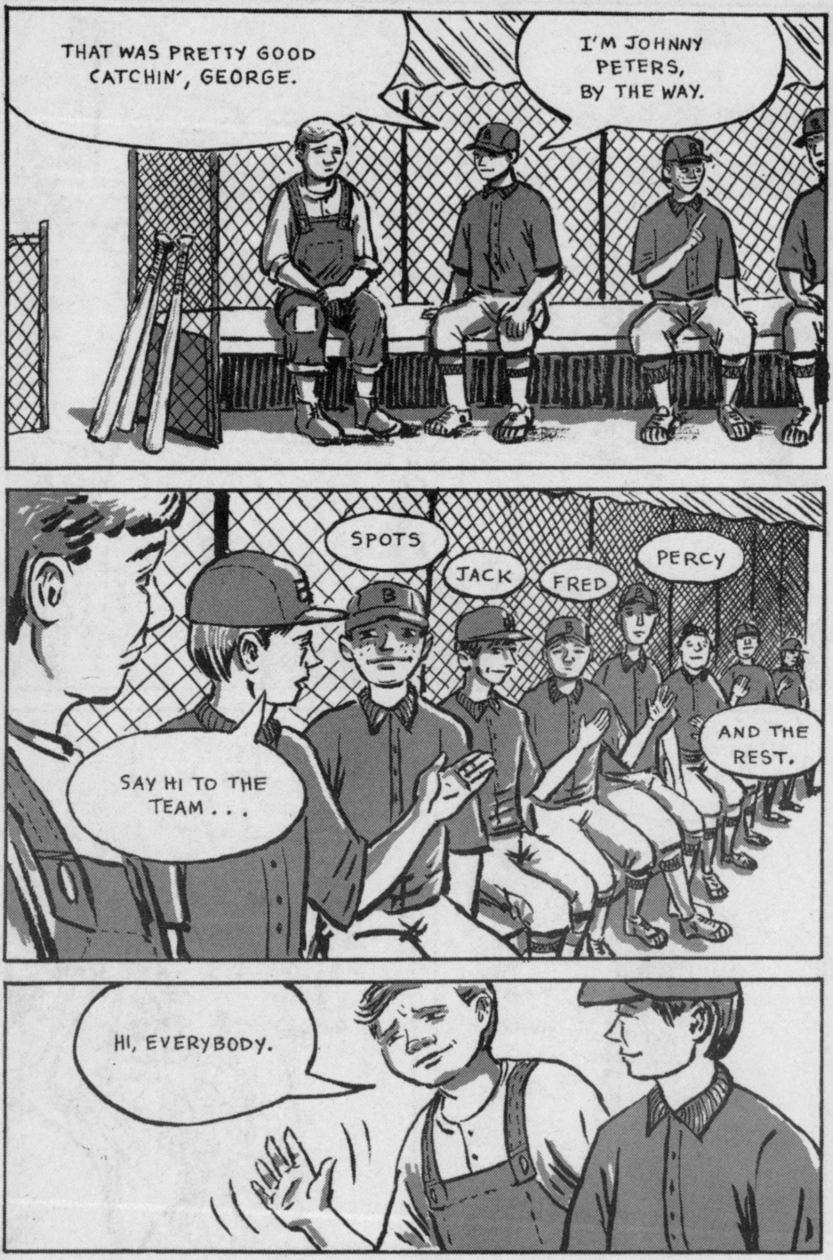
THAT WAS PRETTY GOOD CATCHIN', GEORGE.
I'M JOHNNY PETERS, BY THE WAY.
SAY HI TO THE TEAM . . .
SPOTS
JACK
FRED
PERCY
AND THE REST.
HI, EVERYBODY.

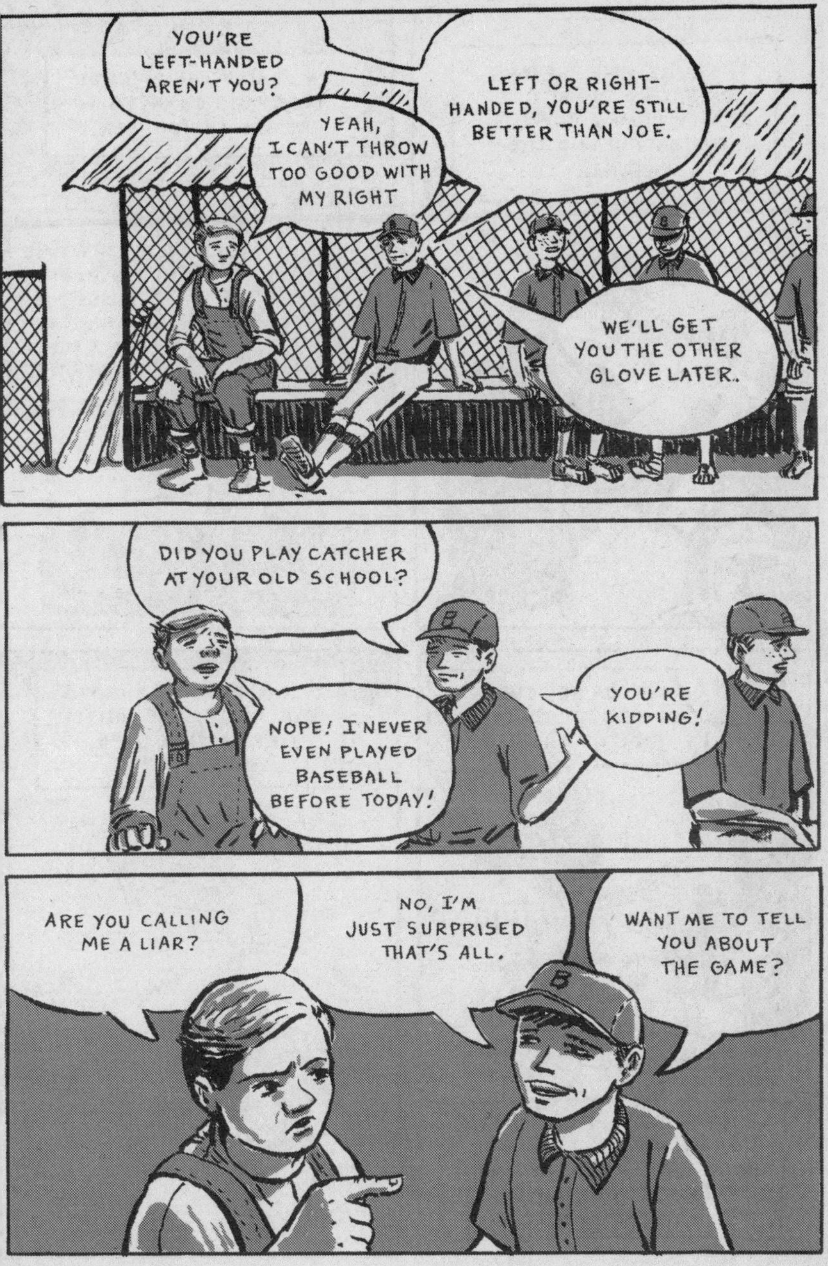
YOU'RE LEFT-HANDED AREN'T YOU?
YEAH, I CAN'T THROW TOO GOOD WITH MY RIGHT
LEFT OR RIGHT-HANDED, YOU'RE STILL BETTER THAN JOE.
WE'LL GET YOU THE OTHER GLOVE LATER.
DID YOU PLAY CATCHER AT YOUR OLD SCHOOL?
NOPE! I NEVER EVEN PLAYED BASEBALL BEFORE TODAY!
YOU'RE KIDDING!
ARE YOU CALLING ME A LIAR?
NO, I'M JUST SURPRISED THAT'S ALL.
WANT ME TO TELL YOU ABOUT THE GAME?

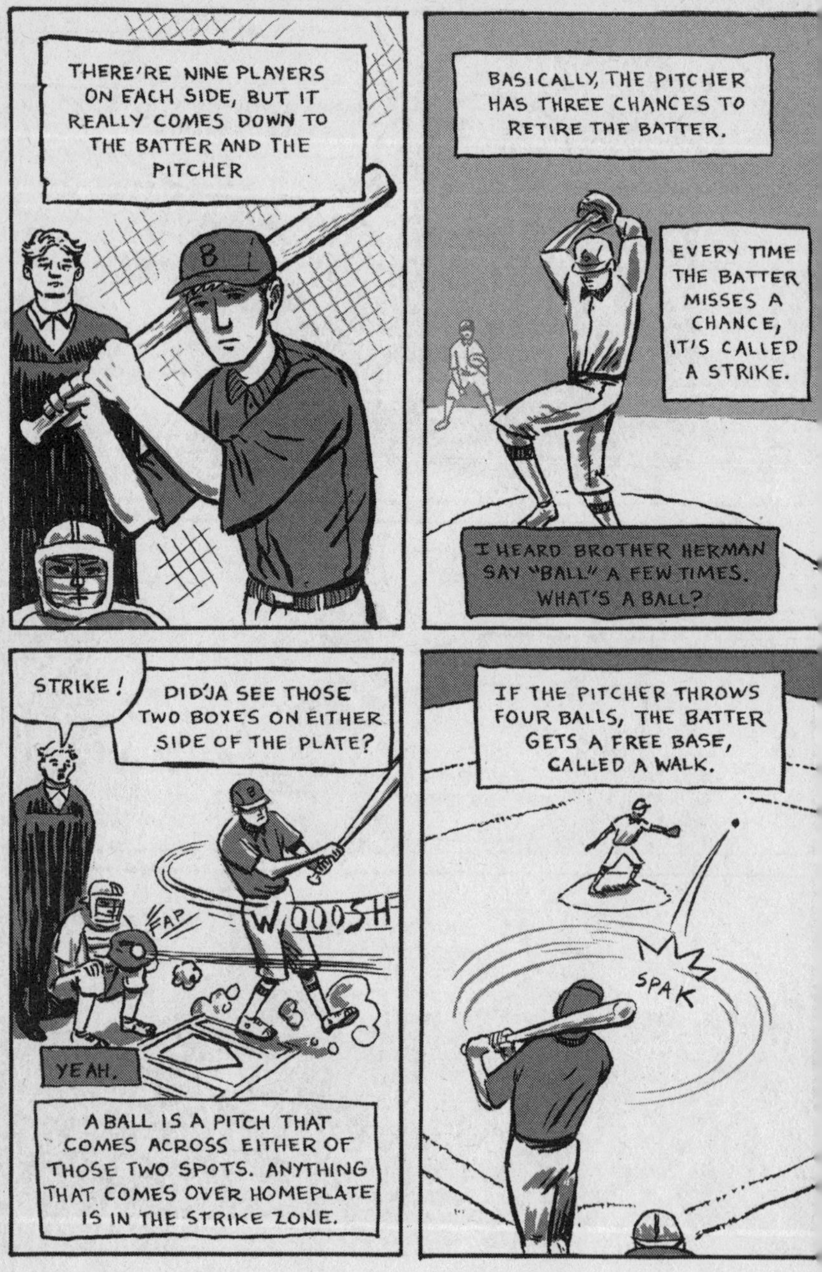
THERE'RE NINE PLAYERS ON EACH SIDE, BUT IT REALLY COMES DOWN TO THE BATTER AND THE PITCHER
BASICALLY, THE PITCHER HAS THREE CHANCES TO RETIRE THE BATTER.
EVERY TIME THE BATTER MISSES A CHANCE, IT'S CALLED A STRIKE.
I HEARD BROTHER HERMAN SAY "BALL" A FEW TIMES. WHAT'S A BALL?
STRIKE!
DID'JA SEE THOSE TWO BOXES ON EITHER SIDE OF THE PLATE?
FAP
WOOOSH
YEAH.
A BALL IS A PITCH THAT COMES ACROSS EITHER OF THOSE TWO SPOTS. ANYTHING THAT COMES OVER HOMEPLATE IS IN THE STRIKE ZONE.
IF THE PITCHER THROWS FOUR BALLS, THE BATTER GETS A FREE BASE, CALLED A WALK.
SPAK

TO SCORE A RUN, A BATTER HAS TO TOUCH ALL FOUR BASES. PERCY JUST HIT A SINGLE, SO HE GOES TO FIRST BASE.

AFTER THREE OUTS, THE TEAM IN THE FIELD GETS A CHANCE AT BATTING AND THE OTHER TEAM HAS TO PLAY DEFENSE.

WOW! THAT KID JUST WALLOPED THE BALL!

KRAK

YEAH, BUT IT WENT OUTSIDE THE FOUL LINE. IT COUNTS AS A STRIKE.

GEEZ, THERE'S A LOT TO REMEMBER.

EH, DON'T WORRY. JUST HAVE FUN!

IT'S JUST A GAME!

GEORGE, YOU'RE UP TO BAT!

DON'T MESS UP, DON'T MESS UP, DON'T MESS UP!
STRIKE ONE!
SMAK
C'MON, GEORGE! KEEP YOUR EYE ON THE BALL!
STRIKE TWO!
WOOOP
SMAK
HA! YOU MISSED BY A MILE!

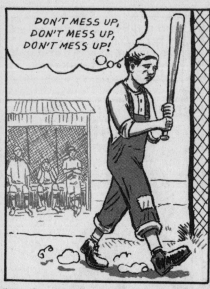

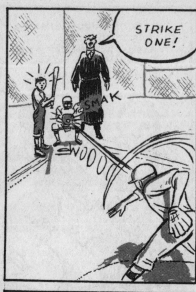

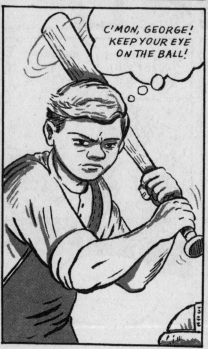

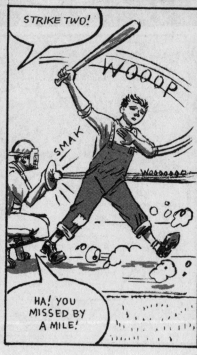

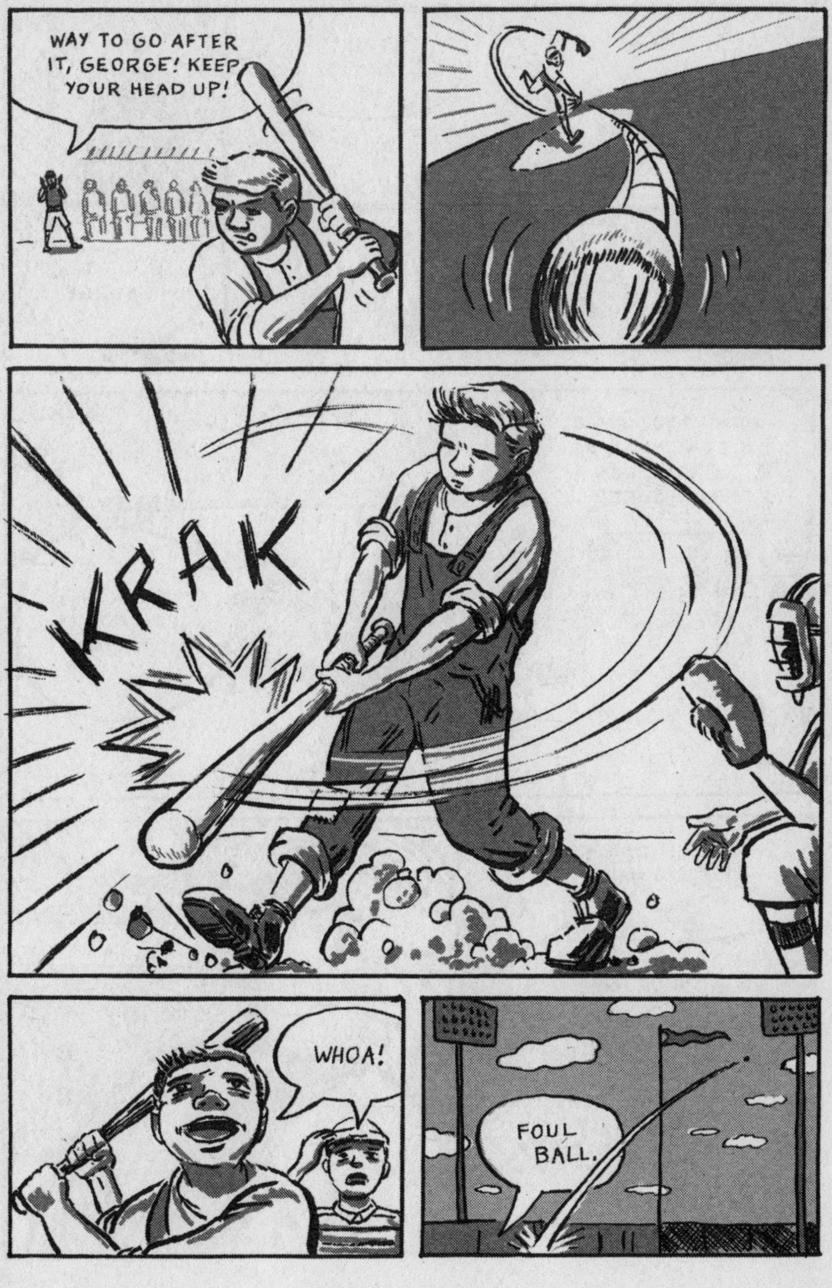
WAY TO GO AFTER IT, GEORGE! KEEP YOUR HEAD UP!
KRAK
WHOA!
FOUL BALL.

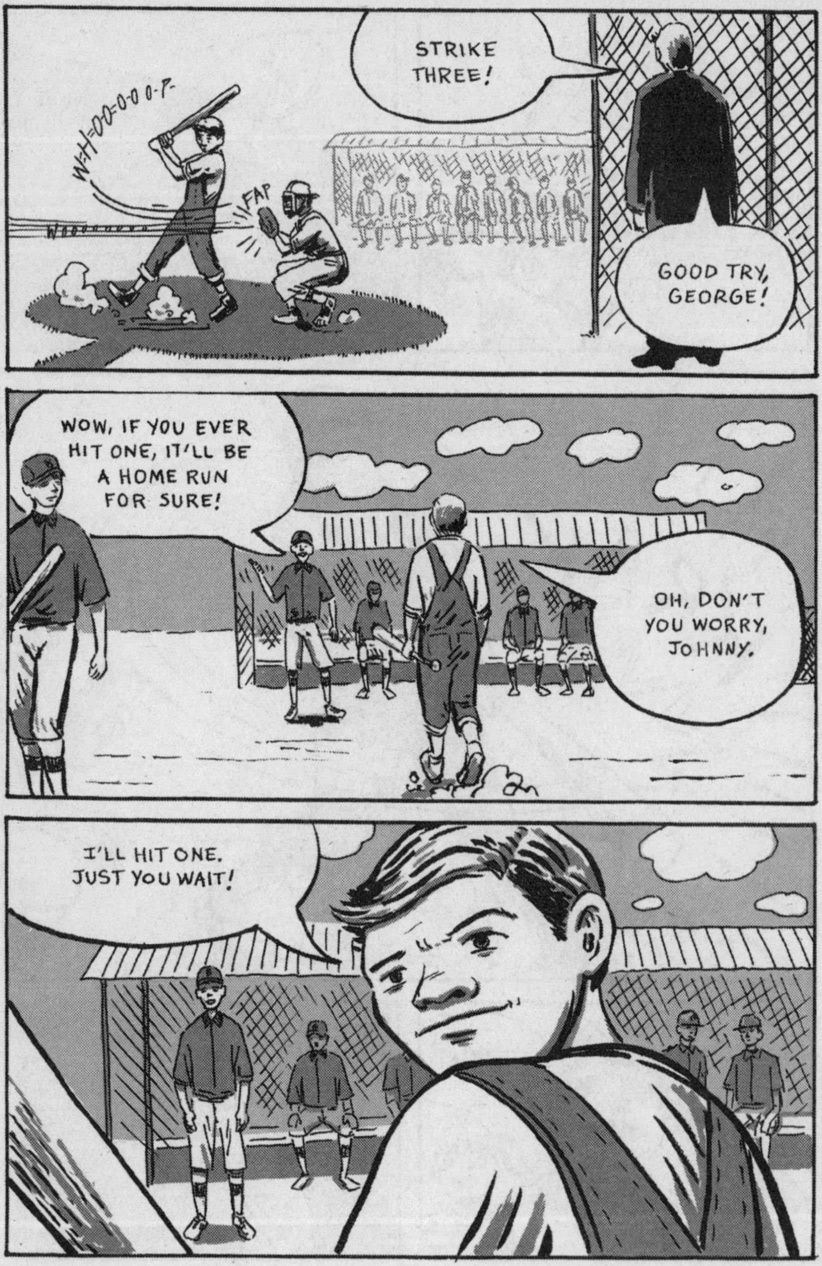
W-H-O-O-O-O-O-P-
WOOOOOOOOO
FAP
STRIKE THREE!
GOOD TRY, GEORGE!
WOW, IF YOU EVER HIT ONE, IT'LL BE A HOME RUN FOR SURE!
OH, DON'T YOU WORRY, JOHNNY.
I'LL HIT ONE. JUST YOU WAIT!

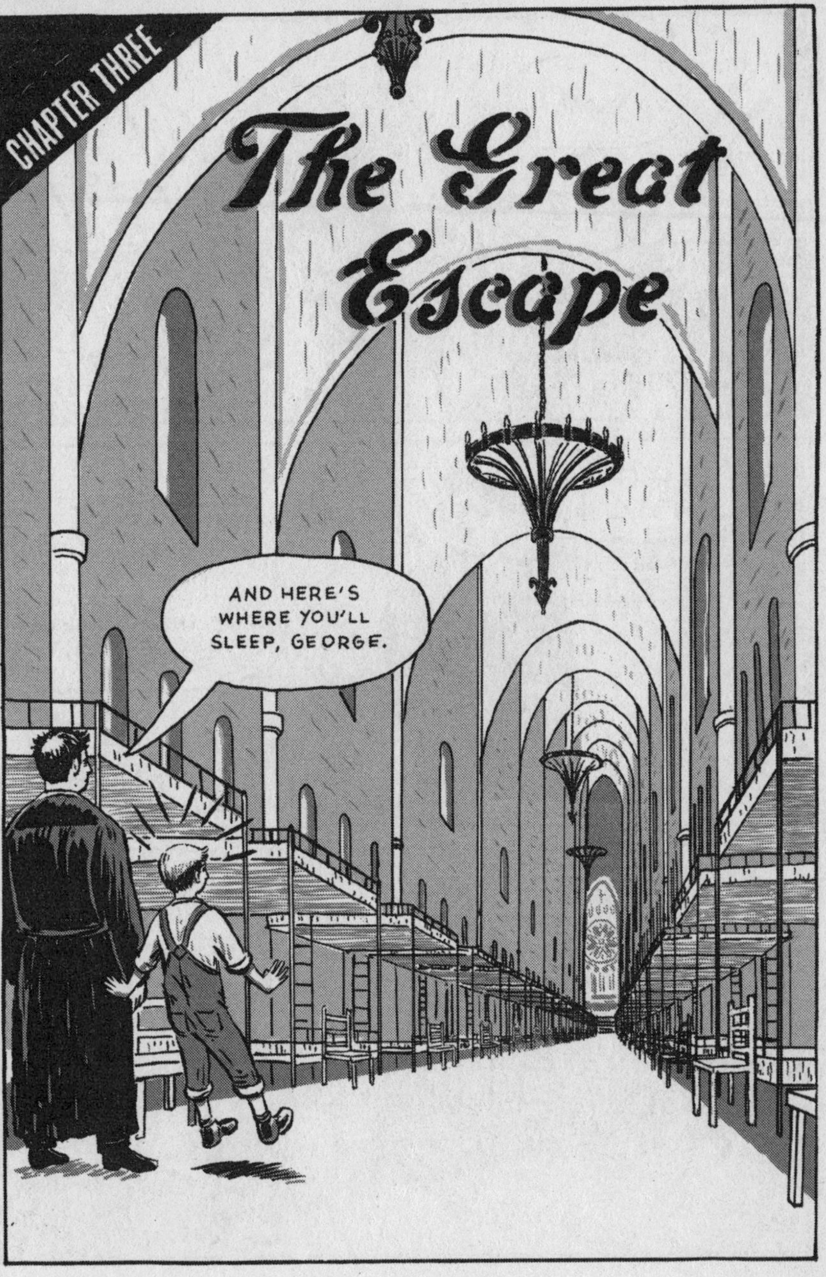
CHAPTER THREE
The Great Escape
AND HERE'S WHERE YOU'LL SLEEP, GEORGE.

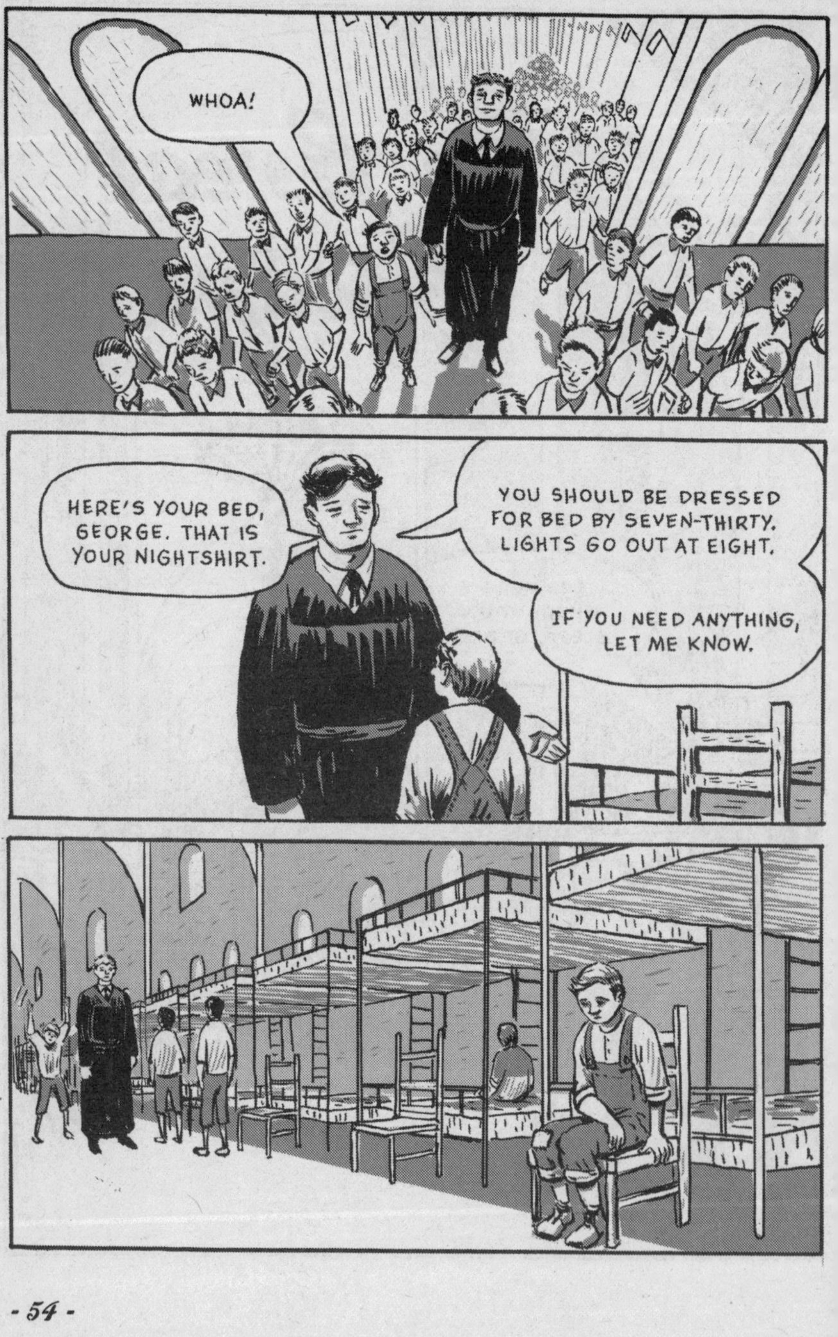
WHOA!
HERE'S YOUR BED, GEORGE. THAT IS YOUR NIGHTSHIRT.
YOU SHOULD BE DRESSED FOR BED BY SEVEN-THIRTY. LIGHTS GO OUT AT EIGHT.
IF YOU NEED ANYTHING, LET ME KNOW.

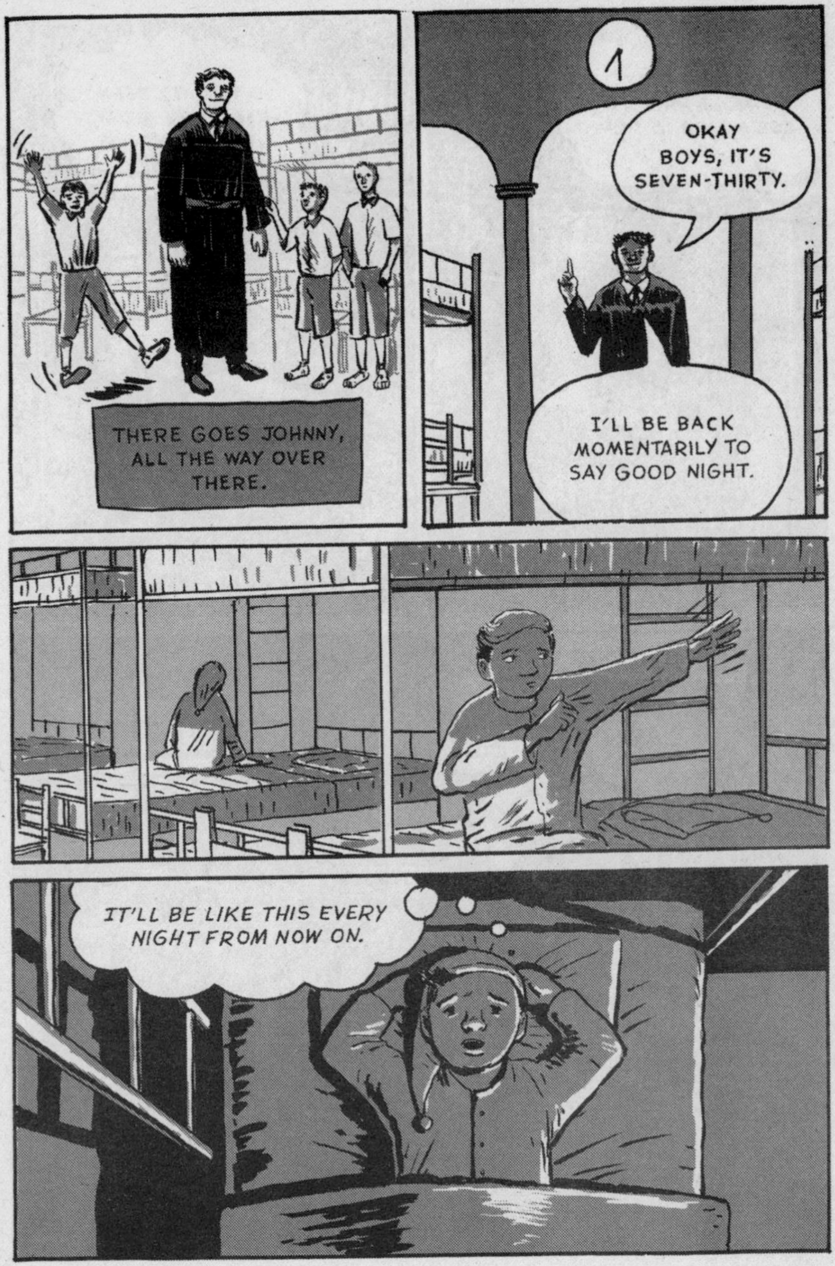
THERE GOES JOHNNY, ALL THE WAY OVER THERE.
OKAY BOYS, IT'S SEVEN-THIRTY.
I'LL BE BACK MOMENTARILY TO SAY GOOD NIGHT.
IT'LL BE LIKE THIS EVERY NIGHT FROM NOW ON.

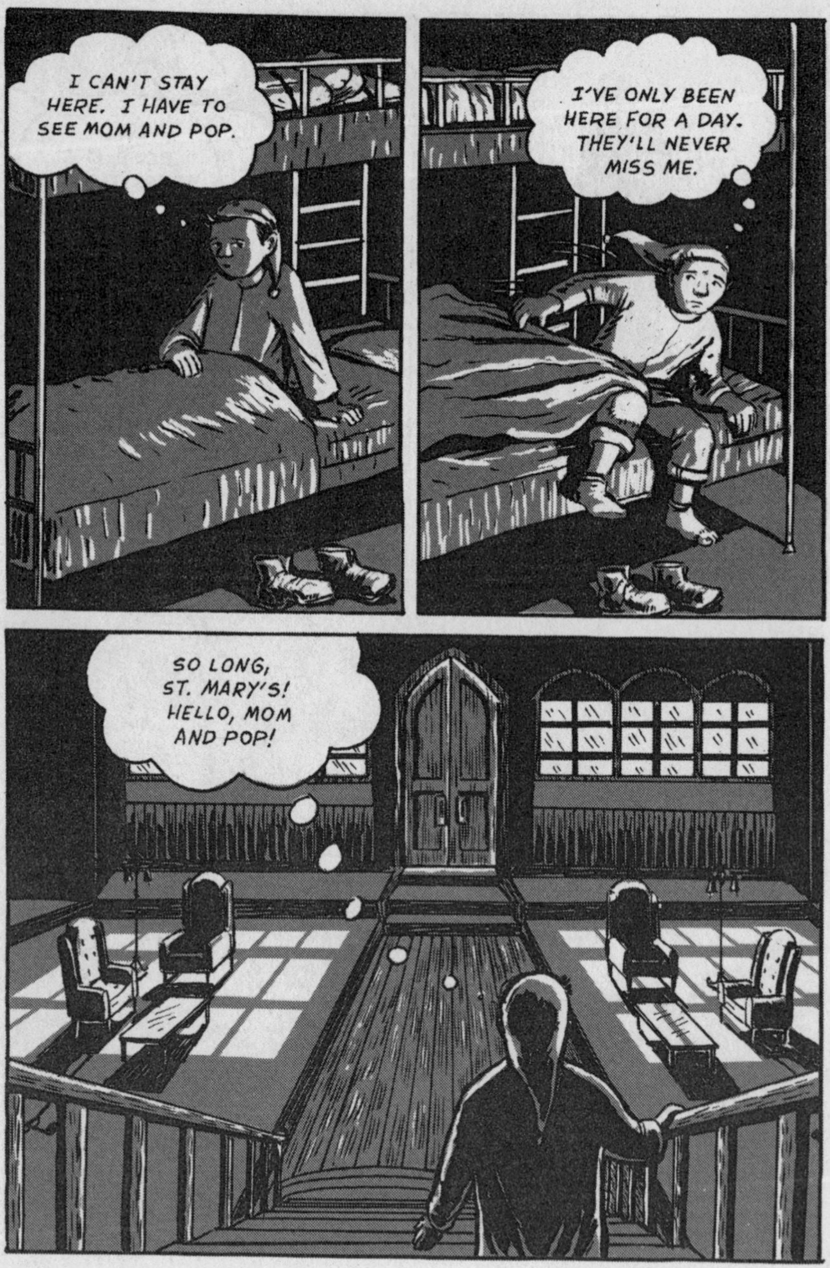
I CAN'T STAY HERE. I HAVE TO SEE MOM AND POP.
I'VE ONLY BEEN HERE FOR A DAY. THEY'LL NEVER MISS ME.
SO LONG, ST. MARY'S! HELLO, MOM AND POP!

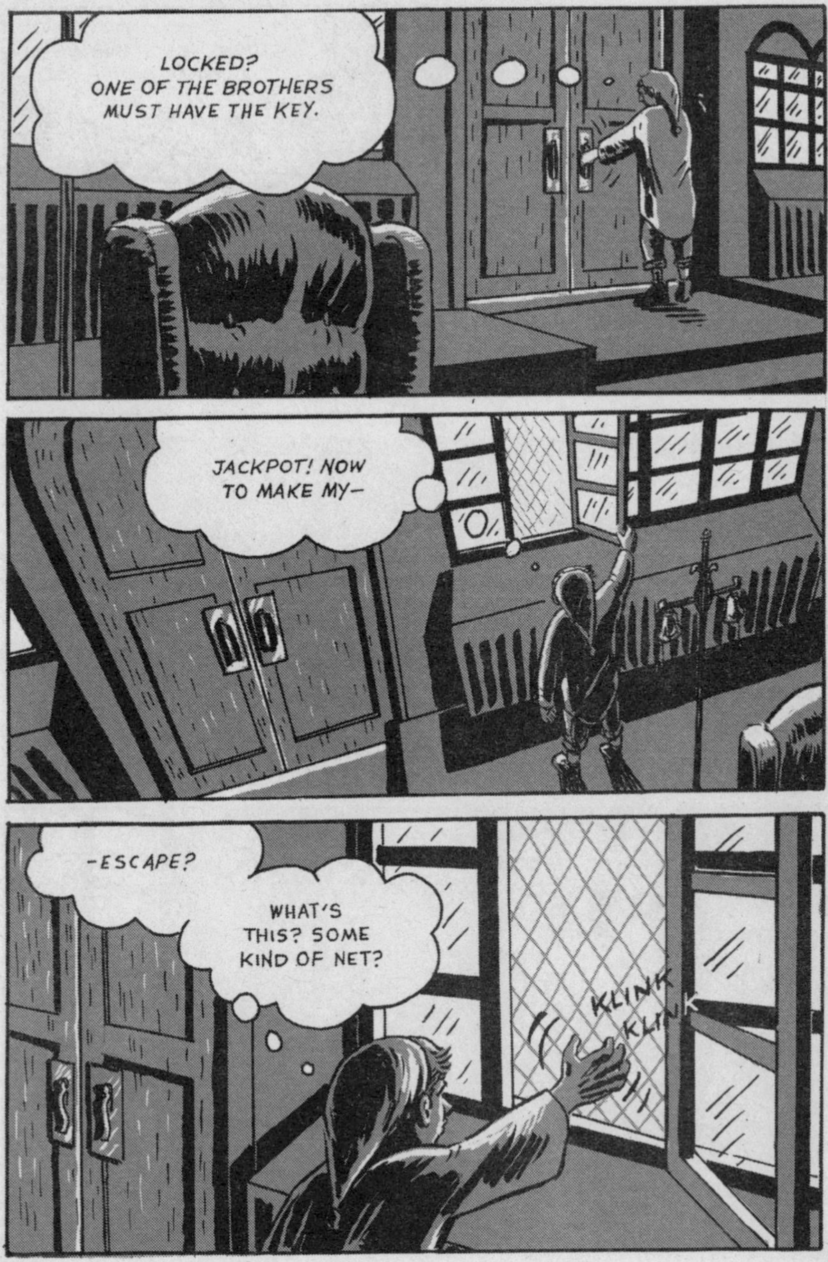
LOCKED?
ONE OF THE BROTHERS
MUST HAVE THE KEY.
JACKPOT! NOW
TO MAKE MY—
-ESCAPE?
WHAT'S
THIS? SOME
KIND OF NET?
KLINK
KLINK

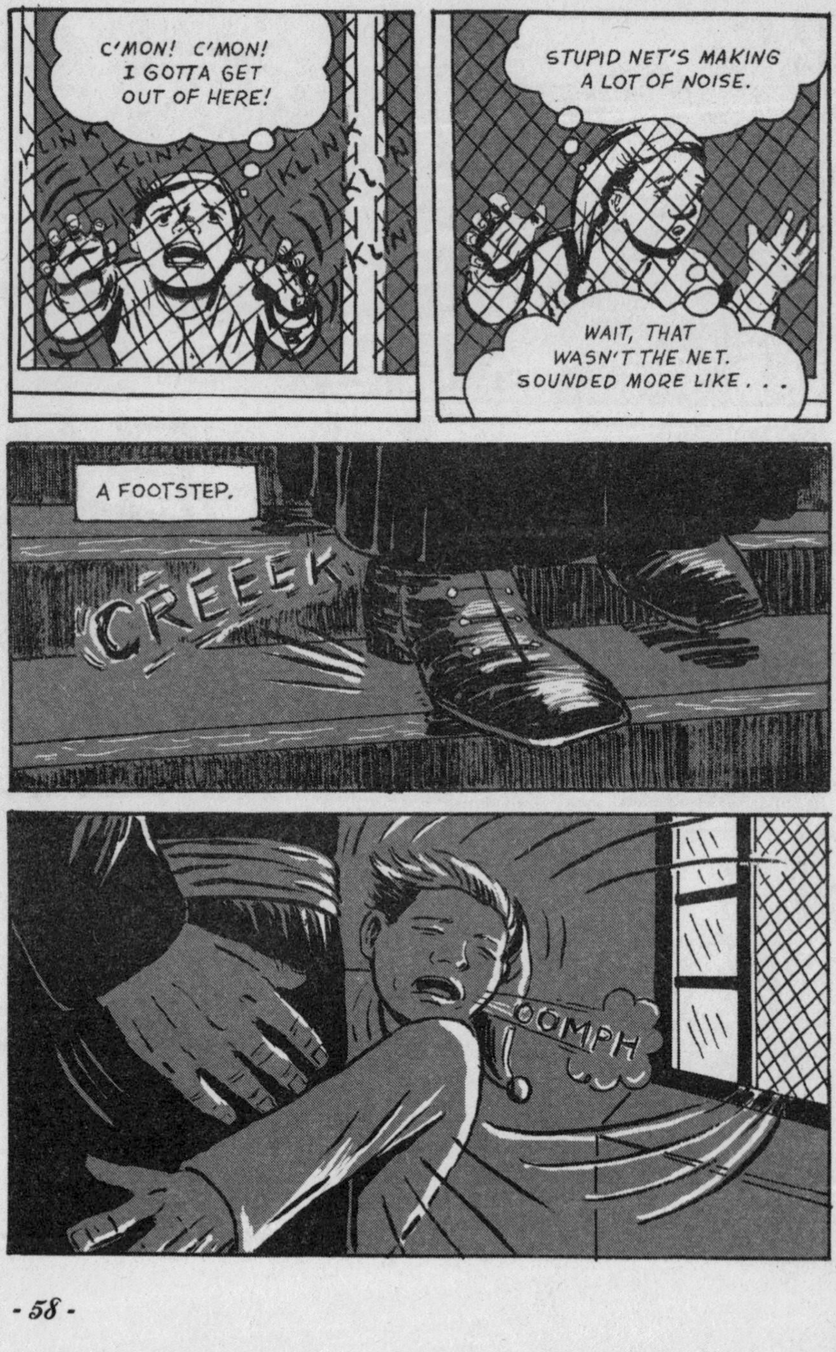
C'MON! C'MON! I GOTTA GET OUT OF HERE!
KLINK KLINK KLINK KLINK KLINK
STUPID NET'S MAKING A LOT OF NOISE.
WAIT, THAT WASN'T THE NET. SOUNDED MORE LIKE . . .
A FOOTSTEP.
CREEEK
OOMPH

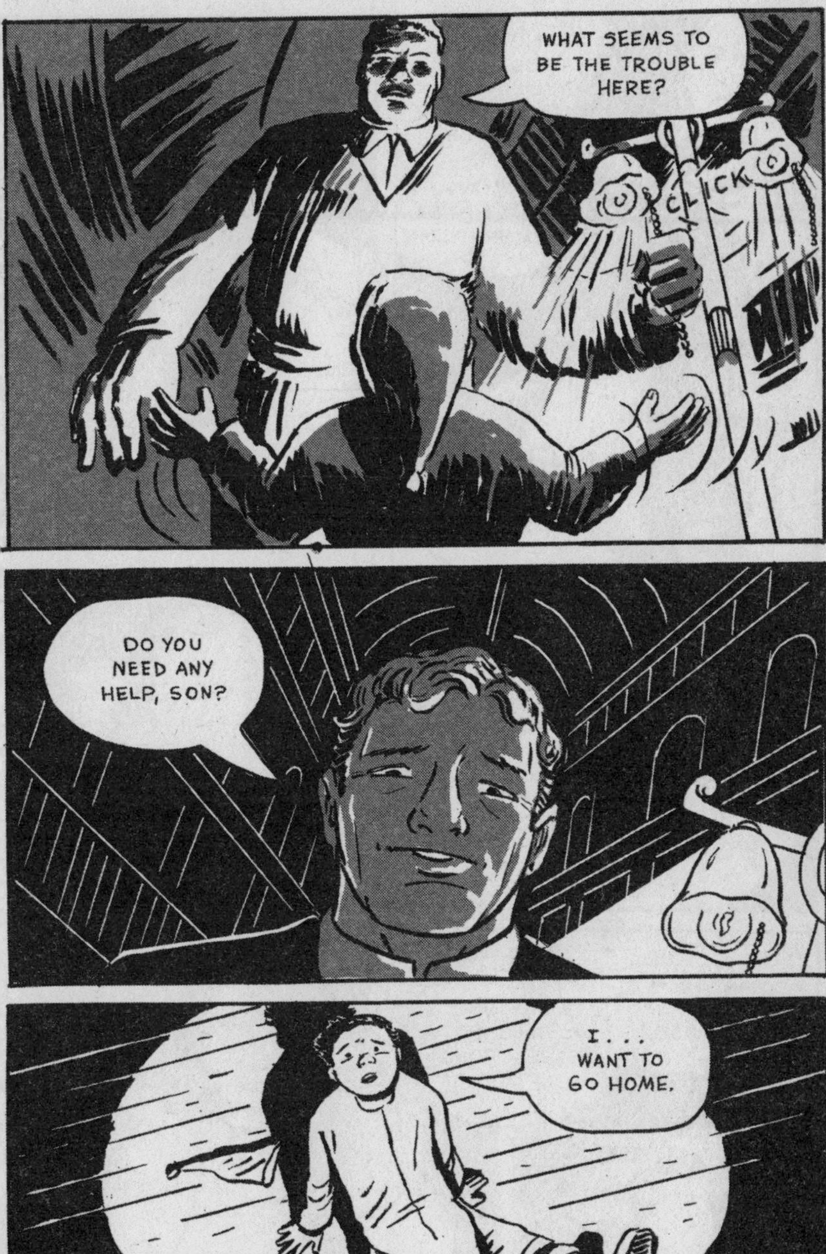
WHAT SEEMS TO BE THE TROUBLE HERE?
CLICK
DO YOU NEED ANY HELP, SON?
I . . . WANT TO GO HOME.

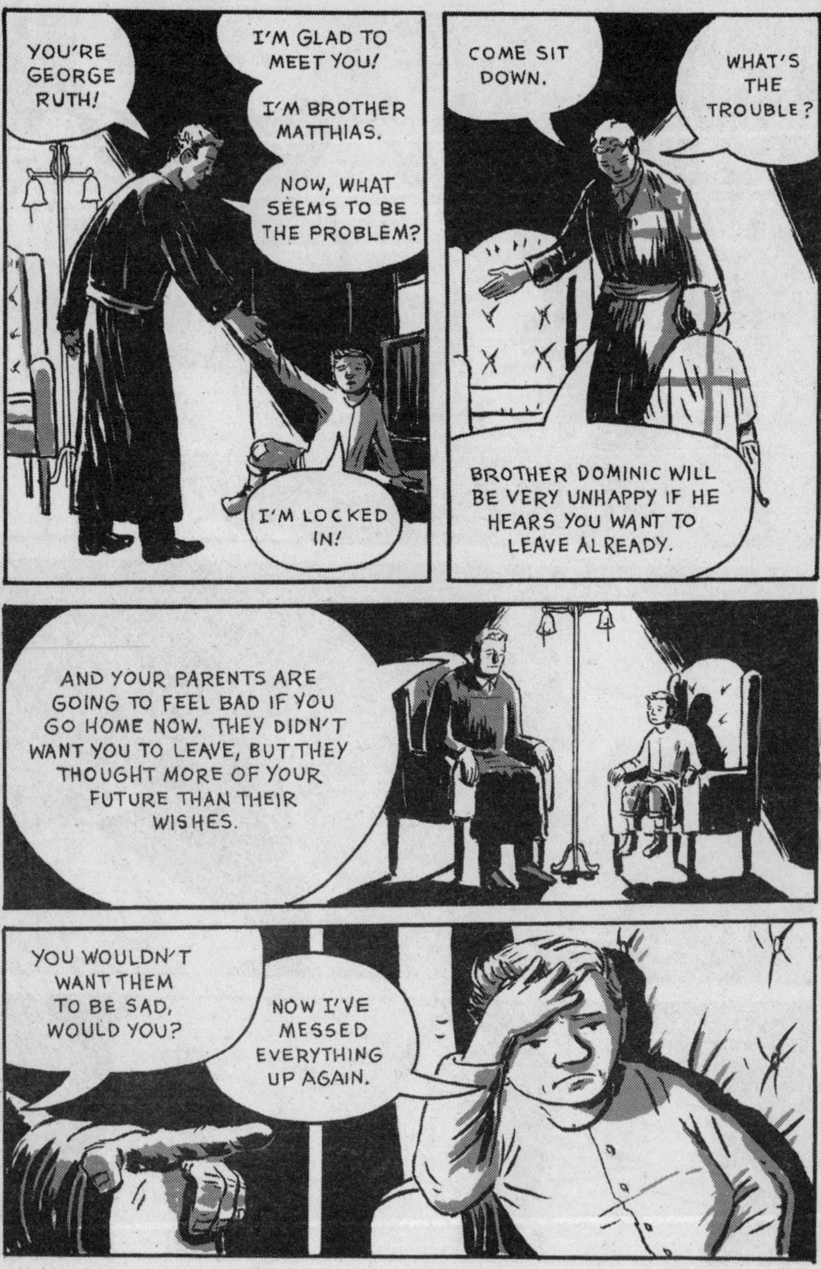

YOU'RE GEORGE RUTH!
I'M GLAD TO MEET YOU!
I'M BROTHER MATTHIAS.
NOW, WHAT SEEMS TO BE THE PROBLEM?
I'M LOCKED IN!
COME SIT DOWN.
WHAT'S THE TROUBLE?
BROTHER DOMINIC WILL BE VERY UNHAPPY IF HE HEARS YOU WANT TO LEAVE ALREADY.
AND YOUR PARENTS ARE GOING TO FEEL BAD IF YOU GO HOME NOW. THEY DIDN'T WANT YOU TO LEAVE, BUT THEY THOUGHT MORE OF YOUR FUTURE THAN THEIR WISHES.
YOU WOULDN'T WANT THEM TO BE SAD, WOULD YOU?
NOW I'VE MESSED EVERYTHING UP AGAIN.

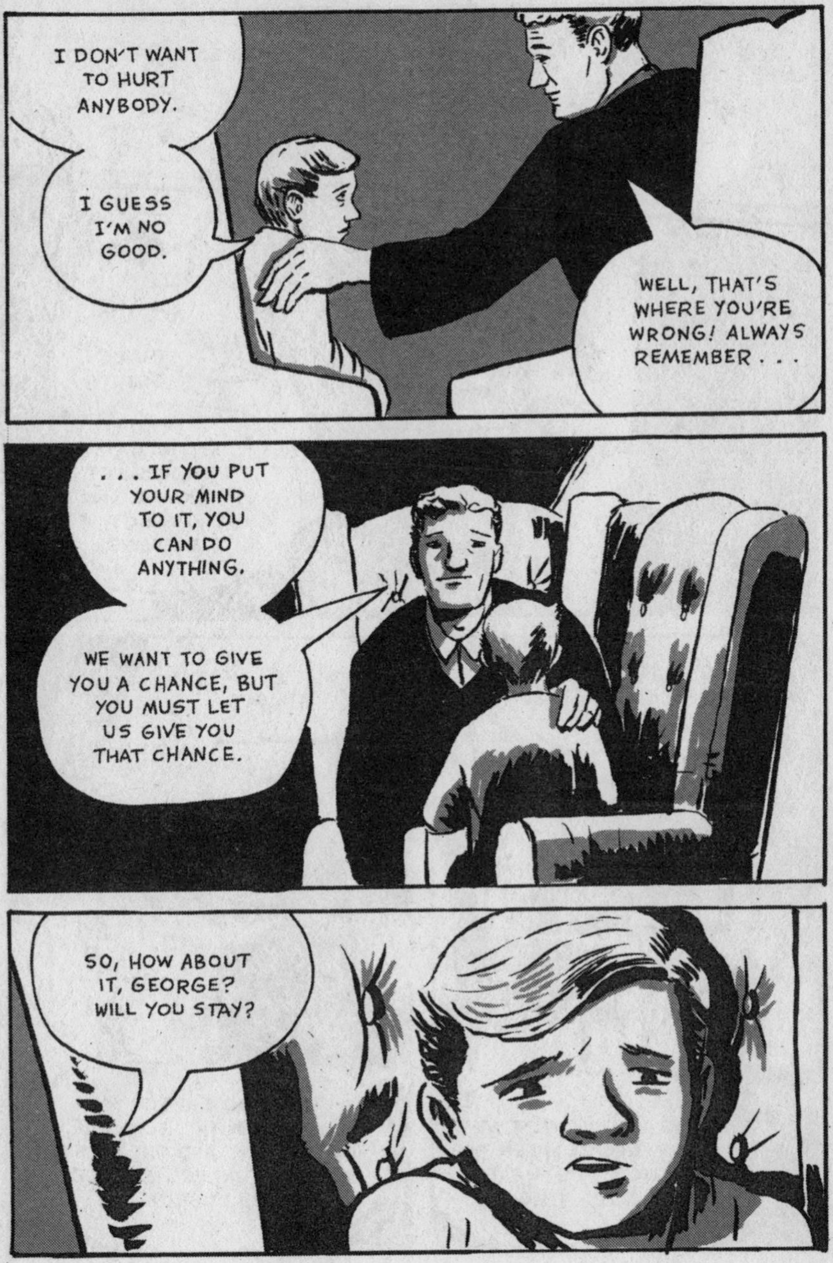
I DON'T WANT TO HURT ANYBODY.
I GUESS I'M NO GOOD.
WELL, THAT'S WHERE YOU'RE WRONG! ALWAYS REMEMBER . . .
. . . IF YOU PUT YOUR MIND TO IT, YOU CAN DO ANYTHING.
WE WANT TO GIVE YOU A CHANCE, BUT YOU MUST LET US GIVE YOU THAT CHANCE.
SO, HOW ABOUT IT, GEORGE? WILL YOU STAY?

SURE! I-I'LL STAY.

THAT'S GREAT!

BY THE WAY, I SHOULD LET YOU KNOW, I'M THE PREFECT OF DISCIPLINE.

DOES THAT MEAN I'M GOING TO GET PUNISHED?

WELL, WHY DON'T WE KEEP THIS BETWEEN THE TWO OF US. WHAT DO YOU THINK?

THAT'S GREAT THANKS!

BUT I DO EXPECT YOU TO FOLLOW THE RULES IN THE FUTURE. AND THE FIRST RULE IS THAT YOU SHOULD BE IN BED!

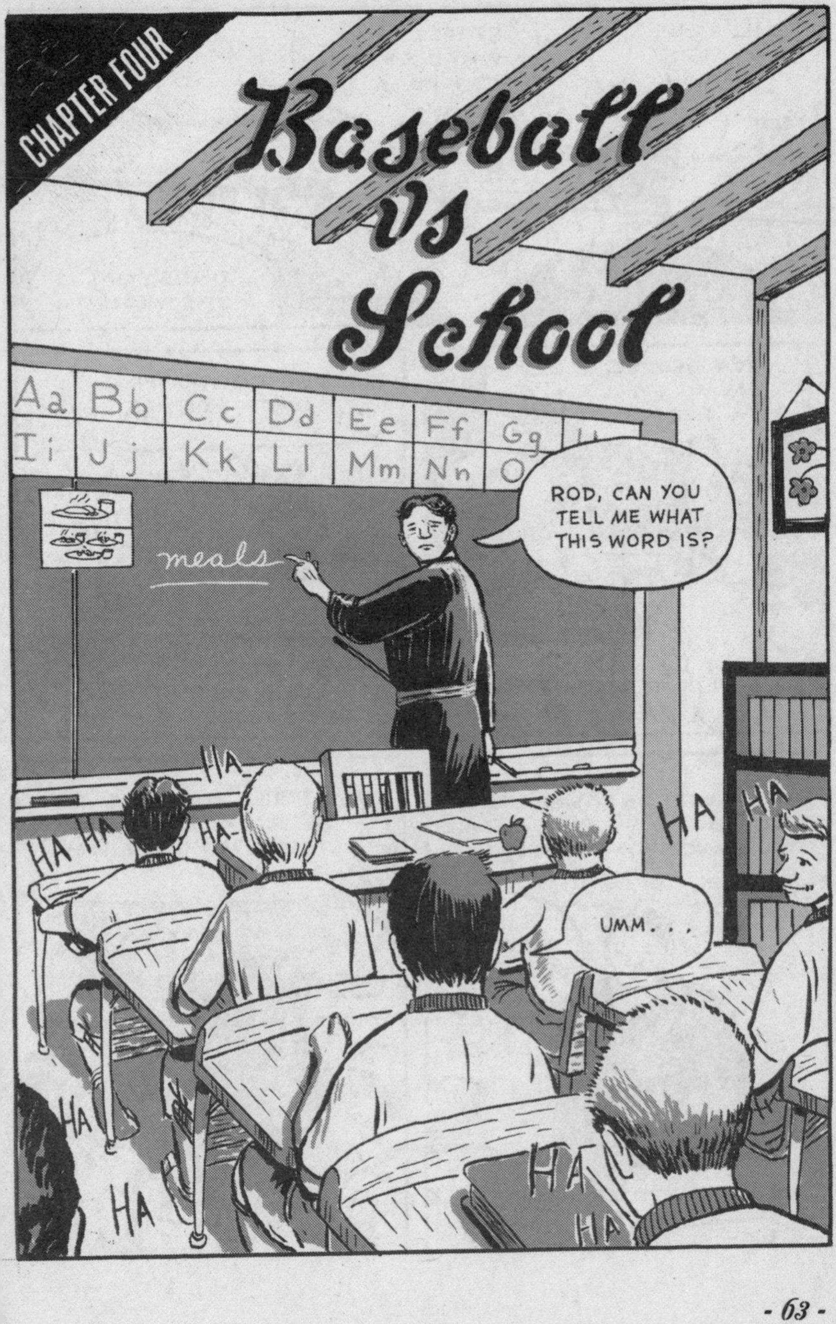
CHAPTER FOUR
Baseball vs School
meals
ROD, CAN YOU TELL ME WHAT THIS WORD IS?
HA HA HA HA HA HA HA
UMM. . .
HA HA HA HA

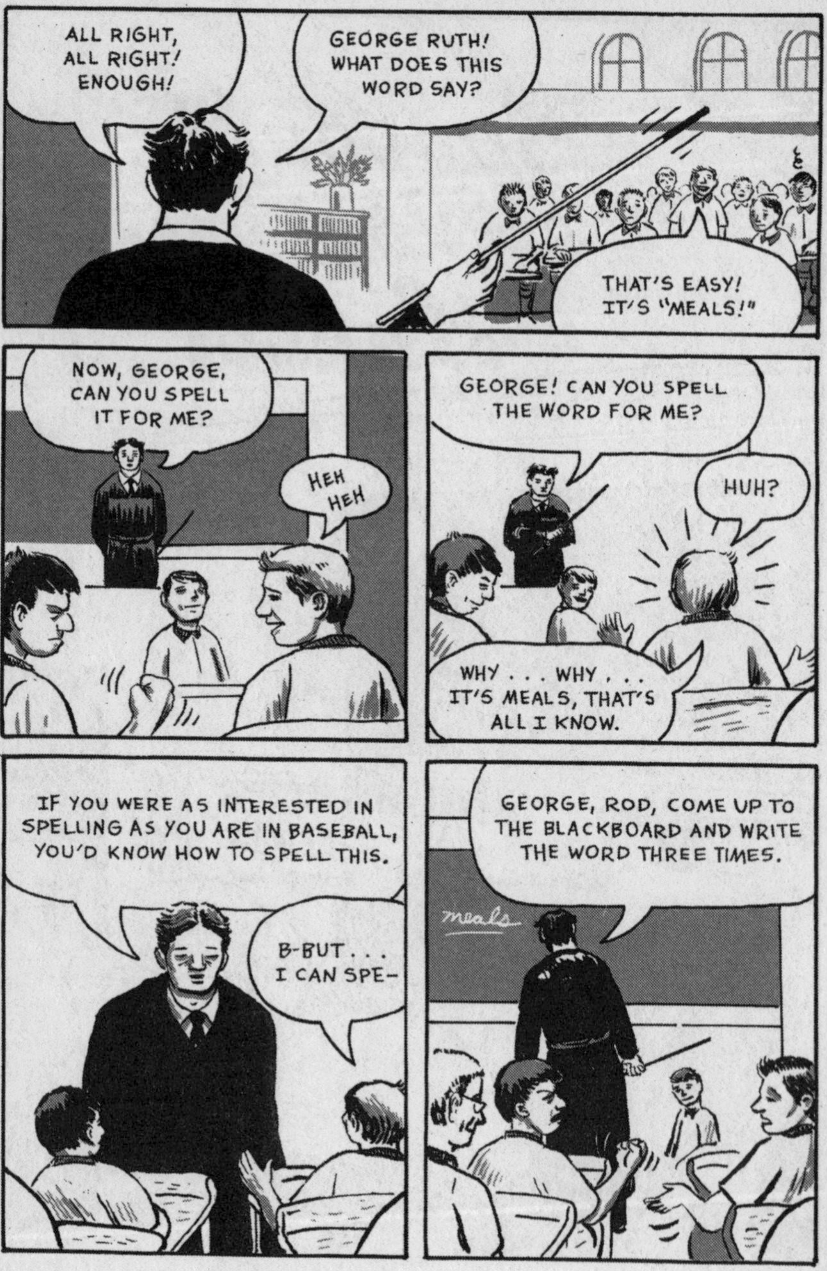
ALL RIGHT, ALL RIGHT! ENOUGH!
GEORGE RUTH! WHAT DOES THIS WORD SAY?
THAT'S EASY! IT'S "MEALS!"
NOW, GEORGE, CAN YOU SPELL IT FOR ME?
HEH HEH
GEORGE! CAN YOU SPELL THE WORD FOR ME?
HUH?
WHY . . . WHY . . . IT'S MEALS, THAT'S ALL I KNOW.
IF YOU WERE AS INTERESTED IN SPELLING AS YOU ARE IN BASEBALL, YOU'D KNOW HOW TO SPELL THIS.
B-BUT . . . I CAN SPE-
GEORGE, ROD, COME UP TO THE BLACKBOARD AND WRITE THE WORD THREE TIMES.
meals

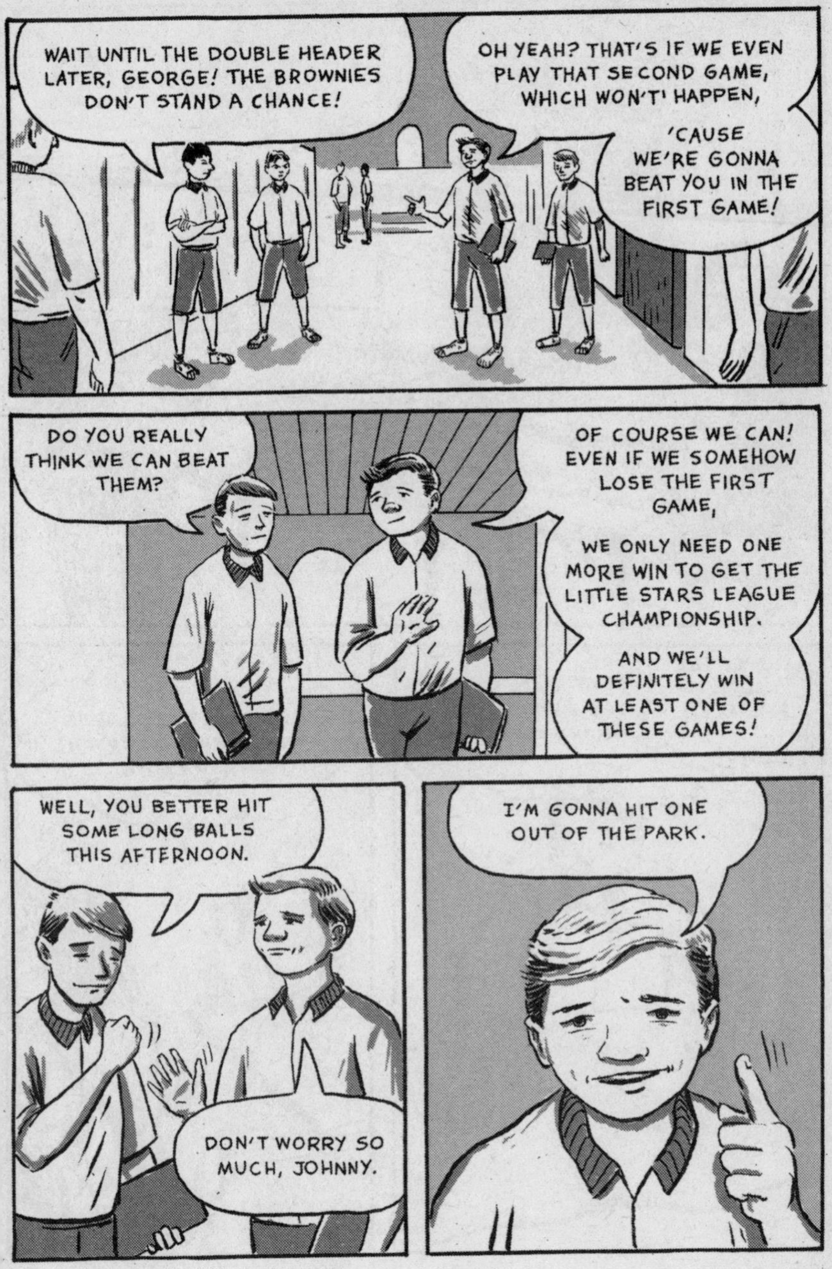
WAIT UNTIL THE DOUBLE HEADER LATER, GEORGE! THE BROWNIES DON'T STAND A CHANCE!
OH YEAH? THAT'S IF WE EVEN PLAY THAT SECOND GAME, WHICH WON'T' HAPPEN,
'CAUSE WE'RE GONNA BEAT YOU IN THE FIRST GAME!
DO YOU REALLY THINK WE CAN BEAT THEM?
OF COURSE WE CAN! EVEN IF WE SOMEHOW LOSE THE FIRST GAME,
WE ONLY NEED ONE MORE WIN TO GET THE LITTLE STARS LEAGUE CHAMPIONSHIP.
AND WE'LL DEFINITELY WIN AT LEAST ONE OF THESE GAMES!
WELL, YOU BETTER HIT SOME LONG BALLS THIS AFTERNOON.
DON'T WORRY SO MUCH, JOHNNY.
I'M GONNA HIT ONE OUT OF THE PARK.

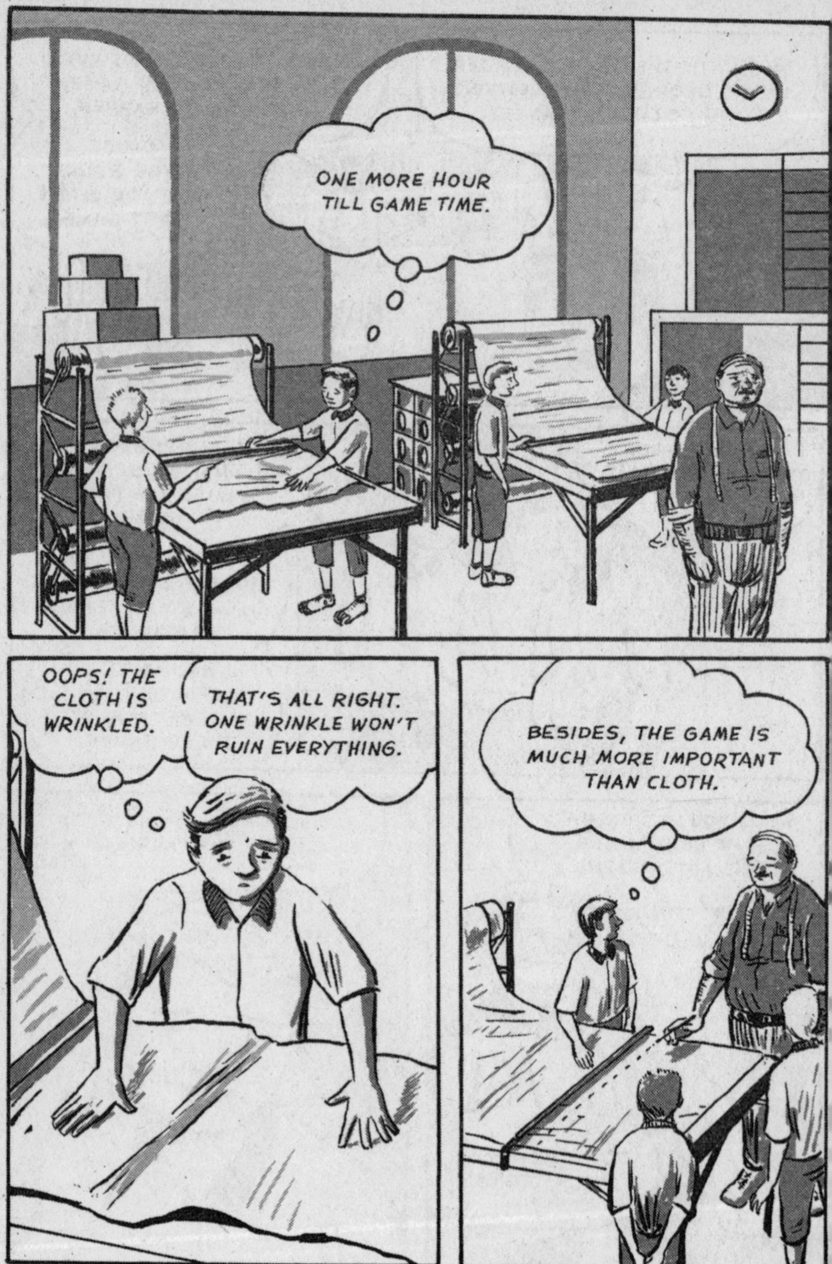
ONE MORE HOUR TILL GAME TIME.
OOPS! THE CLOTH IS WRINKLED.
THAT'S ALL RIGHT. ONE WRINKLE WON'T RUIN EVERYTHING.
BESIDES, THE GAME IS MUCH MORE IMPORTANT THAN CLOTH.

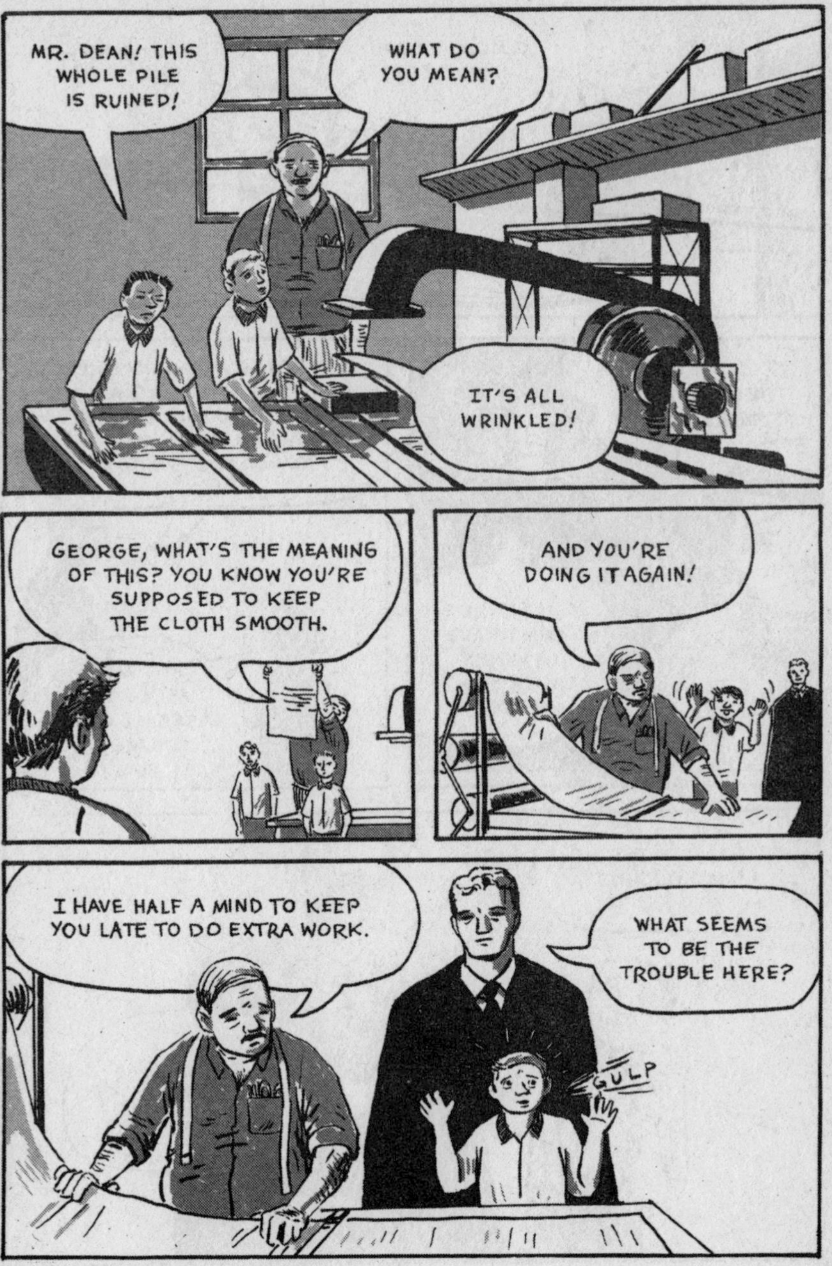
MR. DEAN! THIS WHOLE PILE IS RUINED!
WHAT DO YOU MEAN?
IT'S ALL WRINKLED!
GEORGE, WHAT'S THE MEANING OF THIS? YOU KNOW YOU'RE SUPPOSED TO KEEP THE CLOTH SMOOTH.
AND YOU'RE DOING IT AGAIN!
I HAVE HALF A MIND TO KEEP YOU LATE TO DO EXTRA WORK.
WHAT SEEMS TO BE THE TROUBLE HERE?
GULP

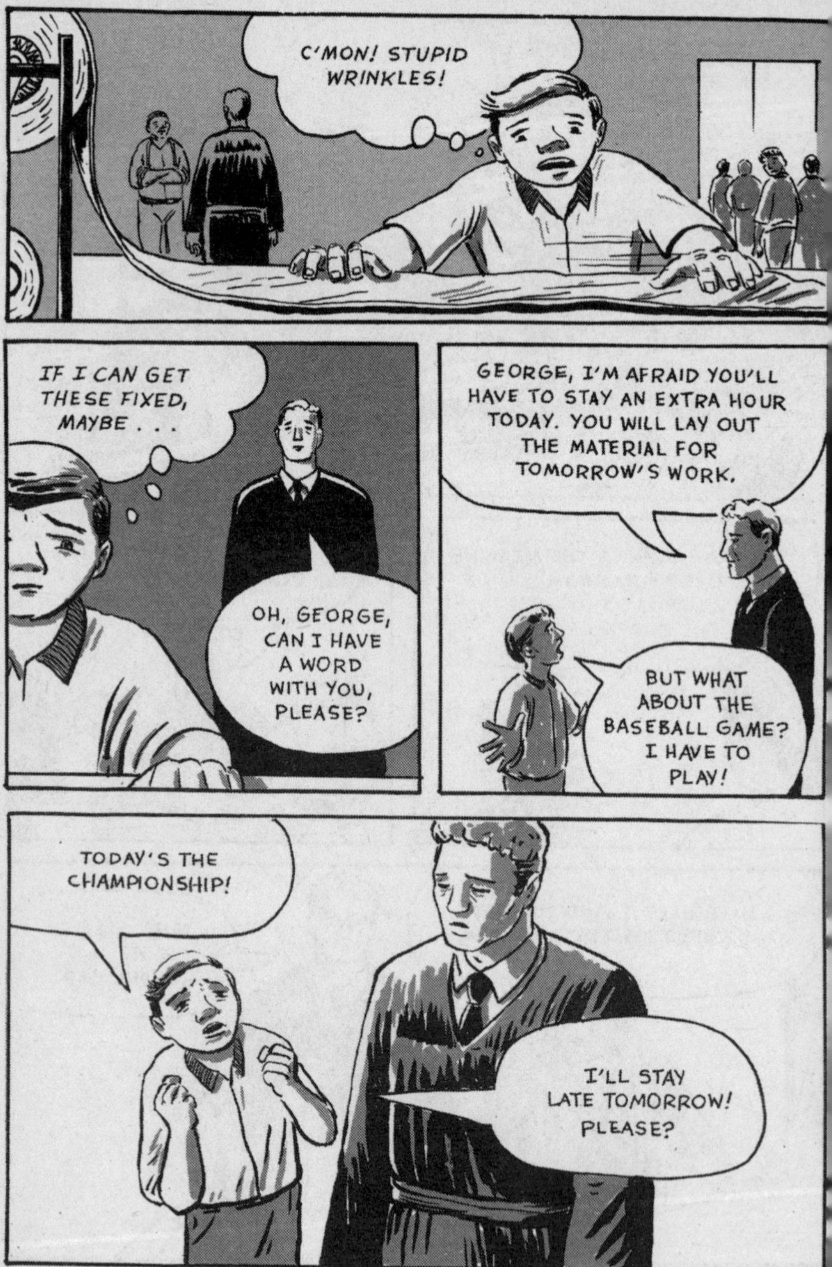
C'MON! STUPID WRINKLES!
IF I CAN GET THESE FIXED, MAYBE . . .
OH, GEORGE, CAN I HAVE A WORD WITH YOU, PLEASE?
GEORGE, I'M AFRAID YOU'LL HAVE TO STAY AN EXTRA HOUR TODAY. YOU WILL LAY OUT THE MATERIAL FOR TOMORROW'S WORK.
BUT WHAT ABOUT THE BASEBALL GAME? I HAVE TO PLAY!
TODAY'S THE CHAMPIONSHIP!
I'LL STAY LATE TOMORROW! PLEASE?

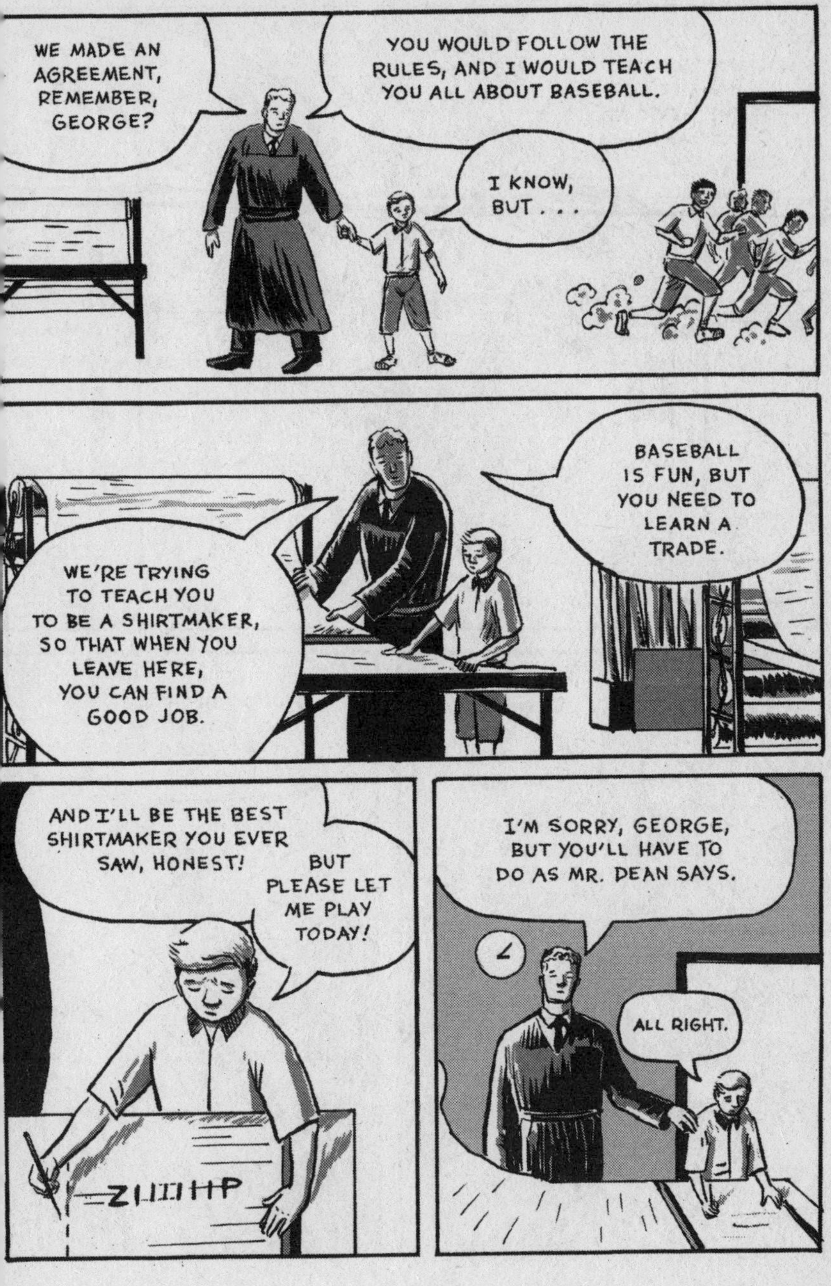
WE MADE AN AGREEMENT, REMEMBER, GEORGE?
YOU WOULD FOLLOW THE RULES, AND I WOULD TEACH YOU ALL ABOUT BASEBALL.
I KNOW, BUT . . .
BASEBALL IS FUN, BUT YOU NEED TO LEARN A TRADE.
WE'RE TRYING TO TEACH YOU TO BE A SHIRTMAKER, SO THAT WHEN YOU LEAVE HERE, YOU CAN FIND A GOOD JOB.
AND I'LL BE THE BEST SHIRTMAKER YOU EVER SAW, HONEST!
BUT PLEASE LET ME PLAY TODAY!
ZIIIIHP
I'M SORRY, GEORGE, BUT YOU'LL HAVE TO DO AS MR. DEAN SAYS.
ALL RIGHT.

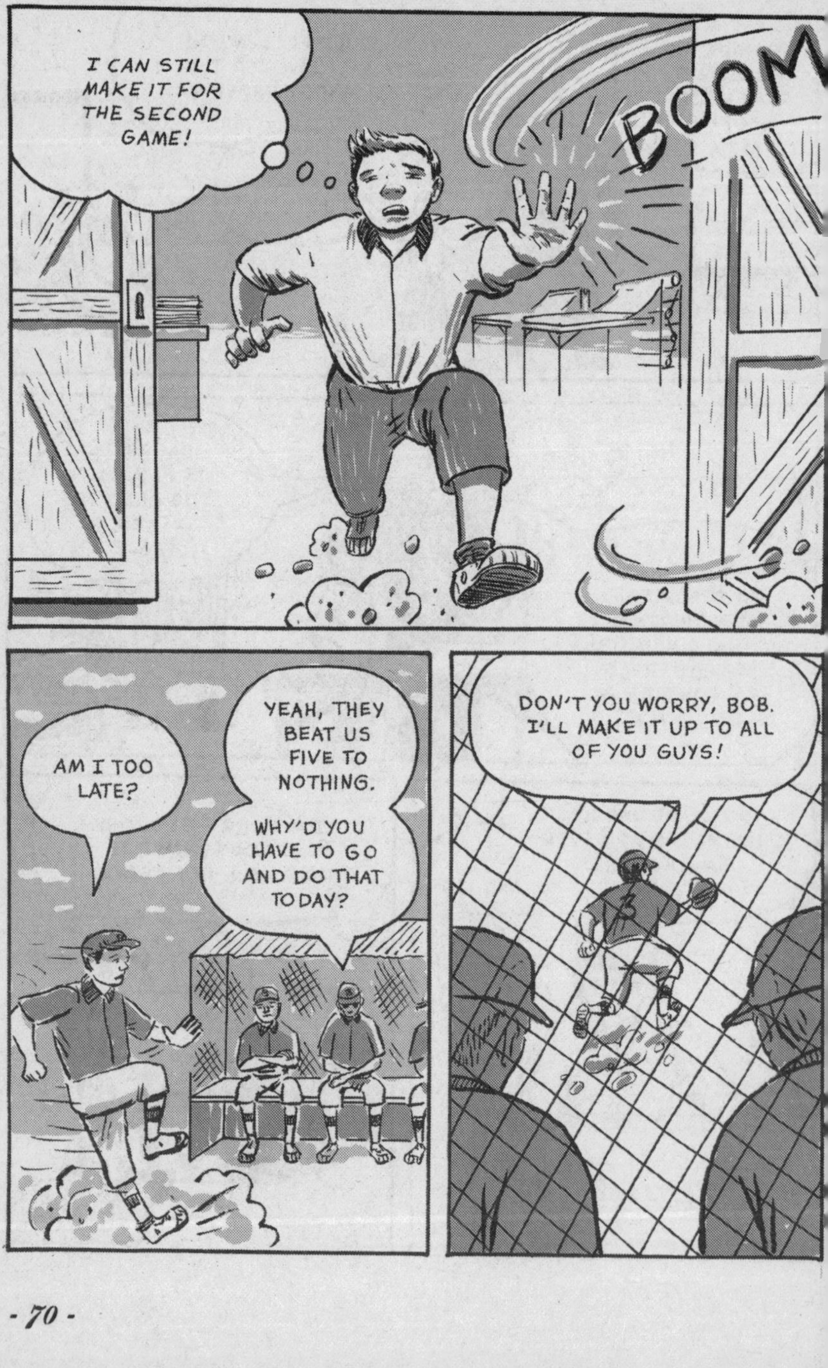
I CAN STILL MAKE IT FOR THE SECOND GAME!
BOOM
AM I TOO LATE?
YEAH, THEY BEAT US FIVE TO NOTHING.
WHY'D YOU HAVE TO GO AND DO THAT TODAY?
DON'T YOU WORRY, BOB. I'LL MAKE IT UP TO ALL OF YOU GUYS!

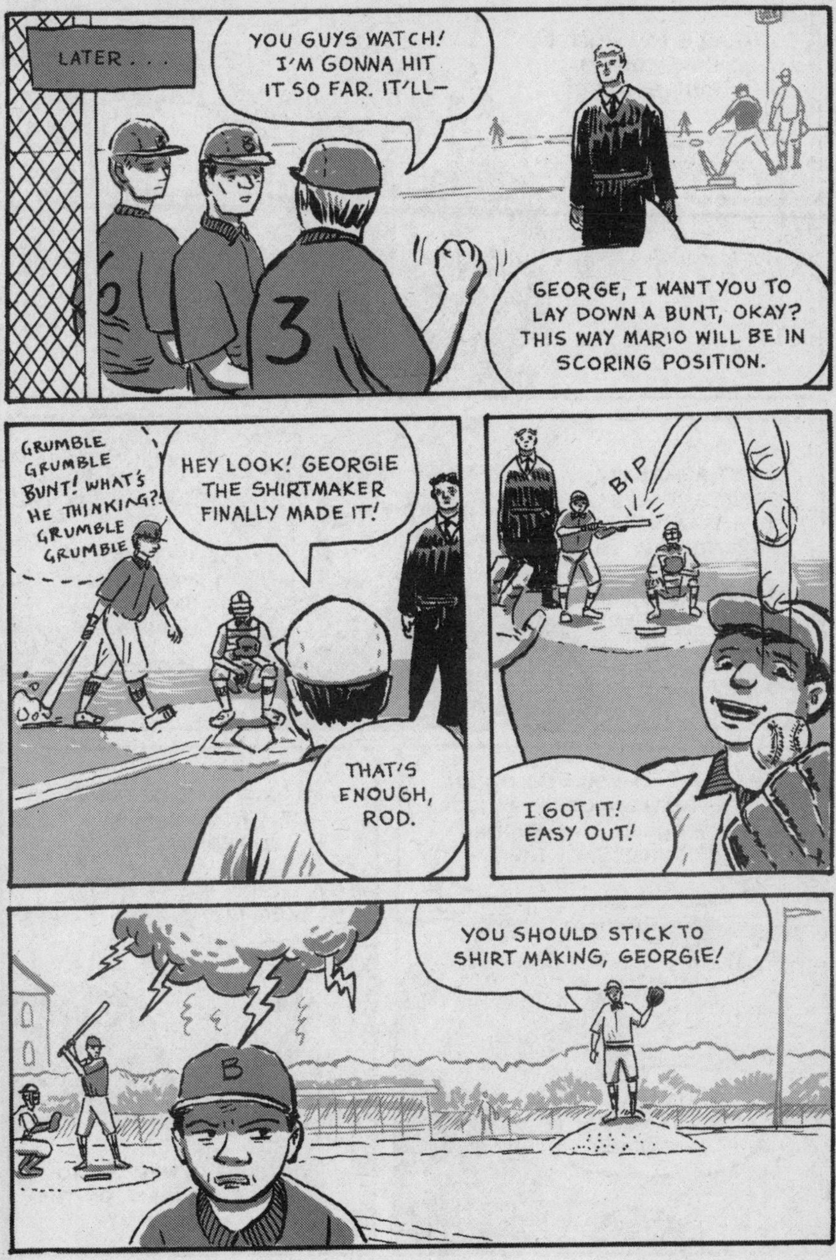
LATER . . .
YOU GUYS WATCH! I'M GONNA HIT IT SO FAR. IT'LL—
GEORGE, I WANT YOU TO LAY DOWN A BUNT, OKAY? THIS WAY MARIO WILL BE IN SCORING POSITION.
GRUMBLE GRUMBLE BUNT! WHAT'S HE THINKING?! GRUMBLE GRUMBLE
HEY LOOK! GEORGIE THE SHIRTMAKER FINALLY MADE IT!
THAT'S ENOUGH, ROD.
BIP
I GOT IT! EASY OUT!
YOU SHOULD STICK TO SHIRT MAKING, GEORGIE!

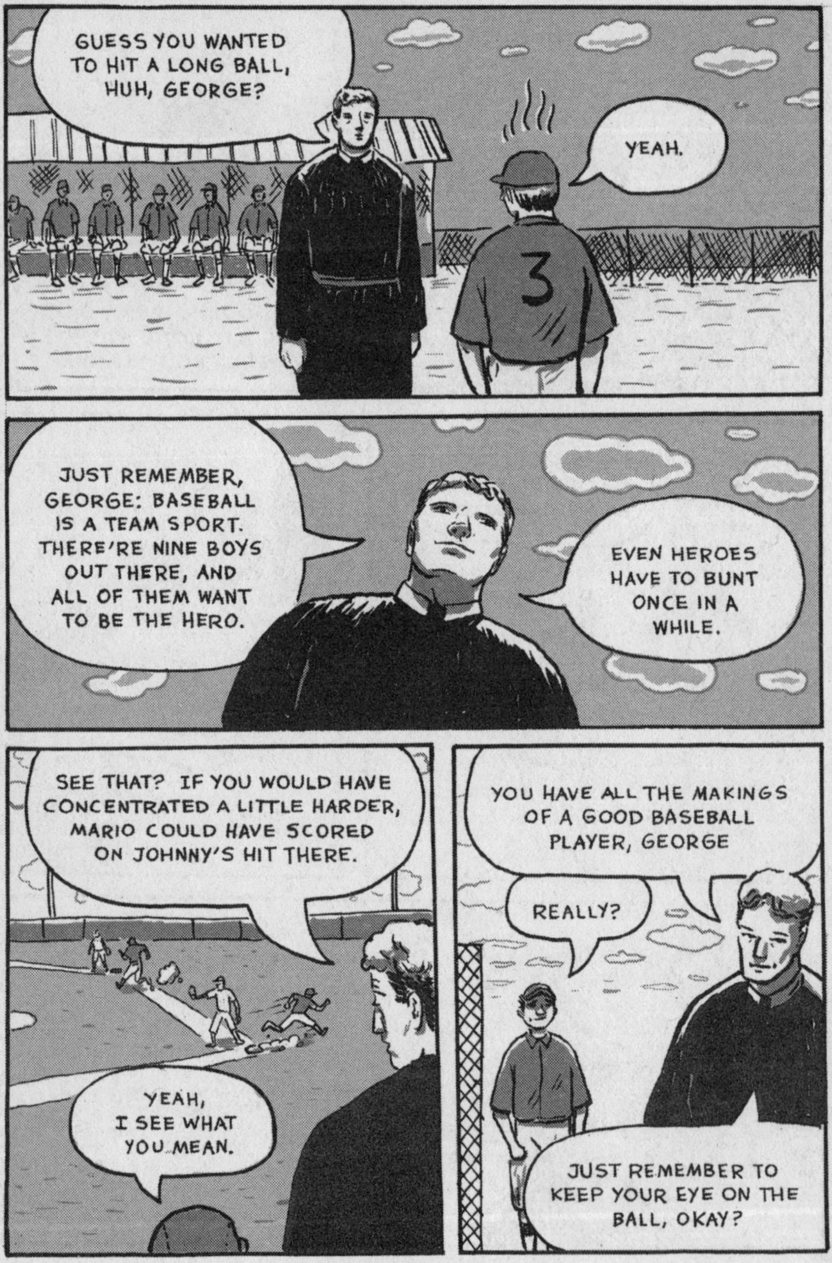
GUESS YOU WANTED TO HIT A LONG BALL, HUH, GEORGE?
YEAH.
JUST REMEMBER, GEORGE: BASEBALL IS A TEAM SPORT. THERE'RE NINE BOYS OUT THERE, AND ALL OF THEM WANT TO BE THE HERO.
EVEN HEROES HAVE TO BUNT ONCE IN A WHILE.
SEE THAT? IF YOU WOULD HAVE CONCENTRATED A LITTLE HARDER, MARIO COULD HAVE SCORED ON JOHNNY'S HIT THERE.
YEAH, I SEE WHAT YOU MEAN.
YOU HAVE ALL THE MAKINGS OF A GOOD BASEBALL PLAYER, GEORGE
REALLY?
JUST REMEMBER TO KEEP YOUR EYE ON THE BALL, OKAY?
3

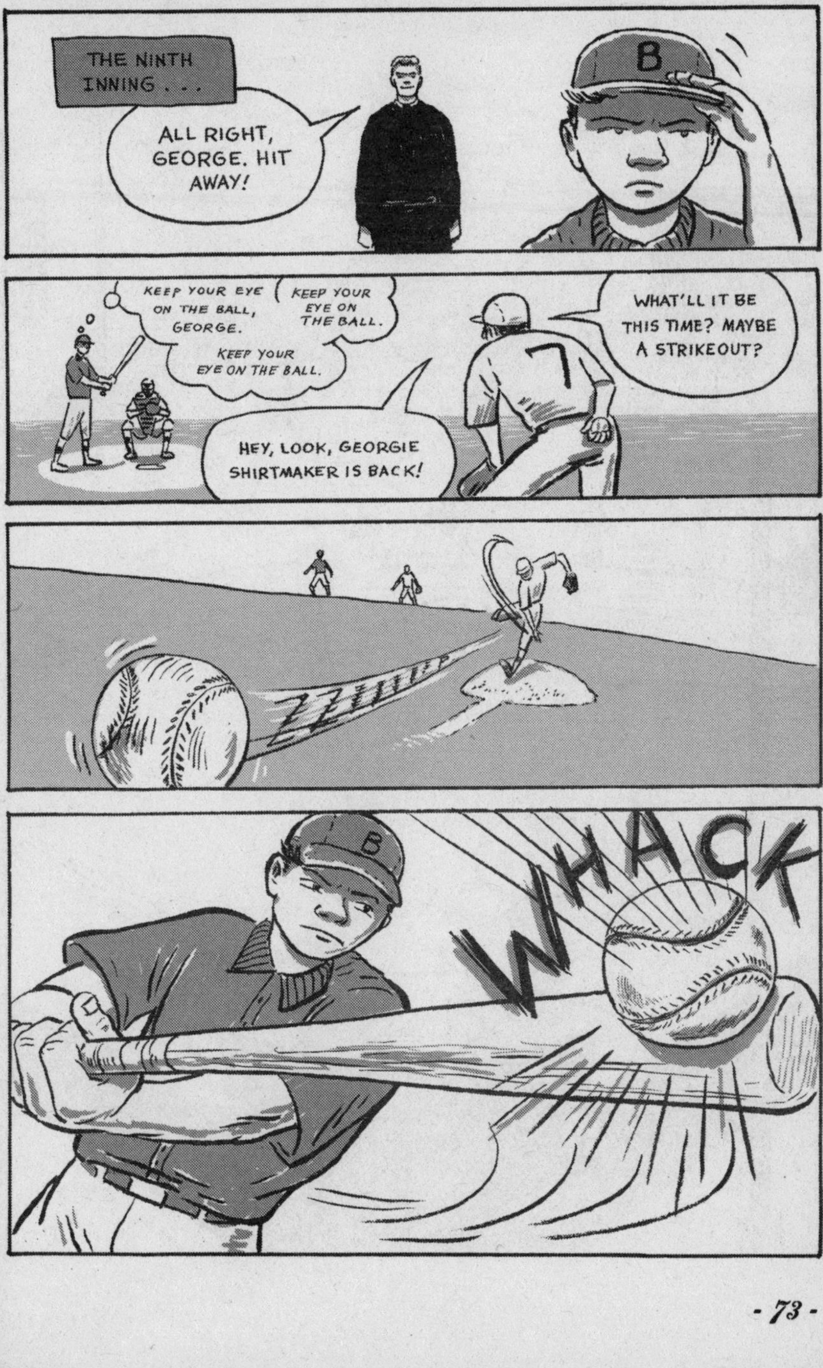

THE NINTH INNING . . .
ALL RIGHT, GEORGE. HIT AWAY!
KEEP YOUR EYE ON THE BALL, GEORGE.
KEEP YOUR EYE ON THE BALL.
KEEP YOUR EYE ON THE BALL.
HEY, LOOK, GEORGIE SHIRTMAKER IS BACK!
WHAT'LL IT BE THIS TIME? MAYBE A STRIKEOUT?
ZZIIIIIP
WHACK

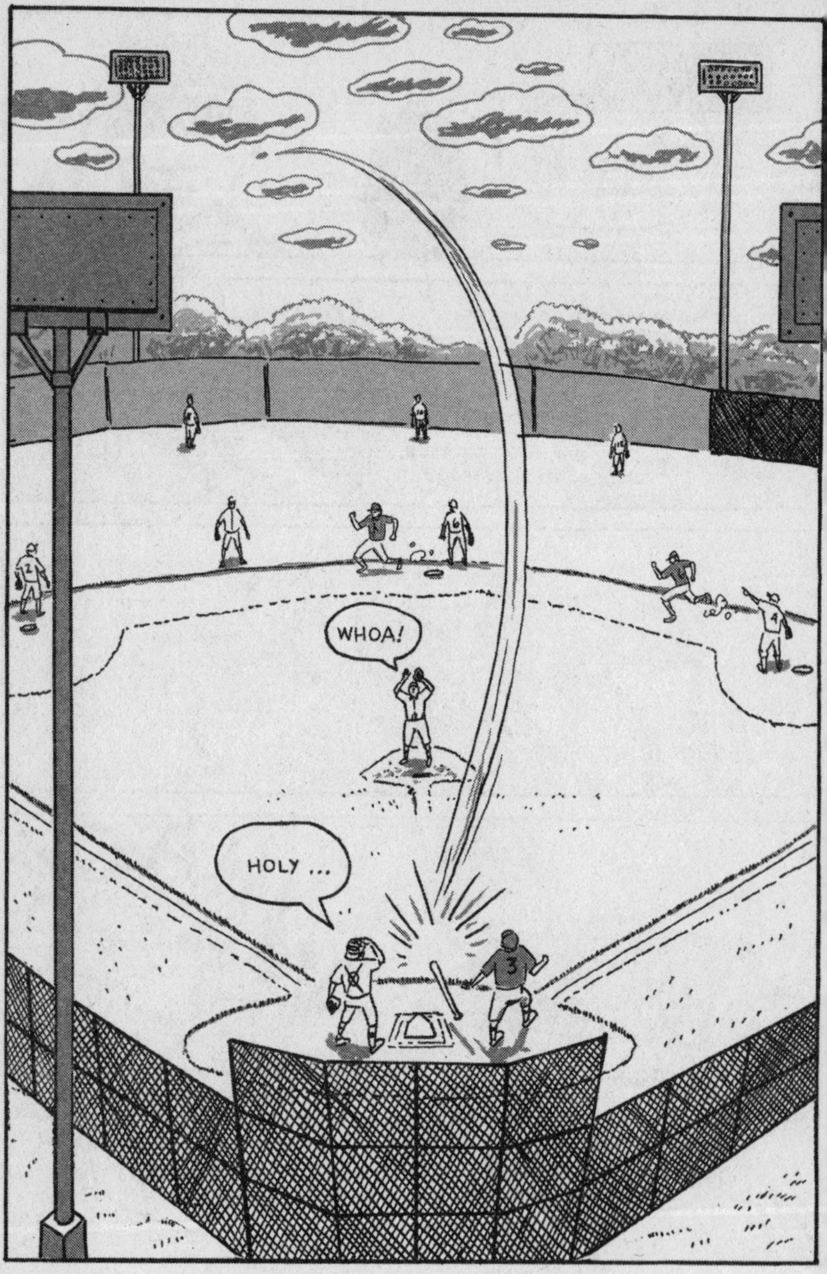
WHOA!
HOLY ...

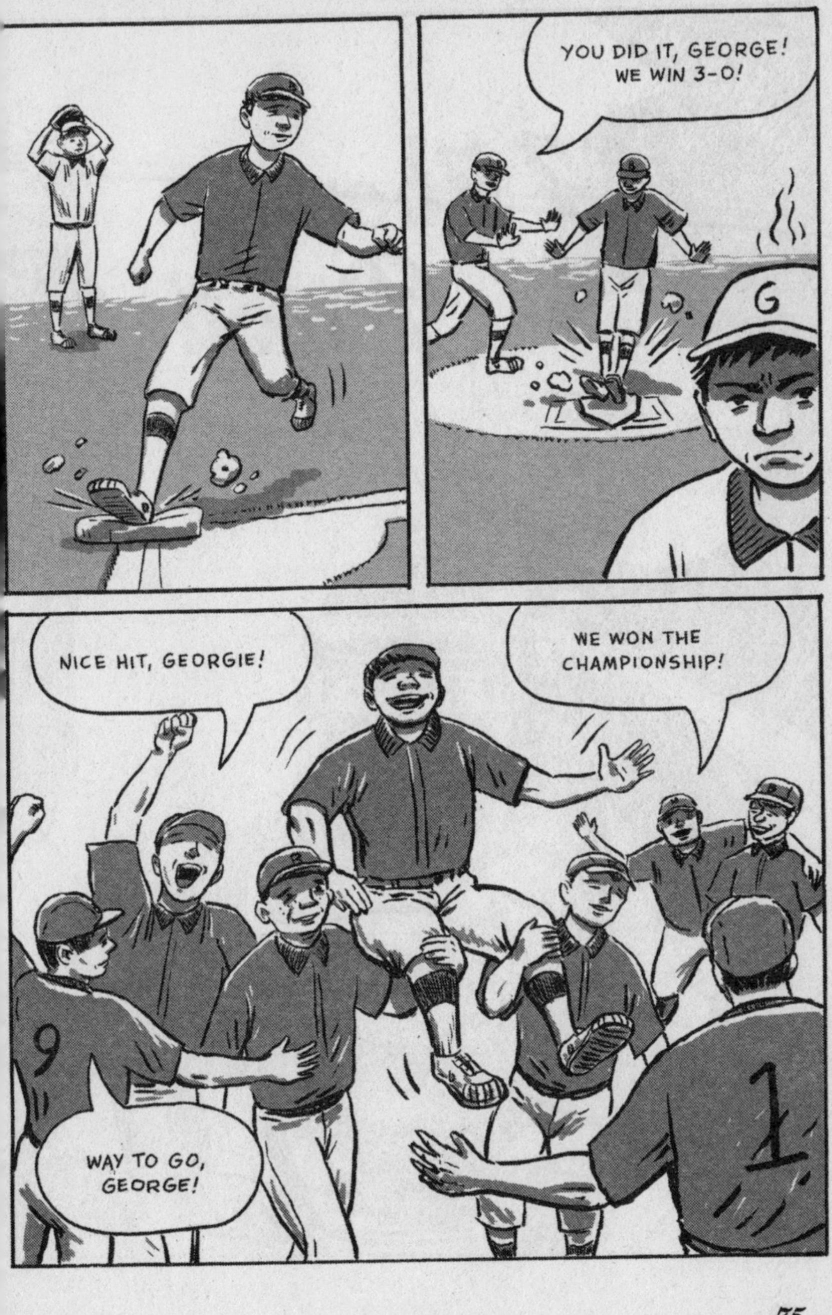
YOU DID IT, GEORGE! WE WIN 3-0!
NICE HIT, GEORGIE!
WE WON THE CHAMPIONSHIP!
WAY TO GO, GEORGE!

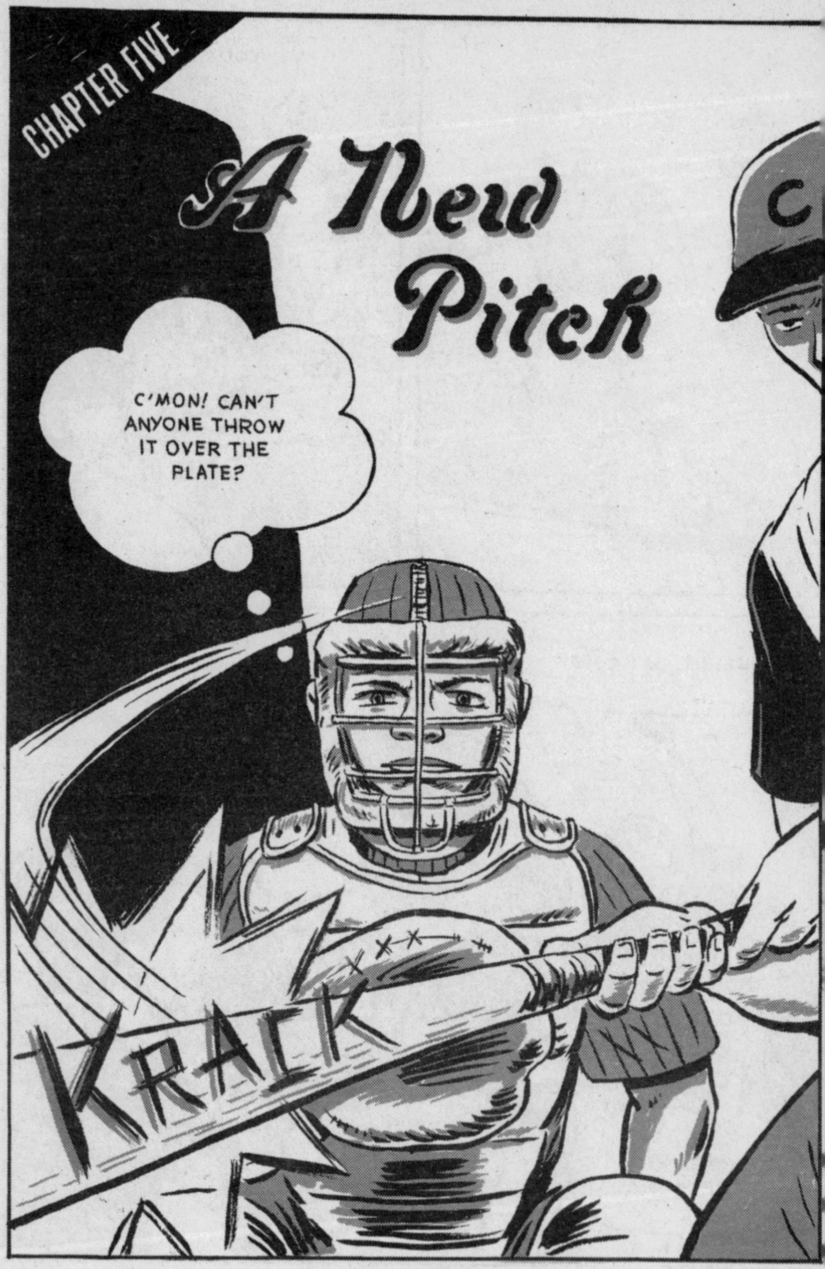
CHAPTER FIVE
A New Pitch
C'MON! CAN'T ANYONE THROW IT OVER THE PLATE?
KRACK

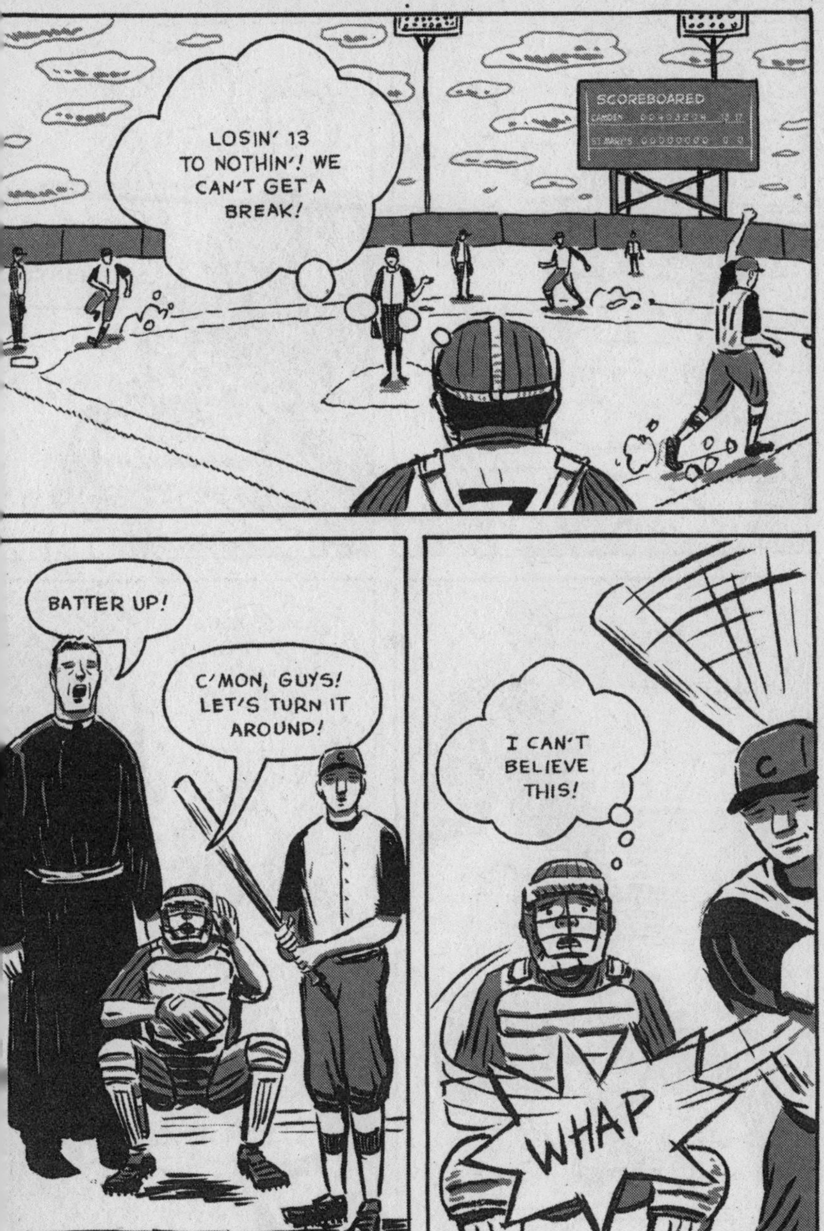
LOSIN' 13 TO NOTHIN'! WE CAN'T GET A BREAK!
SCOREBOARED
BATTER UP!
C'MON, GUYS! LET'S TURN IT AROUND!
I CAN'T BELIEVE THIS!
WHAP

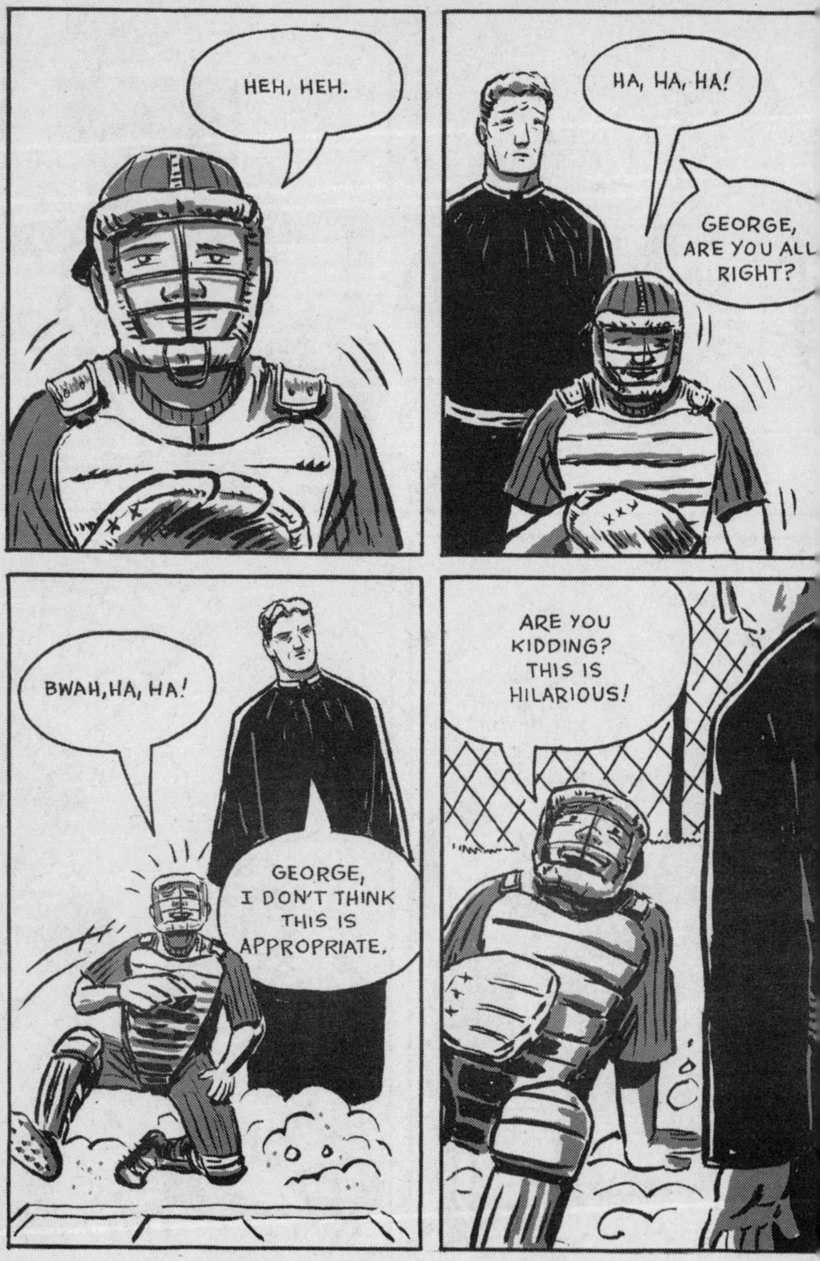
HEH, HEH.
HA, HA, HA!
GEORGE, ARE YOU ALL RIGHT?
BWAH, HA, HA!
GEORGE, I DON'T THINK THIS IS APPROPRIATE.
ARE YOU KIDDING? THIS IS HILARIOUS!

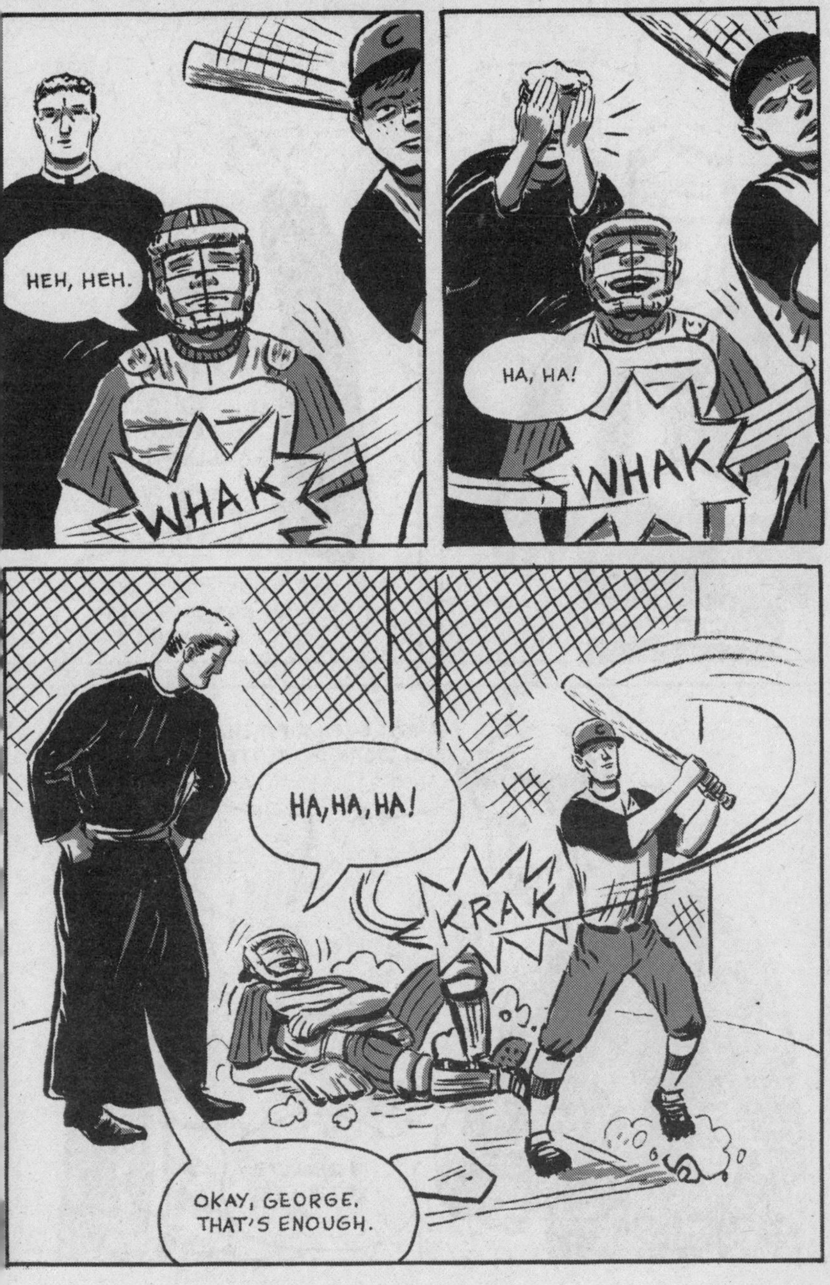
HEH, HEH.
WHAK
HA, HA!
WHAK
HA, HA, HA!
KRAK
OKAY, GEORGE. THAT'S ENOUGH.

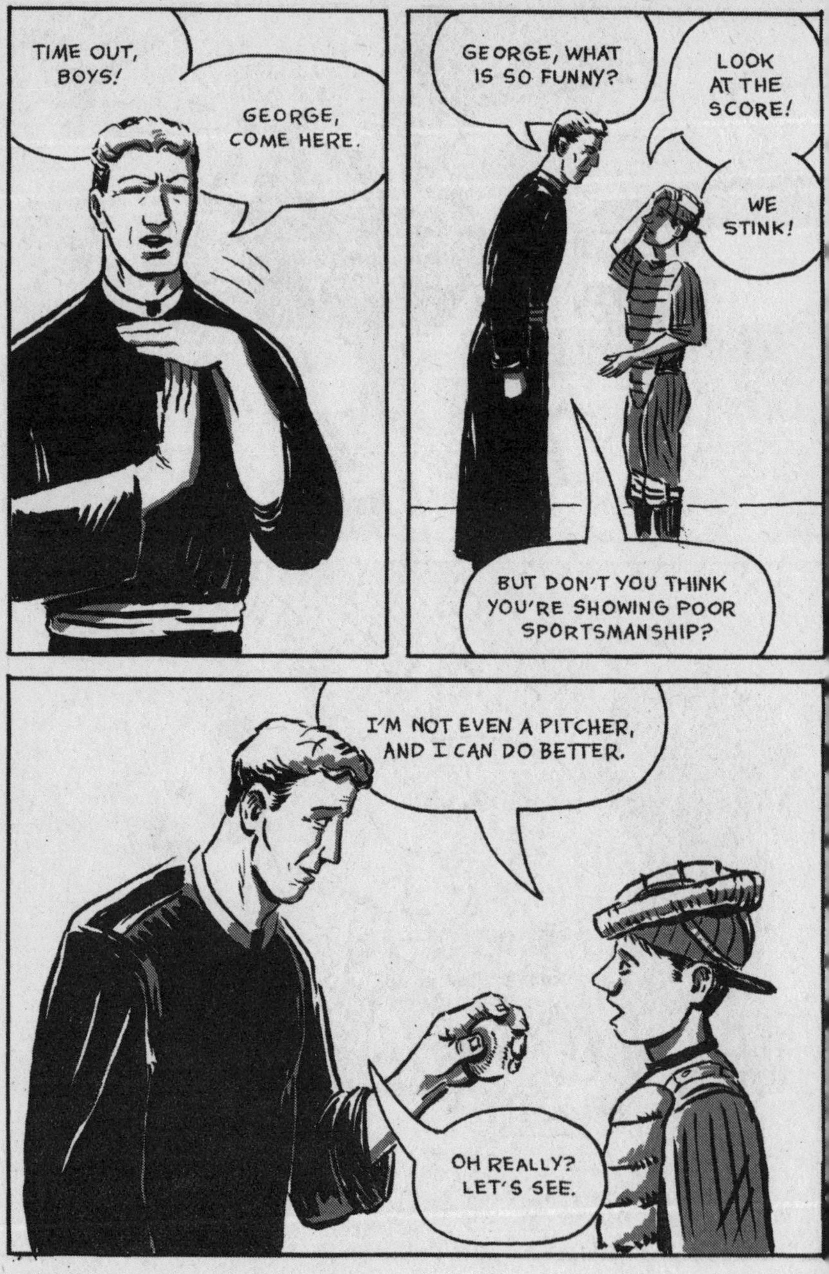
TIME OUT, BOYS!
GEORGE, COME HERE.
GEORGE, WHAT IS SO FUNNY?
LOOK AT THE SCORE!
WE STINK!
BUT DON'T YOU THINK YOU'RE SHOWING POOR SPORTSMANSHIP?
I'M NOT EVEN A PITCHER, AND I CAN DO BETTER.
OH REALLY? LET'S SEE.

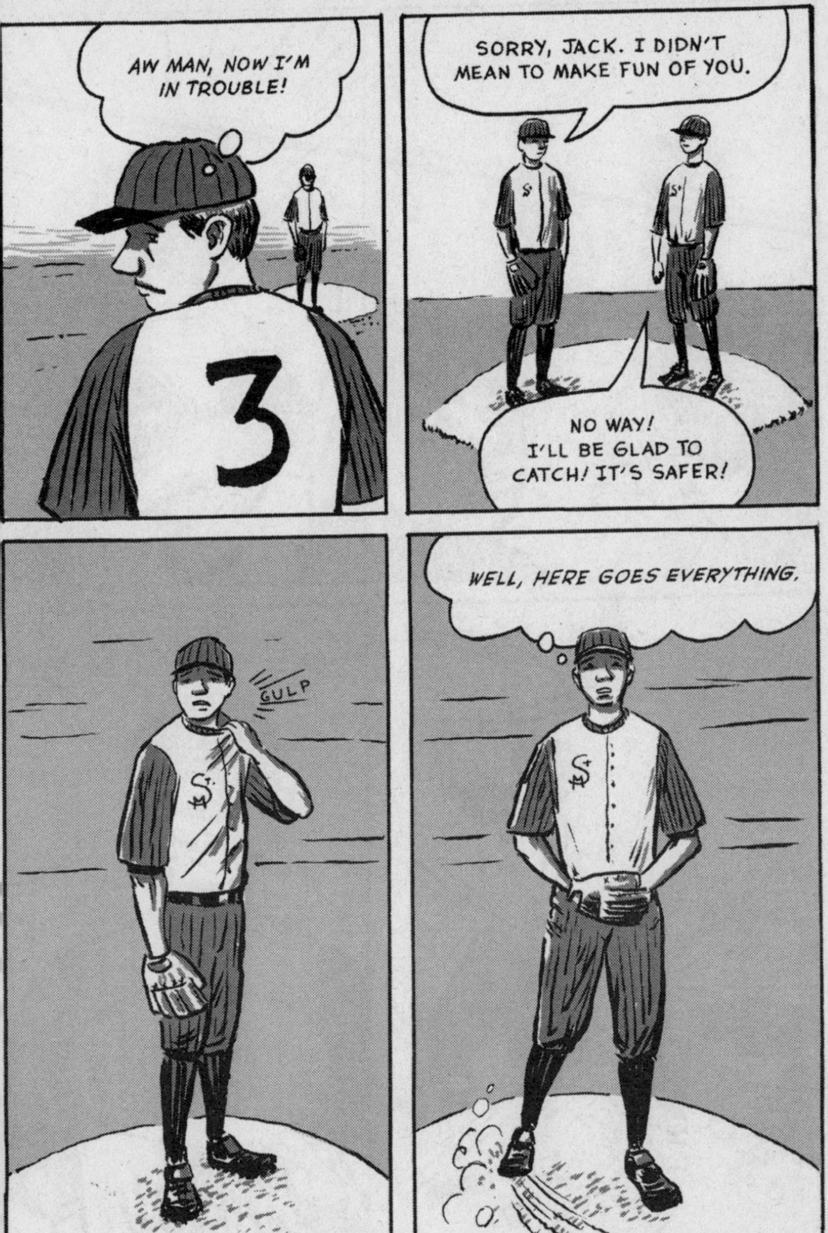
AW MAN, NOW I'M IN TROUBLE!
3
SORRY, JACK. I DIDN'T MEAN TO MAKE FUN OF YOU.
NO WAY! I'LL BE GLAD TO CATCH! IT'S SAFER!
GULP
WELL, HERE GOES EVERYTHING.

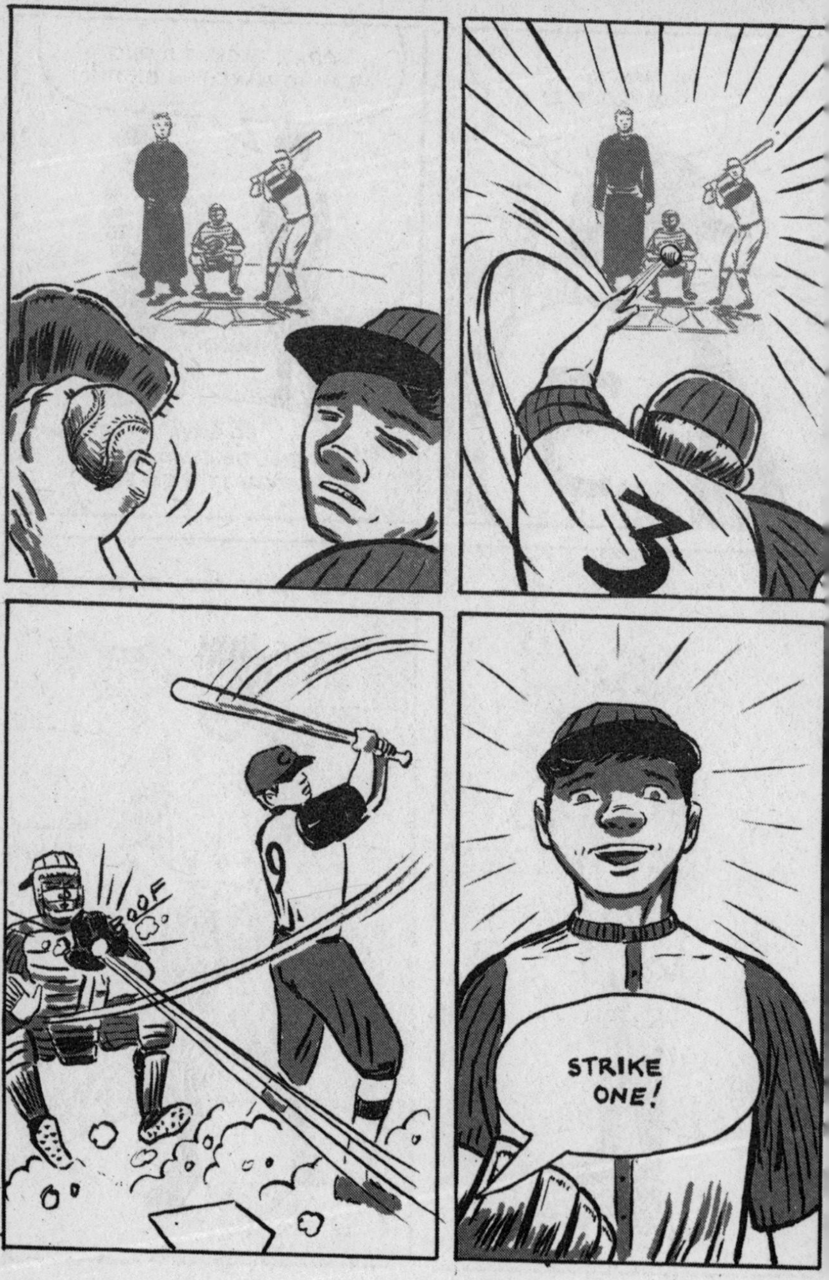
OOF
STRIKE ONE!

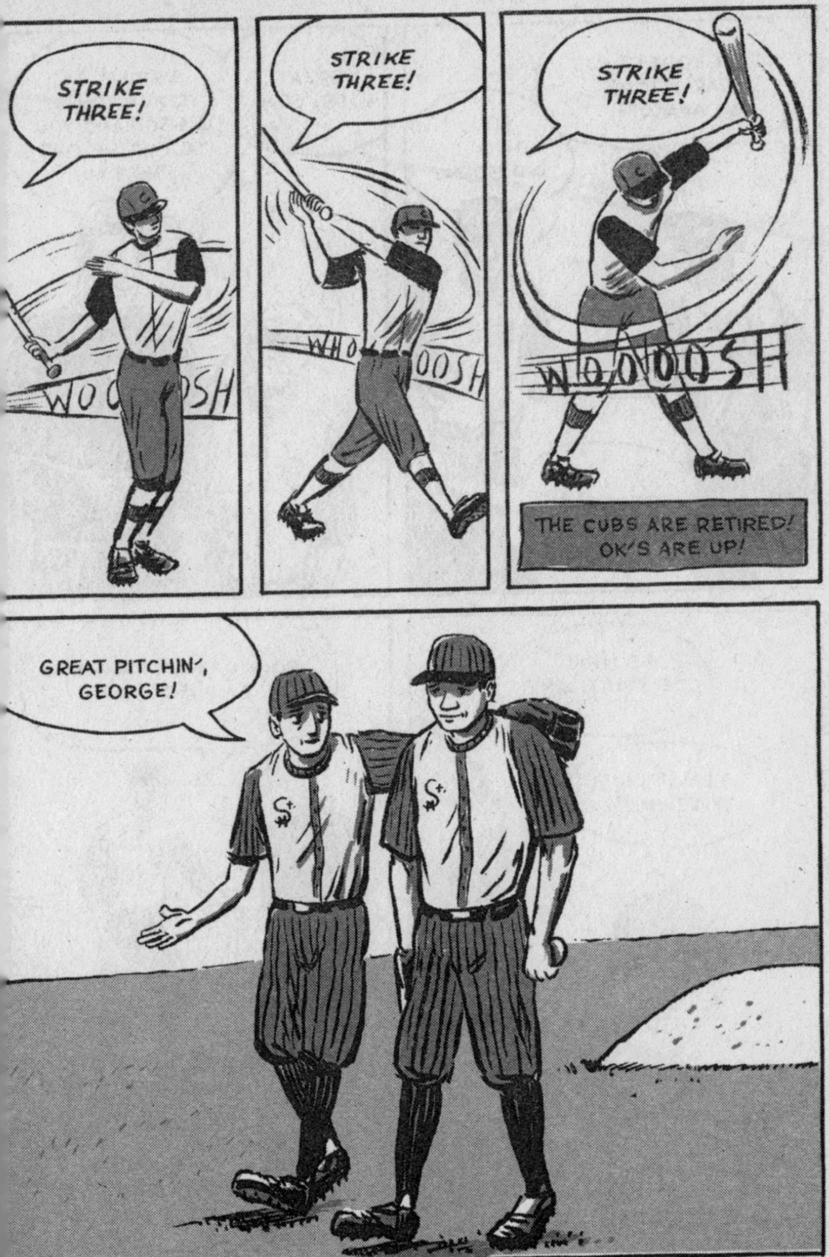
STRIKE THREE!
WOOOOSH
STRIKE THREE!
WHOOOOSH
STRIKE THREE!
WOOOOOSH
THE CUBS ARE RETIRED! OK'S ARE UP!
GREAT PITCHIN', GEORGE!

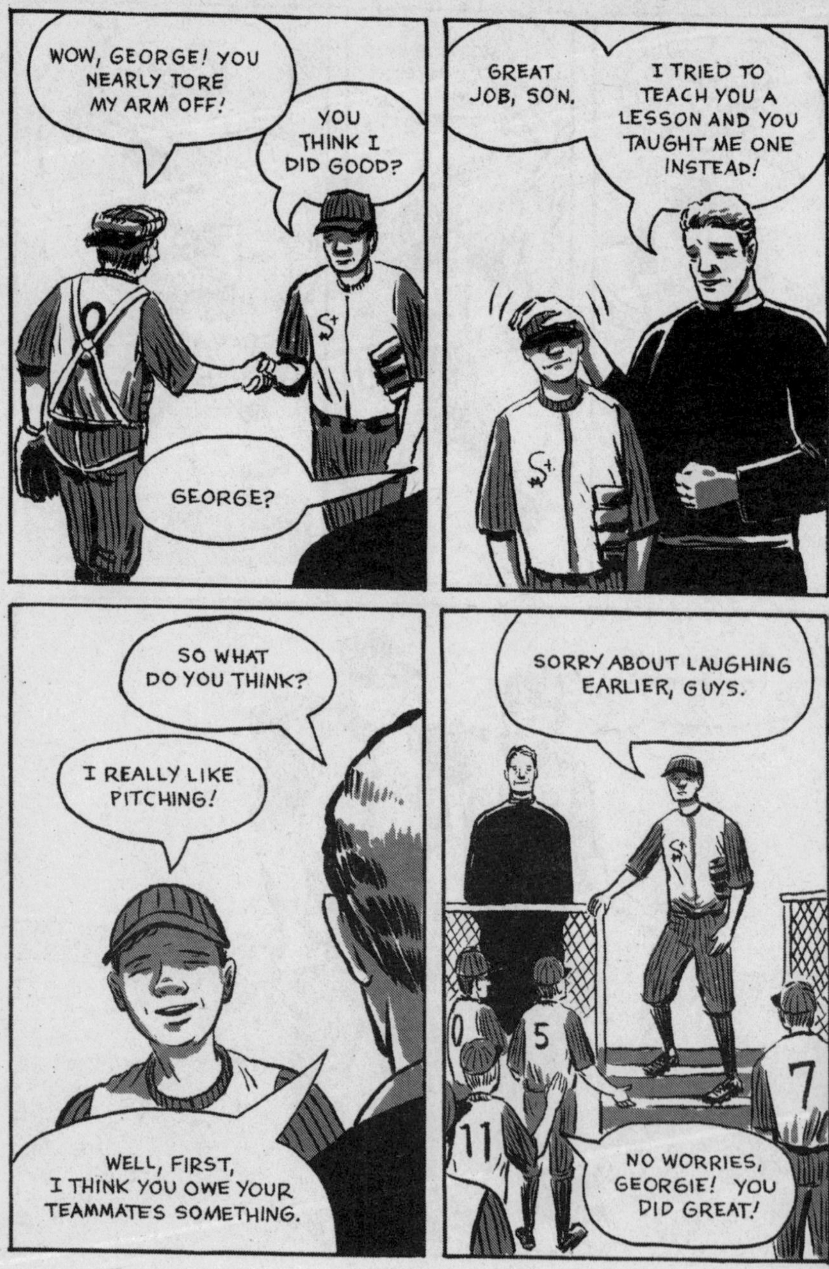
WOW, GEORGE! YOU NEARLY TORE MY ARM OFF!
YOU THINK I DID GOOD?
GEORGE?
GREAT JOB, SON.
I TRIED TO TEACH YOU A LESSON AND YOU TAUGHT ME ONE INSTEAD!
SO WHAT DO YOU THINK?
I REALLY LIKE PITCHING!
WELL, FIRST, I THINK YOU OWE YOUR TEAMMATES SOMETHING.
SORRY ABOUT LAUGHING EARLIER, GUYS.
NO WORRIES, GEORGIE! YOU DID GREAT!

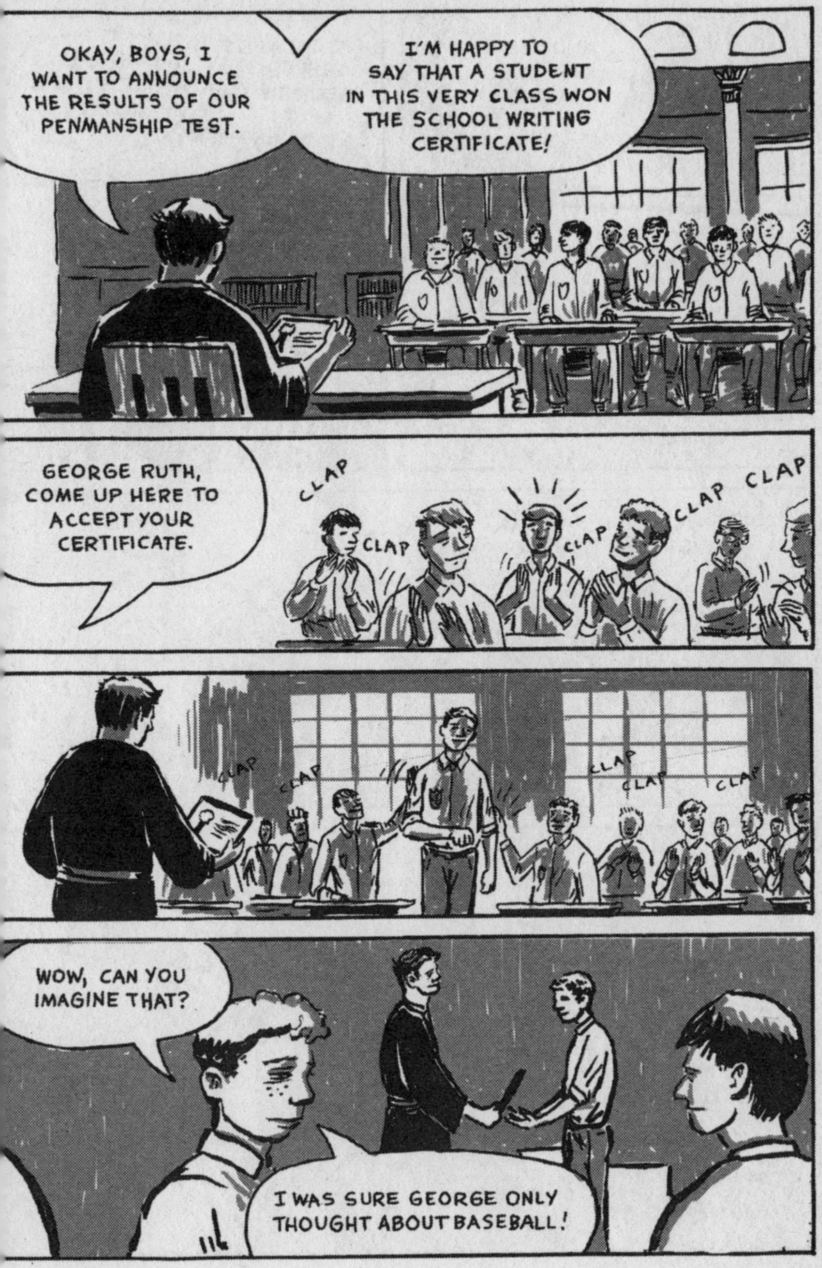
OKAY, BOYS, I WANT TO ANNOUNCE THE RESULTS OF OUR PENMANSHIP TEST.
I'M HAPPY TO SAY THAT A STUDENT IN THIS VERY CLASS WON THE SCHOOL WRITING CERTIFICATE!
GEORGE RUTH, COME UP HERE TO ACCEPT YOUR CERTIFICATE.
CLAP
CLAP
CLAP
CLAP
CLAP
CLAP
CLAP
WOW, CAN YOU IMAGINE THAT?
I WAS SURE GEORGE ONLY THOUGHT ABOUT BASEBALL!

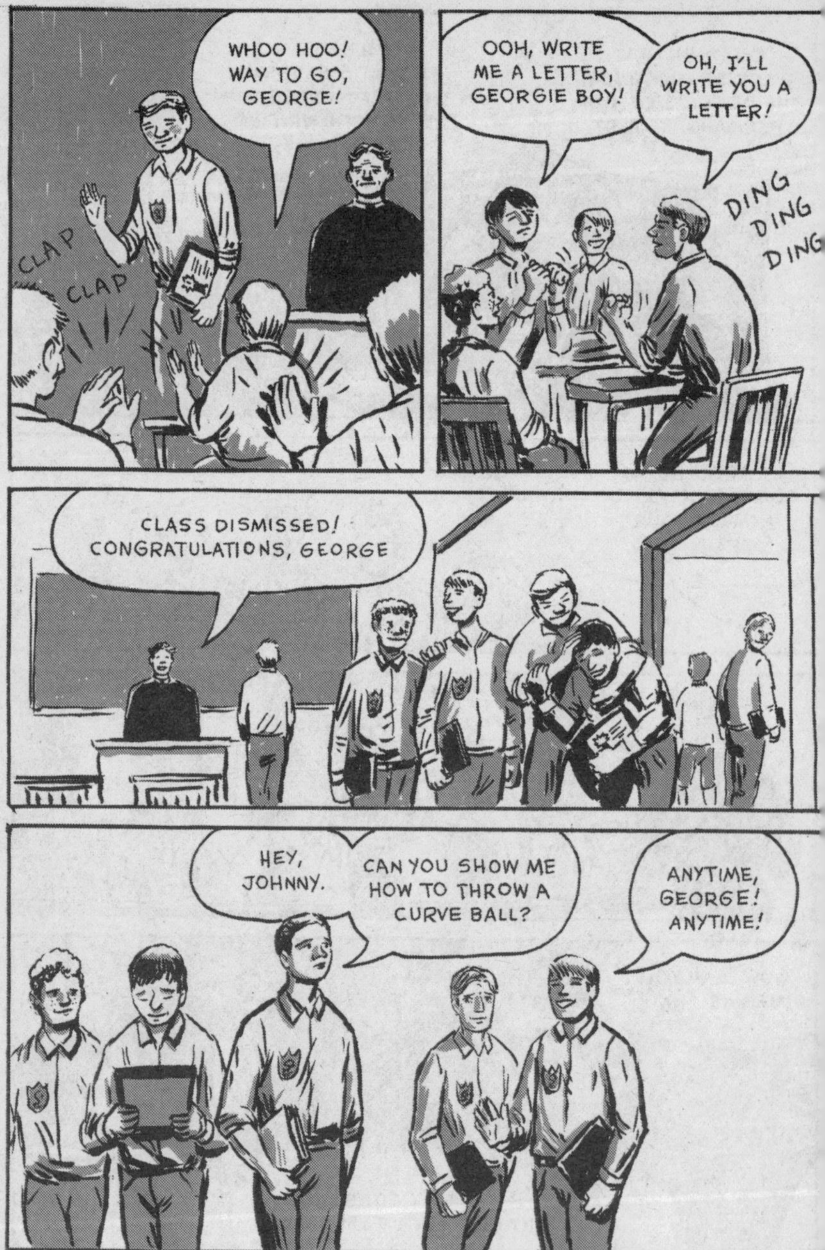
WHOO HOO! WAY TO GO, GEORGE!
CLAP CLAP
OOH, WRITE ME A LETTER, GEORGIE BOY!
OH, I'LL WRITE YOU A LETTER!
DING DING DING
CLASS DISMISSED! CONGRATULATIONS, GEORGE
HEY, JOHNNY.
CAN YOU SHOW ME HOW TO THROW A CURVE BALL?
ANYTIME, GEORGE! ANYTIME!

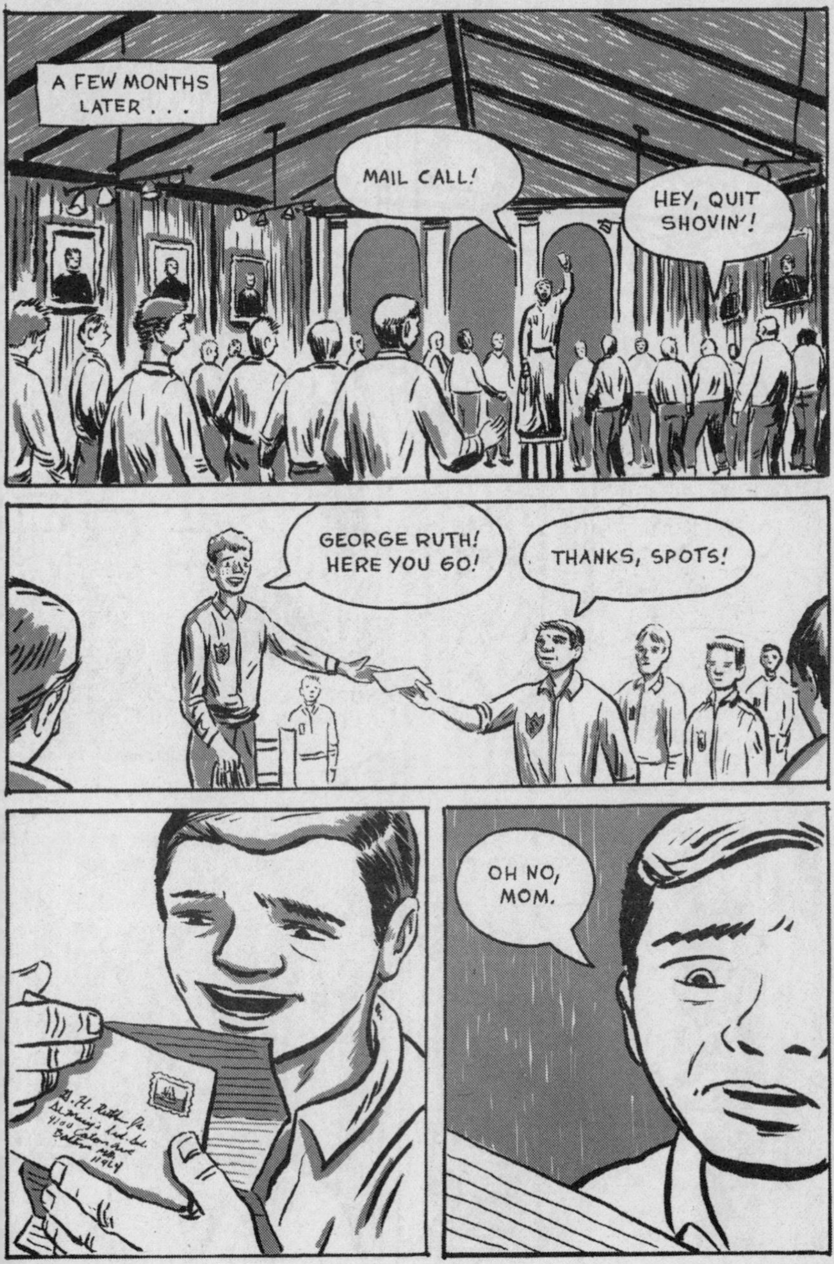
A FEW MONTHS LATER . . .
MAIL CALL!
HEY, QUIT SHOVIN'!
GEORGE RUTH! HERE YOU GO!
THANKS, SPOTS!
OH NO, MOM.

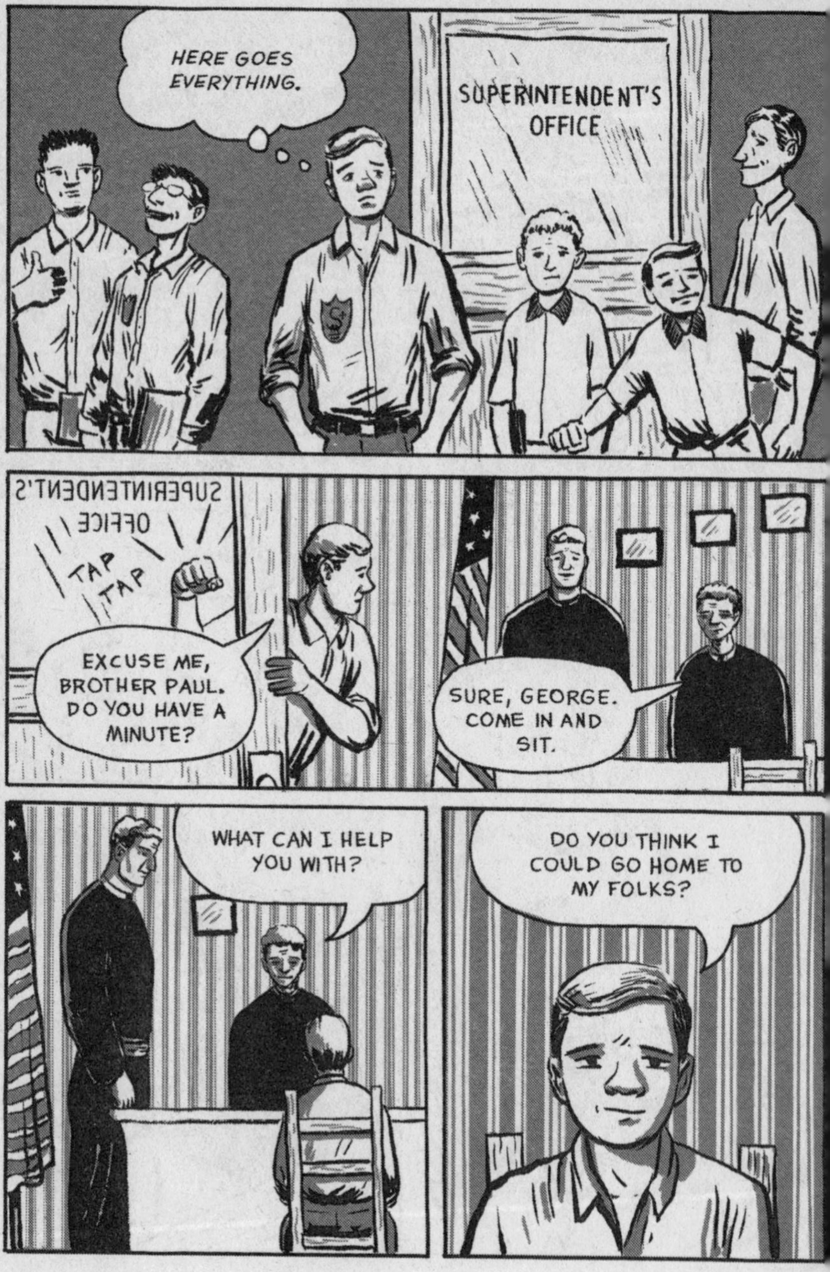
HERE GOES EVERYTHING.
SUPERINTENDENT'S OFFICE
SUPERINTENDENT'S OFFICE
TAP TAP
EXCUSE ME, BROTHER PAUL. DO YOU HAVE A MINUTE?
SURE, GEORGE. COME IN AND SIT.
WHAT CAN I HELP YOU WITH?
DO YOU THINK I COULD GO HOME TO MY FOLKS?

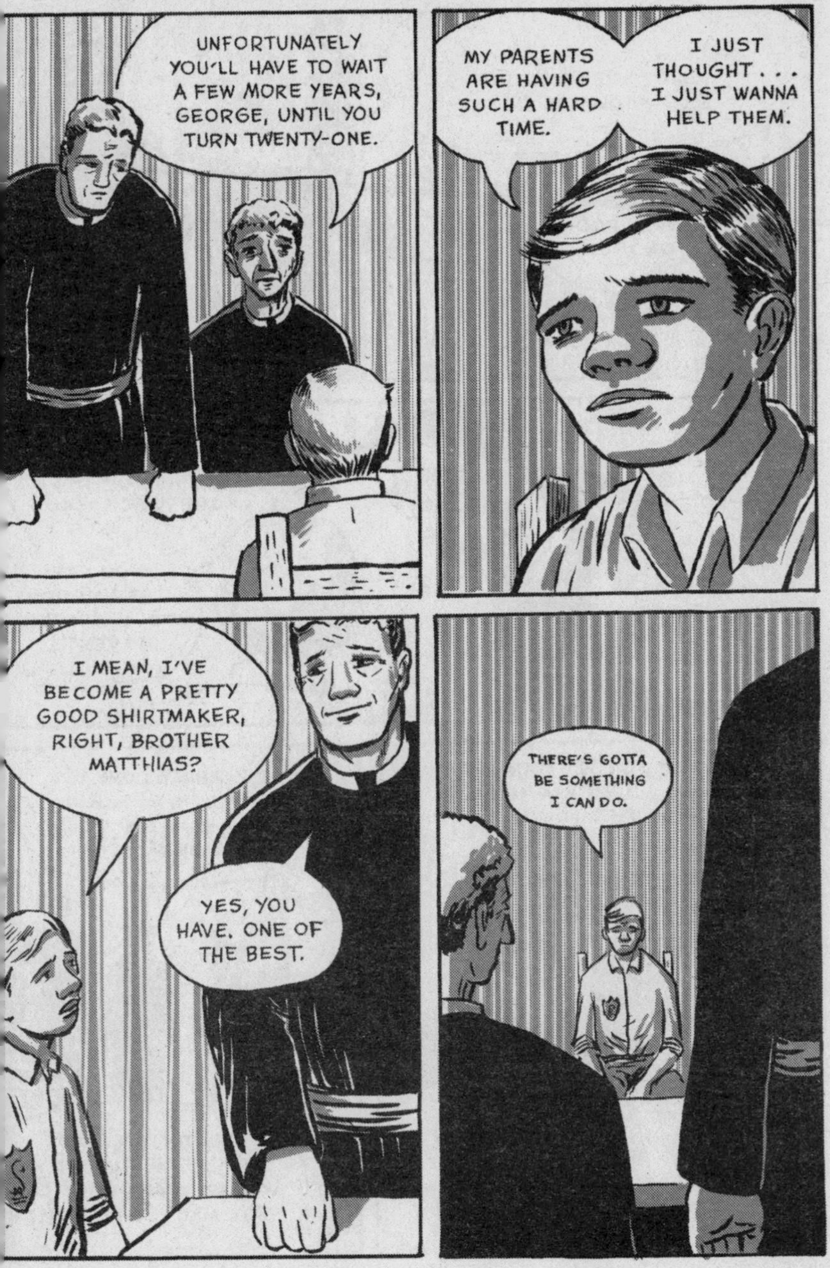
UNFORTUNATELY YOU'LL HAVE TO WAIT A FEW MORE YEARS, GEORGE, UNTIL YOU TURN TWENTY-ONE.
MY PARENTS ARE HAVING SUCH A HARD TIME.
I JUST THOUGHT . . . I JUST WANNA HELP THEM.
I MEAN, I'VE BECOME A PRETTY GOOD SHIRTMAKER, RIGHT, BROTHER MATTHIAS?
YES, YOU HAVE. ONE OF THE BEST.
THERE'S GOTTA BE SOMETHING I CAN DO.

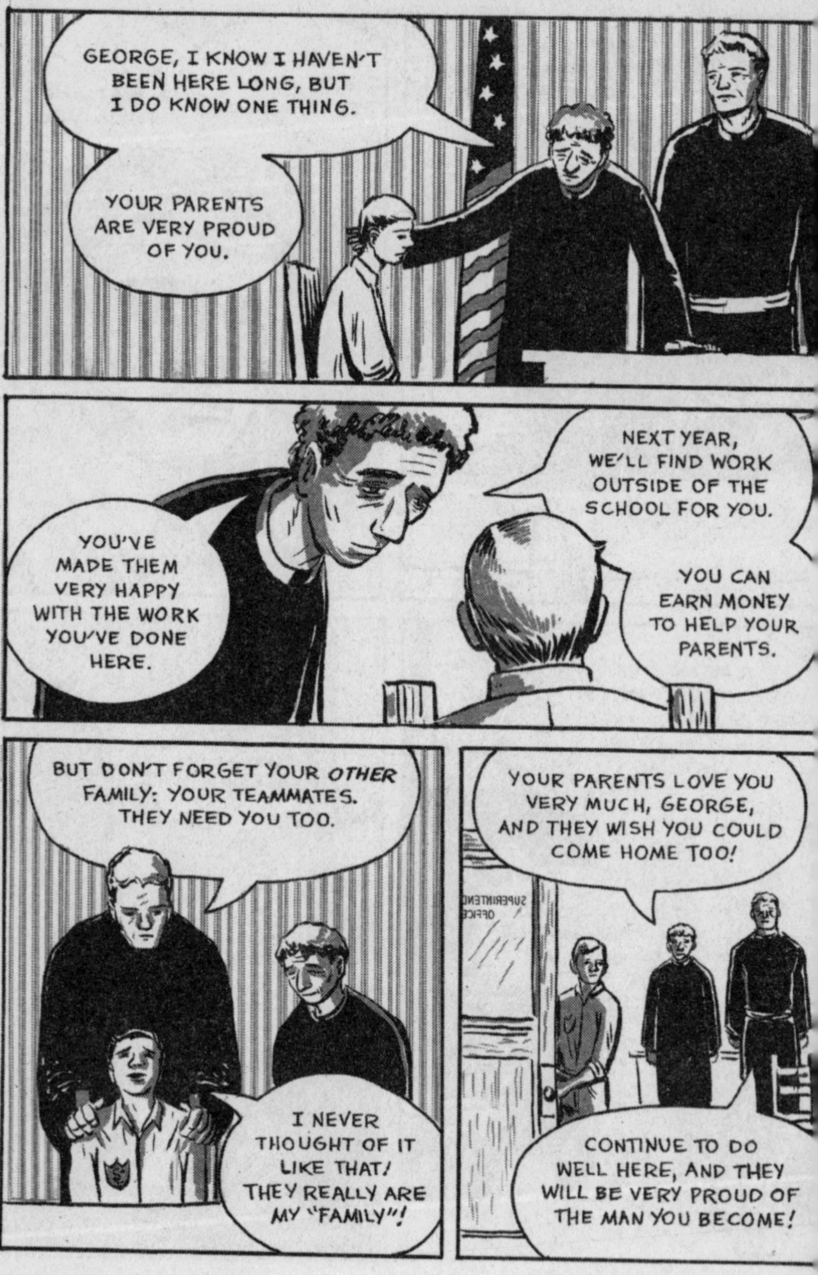
GEORGE, I KNOW I HAVEN'T BEEN HERE LONG, BUT I DO KNOW ONE THING.
YOUR PARENTS ARE VERY PROUD OF YOU.
YOU'VE MADE THEM VERY HAPPY WITH THE WORK YOU'VE DONE HERE.
NEXT YEAR, WE'LL FIND WORK OUTSIDE OF THE SCHOOL FOR YOU.
YOU CAN EARN MONEY TO HELP YOUR PARENTS.
BUT DON'T FORGET YOUR *OTHER* FAMILY: YOUR TEAMMATES. THEY NEED YOU TOO.
I NEVER THOUGHT OF IT LIKE THAT! THEY REALLY ARE MY "FAMILY"!
YOUR PARENTS LOVE YOU VERY MUCH, GEORGE, AND THEY WISH YOU COULD COME HOME TOO!
SUPERINTENDENT OFFICE
CONTINUE TO DO WELL HERE, AND THEY WILL BE VERY PROUD OF THE MAN YOU BECOME!

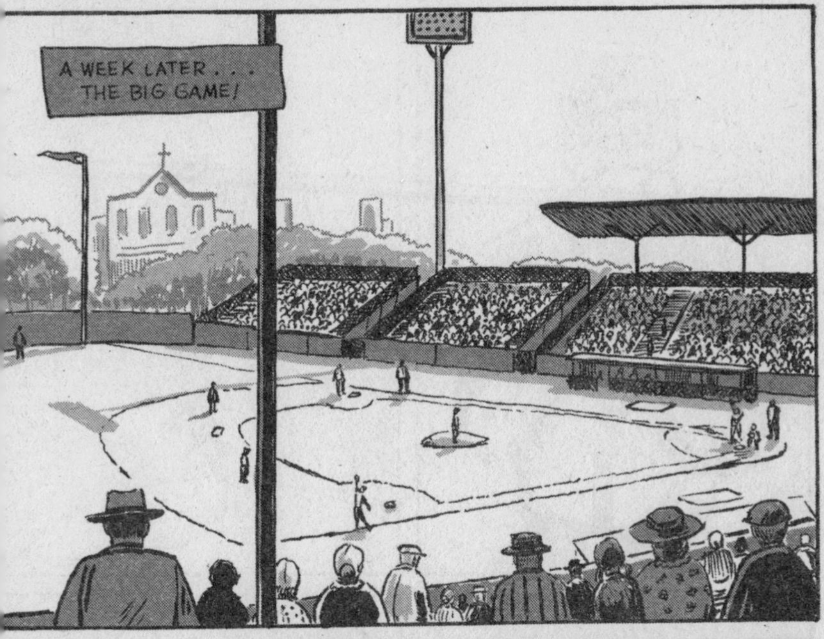
A WEEK LATER . . .
THE BIG GAME!

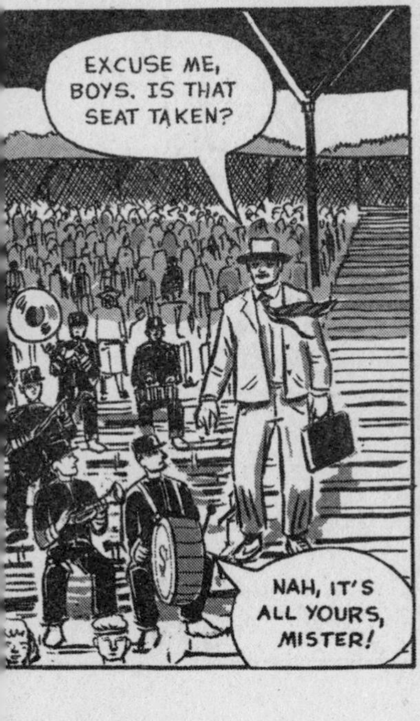
EXCUSE ME, BOYS. IS THAT SEAT TAKEN?
NAH, IT'S ALL YOURS, MISTER!

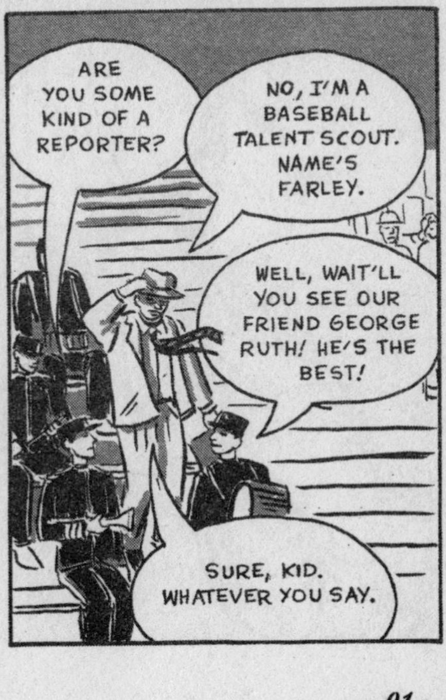
ARE YOU SOME KIND OF A REPORTER?
NO, I'M A BASEBALL TALENT SCOUT. NAME'S FARLEY.
WELL, WAIT'LL YOU SEE OUR FRIEND GEORGE RUTH! HE'S THE BEST!
SURE, KID. WHATEVER YOU SAY.

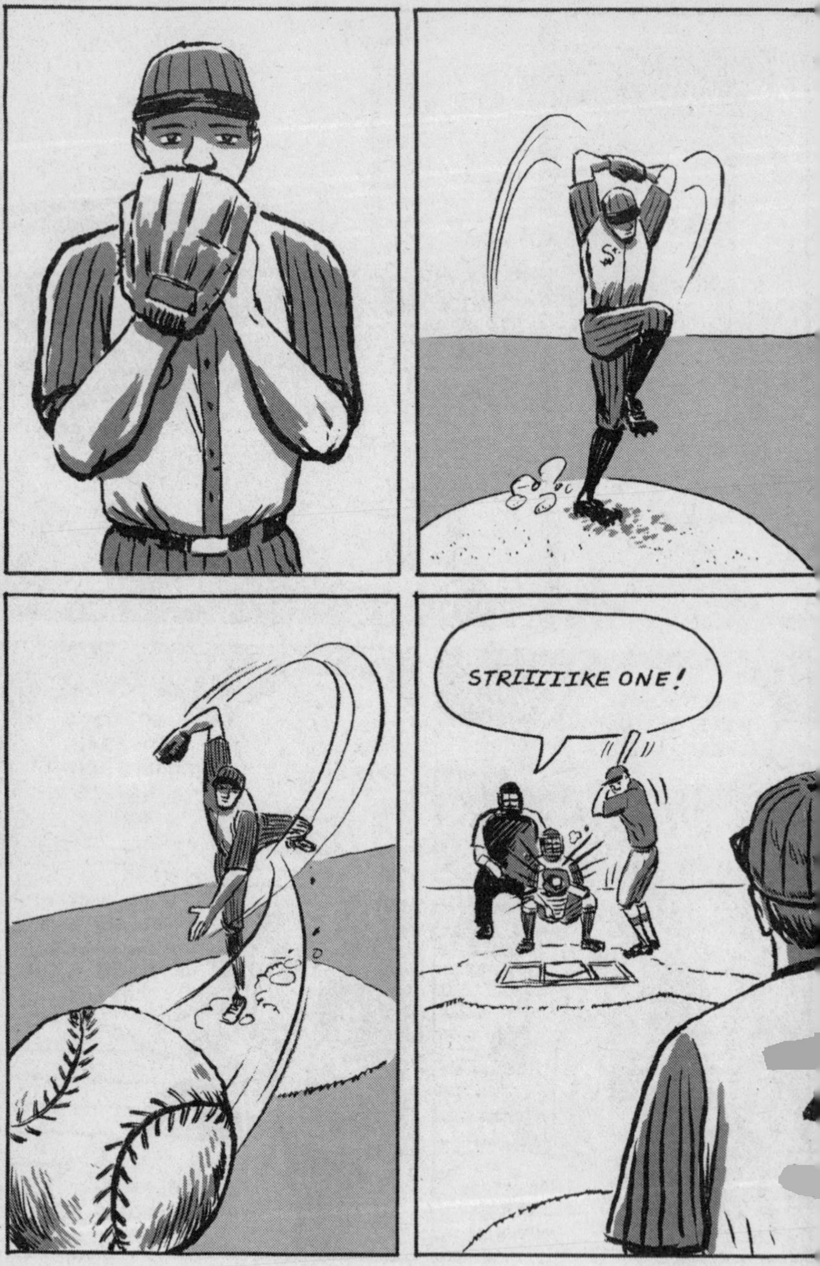
STRIIIIIKE ONE!

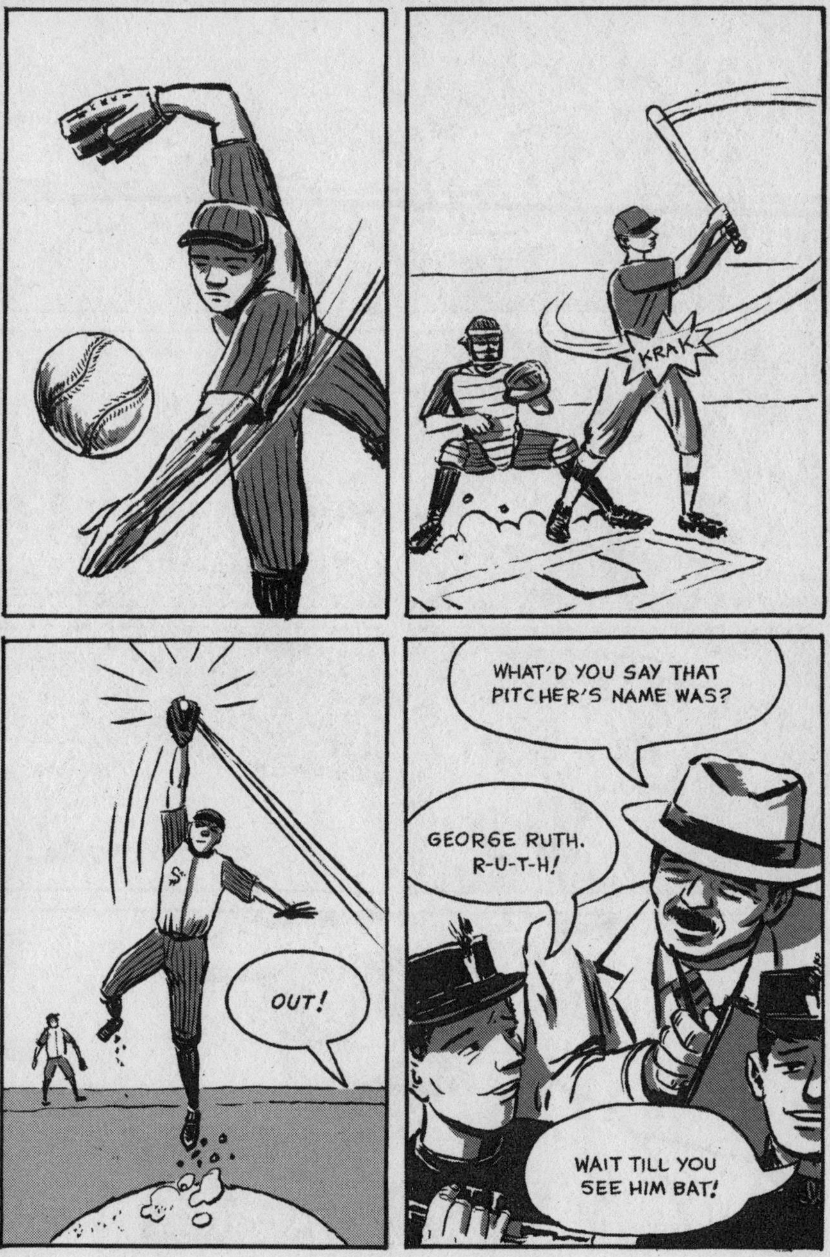
KRAK
OUT!
WHAT'D YOU SAY THAT PITCHER'S NAME WAS?
GEORGE RUTH. R-U-T-H!
WAIT TILL YOU SEE HIM BAT!

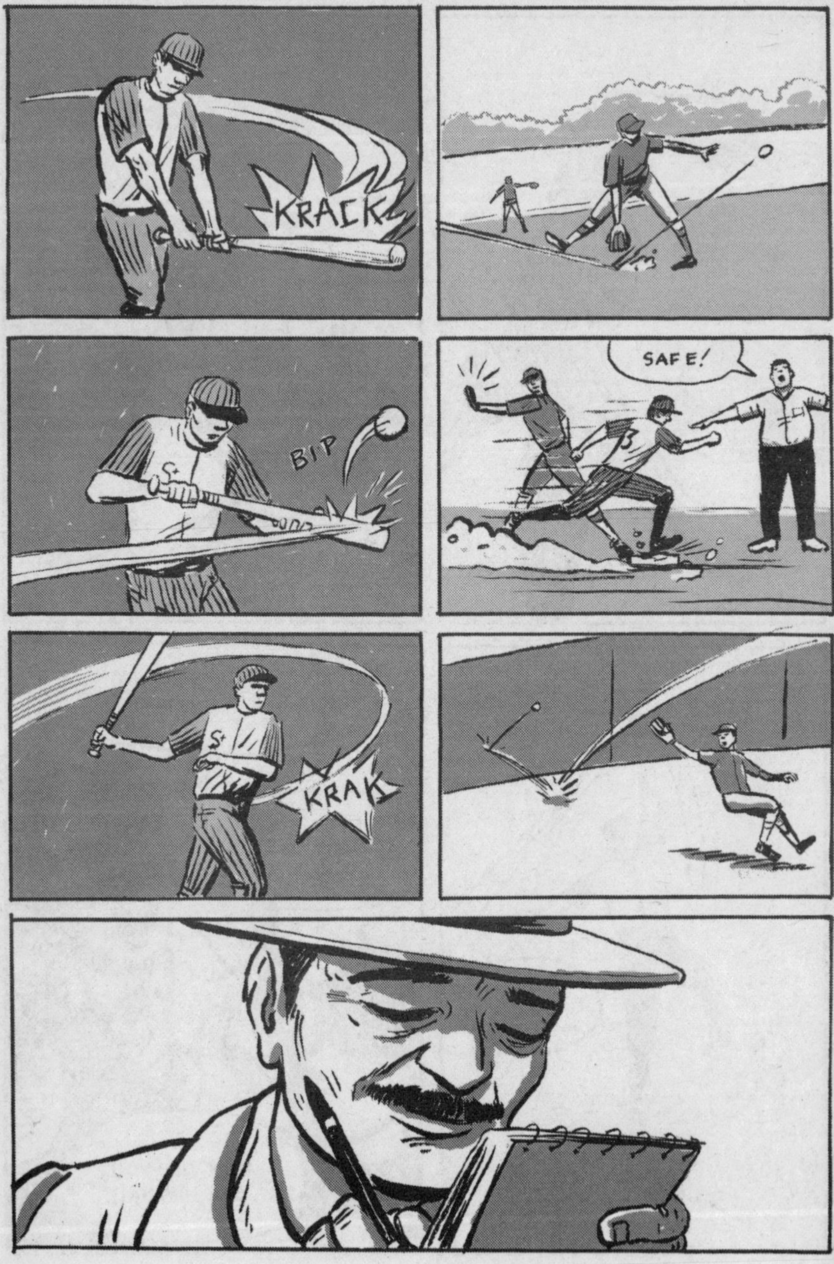
KRACK
BIP
SAFE!
KRAK

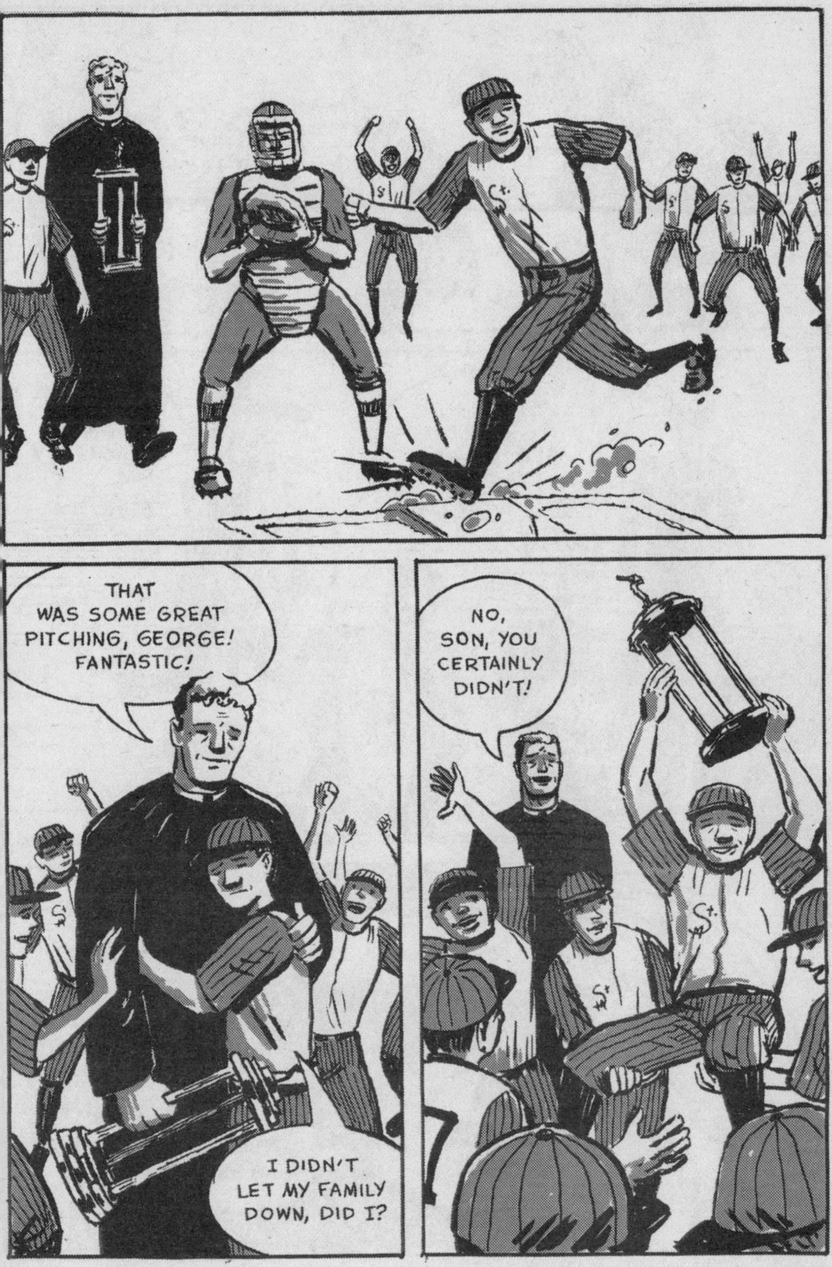
THAT WAS SOME GREAT PITCHING, GEORGE! FANTASTIC!
I DIDN'T LET MY FAMILY DOWN, DID I?
NO, SON, YOU CERTAINLY DIDN'T!

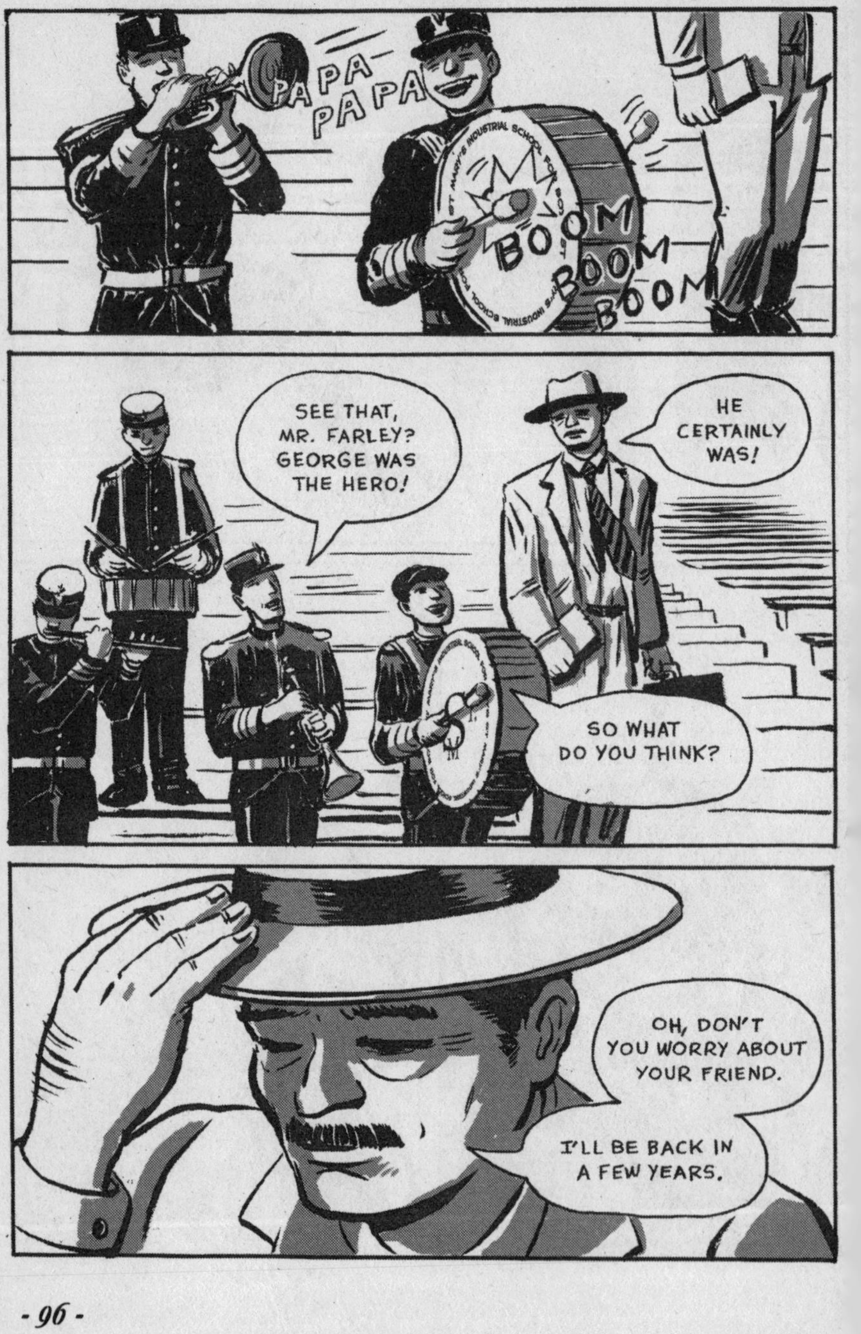

PA PA
PA PA
BOOM
BOOM
BOOM
SEE THAT, MR. FARLEY? GEORGE WAS THE HERO!
HE CERTAINLY WAS!
SO WHAT DO YOU THINK?
OH, DON'T YOU WORRY ABOUT YOUR FRIEND.
I'LL BE BACK IN A FEW YEARS.

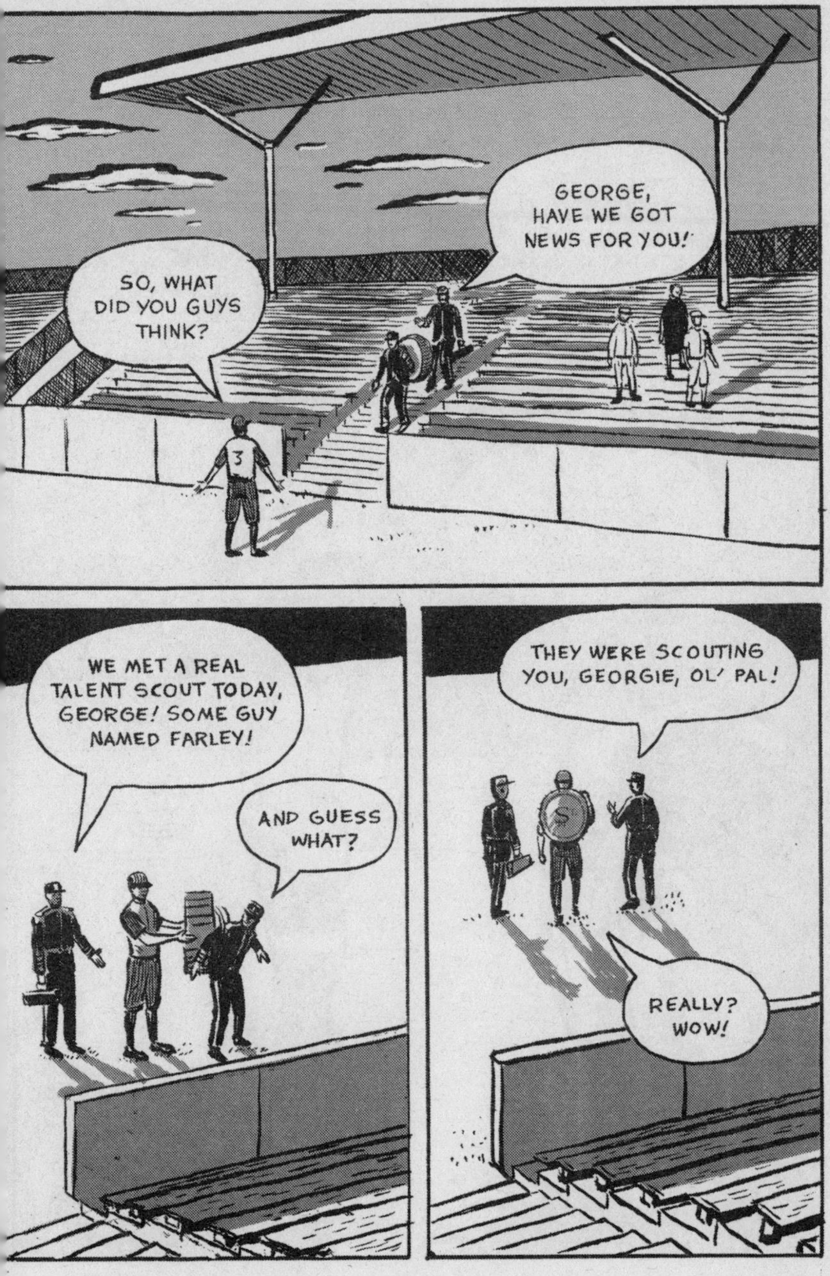
SO, WHAT DID YOU GUYS THINK?
GEORGE, HAVE WE GOT NEWS FOR YOU!
WE MET A REAL TALENT SCOUT TODAY, GEORGE! SOME GUY NAMED FARLEY!
AND GUESS WHAT?
THEY WERE SCOUTING YOU, GEORGIE, OL' PAL!
REALLY? WOW!

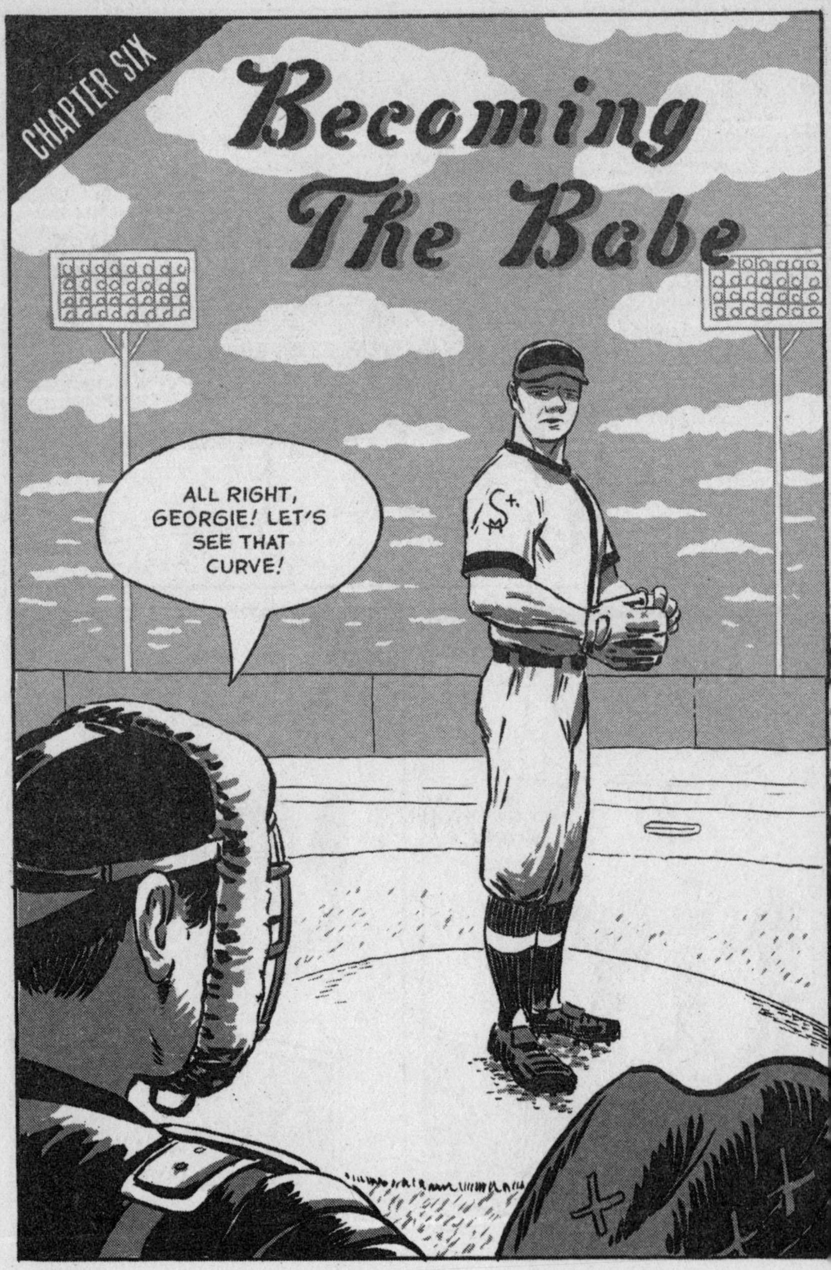
CHAPTER SIX
Becoming The Babe
ALL RIGHT, GEORGIE! LET'S SEE THAT CURVE!

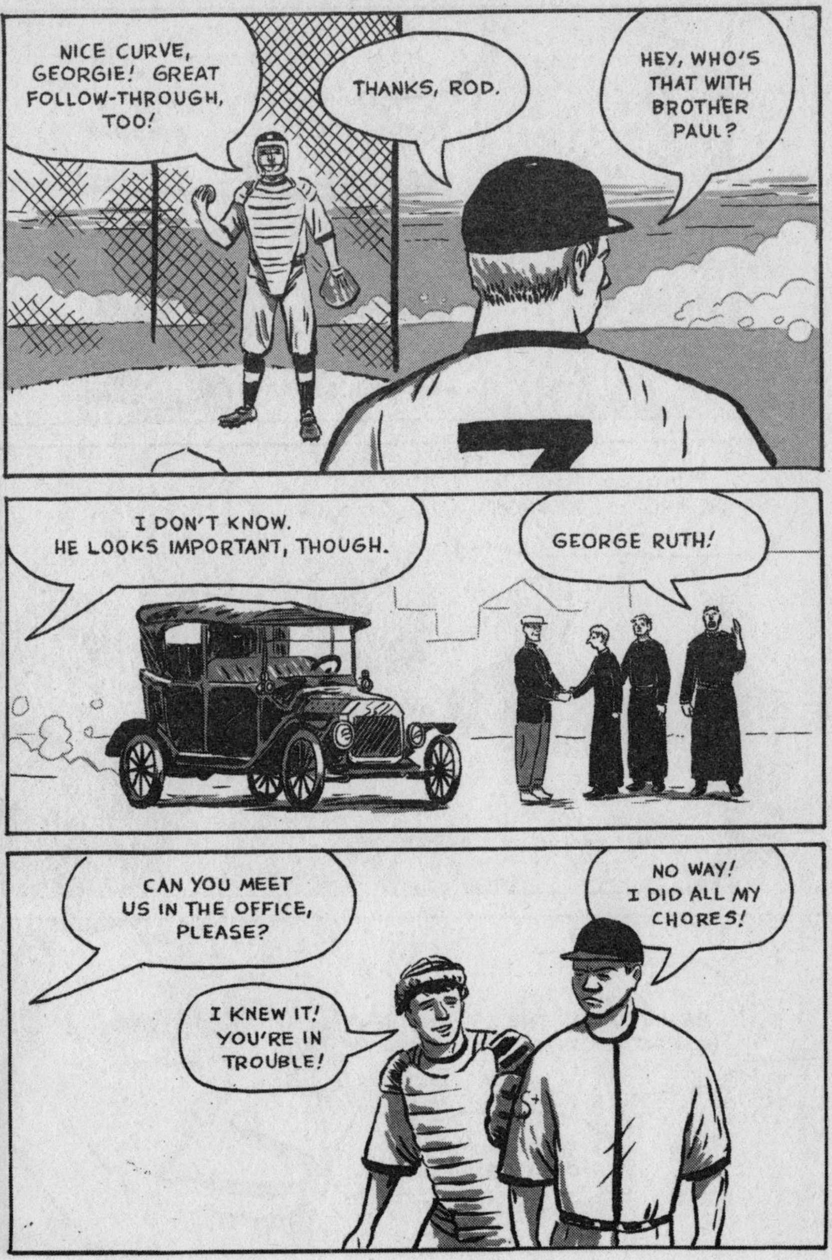
NICE CURVE, GEORGIE! GREAT FOLLOW-THROUGH, TOO!
THANKS, ROD.
HEY, WHO'S THAT WITH BROTHER PAUL?
I DON'T KNOW. HE LOOKS IMPORTANT, THOUGH.
GEORGE RUTH!
CAN YOU MEET US IN THE OFFICE, PLEASE?
NO WAY! I DID ALL MY CHORES!
I KNEW IT! YOU'RE IN TROUBLE!

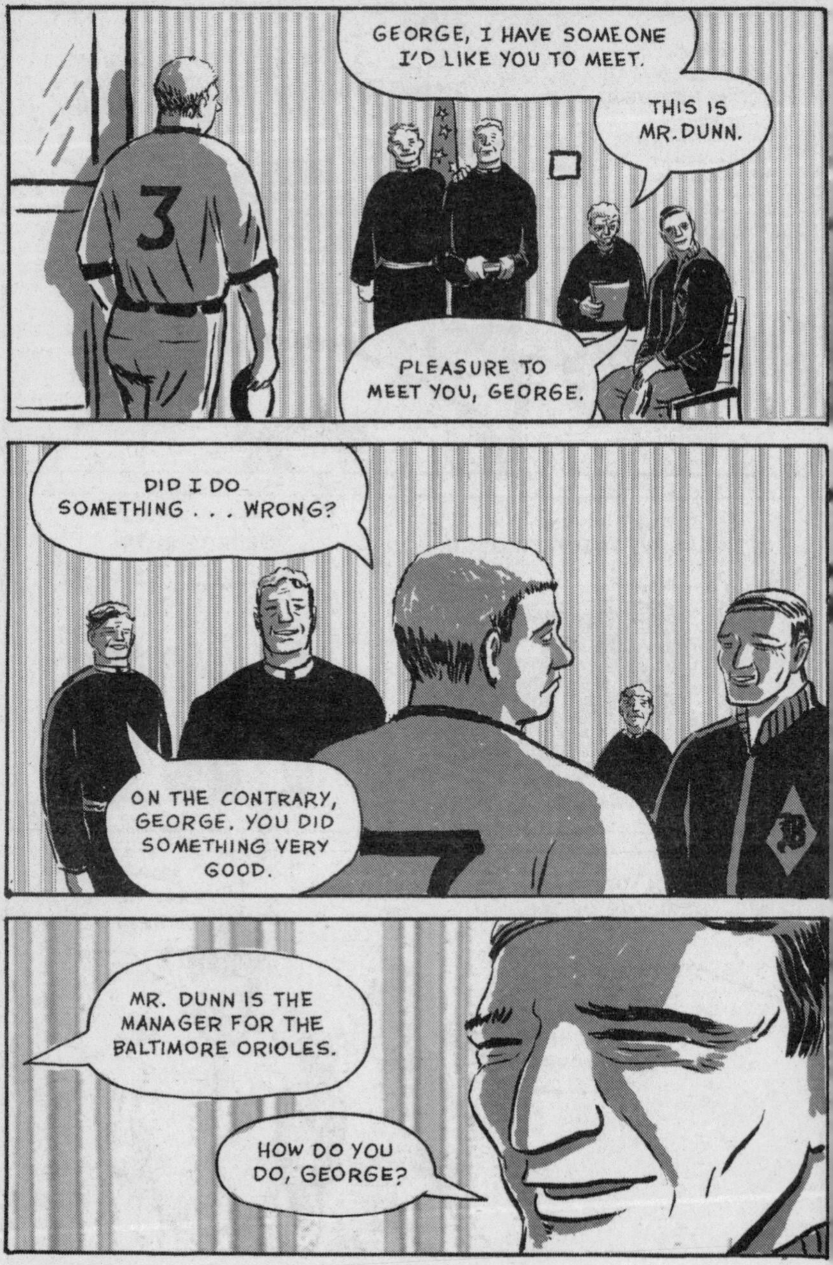
GEORGE, I HAVE SOMEONE I'D LIKE YOU TO MEET.
THIS IS MR. DUNN.
PLEASURE TO MEET YOU, GEORGE.
DID I DO SOMETHING . . . WRONG?
ON THE CONTRARY, GEORGE. YOU DID SOMETHING VERY GOOD.
MR. DUNN IS THE MANAGER FOR THE BALTIMORE ORIOLES.
HOW DO YOU DO, GEORGE?

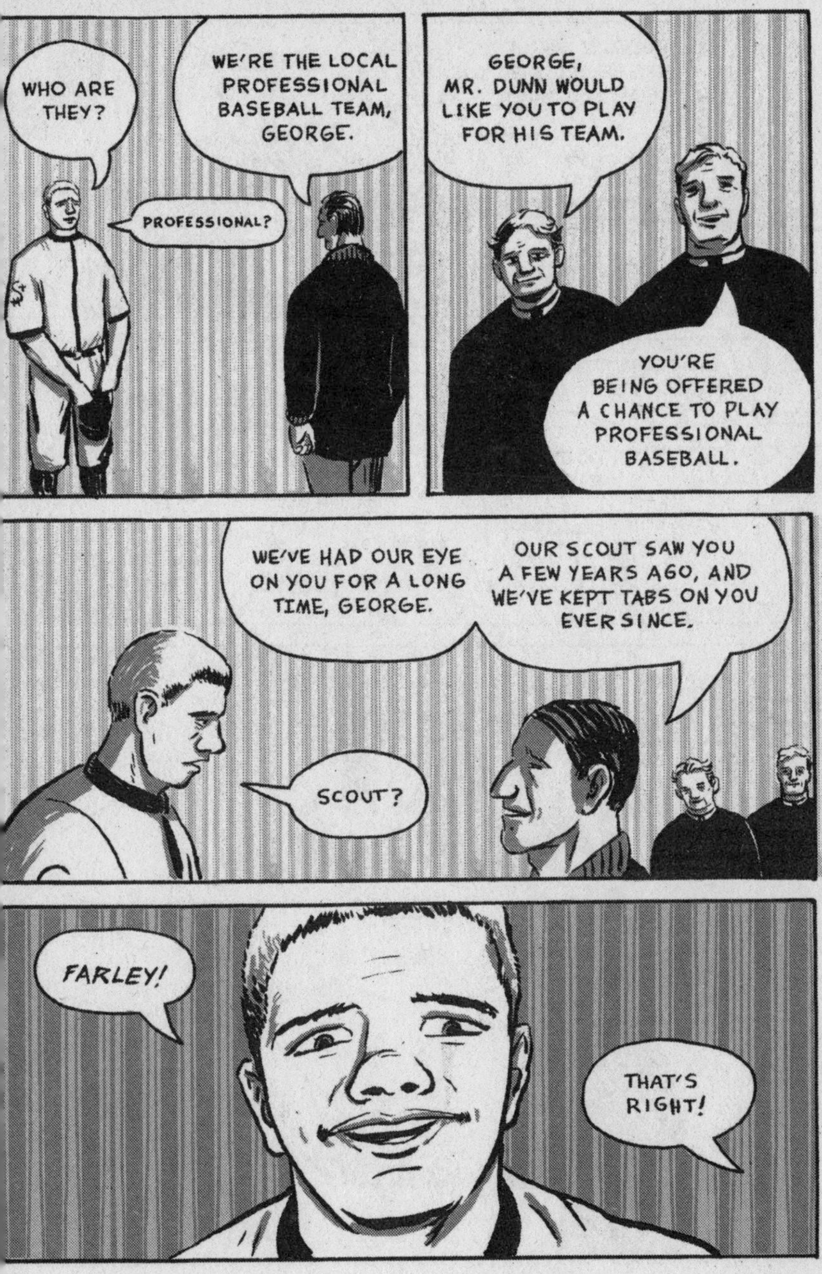
WHO ARE THEY?
WE'RE THE LOCAL PROFESSIONAL BASEBALL TEAM, GEORGE.
PROFESSIONAL?
GEORGE, MR. DUNN WOULD LIKE YOU TO PLAY FOR HIS TEAM.
YOU'RE BEING OFFERED A CHANCE TO PLAY PROFESSIONAL BASEBALL.
WE'VE HAD OUR EYE ON YOU FOR A LONG TIME, GEORGE.
OUR SCOUT SAW YOU A FEW YEARS AGO, AND WE'VE KEPT TABS ON YOU EVER SINCE.
SCOUT?
FARLEY!
THAT'S RIGHT!

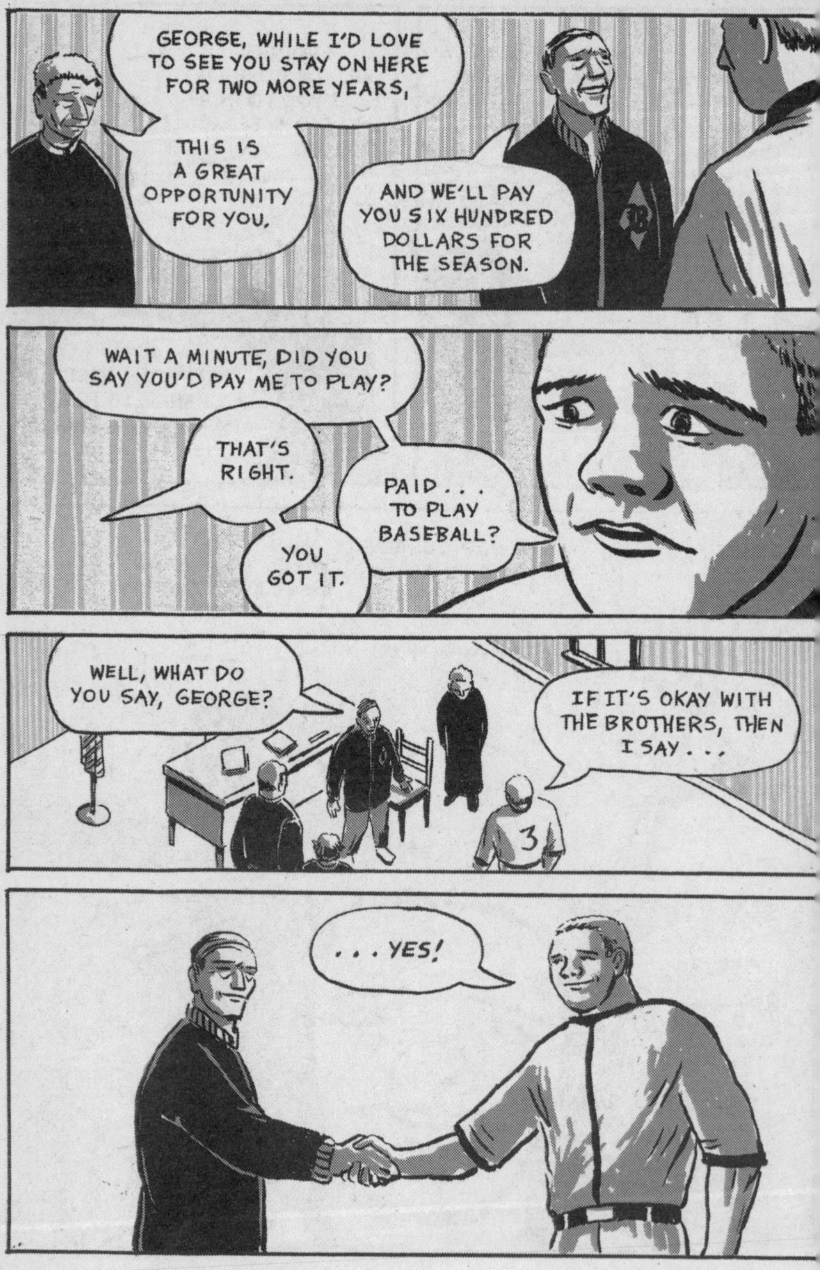
GEORGE, WHILE I'D LOVE TO SEE YOU STAY ON HERE FOR TWO MORE YEARS,
THIS IS A GREAT OPPORTUNITY FOR YOU,
AND WE'LL PAY YOU SIX HUNDRED DOLLARS FOR THE SEASON.
WAIT A MINUTE, DID YOU SAY YOU'D PAY ME TO PLAY?
THAT'S RIGHT.
PAID . . . TO PLAY BASEBALL?
YOU GOT IT.
WELL, WHAT DO YOU SAY, GEORGE?
IF IT'S OKAY WITH THE BROTHERS, THEN I SAY . . .
. . . YES!

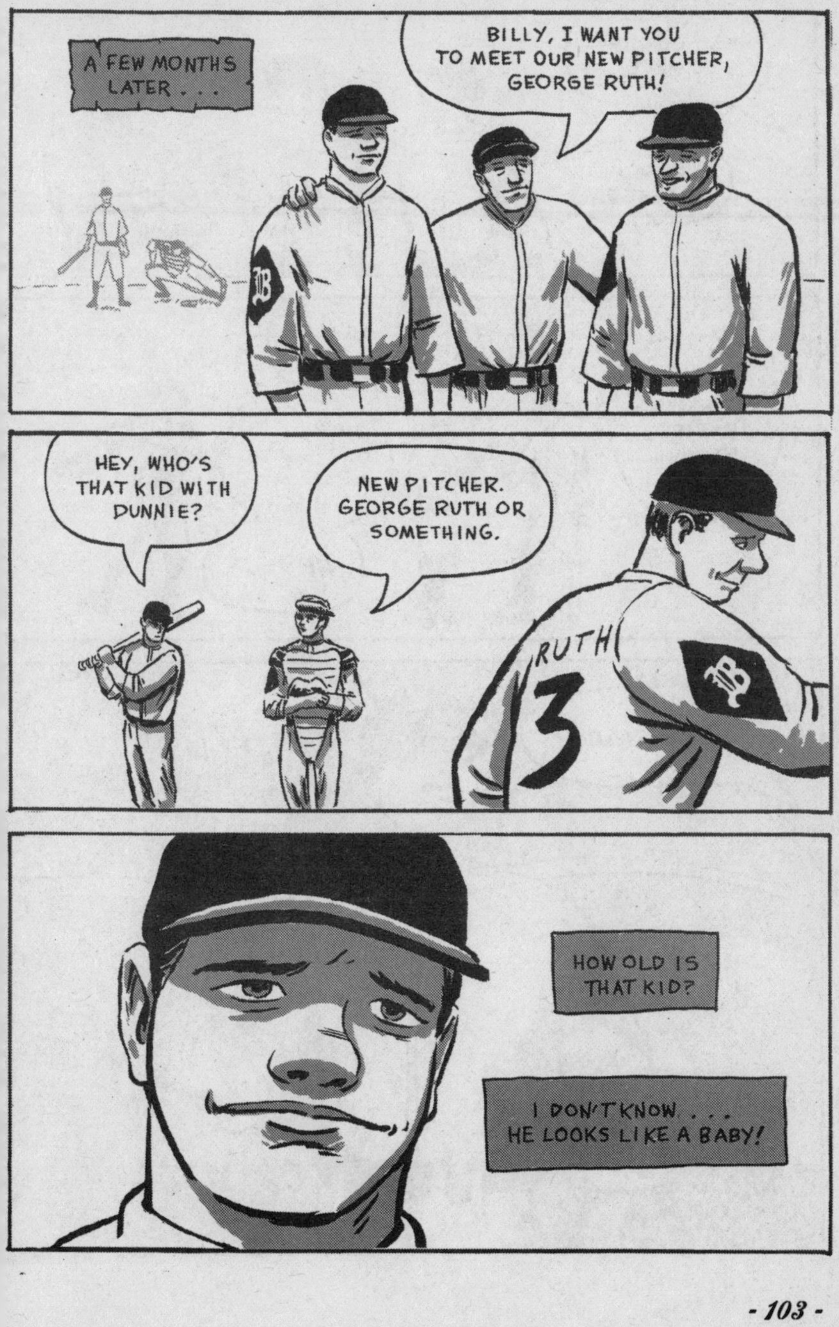
A FEW MONTHS LATER . . .
BILLY, I WANT YOU TO MEET OUR NEW PITCHER, GEORGE RUTH!
HEY, WHO'S THAT KID WITH DUNNIE?
NEW PITCHER. GEORGE RUTH OR SOMETHING.
RUTH 3
HOW OLD IS THAT KID?
I DON'T KNOW . . . HE LOOKS LIKE A BABY!

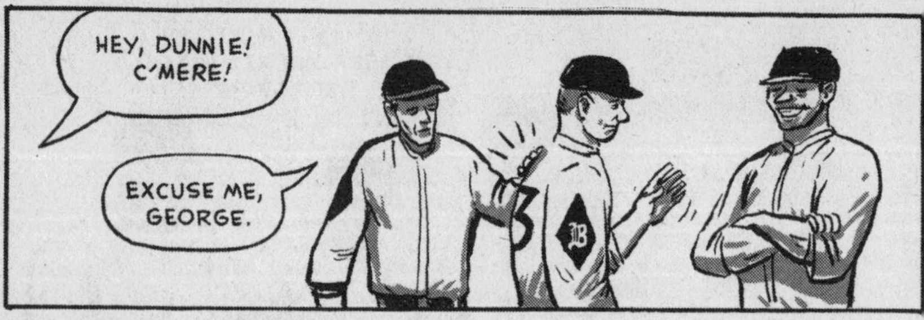
HEY, DUNNIE! C'MERE!
EXCUSE ME, GEORGE.
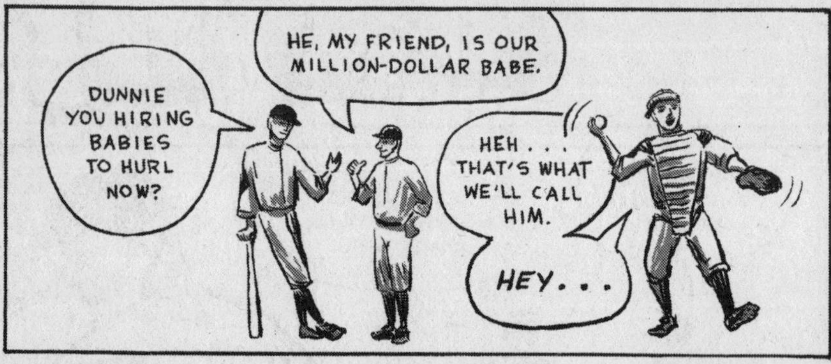
DUNNIE YOU HIRING BABIES TO HURL NOW?
HE, MY FRIEND, IS OUR MILLION-DOLLAR BABE.
HEH . . . THAT'S WHAT WE'LL CALL HIM.
HEY. . .
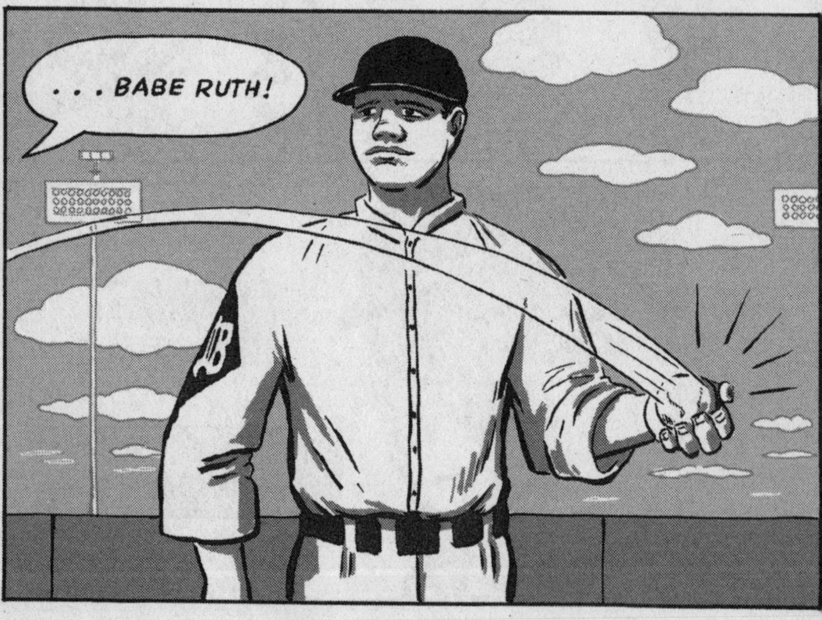
. . . BABE RUTH!

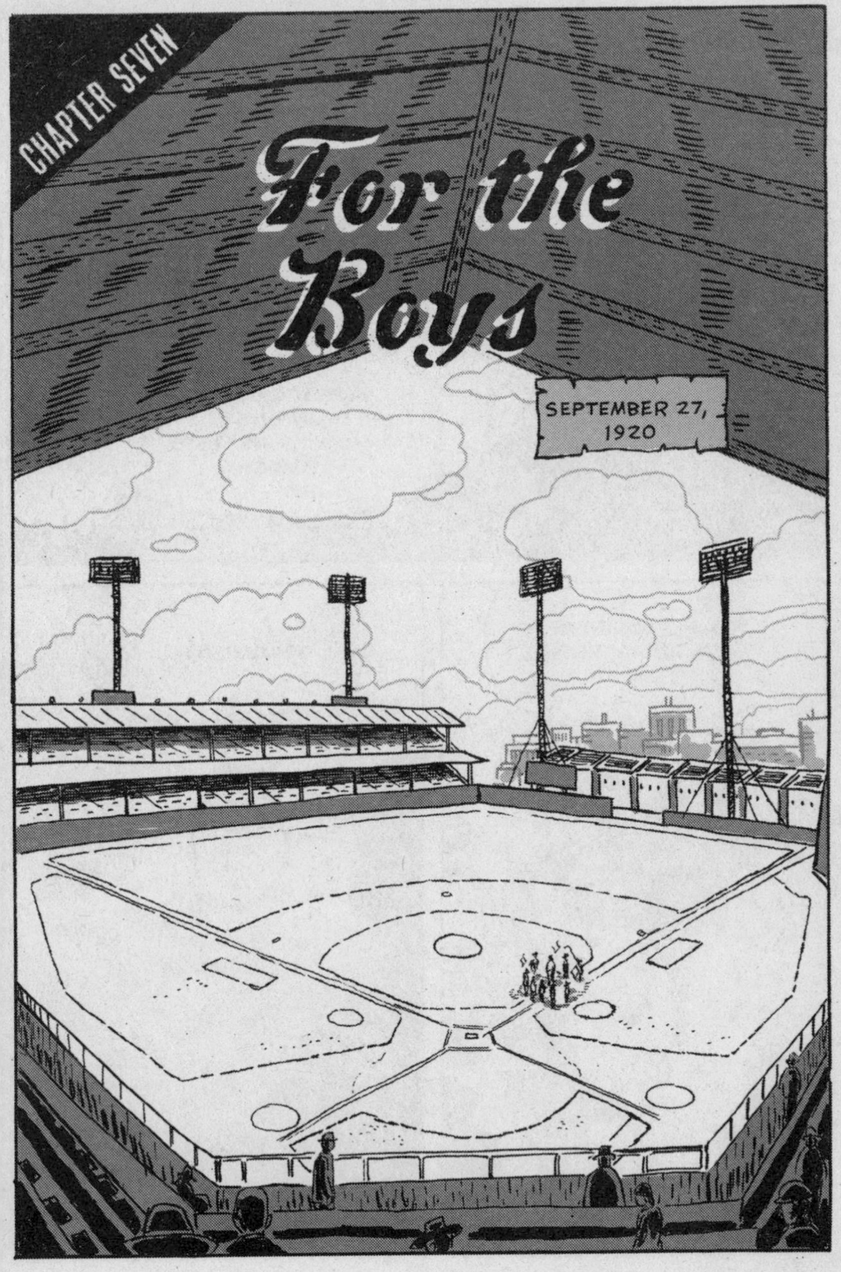
CHAPTER SEVEN
For the Boys
SEPTEMBER 27, 1920

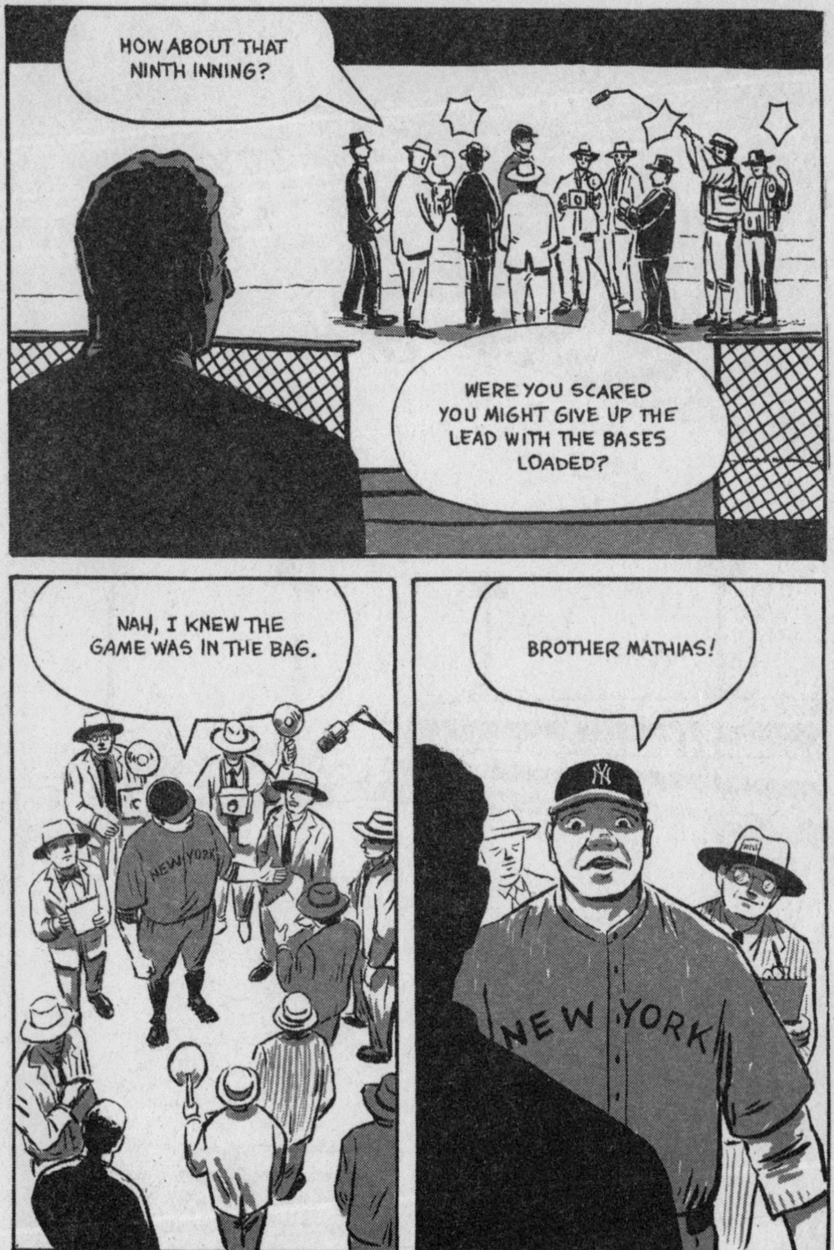
HOW ABOUT THAT NINTH INNING?
WERE YOU SCARED YOU MIGHT GIVE UP THE LEAD WITH THE BASES LOADED?
NAH, I KNEW THE GAME WAS IN THE BAG.
BROTHER MATHIAS!

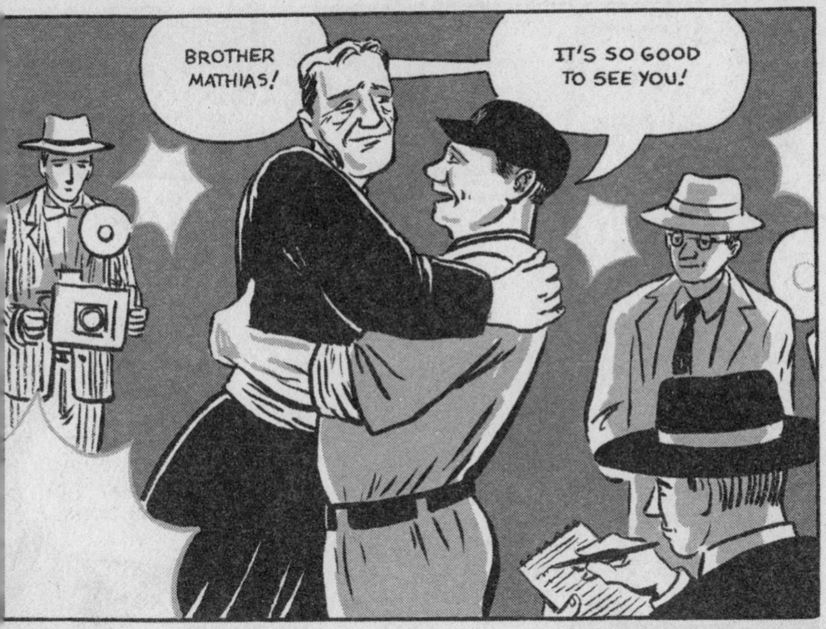
BROTHER MATHIAS!
IT'S SO GOOD TO SEE YOU!

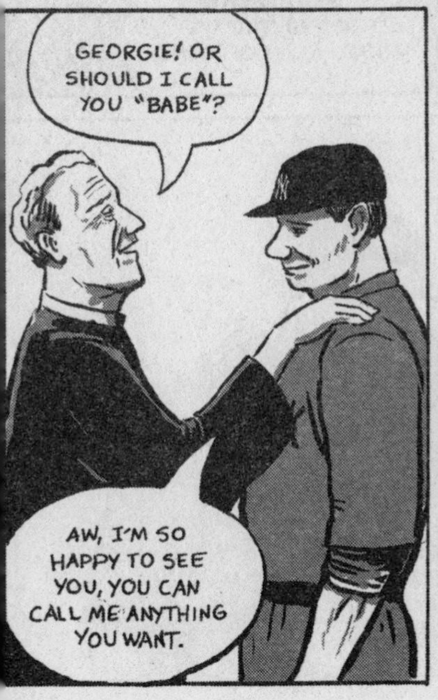
GEORGIE! OR SHOULD I CALL YOU "BABE"?
AW, I'M SO HAPPY TO SEE YOU, YOU CAN CALL ME ANYTHING YOU WANT.

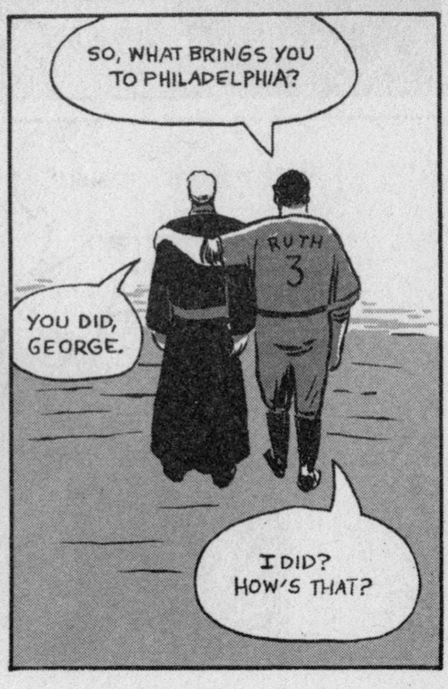
SO, WHAT BRINGS YOU TO PHILADELPHIA?
RUTH
3
YOU DID, GEORGE.
I DID? HOW'S THAT?

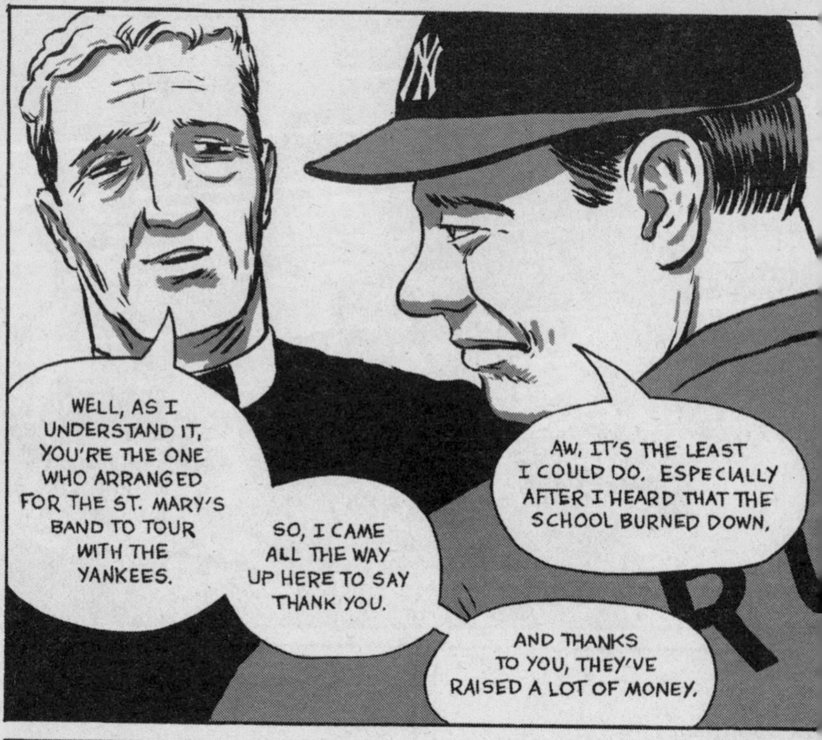
WELL, AS I UNDERSTAND IT, YOU'RE THE ONE WHO ARRANGED FOR THE ST. MARY'S BAND TO TOUR WITH THE YANKEES.
SO, I CAME ALL THE WAY UP HERE TO SAY THANK YOU.
AW, IT'S THE LEAST I COULD DO. ESPECIALLY AFTER I HEARD THAT THE SCHOOL BURNED DOWN.
AND THANKS TO YOU, THEY'VE RAISED A LOT OF MONEY.

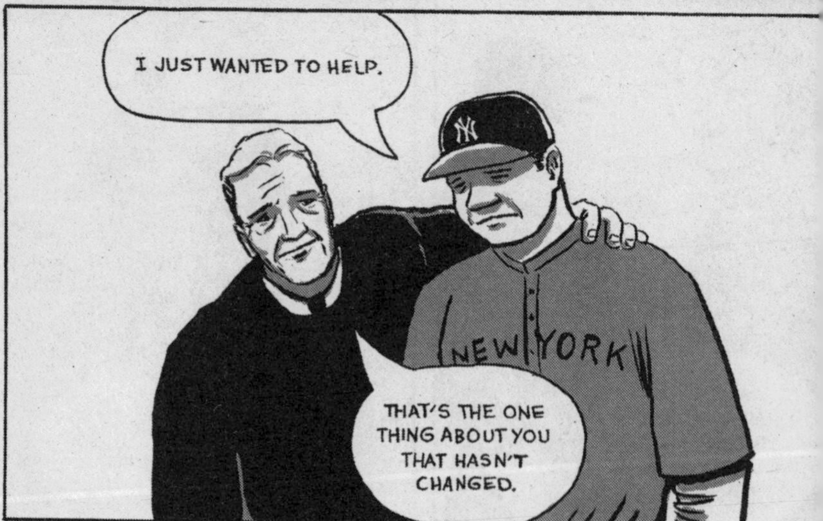
I JUST WANTED TO HELP.
NEW YORK
THAT'S THE ONE THING ABOUT YOU THAT HASN'T CHANGED.

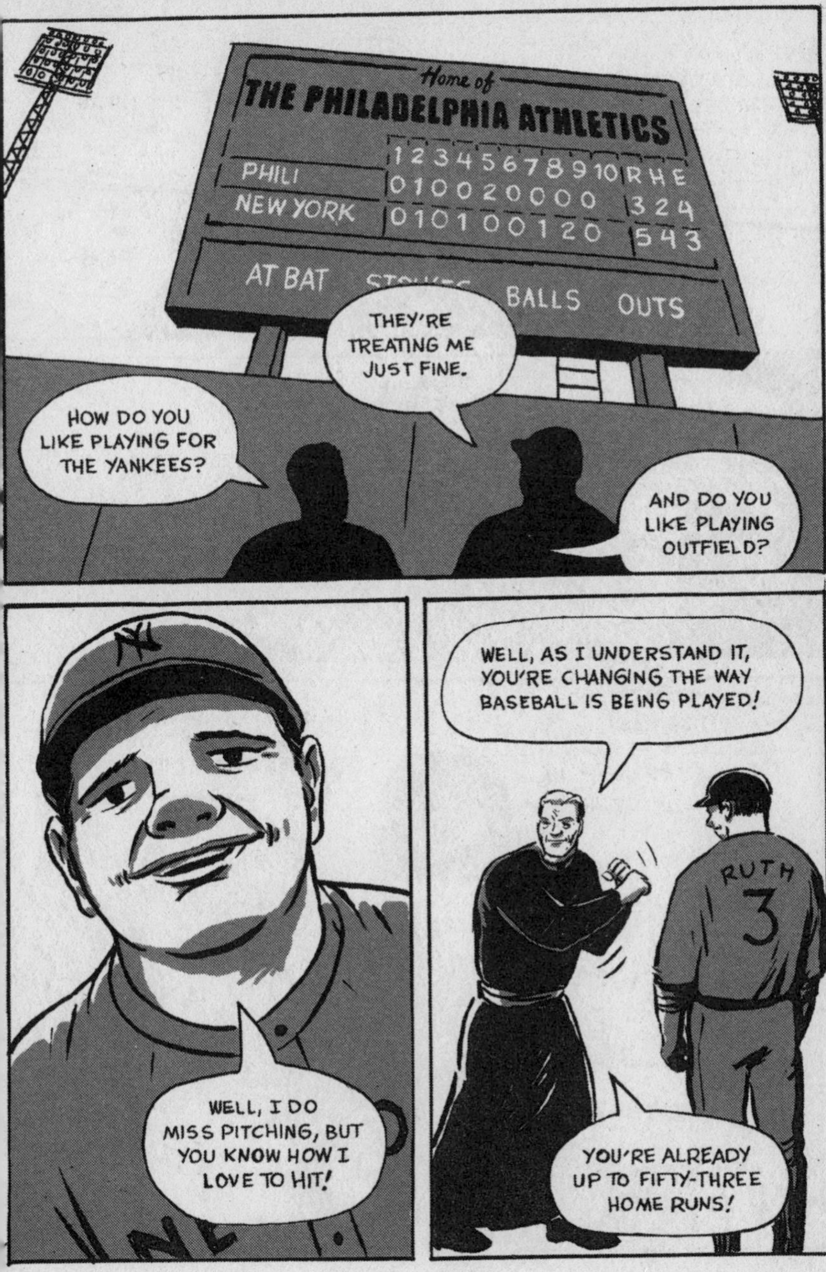
Home of
THE PHILADELPHIA ATHLETICS
1 2 3 4 5 6 7 8 9 10 R H E
PHILI 0 1 0 0 2 0 0 0 0 3 2 4
NEW YORK 0 1 0 1 0 0 1 2 0 5 4 3
AT BAT
BALLS
OUTS
HOW DO YOU LIKE PLAYING FOR THE YANKEES?
THEY'RE TREATING ME JUST FINE.
AND DO YOU LIKE PLAYING OUTFIELD?
WELL, I DO MISS PITCHING, BUT YOU KNOW HOW I LOVE TO HIT!
WELL, AS I UNDERSTAND IT, YOU'RE CHANGING THE WAY BASEBALL IS BEING PLAYED!
RUTH
3
YOU'RE ALREADY UP TO FIFTY-THREE HOME RUNS!

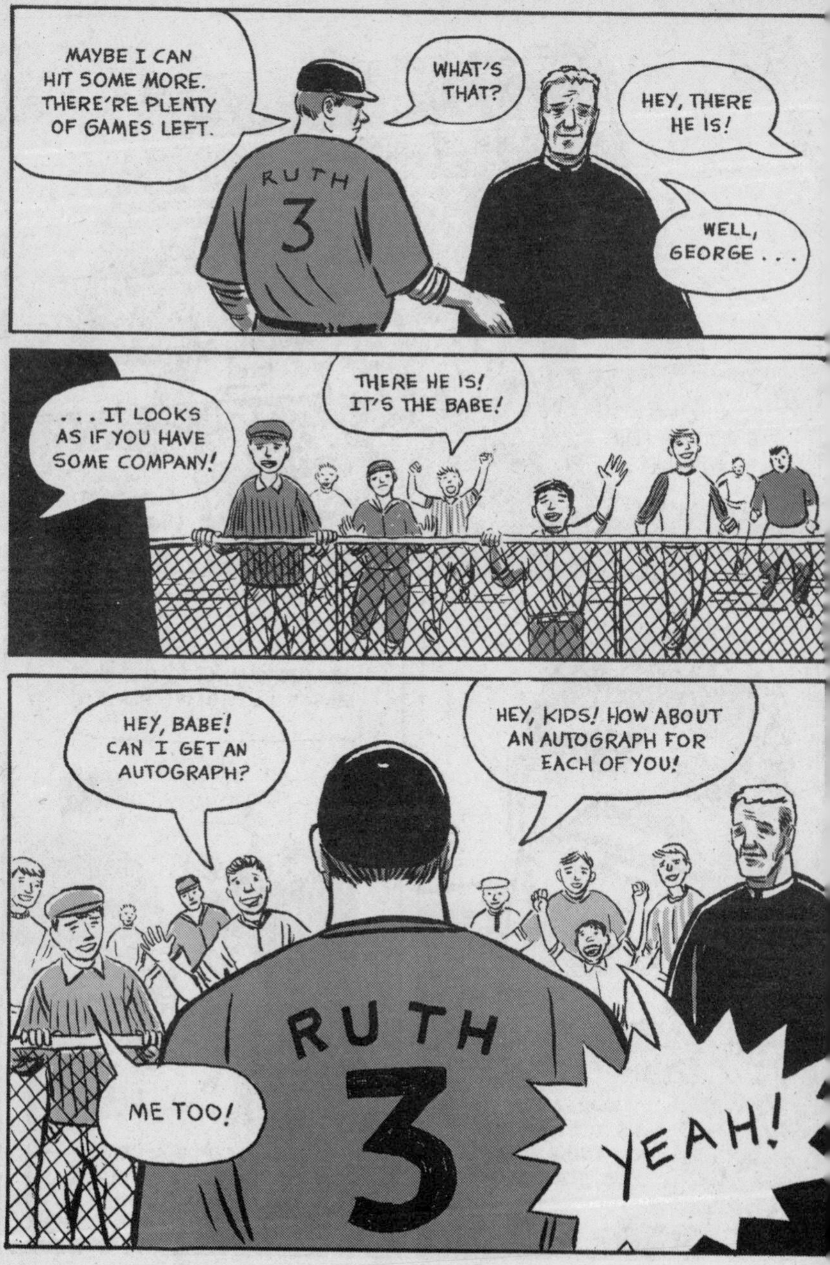
MAYBE I CAN HIT SOME MORE. THERE'RE PLENTY OF GAMES LEFT.
WHAT'S THAT?
HEY, THERE HE IS!
WELL, GEORGE . . .
RUTH 3
. . . IT LOOKS AS IF YOU HAVE SOME COMPANY!
THERE HE IS! IT'S THE BABE!
HEY, BABE! CAN I GET AN AUTOGRAPH?
HEY, KIDS! HOW ABOUT AN AUTOGRAPH FOR EACH OF YOU!
RUTH 3
ME TOO!
YEAH!

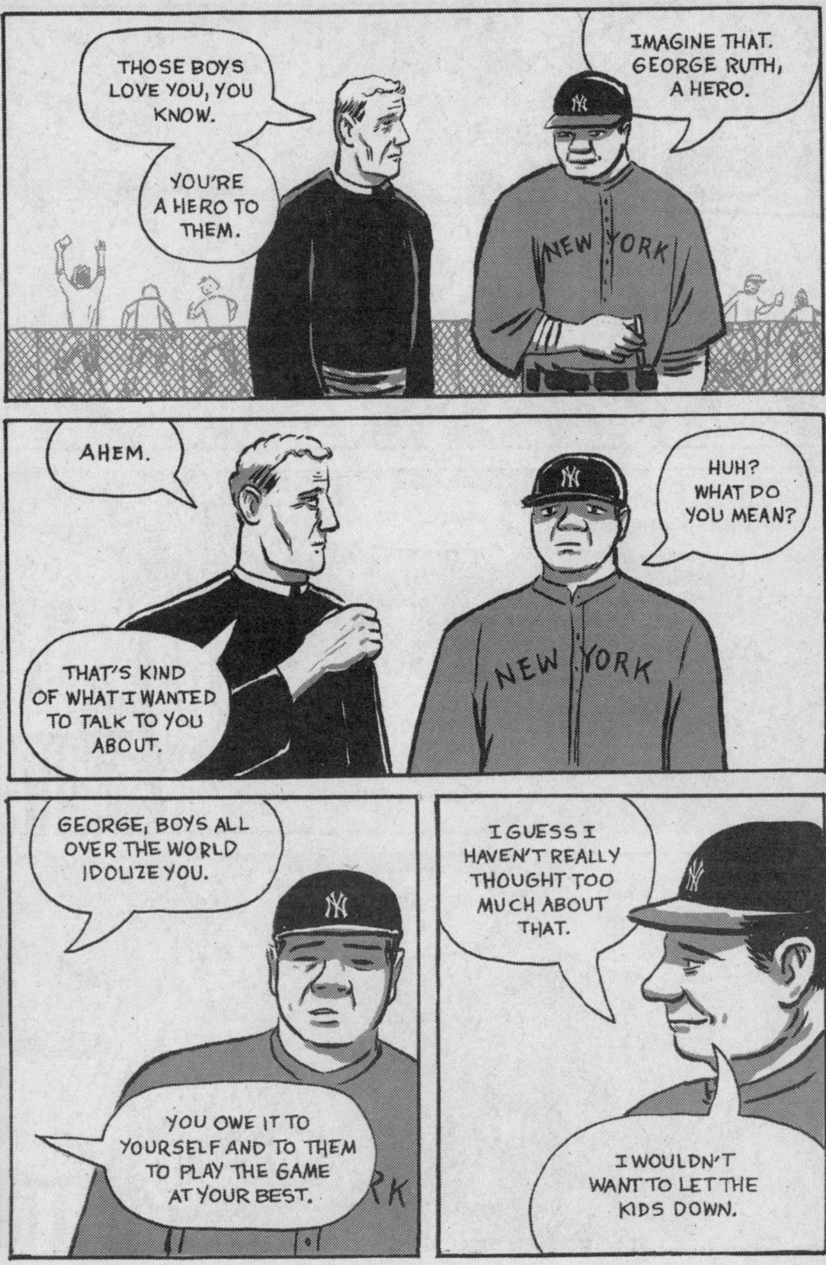
THOSE BOYS LOVE YOU, YOU KNOW.
YOU'RE A HERO TO THEM.
IMAGINE THAT. GEORGE RUTH, A HERO.
NEW YORK
AHEM.
HUH? WHAT DO YOU MEAN?
THAT'S KIND OF WHAT I WANTED TO TALK TO YOU ABOUT.
NEW YORK
GEORGE, BOYS ALL OVER THE WORLD IDOLIZE YOU.
YOU OWE IT TO YOURSELF AND TO THEM TO PLAY THE GAME AT YOUR BEST.
I GUESS I HAVEN'T REALLY THOUGHT TOO MUCH ABOUT THAT.
I WOULDN'T WANT TO LET THE KIDS DOWN.

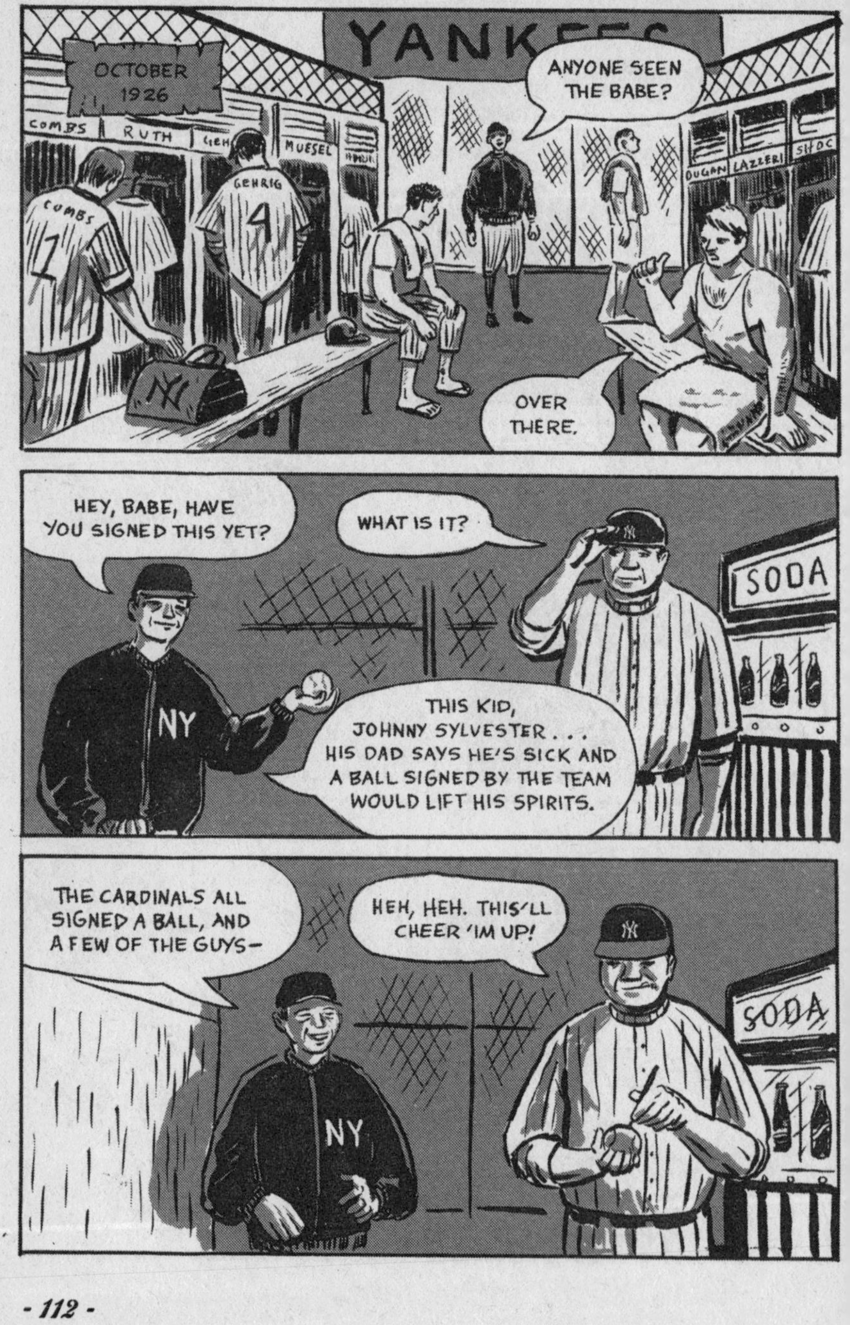
OCTOBER 1926
COMBS
RUTH
MUESEL
GEHRIG
DUGAN
LAZZERI
ANYONE SEEN THE BABE?
OVER THERE.
HEY, BABE, HAVE YOU SIGNED THIS YET?
WHAT IS IT?
SODA
THIS KID, JOHNNY SYLVESTER . . . HIS DAD SAYS HE'S SICK AND A BALL SIGNED BY THE TEAM WOULD LIFT HIS SPIRITS.
THE CARDINALS ALL SIGNED A BALL, AND A FEW OF THE GUYS—
HEH, HEH. THIS'LL CHEER 'IM UP!
SODA

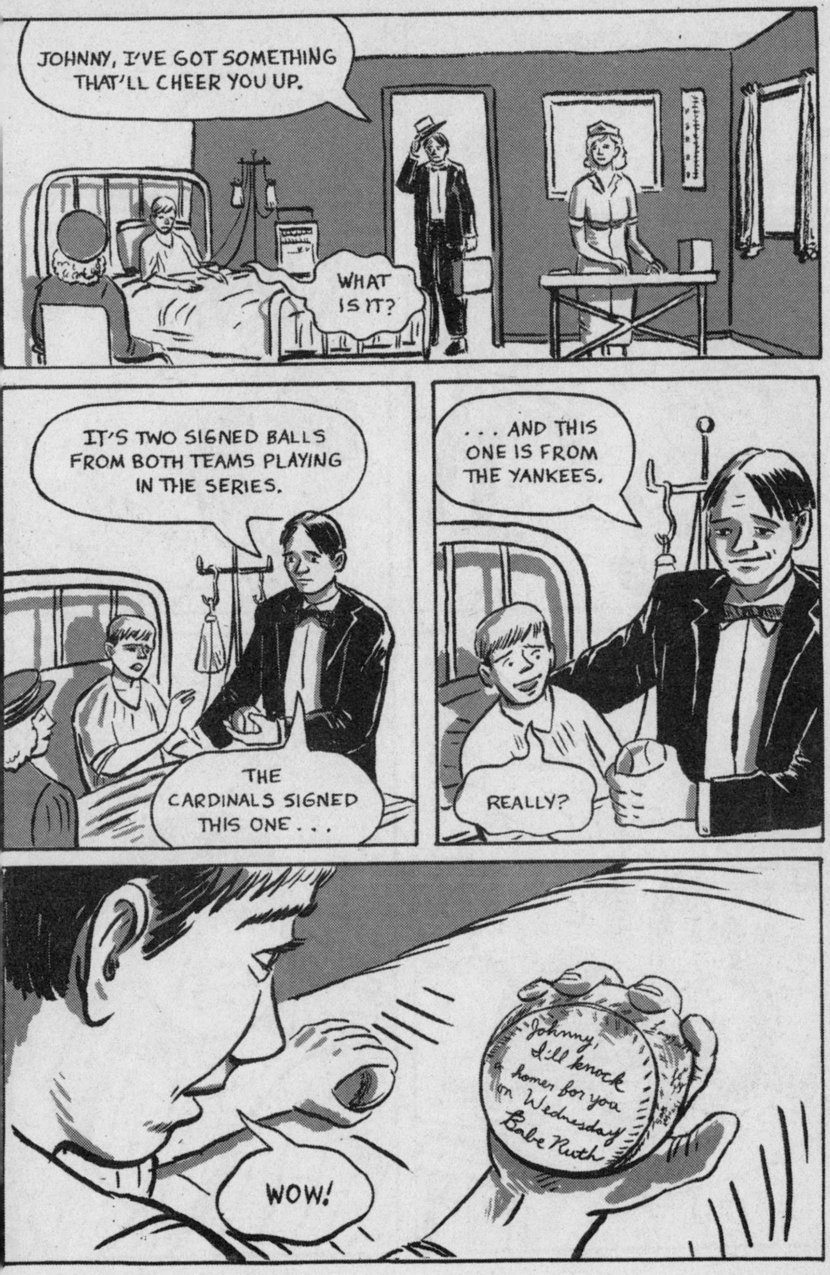
JOHNNY, I'VE GOT SOMETHING THAT'LL CHEER YOU UP.
WHAT IS IT?
IT'S TWO SIGNED BALLS FROM BOTH TEAMS PLAYING IN THE SERIES.
THE CARDINALS SIGNED THIS ONE . . .
. . . AND THIS ONE IS FROM THE YANKEES.
REALLY?
Johnny, I'll knock homer for you on Wednesday Babe Ruth
WOW!

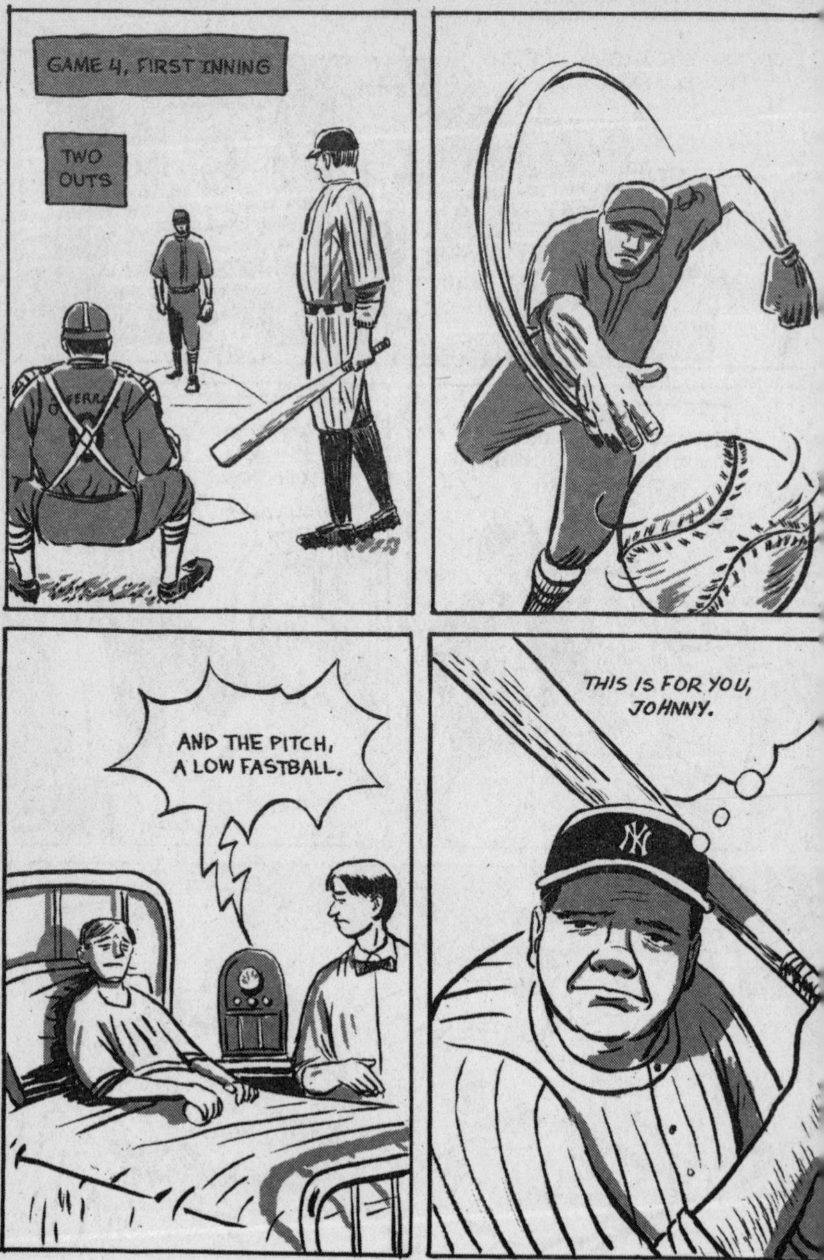
GAME 4, FIRST INNING
TWO OUTS
AND THE PITCH, A LOW FASTBALL.
THIS IS FOR YOU, JOHNNY.

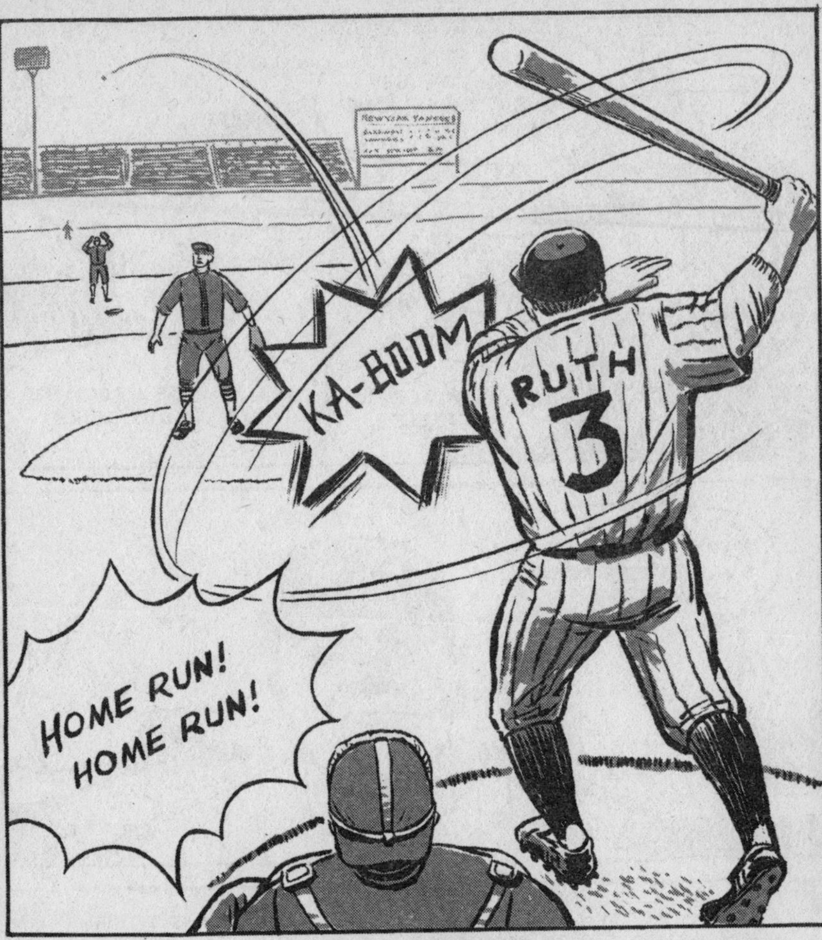
KA-BOOM
RUTH 3
HOME RUN! HOME RUN!

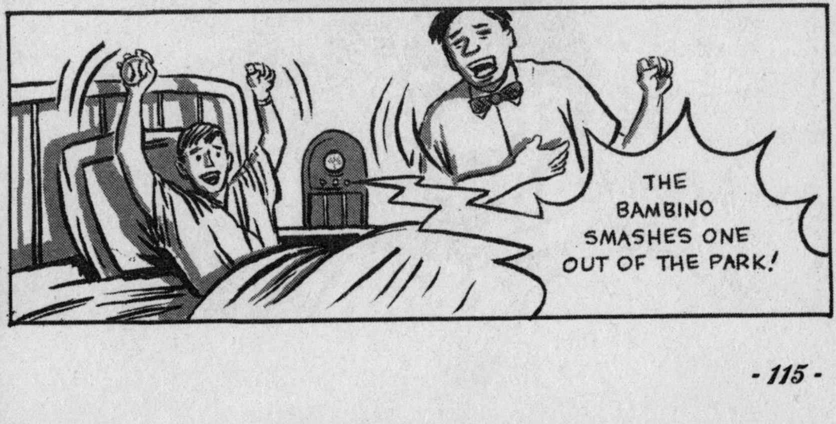
THE BAMBINO SMASHES ONE OUT OF THE PARK!

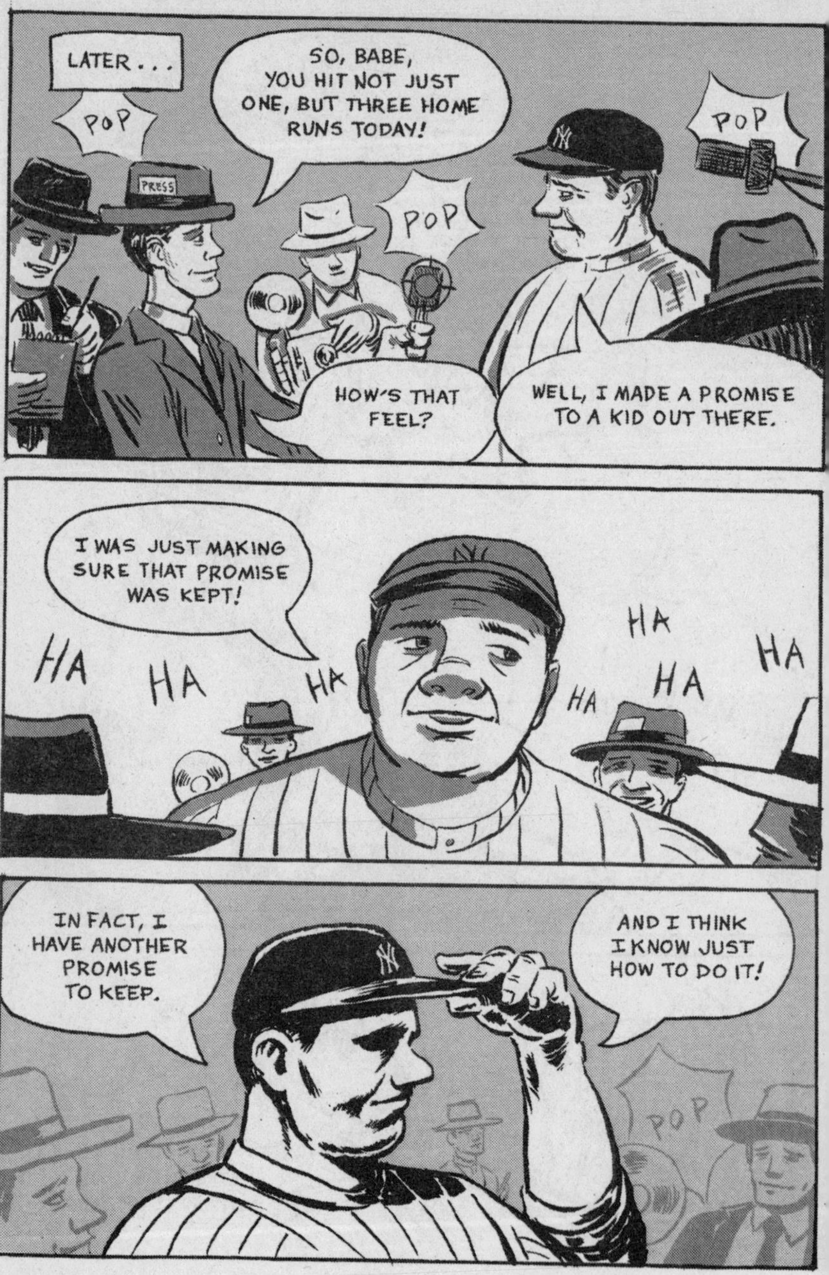
LATER...
SO, BABE, YOU HIT NOT JUST ONE, BUT THREE HOME RUNS TODAY!
POP
PRESS
POP
POP
HOW'S THAT FEEL?
WELL, I MADE A PROMISE TO A KID OUT THERE.
I WAS JUST MAKING SURE THAT PROMISE WAS KEPT!
HA
HA
HA
HA
HA
HA
HA
IN FACT, I HAVE ANOTHER PROMISE TO KEEP.
AND I THINK I KNOW JUST HOW TO DO IT!
POP

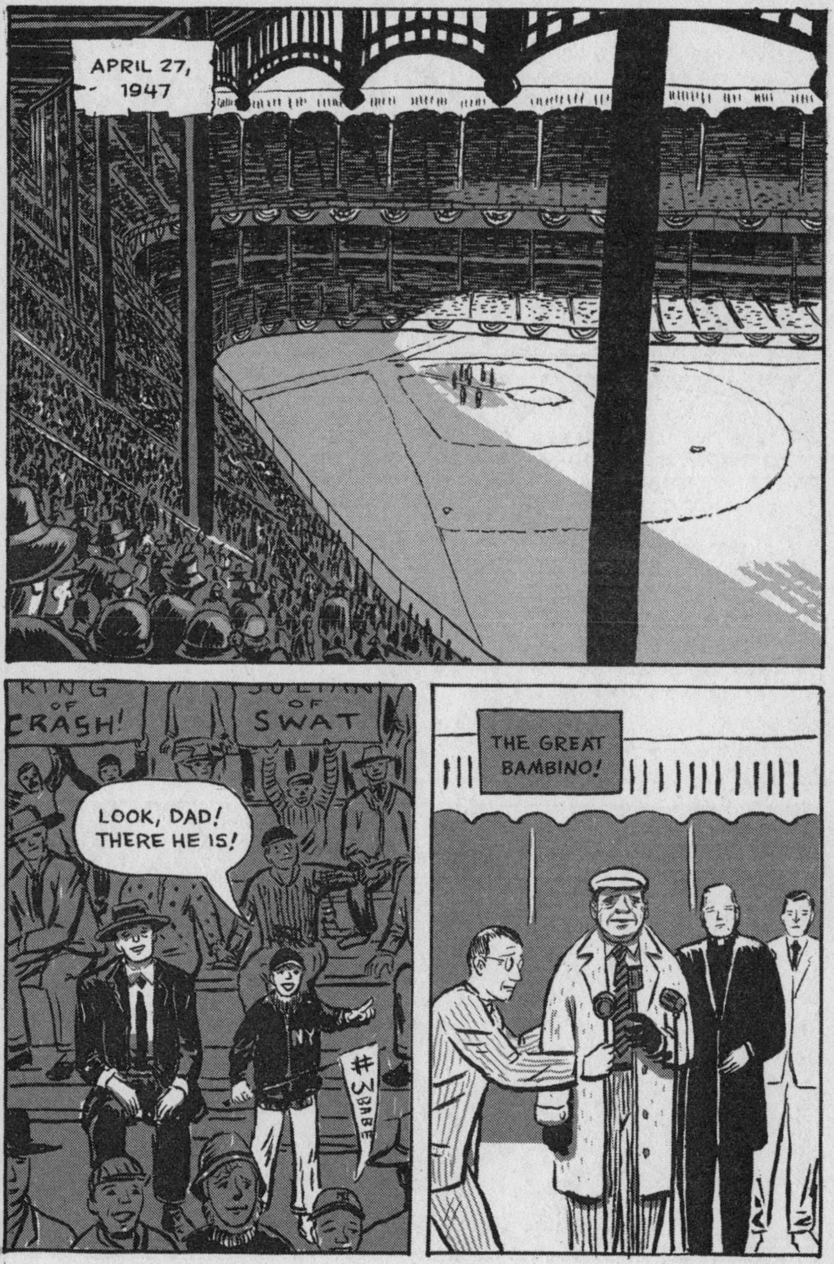
APRIL 27, 1947
OF CRASH!
OF SWAT
LOOK, DAD! THERE HE IS!
NY
#3 BABE
THE GREAT BAMBINO!

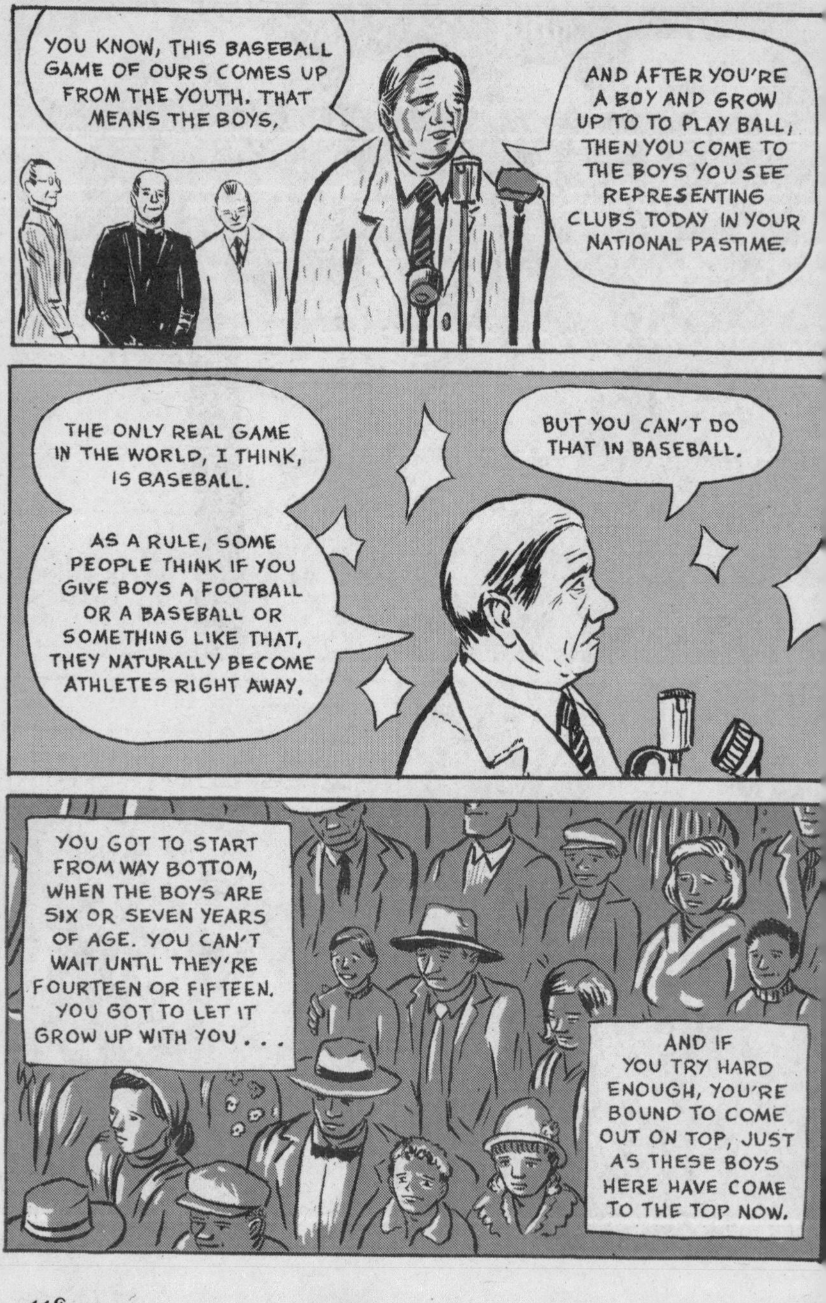
YOU KNOW, THIS BASEBALL GAME OF OURS COMES UP FROM THE YOUTH. THAT MEANS THE BOYS,
AND AFTER YOU'RE A BOY AND GROW UP TO TO PLAY BALL, THEN YOU COME TO THE BOYS YOU SEE REPRESENTING CLUBS TODAY IN YOUR NATIONAL PASTIME.
THE ONLY REAL GAME IN THE WORLD, I THINK, IS BASEBALL.
AS A RULE, SOME PEOPLE THINK IF YOU GIVE BOYS A FOOTBALL OR A BASEBALL OR SOMETHING LIKE THAT, THEY NATURALLY BECOME ATHLETES RIGHT AWAY.
BUT YOU CAN'T DO THAT IN BASEBALL.
YOU GOT TO START FROM WAY BOTTOM, WHEN THE BOYS ARE SIX OR SEVEN YEARS OF AGE. YOU CAN'T WAIT UNTIL THEY'RE FOURTEEN OR FIFTEEN. YOU GOT TO LET IT GROW UP WITH YOU . . .
AND IF YOU TRY HARD ENOUGH, YOU'RE BOUND TO COME OUT ON TOP, JUST AS THESE BOYS HERE HAVE COME TO THE TOP NOW.

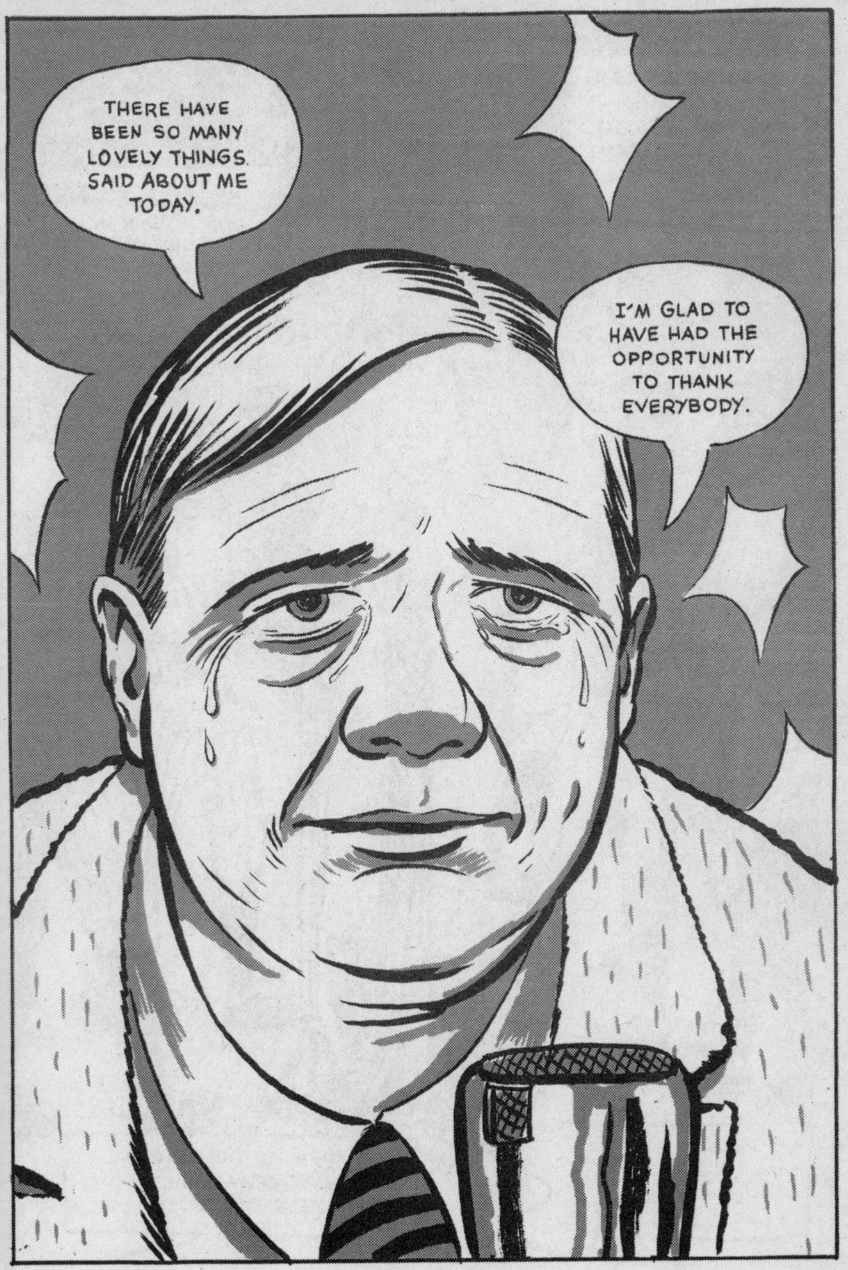
THERE HAVE BEEN SO MANY LOVELY THINGS SAID ABOUT ME TODAY.
I'M GLAD TO HAVE HAD THE OPPORTUNITY TO THANK EVERYBODY.

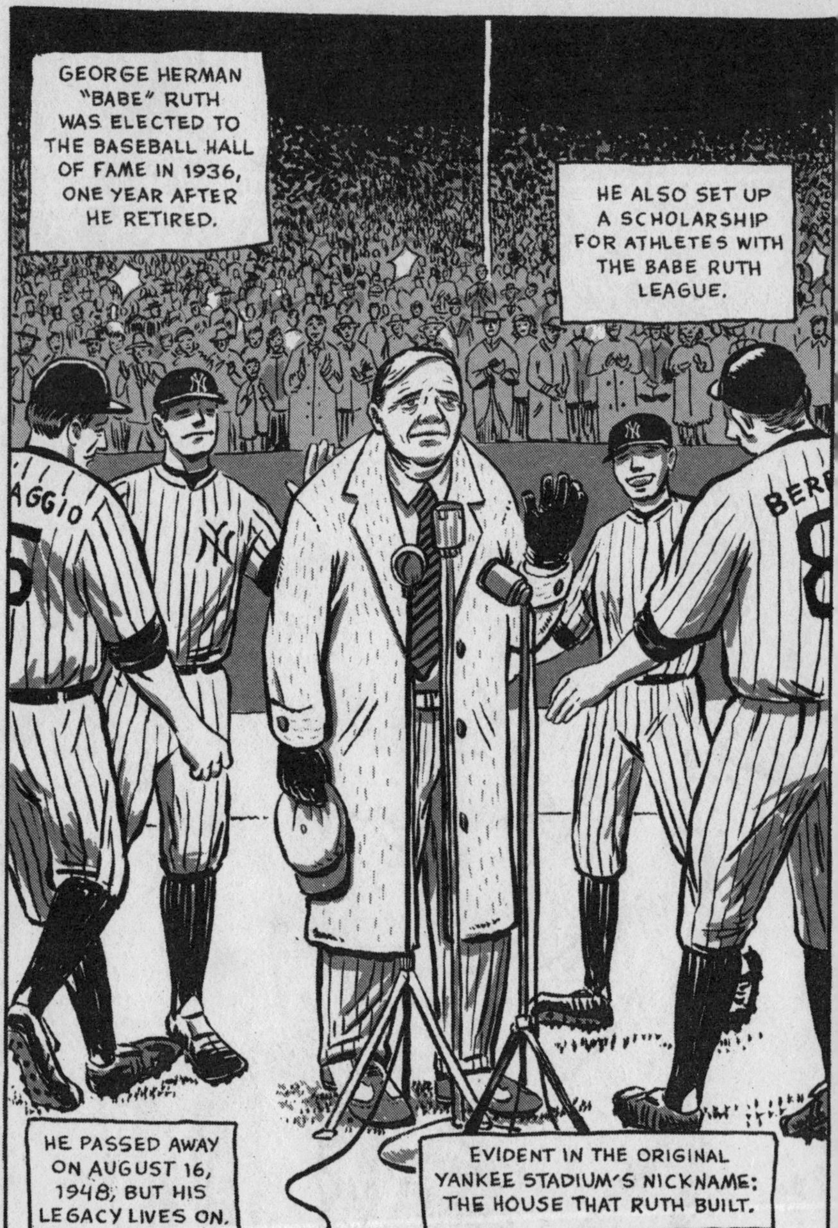
GEORGE HERMAN "BABE" RUTH WAS ELECTED TO THE BASEBALL HALL OF FAME IN 1936, ONE YEAR AFTER HE RETIRED.
HE ALSO SET UP A SCHOLARSHIP FOR ATHLETES WITH THE BABE RUTH LEAGUE.
AGGIO
BERR
HE PASSED AWAY ON AUGUST 16, 1948, BUT HIS LEGACY LIVES ON.
EVIDENT IN THE ORIGINAL YANKEE STADIUM'S NICKNAME: THE HOUSE THAT RUTH BUILT.

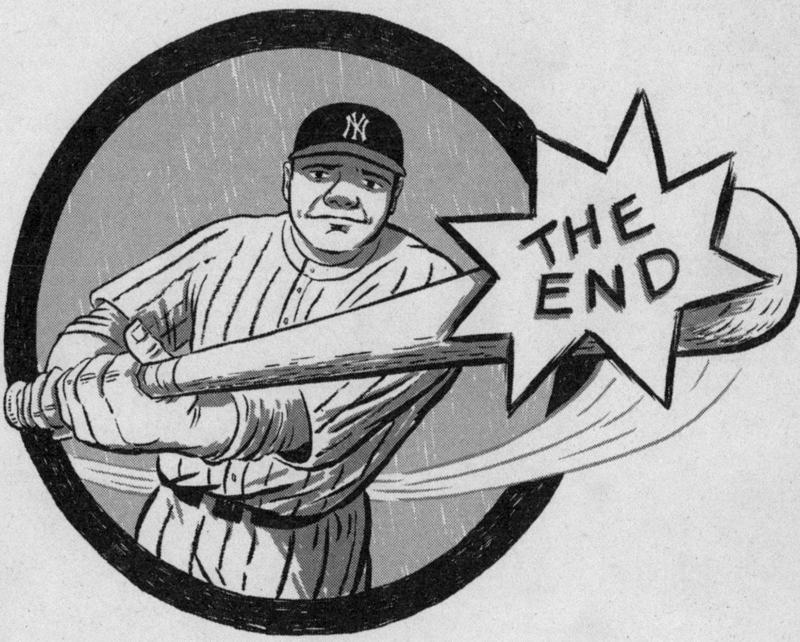
THE END